PRAISE FOR CAROLINE MITCHELL

'For me, this book had everything – an excellent police procedural with tension, pace and a compelling storyline. With the added psychological element, there was nothing more I could have asked for.'

—Angela Marsons

'Fast-paced, twisty, and chilled me to the bone . . . I loved every minute of it!'

—Robert Bryndza

'The writer's conflicted heroine and twisted villain are superb characters.'

—The *Sunday Express* magazine

'Heart-thumping moments that left me desperate to read more.'

—The Book Review Café

'The very definition of a page-turner.'

—John Marrs

'The tension built up and up . . . I devoured every page.'

—Mel Sherratt

'With her police officer experience, Caroline Mitchell is a thriller writer who knows how to deliver on plot, character, and most importantly, emotion in any book she writes. I can't wait to read more.'

—*My Weekly* magazine

THE
SECRET
CHILD

THE
SECRET
CHILD

CAROLINE MITCHELL

Text copyright © 2019 by Caroline Mitchell

Published by Thomas & Mercer, Seattle

www.apub.com

Amazon, the Amazon logo, and Thomas & Mercer are trademarks of Amazon.com, Inc., or its affiliates.

ISBN-13: 9781503905023
ISBN-10: 1503905020

Cover design by Tom Sanderson

Printed in the United States of America

This book is dedicated to my readers,
who enable me to have the best job in the world.

'There are no secrets that time does not reveal.'

Jean Racine

PROLOGUE

The intruder's eyes roved over the little girl's form. How safe she must feel, asleep in her lavish room. How protected. A rumble of hatred rolled from within. The kidnapper's thoughts were dark, consuming all in their path. He could almost sense his brain pulsating, tormented by years of reflection that offered no relief.

Walking his fingers over the dressing table, he took in the luxurious surroundings. His eyes fell on the varnished wooden rocking horse with its real mane and tail. To the sheepskin rug splayed on the carpeted floor. Opening the wardrobe door, he touched the little girl's clothes. Felt the bile rise in his throat. A rabbit-skin hat, a fur-lined coat – ripped off the backs of innocent creatures. The suffering of animals did not bother the occupants of this household.

The same could be said for human pain. The crackle of flames from downstairs infiltrated his consciousness, reminding him of the urgency of his task.

'Who are you?' Ellen blinked as she woke to find him standing at the end of her bed. Moonlight seeped through her bedroom window, providing enough visibility for her to make out his outline.

'Shh,' he said, briefly pressing a finger to his lips. 'It's a secret.'

'Are you the bogeyman?' the little girl asked, sitting upright. Her mouth fell open, her tongue gliding over her front teeth.

The man smiled. She was precocious, unafraid. So unlike other girls her age. Raised in a bubble, four-year-old Ellen was protected from the world and unaware of the dangers she faced . . . until now. Swiping her blonde curls from her eyes, she squinted for a better look.

'The house is on fire,' he said. 'We need to leave.' Taking her glasses from the bedside table, he passed them to her, unable to disguise the shake in his hand. Despite all the planning, he could not believe he was here. Could he go through with it? It was too late to back out now.

Ellen sniffed as she slipped her glasses on. Most children would rush from their beds, their hearts beating wildly at the announcement of such news. But not Ellen. She was different, just like him.

An acrid smell filtered through the bedroom window, endorsing the validity of his warning.

'Time to go,' he whispered, gently pulling back her feather duvet. 'It's not safe here anymore.' He was dressed in black, his eyes a void of nothingness, his scarf and hat hiding much of his face. Not that anyone would find him. He was a dead man, after all.

'Where's Mummy and Daddy?' Ellen asked, her blue eyes cartoonishly big behind her thick spectacles.

'They're safe.' The words grated on his lips. If it were up to him, he would have taken the child without saying a word, but providing reassurance was the best way of keeping her calm. Sweat laced his forehead, his muscles tense as adrenaline raced through his veins. Time was running out, his stress levels were rising and making him twitch. 'We need to go. Now.' Leaning forward, he scooped her up. The time for persuasion was over.

The fire he'd lit had caused a diversion, sending the babysitter spiralling into panic downstairs. Nobody saw him slip out the side door with the child in his arms. It wouldn't stop there. He was on a mission. Soon more children would be silently taken from their homes.

Thoughts of justice finally being served spurred him onwards and he deposited the child in the back seat of the rented car.

'Where are we going?' Ellen said as he strapped her in.

'On an adventure. Now be quiet. I need to concentrate.' He could not afford for his migraine to return. When pain closed in, sanity took a back seat and his actions were driven by a stronger force. The scream of sirens cut through the night, hastening his movements as he jumped into the driver's seat. Starting the car, he floored the accelerator and gravel rattled against the undercarriage as he sped away.

CHAPTER ONE

Ruler in hand, Amy stretched on to her toes as she tried to reach the block of yellow Post-it notes on the top shelf. Cursing her choice of clothing, she checked over her shoulder before nudging the ruler into the depths of the shelf. She groaned. If she had worn her trouser suit instead of her pencil skirt, then she could have jumped on to her desk and grabbed them before being seen. Such hiding places were necessary, as Post-it notes were like gold dust now the admin department had declined her requests for more.

'Gotcha!' she exclaimed as she shot the stack of notes off the shelf. But her triumph was short-lived as she caught sight of her DCI ducking to avoid the yellow missile zooming across the room.

'Not the warmest of welcomes,' Pike said, picking up the block of stationery from Amy's office floor. At least, Amy liked to call it an office. In truth, it was half the size of DCI Pike's, which was on the floor above and had a much better view of the streets below. Amy's space gave her just enough room to fit in a ridiculously high bookcase, a battered filing cabinet, two swivel chairs and her desk.

Dressed in a grey trouser suit, DCI Pike put her frown lines to good use as she glared in Amy's direction. Her brunette hair was lighter than

Amy's, cut into a short choppy style that did little to soften her harsh expression.

'Sorry, ma'am.' Amy blushed, depositing the Post-it notes in her desk drawer. They would hide there, along with other goodies such as highlighter pens, rulers and a diary for the year ahead. Planning was important, as far as Amy was concerned, although lately her life had taken a disturbing deviation from the routine. 'Can I make you a coffee?' she asked, curious about the sudden visit.

Amy's relationship with DCI Pike had been tenuous since their last falling-out. These days, she felt she was on a knife edge every time they were alone. Today was no exception.

'A job has come in,' Pike said, wasting no time in explaining her presence. 'It's high-profile and to be handled with care.'

'Sounds right up my street,' Amy replied, standing behind her desk. 'Tell me more.' Amy was well known in the force for her uncanny gift for dealing with sinister minds. Only recently had she discovered where her insights originated from, having closed the door on her past at an early age. But now the door had been ripped off its hinges, her darkest memories squirming as the truth leaked free. She would use them to her best advantage. Help people who could not help themselves.

The truth was so horrific that she had not yet gone public with the news. Up until the age of four, Amy had been raised by serial killers known as the 'Beasts of Brentwood'. It was a blessing her adoptive parents Robert and Flora Winter had taken her in. Having recently met her biological brothers and sisters, it was clear that Amy had been the lucky one.

All her life, she had compartmentalised her ugly past. But since reuniting with her biological sister, Sally-Ann, she had been bombarded with nightmares of their time in the Grimes family home. She needed to create new, happier memories, and integrate her sister into her present-day life, if she had any hope of moving on.

'Have you heard of Dr Hugh Curtis?' DCI Pike had the voice of someone who had smoked all her life.

Amy tilted her head to one side. 'The name rings a bell. Is he famous?'

Pike's eyes rested on the framed photo of Amy's adoptive father, Superintendent Robert Winter, which was on display on the desk. For a split second, the DCI's grief at his loss was laid bare.

'Yes,' Pike said, taking a sharp breath to compose herself. 'He's just been awarded an OBE.'

Amy nodded. Whatever the job was, it would be perfect for her team, which had been formed to deal with high-priority cases that were bound to hit the press. 'What have we got?'

'Child abduction. Dr Curtis and his wife were at a charity do and their four-year-old, Ellen, was taken from her bedroom. She was in the care of their babysitter. It looks like whoever's responsible lit a fire to cause a diversion.'

'Four-year-old?' Amy said, feeling her throat constrict. 'Really? I've not seen anything in the news.'

Upon waking every morning, she checked the newspapers for the latest headlines. Crimes against children hit her hardest of all.

'The fire authorities alerted us to the arson. We knew nothing of Ellen's disappearance until her grandmother reported it today.'

A short burst of laughter sounded from outside the office. It was DC Molly Baxter. Amy would recognise the shrillness of her giggle anywhere. But a sharp glance from DCI Pike through the window put an end to any joviality.

'She's happy in her work.' Amy smiled, but Pike's expression told her it had been a long time since she'd equated police work with enjoyment. Amy folded her arms across her chest, warding off the chill that had crept into the room. 'Why didn't Ellen's parents report her missing?'

Neglectful parents were one of Amy's bugbears. Discovering the truth about her own biological parents had impacted every aspect of her life.

'That's what I want you to find out,' Pike replied.

'Do you think Ellen's abduction is a front for something darker?' When it came to crimes against children, quite often the perpetrator was known to the victim, be it a friend, a relative or someone closer to home. 'Could her parents be hiding something?'

'Possible, but doubtful.' DCI Pike shifted from one foot to the other. She had yet to take a seat, and although the backs of Amy's legs were tiring she mirrored Pike, remaining rigid in her stance. Even now, her competitive streak came into play.

Pike continued: 'Dr Curtis is an intelligent man. Had he set this up, he'd be more likely to act like any other worried parent and inform us straight away.'

'Of course,' Amy said, slightly embarrassed she had been slow to work this out. 'Couldn't Ellen have been scared of the fire and run away?'

'Her grandmother is adamant she wouldn't have – and, given Ellen's age, I'm inclined to agree. The babysitter said she read her a bedtime story, and when she peeped in on her at nine she was fast asleep.'

'Sounds like abduction all right,' Amy said. 'Her parents were reluctant to involve the police, which means they may have already been sent a ransom note.'

'It's looking that way.' DCI Pike checked her watch. 'You've been tagged as dealing with the incident. Keep me updated.'

Numerous ideas jostled for Amy's attention as her mind raced ahead. She would have loved to explore them with Pike as they both visited the scene. They were fortunate their roles allowed them more freedom than regular officers of their rank, but it was not something Pike seemed willing to take advantage of. 'Office-bound,' Paddy had once called her, and today Amy could see why. 'Have statements been taken?' she asked as Pike turned to leave.

'Officers are at the scene now,' she replied, her fingers curling around the door handle as if nothing would stop her leaving. She gave one last glance in Amy's direction. 'I'd like you to attend. You've got excellent insight into this sort of thing.' She opened the door. 'But remember, discretion is key.'

'Absolutely,' Amy said, feeling a bolt of excitement at the thought of taking on such a big case. Early in her career, she had felt guilty for siphoning enjoyment from people's misery. But she had come to accept that her heightened senses and her personal experiences helped her spot things other officers missed. Gazing at her father's photo, she felt a swell of pride. Despite everything that had happened this year – her father's death and her biological mother coming out of the woodwork – she had kept it together. Yes, there were times when Lillian came close to breaking her, and the battle between them was not over yet.

Today, she was going to focus on the job ahead. She had a good team behind her: half a dozen officers with different personalities, each one carefully chosen for what they brought to the table. As they'd settled into a routine, they had all come to know each other's little ways. It was beginning to feel like she was at the controls of a finely tuned machine. She had confidence in her team and trusted every one of them, even DC Steve Moss, who'd had a bumpy start but had worked hard to prove his worth. No two days in her job were the same. The role demanded everything she had to offer and more.

'Molly, I want you to come with me,' Amy said after bringing her team up to speed. 'Guys, you know what to do. Get the ball rolling with background investigations, and if anything interesting comes up, then make me aware. Call me on my mobile rather than clogging up the airwaves.'

She paused, casting a determined gaze around the room. 'We're bring-ing Ellen home.' Pulling on her jacket, she waited for Molly to sign out the keys of the unmarked car. She would not lose sight that the beating heart of the case was a missing four-year-old girl. A child victim herself, Amy understood the trauma and confusion that Ellen Curtis must be feeling. She had Jack and Lillian Grimes to thank for that.

Amy was not alone in her suffering. Up until recently, the whole world had believed her older sister was another tragic victim, murdered by Jack and Lillian. The fact that Sally-Ann was their daughter added an extra layer of horror to an already gruesome case.

The discovery that she was alive changed everything. Her existence was welcome, but also one of the many facets of the past that Amy was still coming to terms with. How had Sally-Ann stayed in the shadows for so long? Why come forward now? But asking such questions would mean pulling the scab off an old wound. It was easier for Amy to throw herself into work than to allow herself to be consumed by past events.

CHAPTER TWO

Novokuznetsk, Soviet Union, 1984

As he sat at the makeshift kitchen table, Ivan's head hung low. 'I've never worked so hard to be so poor.' He spoke on the exhale, his words peppered with cigarette smoke. Having finished his shift in the coal mine, he watched his wife, Sasha, prepare their food. As always, he spoke in Russian, and the words could be easily translated into English in Luka's mind. Proud of her British heritage, Sasha had pushed the language upon her son from an early age.

At just six years of age, Lukasha Ivanovich Volkov knew only hardship, yet his teachers said that he was one of the lucky ones. His papa had a job and was fit to work. His mother was educated and resourceful. As for Luka . . . he was bright. 'Advanced beyond his years', according to his teachers.

Most importantly of all, his family loved each other, which was more than could be said for many on their street. Poverty bred frustration, and violence was commonplace in his neighbourhood. While Luka and his family lived in a small apartment purposely built for miners, others shared communal living spaces without gas, heat or running water. The fireplace in their kitchen-cum-living room was better than nothing, and most days they had enough kindling and wood to cook food and keep themselves warm.

But yet his mother complained, 'Why, among all the mines and steel mills, is there so much poverty? I waited hours in the rain for this sliver of meat.' She stirred the stew, her brows knitted in a frown. Life in Novokuznetsk was tough, and those unable to work struggled to feed their children. Grim-faced and poverty-stricken, many youngsters fled their homes, living among the wild dogs as they begged for scraps of food. Most people did not have the luxury of pets, and those that did had turned them loose long ago. Drugs were a problem in their area, a temporary solution for teenagers with no hope and no support. But among the glue sniffers and the destitute were small pockets of people who genuinely cared for each other. A reassuring smile, a word of encouragement; they had to stick together because otherwise there was no point in going on.

Luka tried not to concern himself with such things as he played with his toy aeroplane. He imagined himself travelling on it, visiting the faraway lands that he read about in books. How wonderful it must feel to fly like a bird in the sky.

'Luka, come and get your food,' his mother said. 'And wash your hands.'

'Yes, *mamochka*,' he said, rising from the floor. His stomach rumbled as he tucked into his stew and his eyes flicked to Mama's portion, which was half the size of his.

But Mama was busy focusing on winning his father round. 'We wouldn't have all these worries if you let me apply for the scholarship,' she said. With her wavy black hair and long dark lashes, Mama was pretty when she smiled. But today her features were taut, her words imbued with dogged determination.

Papa rolled his eyes, broth dripping from his spoon as he held it in mid-air. His face was stained with coal dust, accentuating the wrinkles too plentiful for his age. 'I told you. If it's too good to be true, then it usually is.'

'But the Curtis Institute would be our passport to England. Can you imagine seeing London? Those bright red buses, the colourful clothes and shops. All the tourist attractions. The Tower of London and Windsor Castle.'

'And how could you afford to visit these places? You think this Dr Curtis is going to show you around London and expect nothing in return?'

'But he's not getting nothing, is he? Luka's bright. The teachers say he's gifted.' Sasha edged towards her husband. 'I can get a job, earn money while he takes part in the trial. It could pave the way to a better life for us all.'

'And he couldn't find these gifted children in London?'

'They want children from all over. Please. Let me apply and see what happens after that.'

Exhaling loudly, Ivan dropped his spoon into his bowl. 'Fine, if it makes you happy, but don't get your hopes up. Nice things don't happen to people like us.'

Luka wiped the dribble of broth that edged down his chin. Soon his stomach would grumble again but for the moment hope was on his horizon. 'Are we going to England?' His heart gave a little flutter at the thought.

His mother turned to him, her smile lighting up the room. 'Perhaps, *sinochka*. Perhaps.'

CHAPTER THREE

Amy had barely entered her office when her phone rang. 'Hello?' she said, without checking the caller display. She grabbed her police-issue harness from the back of her chair, visibly withering as she recognised her caller's voice.

'At last, my darling daughter sees fit to answer my calls.' Like liquid poison, Lillian Grimes's voice seeped down the line.

Amy's spirits plummeted. It was bad enough the woman haunted her nightmares; why must she insist on ringing her at work? 'Go to hell!' she said, before slamming down the phone. She had a scene to attend and there was no point in expending any more energy on Lillian Grimes. As the phone rang for the second time, she unleashed her annoyance.

'Didn't you hear what I said? Sod off, or I'll do you for harassment!'

'Steady on . . . what did I do to deserve this?' The voice on the other end was friendly and warm, in total contrast to the scheming caller seconds before. A recent acquaintance, DI Donovan of Essex Police had got to know Amy well. Too well.

Amy sighed. Her relationship with her ex, Adam, had reinforced the idea that she was better off alone.

'Oh. Sorry, I thought you were someone else.'

'That's a relief.' A smile was carried on his words. 'Everything OK? You haven't returned my calls.'

'Sorry.' Peering out of her office window, Amy watched her team hard at work. 'I've been up to my eyes in it. I didn't finish until nearly two this morning and I was back at the crack of dawn.'

'Ah, the life of a bobby – who'd want it?'

'I guess we're gluttons for punishment. Look, I can't talk right now. Is it important?' She was still irritated by Lillian's call, and the planner on her desk was jam-packed with things to do.

'No . . . I'll be in your neck of the woods soon, maybe we could meet up then?'

'Yeah, sure.' Her eyes flickered to Molly's as the young officer approached her office door, car keys in hand.

'Um, sorry, I've . . .'

'. . . got to go.' Donovan finished her sentence. 'No problem. Speak soon.'

Ending the call, Amy paused for breath. She was too wrapped up in work to talk about hooking up. Inside, she was buzzing from the tingle of urgency that heralded each new case. As Molly drove them to the scene, Amy used the time to think.

Amy's position as DI of the high-priority crime unit offered up a variety of backdrops to her day. She often visited luxurious London homes, but rarely did she envy the homeowners. Their grief was just as real as those with barely a penny to their name. Such seemed the case today as she spoke to the Curtis family about the disappearance of their child.

At five foot eight, Dr Curtis was not a tall man, but his command-ing presence hinted that he was used to getting his own way. His silver-grey beard was neatly trimmed, his sky-blue eyes intense in their gaze.

Walking ahead of Amy and Molly, he led them past a spiral staircase into the living room. Plaques and family photos were dotted across the walls, and the delicate scent of Dr Vranjes Ginger Lime infusers permeated the room. When she'd visited Harrods with Sally-Ann the week before, Amy had lingered over them with an intent to buy – until she saw the price tag attached. But judging by the furnishings in their household, the seventy-five-pound diffusers were the cheapest items in the room.

As Amy took a seat across from the doctor, her attention was drawn to his wife. Aged thirty-eight, Nicole Curtis was twenty-seven years her husband's junior, and wife number three. Her wavy brunette hair was scooped up into a high ponytail, her slim build accentuated by her fitted black dress. Wringing her hands, she sat next to Dr Curtis, her eyes darting from his face to Amy's as they spoke in turn. The antithesis of her husband, this woman was clearly accustomed to taking a back seat.

Amy's cool grey eyes were sharp and focused as she pinned Mrs Curtis with her gaze. 'Why haven't you reported Ellen missing? I've read your statements, but I've yet to find any explanation as to why you didn't make the call.'

'You're here, aren't you?' the doctor said tersely. 'Therefore, she has been reported missing.'

'But not by you,' Amy replied, still staring at his wife. 'Which makes me wonder why.' She watched Mrs Curtis squirm. 'It could be any number of things. We'll get to the bottom of it eventually.'

Nicole's lips parted to speak, but her voice was drowned out by that of her husband.

'I can assure you we're not withholding information—'

But Dr Curtis was not the only person who could interrupt. Amy carried on as if he hadn't said a word. 'There's a couple of reasons why parents don't report their child missing. I'm sorry to say I've encountered both.'

'When you say "sorry" . . .' Nicole said, her voice faint.

'Neither ended well,' Amy replied, without further explanation. 'Now, you could have been warned not to speak to the police because someone is issuing demands. Or you could be responsible, and trying to cover it up . . .' She raised a hand, silencing Dr Curtis as he began to protest. 'Either way, I'm not leaving this room until you tell me what's going on.'

Beside her, Amy heard Molly swallow, her knees pressed tightly together and her black leather pocket notebook flipped open to take notes. Amy liked Molly. She was as good an investigator as some of the old sweats on her team. But she had a habit of being in awe of those in the public eye, something Amy was keen to eliminate. Celebrities were no less culpable for their crimes than anyone else.

'We have not laid a finger on our child.' His face taut, Dr Curtis rose from his chair. 'Ellen was safely tucked up in bed when we left for a social engagement. The babysitter checked in on her at nine o'clock, and she was fast asleep. She called 999 at ten o'clock when the fire broke out. When she went upstairs to wake Ellen, she was gone.' He paced the room as he spoke, his words mirroring those in the statement he had given to the police.

'You're not answering my question,' Amy said.

'That's because there's nothing more to say.' Pausing at the Victorian fireplace, Dr Curtis stared into nothingness.

'When it comes to the whereabouts of a missing child there is plenty more to say.' Amy stood, her chin held high. 'Either tell me now or we'll discuss it down at the station.' She turned to Mrs Curtis. With her legs and arms crossed, Nicole appeared to have tied herself up in knots.

'We haven't hurt her,' she blurted out. 'And we haven't received a ransom note. At least . . . not yet.'

Amy nodded soberly. At last, she was getting somewhere. She heard Molly click her pen, ready to take notes. 'Do you know her abductor?'

Dr Curtis scowled at his wife before answering on her behalf. 'Perhaps.'

'Would you care to enlighten me?' Amy said.

'By doing so, I would be signing Ellen's death warrant,' he replied.

Amy sighed. 'So you pay them off and get Ellen back safely? You think it's that easy?'

Dr Curtis shook his head. 'There may not be a ransom note, but involving the police will make things a whole lot worse.'

'For whom?' Amy asked. 'I take it there's been some kind of contact, otherwise you would have called us straight away.'

Amy narrowed her eyes as she caught Dr Curtis deliver a warning shake of the head to his wife. 'Believe me when I tell you I only want what's best for my child. I can't risk aggravating this person any more than they already are.'

Giving up on Nicole, Amy took a step towards him. 'You underestimate my team. You'll have a far better outcome with our support. At least give us enough to make some background checks. You can't do this on your own.'

'Tell her,' Nicole said, clutching her hands to her chest. 'We know who he is.'

Amy turned to Dr Curtis, but he remained tight-lipped. 'I could arrest you both for obstruction, then carry on our chat at the police station?'

'You misunderstand me, Officer.' Dr Curtis faced her. 'I can't tell you who took our daughter, because the man my wife's referring to is dead.'

CHAPTER FOUR

Deborah McCauley strained to understand the woman on the other end of the phone. Her voice was punctuated by sobs, her breath coming in judders as she shrieked down the line.

'He's got her, I know it! He said he'd get his revenge, and he has!'

'Calm down. Only dogs can hear you at this pitch. Now, take a slow breath . . .' Deborah tried to calm the fretting mother. 'And another . . .' She was used to dealing with hysterical women. During her career as a psychiatrist, she had come across people in all sorts of turmoil, but Nicole Curtis was in a class of her own.

Pouring herself a cup of black filter coffee, Deborah sat at her kitchen breakfast bar and crossed her long, slim legs. Her cane was propped up beside her. It was long and glittery, just like the shoe bobbing from the tip of her foot. She wondered why every phone call from Nicole involved a drama of some kind.

'It's Ellen. He's taken my little girl. And now the police are treating us like criminals. Hu—' Nicole stuttered, her words tripping over her sobs. 'Hugh told me not to call but I . . . I don't know what to do.'

The esteemed Dr Hugh Curtis, Deborah thought, rolling her eyes. If only people knew. She'd been in her early twenties when they first worked together, and now, decades later, he was incapable of shocking her. It was a quality yet to be afforded to his third wife.

Deborah's blonde hair was now streaked with silver and her health had taken a nosedive. But her memories of her time at the Curtis Institute were still as sharp as a blade. She took a breath, preparing to issue the comfort that Dr Curtis was incapable of providing. 'I told you before, Luka's dead. He can't hurt you.'

'But he *can* hurt Ellen. Who else would have taken her? It's got to be him.' An anguished moan escaped Nicole's lips. 'Hugh said we should hang tight and wait for the kidnapper to call. But what if Ellen's hurt . . . or worse?'

'Just . . .' Deborah frowned, trying to make sense of it all. 'Just start from the beginning. When was the last time you saw her?'

Nicole repeated her account of events.

'How?' Deborah replied. 'How did he take her without being seen?'

'The side door had been jemmied open. The police think he used the fire as a diversion to slip away. He's alive, Deborah. All this time, I've been trying to tell you . . . do you believe me now?'

It was true, Nicole *had* warned them, but her concerns were never reported to the police. Starting five years ago, Nicole and Hugh had received a bunch of flowers at their home on the same date each year. The message that accompanied them was particularly chilling . . . and now he had carried out his threat.

Deborah knew better than to ask why Ellen hadn't screamed. Her reactions were different to those of ordinary children, but that was down to her upbringing more than anything else. Deborah's thoughts wandered briefly to Luka and a pang of guilt hit home. 'I thought you had CCTV?' she said, reining in her emotions.

Nicole sniffed, her sobs finally subsiding. 'It doesn't record. You can check it live on the app, but it doesn't keep anything.'

'Of course it bloody doesn't.' Deborah stared down at her cup of coffee, which was now turning cold. Behind her, the washing machine began the rhythm of a spin cycle. Listening to Nicole, her stomach was beginning to feel the same way. Luka was damaged, there was no doubting that – and it was hardly surprising after what they had put him through. She bowed her head as Nicole's anguished cries bored into her brain. 'Are you sure Ellen didn't get scared of the fire and run? You can't expect her to react like other children. She has no concept of danger.'

Nicole's response was instant, set in another high-pitched tone. 'Don't you think I know that? I'm her mother. You don't need to tell me what my daughter is and isn't aware of. I told Hugh this would happen. How's she going to fend for herself? She's only four.'

'Hey, *you* called *me*, remember? There's no need to snap my head off.'

'Sorry,' Nicole replied in a quiet voice.

That's better, Deborah thought, having put her back in her box. Hugh's voice rang clear in her memory: *The parents of test subjects need to be controlled.* Oh, the irony. How did he feel now he was the one being scrutinised? Another thought sent a dart of worry. It was only a matter of time before the authorities turned their attention towards her. Deborah rubbed her forehead, now coated in a light sheen of sweat. 'And you haven't mentioned Luka to the police? You know what will happen if they start digging . . .'

'But why shouldn't we tell them if it helps bring Ellen home? He's back. I don't know how, but he's alive and he's taken my little girl . . .' An exhalation of breath ruffled the phone line. 'You knew him better than anyone. What should I do?'

'Listen to me. Luka's dead. The police are aware. Just sit tight for now.' Deborah clutched the telephone handset, staring into space. 'There's no point digging into the past. Tell them as little as possible, or we'll all be facing jail.'

She ended the call. Why Hugh had to confide in Nicole, of all people, she did not know.

Deborah's Apple Watch raised an alert that her heart was beating far too fast. Like a tangled web, past and present were weaving themselves around her, making it difficult to breathe.

The receiver still warm in her hand, she attempted to make a group call to her old colleagues – Stuart and Christina were no doubt panicking. The ties of the past kept them tightly bound together, even though she had not seen them in years. The four of them had stayed true to their word. But for how much longer? If their secret came out . . . Her hold on the receiver tightened.

It would mean the end of her.

CHAPTER FIVE

The bruise was yellow and the size of a small buttercup on Ellen's skin. Her kidnapper frowned. He had forgotten how delicate children were. Spending time in their presence gave him the creeps.

'I want my mummy.' Snatching back her wrist, Ellen petulantly folded her arms. The tracksuit was a size too big and he'd had to bribe her with a Mars bar to put it on.

'Here,' he said, picking up the plastic shopping bag and rummaging for another bar of chocolate. 'Try this. It'll make you feel better.' A hint of a Russian accent coloured his words.

'Mummy says chocolate is bad for my teef,' Ellen said, clearly unaccustomed to the joys of a Mars bar. The thought of breaking her meticulously planned diet made the man smile. Compromises needed to be made with a child in captivity. It was something he understood only too well.

'I won't tell her if you don't,' he replied. His thoughts darkened. Ellen would not live long enough to tell any tales. Rising from the sofa, he glanced around the room. Photographs, maps and plans had, until recently, adorned the walls. He remembered the first day he got here, how everything had seemed so bare.

A flat-screen television was positioned next to where the plans of Ellen's home had hung. Tiny blobs of Blu-Tack still clung to the paintwork where the photographs of the other children had been displayed. Now all that remained were four windowless white walls.

Ellen sucked on her Mars bar, her eyes growing wide as she tried to comprehend the impending threat. Yes, she had been brought up shielded from the world, but he knew from the books in her bedroom that she was no stranger to a fairy tale or two. A smile spread on his lips as he decided to breathe life into an old Russian folk tale. 'I'm keeping you safe from Baba Yaga,' he whispered conspiratorially, looking over his shoulder as if to check whether she was there.

Temporarily unplugging the chocolate bar from her mouth, Ellen licked her lips. 'Who?'

'Haven't you heard? Baba Yaga – the witch who set fire to your house. In Russia they call her Baba Yaga Kostianaya Noga.' His features became animated as he recounted the tale. 'She's got a long, thin nose which scratches the ceiling when she snores. Her legs are pure bone, her teeth as sharp as knives, and she lives in a house on chicken legs.' He relished the look of fresh fear in Ellen's eyes. 'That's why I brought you to my special place. See?' He pointed to the walls of their room. 'No windows.' Leaning towards her, he whispered for effect: 'She flies around in the night, feasting on children whose parents have been bad. Whenever she is near, the birds become silent and the wind screeches a warning to those far and wide.'

'Mummy and Daddy aren't b-bad,' she said, a sob catching in her throat. The man had improvised that part of the story and was enjoying its effect.

'But they are,' he rasped, 'which is why they asked me to hide you. Do you understand? That's why you must do as I say.'

Ellen nodded solemnly, chocolate dribbling between her dimpled fingers. She had no reason to disbelieve him. A product of her father's upbringing, she was untainted by the outside world. Every word the man spoke was taken literally and she offered him her complete trust. He watched as she began to sob, half-heartedly returning the Mars bar to her lips.

'No crying.' He reached for a packet of wet wipes from the coffee table. 'She'll hear you. Now eat up. You don't need to worry. As long as you're quiet, you're safe.'

'Who *are* you?' she said, clumsily swiping away the chocolate from her chin.

'You can call me Luka,' he replied, overcome by a sense of surrealness. Kidnap carried a hefty prison sentence. But he wasn't planning on getting caught. He looked at the child, his resolve strengthening. It had to be done.

'W-where are you going?' She pushed her spectacles up her nose, her big blue eyes following his movements as he strode towards the door.

'To keep a lookout, of course. And remember – not a sound.' He closed the heavy door behind him, blocking out Ellen's sobs. The soundproof room would afford him some peace, and she had enough food and fizzy drinks to last her the day. Leaning against the bookcase, he pushed it back so it was against the wall. So this was what it felt like to be the one in control. But what had started off as a source of mild amusement had turned sour on his tongue. Frightening a four-year-old girl was a hollow victory. Besides, he had things to do. The next part of his plan was ready to be put into action. Ellen would not be here for very long.

CHAPTER SIX

Flicking on the kettle, Amy spooned coffee and sugar into her favourite James Bond mug. There was a crack in the handle and a tidemark that was impossible to remove, but it had been a gift from her father. Her lucky mug. His guidance was sorely missed. She sniffed the carton of milk from the fridge before adding a dollop on to the coffee granules and pouring the boiling water. In a rare moment to herself, she stared at the undissolved coffee granules floating on top. She could almost hear her father groan that she was making it all wrong.

She was doing this a lot lately, keeping his memory alive by imagining what he would say. His absence had left a huge hole in her life, and the last thing she needed was Lillian Grimes trying to fill the space. Months had passed since Amy had discovered the devastating truth, and Lillian seemed determined to have her say. The echoes of Jack and Lillian's laughter still rang in the chambers of Amy's memories, along with the screams of the victims they had taken captive over thirty years ago.

Was four-year-old Ellen Curtis screaming in a basement somewhere? Or had her body been disposed of like a piece of rubbish, or buried in the grounds of her parents' home? Amy's thoughts roamed, unwanted

invaders scuttling in her brain. Lately, every snatched moment of soli-
tude returned her to the past: a place of unfinished business, with ugly
memories waiting for release.

DS Paddy Byrne sidled into the office kitchen beside her, empty
mug in hand. He seemed happier in his work now his life was back on
an even keel. They had yet to have a proper chat about the recent turn
of events regarding Lillian Grimes, but work was relentless and their
personal lives would have to wait.

'The kettle's just boiled.' Amy smiled, grateful for some respite from
her thoughts. 'Manage to dig anything up?' she added, referring to the
case. Dr Curtis's comment about Ellen's kidnapper being a dead man
was bizarre, but further questioning had been fruitless and Amy had
instructed the team to investigate his past.

Having become famous through his career as an experimental
psychologist, Dr Curtis had gained further notoriety after releasing a
string of bestselling books on childhood behaviour. His face was often
on television as he was regularly consulted on the topic, although his
charismatic on-screen persona was far removed from the character Amy
had encountered today. It was hardly surprising, given the stress he was
under, but Amy sensed there was more to Ellen's disappearance than
Dr Curtis was letting on.

Paddy's spoon clinked against his cup as he stirred sugar into his
tea. 'Curtis did a brief stint in an animal-testing lab before moving on
to child psychology. It was forty years ago, though, so I can't see that
it's relevant to this case.'

'We need to know everything. A full résumé of his background,
and Nicole's too. Their childhoods, their parents, their social circles. Are
either of them having an affair? Do they owe anyone money? Something
stinks in that house, and I want to know what it is.'

It was bad enough they were playing catch-up, as the kidnapping
had been reported late. Amy had requested undercover surveillance of
the Curtis family home, but, given a lot of their budget had been blown

on their last big case, chances were she would be turned down. At the moment, the Curtis family were victims, but Amy knew from experience how quickly things could turn.

Paddy sipped his tea. 'The officers involved in the house search said that Ellen's room was spotless. The whole place was like a show home, nothing out of place.'

'I guess when you're as rich as Curtis you can afford to pay cleaners to pick up after you.' Amy wondered how scrupulously their home had been cleaned after Ellen disappeared. She sipped her coffee, conscious of the time. 'There was something very *Stepford Wives* about Nicole,' she continued. 'You should have seen the way Curtis looked at her. We need to speak to her on her own.' But all attempts to do so had failed and, unless the parents became suspects, it was something Amy could not force. She checked her watch. Time for the briefing.

Side by side, she walked with Paddy to the conference room, mug of coffee in hand. Even in her heels she was dwarfed by Paddy's form. Their relationship had been strengthened since Sally-Ann's identity was revealed. Not only was Paddy one of Amy's closest friends, he was living with her sister too. He had been as surprised as anyone to discover who she really was. They were all a little shell-shocked, going through the motions until they found a better way to cope.

Within minutes, her team had filed in, and Amy began briefing the specialist officers assigned to the case. She glared at the desk phone as it rang with persistence, interrupting her flow. Front-counter staff knew better than to transfer calls to this number, so who were they trying to put through?

'Quiet for a minute,' she said, halting the background chatter as she picked up the receiver. 'DI Winter speaking. We're mid-briefing. This better be good.'

'Sorry to interrupt, ma'am, but I've got a caller here who insists on speaking only to you.' Daphne from the front desk sounded somewhat affronted. 'I tried your airwaves but you weren't picking up.'

Amy's radio was sitting on her office desk but, to be fair, she switched it on more than most. Uniformed officers were expected to have theirs on at all times, but detectives could get away with having one transmitting in the background, as long as they were contactable by phone. Besides, their rechargeable batteries barely lasted the day and, like everything else, were in short supply.

'Can you take a message?' Amy presumed it was another follow-up. Their appeal had just hit the press, meaning crank calls and dead-end leads weren't far behind. She sighed. They would never get through the briefing at this rate and she was acutely aware that all eyes were on her.

'I'm afraid not,' Daphne replied. 'He's saying he has Dr Curtis's child.'

'So you're telling me the kidnapper is on the line.' Amy raised her voice for everyone in the room to hear. Their low mumblings came to an immediate end. 'What are you waiting for? Put him through!' Raising her finger to her lips, she signalled to her colleagues to be quiet as she activated the speakerphone. Amy would never win awards for her phone manner. She mused that it was probably a crank call, but it would not do any harm for them to listen, just in case. She watched as Paddy slipped his phone from his pocket, pressed the record button and slid it across the table in her direction. Molly stretched in her seat to reach for her notepad, pen in her other hand. They would take note of every word said.

The call seemed like a gift that had dropped into her lap. Was Ellen's kidnapper really on the line?

CHAPTER SEVEN

Nicole stared mournfully out the window. Losing Ellen had made her re-evaluate everything. She had thrown everyone out, telling them she needed time to think. Hugh had gone searching for their daughter and instructed her to stay at home in case Ellen returned. As if it would be that easy. The very thing that had attracted Nicole to her much older husband had also led to their downfall. It was his fault Ellen had been scooped from her bed. His actions that had put her in danger.

Luka was alive. She was convinced of it. Who else would send them a wreath on the anniversary of his death each year? And the words on the card inside the stiff black envelope pinned to the front . . . they chilled her to the bone.

From what she gathered, she was not the only one to receive such communications. Her husband's hushed phone calls told her that Deborah, Stuart and Christina received the yearly reminders too.

She turned the card over in her fingers as she read the message once more.

Ladybird, ladybird, fly away home

Your house is on fire

Your child is gone . . .

Luka

She should have handed it to DI Winter, but instead it had burned a hole in the pocket of her dress. Why hadn't she listened to Hugh when he told her to throw it away? He would be furious to know she had kept it all this time. The note was a warning of what was to come – payback for the practices at her husband's institution. He had been drunk when he'd confided in her and now they were too scared to go to the police. Each year after the flowers, everything went quiet and they fooled themselves into believing their tormentor was making empty threats. When had he first planned Ellen's abduction? How could he hurt an innocent child? *An eye for an eye . . .* The words filtered into her consciousness, loaded with gloomy foreboding.

It was so hard, not having anyone to talk to. Hugh claimed to love Ellen, but theirs was not a typical father/daughter relationship. Each night he sat in his private office making notes, writing in his journals, updating his peers. Ellen was a test subject, like so many before her. A canary in a gilded cage. Nicole had thought about leaving him, taking Ellen far away and starting again. But with what? As long as she lived with Hugh she was well cared for – both of them were. He had reassured her that Ellen was different and that he had her best interests at heart, but what about now? She should never have put money before her daughter's freedom . . .

Nicole's thoughts were stilled by the shrill ring of the doorbell. *Could it be?* Her heart jerked in her chest. Was it Ellen? Or were the police bringing bad news?

31

Time seemed to move in slow motion as she answered the front door. The last thing she expected to see was a leather-clad courier on her doorstep, his bulky frame blocking out the light from outside. 'Yes?' she said, her eyes wide and unblinking as she waited for him to speak.

His face obscured by the tinted helmet, he silently offered her the parcel in his hands.

Nicole accepted the package, her mouth falling open as she realised this was no ordinary delivery. For one thing, most courier firms used a van, and there was something about the way the man loomed over her that made her uneasy.

He thrust the parcel into her hands before walking away.

'Do you need me to sign for it?' Nicole called after him, but he failed to acknowledge her words.

Nicole looked beyond him into the empty courtyard as he stood next to his motorbike. It was a small mercy that the media had not yet found their address, as their appeal had just hit the press. Was Luka watching? Was *he* Luka?

Nicole's expression changed. 'Is this a ransom note?' she called, feeling suddenly afraid. Surely it wouldn't be delivered here, in broad daylight? But the courier ignored her question and the roar of his motorbike drowned out her words as he rode away.

Returning to the confines of her home, Nicole tugged at the brown-paper packaging, her hands shaking as a small cardboard box was revealed. Her eyes were immediately drawn to the black envelope resting on top. The same black envelope containing the card signed *Luka* that she received each year. It was expensive, made of thick, bonded paper.

Slowly opening the envelope, she thought about stories she had read of terrorists who sent explosives in the post. Biting her bottom lip, she slid out the white card within, instantly recognising the childish scrawl of the signature below. Her eyes darting from left to right, she read the words.

There are four phials in this package.

One is poisoned. Three are safe.

Drink one for me to notify police about Ellen's location.

Risk your life for the one you love – a choice not afforded to me.

Luka

'I don't understand,' she said aloud, her heart beating so hard she could feel it through the thin material of her dress. She closed the door behind her, shutting out the outside world. Luka was alive, she was convinced of it. But what did he mean, *a choice not afforded to me*?

Nicole explored the box. The contents consisted of four glass phials which glinted in the light. Three contained blue liquid. The fourth was red. Her fingers brushed against the black sponge base that held the phials in place. It was clear that Luka had prepared for this day. Everything about this moment felt too monumental for Nicole to process it on her own. She walked into the living room, her body moving on autopilot. Where was Hugh? She wasn't used to making decisions for herself. She needed him to . . .

The box vibrated in her hand, making her yelp as it came to life. Steadying herself, Nicole listened to a ringtone coming from within. Cautiously, she worked her fingers into a gap between the sponge and the cardboard and pulled out a black iPhone. It was scuffed from use, and *Answer me* flashed up on the screen as a request for a FaceTime call came through. A sob clogged Nicole's throat as she stared in disbelief at the battered phone. Was she about to come face to face with her daughter's kidnapper? Was Ellen there? She pressed the icon to accept the call.

'You've got one minute.' A gravelly voice made her jump as the face of a man filled the screen. At least, she thought it was a man. His face was cloaked by a semi-transparent face mask, its painted orange lips and thick black eyebrows giving him a sinister edge.

Nicole stared at him, overcome by emotion as she tried to deal with the situation she found herself in. 'Who are you? What have you done with Ellen?' It did not take a genius to work out that this man was involved in her daughter's kidnapping. Summoning all of her courage, she demanded to speak to Ellen. But the deadness behind his eyes made her words wither in her throat. 'Please,' she squeaked. 'Let me see her?'

'Read the letter,' he said in a menacing tone. 'You've got three minutes . . . starting now.'

Nicole stared from the screen to the written demand. *Drink one for me to notify police of Ellen's location.*

Her tears made a warm trail down her cheeks as she found her voice. 'Let me see my baby! I need to see her now!'

The man stared, unblinking, before opening a door and turning the camera around. Had she seen those eyes before? But the thought quickly evaporated as her daughter's face came into view.

The sight of Ellen's face made Nicole's heart feel like it was physically breaking in two. Ellen rarely had anything to cry about, but today big fat tears rolled down her cheeks as she gulped for breath. Her hair was dishevelled, her face streaked with dirt. 'I don't like it here,' she sobbed, looking beyond the camera to the person whose face was out of view. 'I want to go home.'

'Baby, I'm here! Mummy's here!' Nicole cried, swallowing back her tears. But Ellen was not wearing her glasses and Nicole's words seemed to go unheard. Had he muted the call?

The door closed and a digital stopwatch was held up to the screen, to signal that their conversation was coming to an end. Mercilessly, the seconds ticked away. She knew then, as they counted down to twenty and then ten, that this was part of Luka's sick game. Hugh's deeds were coming back to haunt him, but neither she nor Ellen were to blame. Luka wanted to frighten them, that's all. To teach them an elaborate lesson they would never forget. The liquid was probably harmless. But which one should she choose? Ten . . . nine . . . eight . . . the seconds ticked away. Her hand hovered over the phials. Soon the timer would come to an end. She might never see her little girl again. Five . . . four . . . three . . .

'OK, OK!' she screamed, snatching one of the phials. She chose the blue liquid because red signalled danger – didn't it? Popping off the stopper, she threw back her head and swallowed the contents, ensuring her actions were in view. The liquid was tasteless and odourless but warmed her throat on the way down.

'Done,' she said, her voice shaking as she stared into the phone. 'What happens now?' She still felt the same. Perhaps everything was going to be all right.

But the man behind the mask stared wordlessly before ending the call.

'Wait . . . no, don't go!' Nicole said. 'I've done what you asked. Where are you keeping her?'

But the line was dead and, despite jabbing the buttons, she could not return the call. She threw down the phone, her head bowed as she paced the room. At least Ellen was alive – but for how much longer? Would her kidnapper let her go? Nicole began to feel nauseous and the dull throb of a headache made itself known. Should she call Hugh? Let him know what had happened? She picked up the phone and brought up his number, but after a few seconds it went to voicemail. What now? She thought about the detective inspector who had come to her home earlier. Luka's note said *he* would call the police. Should she make her aware? Nicole frowned. There was no point in jeopardising everything now. She clasped her fingers together, her knuckles white as she squeezed them tight. Soon Ellen would be home. They'd move away from this place, just the two of them . . .

Her thoughts were interrupted by a sudden, trickling sensation. She wobbled slightly on her feet. It felt like someone was pushing pins into her brain. Touching the bottom of her nostril, she stared at the tips of her fingers. 'No!' She gasped at the sight of it. Was this because of the drink? Warm and moist on her fingertips was a bead of blood.

CHAPTER EIGHT

'This is DI Winter.' Standing in the briefing room, Amy spoke with force. She was in no mood to be messed around. 'With whom am I speaking?'

'My name is Luka Volkov. But surely you know that, don't you?' The sound of his Russian accent sent the hairs prickling on the back of Amy's neck. Her team had been thorough in their investigations since her visit to Dr Curtis and his wife. Luka Ivanovich Volkov had been one of the children involved in experimental psychological trials during the eighties. He was also the subject of the team briefing she was about to give – and of particular interest because he was dead.

Amy gave Paddy a knowing look. Her caller could have said he was Santa Claus and she would have gone along with it. He clearly knew too much to be a time-waster and she would appease him for now. 'I've been told you have Ellen Curtis.'

'Yes. And I will speak only to you.'

'Fine by me,' Amy replied. 'Where is she?'

'I read about you in the newspaper . . .' he said, in no hurry to give up the information. 'Amazing work, discovering the bodies of those girls decades after they were murdered. I thought you must be very clever to do that, and wouldn't it be good if you could rise to the challenge again?'

Amy knew he was referring to the case involving Lillian Grimes. But rather than deterring her, it set her pulse racing. Like a moth to the flame, she found herself being drawn in. Too much time had passed since Ellen's kidnapping, and she would crawl over hot coals if it brought the little girl home. 'And what challenge would that be?'

'To find Ellen, of course. Fate has thrown us together.'

'Where are you?' she asked, glancing around the room. One of her colleagues was on the phone, quietly updating Control about the call. Molly was scribbling in her investigator's book, and Paddy was standing near the door, leg jiggling, waiting to charge off at a moment's notice.

'I credited you with more intelligence. Do you really think I'd go through all this just to hand Ellen back?' He paused as if mentally forming his words. There were no background noises, just the sound of his breathing as he prepared to make his next move. 'We are all pawns in this game. Ellen's mother played her part, affording you this call. But now it's your turn.'

Memories of Lillian Grimes came to the forefront of Amy's mind. In order to find the bodies buried by her parents, she'd had to jump through hoops. And now, having read of her exploits in the newspaper, was another psychopath toying with her?

'Why don't you get to the point and tell me where she is?' Amy knew she was being optimistic, hoping for such a quick resolution.

'Because I can't,' the caller replied. 'At least, not yet. I know I'm on loudspeaker. That's fine, as long as you take the lead. You see, I want your team behind this. I want you to understand why I came back from the dead to put things right.'

Amy pinched the bridge of her nose. Her caller may have *thought* he was Luka Volkov, but she was pretty sure no resurrection had taken place. 'How do I know this isn't a hoax?'

'Nicole Curtis believed me. It's thanks to her that I'm calling you now.'

Nicole? Amy thought. *What involvement has she had in this?* She paused for breath. 'What do you need? Tell me, we can sort this out.'

'I hate children,' the man muttered. 'Their whiny voices and sticky fingers invading my space.'

'Then for God's sake let her go.' Amy's voice raised in volume as frustration crept in.

'Not until the world knows just how sick and twisted Dr Curtis really is. I want headlines. Front page. Every year, I send letters to the papers but they've ignored me . . . until now. I'm sure a hotshot detective like you can make them listen when they get my next one. It's already winging its way to them.'

'Letters?' Amy frowned. 'What letters?'

'You'll know soon enough. Give me your mobile number.'

Amy reeled off her number without hesitation. 'How do we know Ellen's still alive? I need proof.' She looked around the room, reading the tension on her colleagues' faces. The atmosphere felt on a knife edge.

The caller sighed, before speaking in a matter-of-fact way. 'Her nightdress is blue with a pink ribbon. She has curly blonde hair. We took her glasses when we left because she can't see without them. I left her slippers behind because they're lined with rabbit fur. She's a chatterbox – although her ability to speak has been somewhat limited since I took her into my care. I'll call tomorrow. Be ready.'

An ominous silence filled the briefing room as the call came to an end. Amy turned to her team. 'Find out if they've had any luck tracing that call.' Swivelling her head, she spoke to Paddy. 'Bring the car around. We're paying another visit to Nicole Curtis. We need to verify what he said about Ellen.' She turned to Steve. 'His comment about fur-lined slippers was a bit odd. Find out if there's been any recent contact between Dr Curtis and animal-rights activists.'

Already on it,' DC Steve Moss replied, tearing off the sheet of note-paper he had been scribbling on then rushing out of the door.

'Molly, I want you with me on this tomorrow. Clear your workload for when he makes that return call.'

'Yes, ma'am.' Molly nodded, her eyebrows raised. 'What did he mean about Ellen's ability to speak being limited?'

Amy shook her head. She was trying hard not to think about that right now. 'Hopefully, it just means she's been gagged.' She sighed. 'Or it could mean her tongue is winging its way to her parents right now.' An old case flashed in her memory in which body parts had been sent through the post. Ransom cases were unpredictable and could go either way. But Ellen's kidnapper was communicative, and that in itself offered a small but much-needed crumb of hope.

CHAPTER NINE

'How are we going to play this?' Paddy tapped the steering wheel as the traffic lights turned red. Wearing his crumpled blue shirt and colourful novelty tie, he was not what you would call a sharp dresser, but behind his sloppy exterior was a man who was wholly dedicated to his team. Amy valued his opinion. She had a lot to thank him for, given that he had taken her under his wing when she first joined the police. Sitting forward in the passenger seat, she contemplated their next move. They had been all set to discuss Luka in the briefing, but now her team were racing to find answers due to the unexpected call.

'I'll be having a stern word with Nicole,' she replied, wishing she'd had the opportunity to speak to her alone before now. DCI Pike was so scared of upsetting the esteemed Dr Curtis and his high-profile circle of friends that she had pooh-poohed the idea of bringing his wife in for questioning. Such favouritism left a bitter taste on Amy's tongue. Why should such people be treated differently to everyone else?

An update from Control came through the police airwaves in the car, informing her there had been no recent calls to the police from the Curtis family home. 'Received,' Paddy replied, activating the buttons on the steering wheel to deliver his response.

Amy turned down the radio as officers updated Control on their own locations and tasks. 'What do you make of it all?' she said, bringing her attention back to the phone call. 'We've read the reports. Luka died in that fire. So why would anyone go out of their way to make us think he's alive?'

'Could be some nutcase.' Paddy shrugged. 'It's all very odd.' He pushed the car into gear as the traffic lights turned green. 'It doesn't help that everyone's so tight-lipped about the past.'

Amy agreed. Her team had obtained records of Luka and his mother, Sasha, coming to the UK in 1984 on a scholarship programme, but there were scant details about him participating in the psychological trials. 'It's tragic, isn't it? How they both died.' She was referring to Luka and his mother and the fire that had claimed their lives. 'And all the records going up in smoke.' She paused, speaking her thoughts aloud. 'The fact that they were cremated seems very convenient too.'

Paddy gave her a sideways glance that suggested she was out of her tree. 'You don't seriously believe that nutter, do you? He's not Luka. He's yanking your chain.'

Just the same, Amy wondered what had gone on behind the scenes at the Curtis Institute. She needed details of the experiments and further information on the deaths of Luka and his mother.

'I reckon Nicole has been in contact with him from the off.' Paddy manoeuvred the car through traffic. To his left, a city bus rumbled past, almost drowning out his words.

Amy knew he was talking about their suspect. Minutes passed before she spoke, having assembled her thoughts. 'He mentioned Nicole for a reason. He wants us to give chase.' She gazed out of the car window as Paddy took the road to the Curtis family's residence. 'It wouldn't surprise me if he's watching the house.' A point-to-point call on the police radio informed her that officers had tried but failed to get an answer on the landline. A prickle of concern grew. She did not know enough about Ellen's kidnapper to build a profile of him, but it was obvious he took pleasure in playing games. That's why he'd been drawn to Amy after reading about her latest case in the press.

On reaching the Curtis house, she opened her car door before Paddy had even put on the handbrake, unable to wait a second longer to find out what was going on.

Gravel crunched underfoot as they approached the expansive drive, and Amy frowned at the appearance of a single skid mark in a perfectly formed arc. A motorbike, perhaps? Someone who had turned in a hurry to leave? Next to it was Dr Curtis's Mercedes.

Paddy pointed to the cherished licence plate: CUR711S. 'I bet that cost a few quid.'

Amy was unimpressed, although it did serve to tell her that Curtis was home after all. She touched the hood. Warm. As she approached the front door, a howl rose from within, making Paddy and Amy exchange a look. Raising her finger, Amy signalled for Paddy to go around the back, conscious that if there was an intruder present it would be their first means of escape.

Patting his jacket pockets, Paddy's face fell. 'My radio . . . I left it at the nick.'

It was not the first time he had forgotten it. Unclicking her radio from her shoulder harness, Amy threw it in his direction. If necessary, she could make use of the airwaves in the car.

Inside, the howling came to an abrupt stop. There was no time to spare. 'Open up!' Amy commanded, keeping her finger pressed on the doorbell. No response. Crouching, she peered through the letterbox. Down the hall, she could see Dr Curtis standing, his head in his hands.

'Police. Open up!' Amy's voice carried through the letterbox.

Slowly, he glanced up at her, each movement a monumental effort. Rising to her feet, Amy acknowledged Paddy as he returned.

'It's all locked up,' he said, just as Dr Curtis opened the door. The tears wetting his face conveyed that something was very wrong.

'She's dead,' he blurted as they followed him inside.

'What? Who? Are you talking about Ellen?' Amy said, trying to fuse together the pieces of the puzzle. 'Have you spoken to her kidnapper?'

Dr Curtis's mouth hung open as he looked from Amy to Paddy. His grey hair stood in tufts on his head, his skin was pallid. 'Ki-kidnapper?' he stuttered.

'Where's Nicole?' Amy said, brushing past him to check the rest of the house.

Raising a shaking hand, Dr Curtis pointed towards the living room.

Relaying his call sign, Paddy updated Control.

Amy's heart skittered in her chest as she caught sight of a pair of feet sticking out from behind the sofa. A kitten-heeled shoe lay on its side and, in the oddest of moments, she noticed that Nicole's toenails were painted metallic blue. It was strange how, in the most panic-stricken times, the smallest details came into view. As she rushed to the body, her police training took over, but later in the night when she could not sleep, those blue-painted toenails would resurface in her thoughts.

Lifeless, Nicole lay on her back, jagged paths of dried blood crusting her nostrils and mouth. The cream carpet was covered in splatters from where she must have coughed before she crumpled to the floor. With two fingers, Amy touched the side of her neck. Her skin was graveyard-cold. It could not end like this. Amy's jaw clenched as she tilted back Nicole's head and prepared to resuscitate. She had carried out CPR many times in her career and was not about to give up now. Her chest compressions were quick and firm and she resisted Paddy's offer of help.

'You stay with Curtis and show the paramedics in,' she said. There would be no contamination of evidence on her watch. She had seen the discarded mobile phone on the ground, too battered and scuffed to be Nicole's. To the side lay what looked like small glass phials, next to a box that had been torn open with force. Pinching Nicole's nose, Amy put her thoughts on pause as she sealed her mouth over it and delivered two breaths. After another round of CPR she detected the faintest of pulses beneath the skin. 'She's still alive!' Amy called to Paddy, who had detained Dr Curtis in the hall. It was how they worked. One officer worked while the other watched their back.

Curtis was looking very sheepish right now. He had medical training. Why hadn't he administered CPR? Gently and swiftly, Amy turned Nicole into the recovery position, closely monitoring every breath.

When the paramedics arrived, Amy stood and gave a quick explanation of events. In the corridor, Dr Curtis sniffed.

Amy and Paddy had walked in on something they did not understand. Why had Nicole been almost murdered when their caller had said she'd cooperated with him? Amy checked her watch, making a mental note of the time. She would have to provide a police statement. It was the best way of remembering crucial details that might be forgotten later on.

Outside, car doors slammed as uniformed officers arrived at the scene. Updating Control, Amy instructed that nobody else enter until everything had been cordoned off.

She nodded at Paddy as unspoken words passed between them. It was the second time Dr Curtis had failed to telephone the police. And why hadn't he been trying to save his wife when they arrived? If it had been left to him, Nicole would have died.

There was only one thing left to do.

'I'm arresting you on suspicion of attempted murder.' Paddy's words flowed confidently as he took a firm grip of Dr Curtis's arm. Reciting the caution, he led him outside, towards a marked car. Curtis followed meekly, as if in a state of shock.

Shoulders hunched, features taut, Dr Curtis's body language mirrored that of many before him as he sat on the plastic chair in the interview room. The decision to arrest him had not been taken lightly. If the press got hold of this, it could ruin Dr Curtis's career.

A Styrofoam cup of tepid tea sat on the table, untouched. It was hardly what Dr Curtis was used to. Amy watched from another room as Molly and Steve conducted the interview, leading him through the usual introductions before they began. This was termed a 'first account' interview. Further in-depth questioning would follow as they examined every detail of the events leading up to his arrest.

Harvey Forshaw of law firm Forshaw & Smith began to take notes. He was a broad, well-tailored man, and Amy's team had encountered him more than once. The esteemed firm of lawyers was known for defending celebrity clients and were regularly in the press. Amy disliked Forshaw because of his stalling techniques. With painful deliberation he had thumbed through the custody report before taking over an hour in the consultation room with his client. Each action was designed to wind down their custody clock, leaving officers with less time for the interview.

Amy's team had twenty-four hours to detain Curtis, and that included his designated eight hours' sleep. An extension was unlikely to be granted. It was better to interview then bail, rather than keep him in overnight and wind down the custody clock. It was unusual for bail to be granted for such a serious offence, but Dr Curtis's record was pristine and he was unlikely to abscond.

Amy snapped out of her thoughts. They had barely begun interviewing and she had already forecasted the gloomy conclusion. Curtis had not been arrested on suspicion of kidnapping his daughter, so their questioning of him on that matter was curtailed. But if she could pick up anything – the slightest clue as to Ellen's whereabouts – it would make the fallout of his arrest worthwhile. But judging by his body language, Curtis was not ready to open up.

Introductions out of the way, Steve delivered his opening question, asking Curtis to explain his movements that day.

'I've told the officers already,' Curtis sighed wearily. 'I was looking for Ellen, visiting parks where I've taken her in the past. When I got home I called out to Nicole but there was no answer. I'd just found her when the police started banging on my door.'

'Was anyone else in the house? Any signs of forced entry?'

'No . . . We have housekeepers but Nicole sent them home. Speak to them if you don't believe me. It's why I left. She said she needed some space.'

'She was upset?' Steve sought confirmation.

'Of course she was upset – what sort of question is that?'

Steve ignored the doctor's outburst. 'Had you argued?'

Curtis shifted in his chair. 'Her nerves were frayed. Voices were raised.'

'What about the phone and the phials of liquid we found at your address? What do you know about them?'

'Nothing,' Dr Curtis replied. 'They're not ours. I don't know where they came from.'

'So we won't find your fingerprints on them?'

'No.'

'But there's something you're not telling us, isn't there?' Steve regarded him with a cynical eye. 'Why did you shut your wife down when she told officers Luka was responsible for Ellen's kidnapping?'

'Luka is dead. I didn't want her wasting police time.' He folded and unfolded his arms, unable to sit still.

'He's causing an awful lot of trouble for someone who's dead,' Steve replied. Sliding a clear plastic exhibit bag across the table, he looked Curtis squarely in the eye. 'I refer to exhibit CC05, a card found in your wife's pocket. What can you tell us about this?'

Dr Curtis leaned forward and stared at it, the colour draining from his face. It was the card quoting the 'Ladybird, Ladybird' poem with Luka's signature underneath.

'Do you need further consultation?' his solicitor interceded, clearly unaware of this latest turn of events. 'We can pause the interview . . .'

47

From the privacy of the monitoring room, Amy rolled her eyes. How much longer was he going to drag this out?

Curtis cleared his throat. 'No. I want to get this over with so they can concentrate on looking for Ellen and whoever did this to my wife.' He prodded the air with his finger. 'Have you had any more updates? I should be by her side.'

'Can you answer the question?' Steve interjected.

Curtis glared at DC Moss, finally delivering his response. 'No comment.'

A vein throbbed in Amy's forehead as the stress of the investigation hit home. Right now, Nicole was in an induced coma with suspected poisoning. It was not known at this stage if she would pull through.

Steve raised an eyebrow, unaware of Amy's concerns. 'You do understand that by responding "no comment" to this question, the court can draw an inference – in other words, they may wonder why you're unable to—'

'I'm an educated man, Detective,' Dr Curtis interrupted, folding his arms once more across his chest. 'I know what an inference is. Now, I'd appreciate it if you'd move things along.'

But Steve refused to budge. 'I want to talk about your work at the Curtis Institute in 1984 and 1985. Tell me about your time with Luka.'

'No comment.'

Amy leaned back in her chair as Curtis continued to answer 'no comment' to the remainder of Steve and Molly's questions. She watched as he removed a handkerchief from his pocket and mopped his brow. The very sight of the note had sent the doctor into a cold sweat. Peering more closely at the monitor, Amy tuned into her intuitions, staring at the man under scrutiny from her team. His arms were wrapped around his torso as he leaned forward. Hunched in his chair, his breathing was rapid, his nostrils flared. Amy had encountered enough victims to read the signs. Dr Curtis was scared.

CHAPTER TEN

Novokuznetsk, Soviet Union, 1984

It had been two hours and ten minutes since the letter was delivered. In all that time, Mama had not stopped pacing the floor. Her eyes were bright, her voice animated. 'Just think,' she said. 'The Tower of London, the Changing of the Guards . . . You're going to love it!'

'But Papa said . . .' Luka replied, barely daring to believe that such a trip was possible. And without his father too. There was no way Papa would allow the family unit to be split up – would he?

It seemed his question would soon be answered, as Ivan walked through the door. Up until today, going to London had seemed as unlikely as the fairy stories his mother read to him at bedtime. It had all begun when his teacher asked the class to complete some psychometric tests. He was the only boy in his class who could not just spell the word but fully understood what it meant. It was on the back of his good results that Mama had plucked up the courage to apply to the Curtis Institute for them both to attend.

The letter his mother clutched in her fingers was from a man called Dr Curtis. Luka had been invited to join his study group in London for six whole months. According to Mama, a scholarship meant they would stay in the dorms and he would receive the best schooling under their care.

At six years of age, Luka knew far more than his friends. Fluent in both English and Russian, he could also solve the algebra problems his teachers set. Yet there were things he did not understand. Papa had said more than once that he lacked common sense. Despite Luka inheriting his broad stature and cheery demeanour, Ivan insisted that life in the mines was not for him. Mama agreed, which was why she had gone to so much trouble with tonight's chicken dish. It had warranted another trip to the market, and Luka's fingers were red and sore from plucking the feathers embedded in the bird's skin. As usual, nothing would be wasted. She would keep the bones, claws and head to form the base of a stew tomorrow night. Luka imagined that they would not have to go to such lengths when it came to food in England.

'Please, Ivan,' Mama pleaded with his father when they sat down at the table to eat. All of their arguments took place over dinner. Not that it was ever much of an argument. She had only the time it took to eat the meal to get her point across. By the time Papa had finished eating, his mind would be made up and there would be no changing it.

'What sort of study group is this?' Papa replied. 'You hear about human trafficking. You could be sold off as slaves, for all I know.'

'Look!' Mama said, waving the letter in front of his face. 'It's from a real institute, backed by the government – legal and above board. Only the brightest children are being offered a place.'

'And what if it doesn't work out?' Papa paused to chew his chicken. 'What then?'

'We come home. Only this time we'll have money lining our pockets.' Mama smiled, pushing a stray hair from her face.

'Very well.' Ivan sighed. 'But I worry about you. Yes, Luka is clever. Far cleverer than me. But you both lack common sense.' Still grumbling, he picked up his bowl and slurped the remains. Luka was glad his papa didn't drink alcohol, like some of his friends' fathers. Some distilled it from rotten potatoes and beets. Others drank cologne, which was a tenth of the cost of the vodka sold in the shops. Last week, one of the people in their block of flats had died from drinking anti-freeze. Such examples were often given by Luka's mother as reasons why they should move to the UK. But his father was still rambling on, explaining why they should stay.

Luka frowned at his father's use of the Russian word *naivnyy* as he continued to voice his concerns. It took him a few seconds to translate it into its English counterpart. Naive. Innocent. Simple. A spark of annoyance rose from within. Who was he calling simple? Then he saw the expression on his father's face. Full of concern, his skin weathered from years of hard work. Up until now, Papa's life had been hard but safe. He didn't want to fly in an aeroplane or see the world. *He* was the simple one.

'I want to go,' Luka piped up. 'Please. My friends are jealous. They wish they were me.'

'Ack!' Papa frowned, returning his glance to his wife. 'Don't you see? When people give you nice things for free, it means they want something in return. Say little. Make your silence a source of strength. In time, they will let down their guard. Only then will you know their motivations.'

Mama narrowed her eyes. 'You're so suspicious.'

'And you're too trusting.' His voice softened. Rising from his chair, he took her by the hand. 'Promise me, please. Be swift to hear and slow to speak. Make me a vow.'

'So be it.' She sighed, her earlier excitement having fizzled away. She turned to Luka. 'Go to your room and sort through your clothes. We don't need much. Pick out what still fits you and put it on your bed so I can wash and darn it in time.'

'When are we going, Mama?' Luka said, his conflicting emotions twisting his stomach in knots.

'In two weeks,' she replied, smoothing open the letter. 'Enough time to say goodbye to your friends.'

Luka responded with a weak smile. Now the opportunity had presented itself, he was unsure if he wanted to go. Leaving home without Papa made him feel ill at ease. If he voiced his concerns, then Papa would put a stop to it for sure. Nibbling on his bottom lip, he watched his mama gather up their bowls, a serene smile on her face. He loved her too much to shatter her dreams.

CHAPTER ELEVEN

A seasoned journalist, Adam was unaccustomed to feeling so nervous. He waited in the prison visiting room, his right knee shaking as the heel of his boot danced against the floor. It was the link to Amy that had brought him here. He still loved her, no matter how hard he tried not to. What had Lillian Grimes meant when she'd hinted at a connection? Despite his misgivings, he was about to meet the woman who had shocked the nation with her acts. He had reported Lillian Grimes to be a monster, capable of the most despicable crimes. Would she be angry with him?

He thought of the letter he had received in the post. He had memorised every word. Each time he closed his eyes, it floated before his face.

> *Dear Adam,*
>
> *I imagine my correspondence will come as a surprise. I have been following your newspaper reports with interest. I feel that we're going to get along.*
>
> *Did you know we were almost related, you and me? It's a shame your engagement to Amy failed. It would have been nice to have a journalist in the family. Then*

again, perhaps when you know who she really is you'll count your parting as a blessing.

I have arranged for you to visit me tomorrow. I'm sure you'll find it useful, and I'm prepared to tell all. There are just a couple of things I need you to do for me first.

Yours, always,

Lillian Grimes

He had not visited the next day, as instructed. In fact, the letter had been sent months ago. His reluctance to take the bait had surprised even him. An exclusive with Lillian Grimes was something he could have only dreamt about before now. But this affected Amy and needed careful consideration. What had Lillian meant about having a journalist in the family? Were she and Amy related? Curiosity had got the better of him and, when she next requested a visit, he'd seized the opportunity to get answers once and for all.

He fidgeted with his hands. Had he done the right thing? Should he have told Amy about the letter? Since their split, they'd not been on the best of terms.

He sprang from his seat as his vision was filled with the sight of Lillian Grimes. She did not hold out her hand to shake his, obviously used to people keeping their distance. Her hair was shoulder-length, cut in a bob, and a half-smile played on her lips. She had an attractive face, which could easily lure people in, but if there was any resemblance to Amy it was nothing more than a shadow of one. Where Amy had depth, Lillian held a deadness behind her eyes.

Adam waited for her to take a seat across from him before sitting back down. She assessed him for a few seconds before speaking, her right leg gently bobbing in time with his. Adam realised that she was watching him very intently, and he stilled his movements as he waited for her to speak.

'So you're the famous Adam Rossi.' Her head tilted to one side, her gaze crawling over his form.

'Famous in what way?' Adam replied, his throat tight as he swallowed. It was an unorthodox introduction, but they both knew who the other one was.

'I have you to thank for all this attention in the press, don't I? "The Beast of Brentwood" – what a frightening headline that was.' She raised her hand as he opened his mouth in protest. 'Yes, I know, you weren't the first to use it. That started a very long time ago. But you were quite happy to resurrect it when the time came.'

'Why did you write to me?' he said, hoping she would get to the point.

'Amy is my daughter. I thought you had a right to know.' She paused, her dark eyes boring into him. 'I can see why she took a fancy to you; you're not a bad-looking young man. Shame you couldn't keep your dick in your trousers.'

Adam raised his eyebrows, for once lost for words.

'Oh, don't worry, I'm not judging you. In fact, I'm all for sexual freedom. It's a shame my daughter didn't inherit my tastes.' Smiling, she fluttered her eyelashes in a coquettish fashion. 'When I was her age I would have eaten you whole. And not just me . . . if my husband were alive, he'd have loved watching us.'

Adam felt like he was twelve years old as Lillian's voice became dark and thick in her throat. Her eyes glittering like two black diamonds, she stared at him like a viper about to strike. She and her husband, Jack Grimes, had conducted a campaign of terror, killing innocent young women and children as they satisfied their perverse sexual needs. It was a small mercy that Jack had died of an undetected heart condition while awaiting trial.

Adam cleared his throat. He had never met a woman like this in his life. She was creepy yet intoxicating, and the journalist in him wanted to know more about her past. 'Why go public now, about you being Amy's mother? Is it really true?'

'I'm appealing my case,' she replied, 'and I need all the help I can get. Amy got in touch a while ago asking for the burial places of three of Jack's victims. But as soon as I gave her what she wanted she cut me out of her life.'

Adam nodded. It was on the tip of his tongue to say he knew how Lillian felt on that one. But the jury was out on Lillian Grimes. He could not bring himself to sympathise with such a vile human being just yet.

Lillian's mouth curled upwards in a smile as she caught the faint nod. 'If Amy had her way, I'd rot in prison. But I'm no murderer. Ask her. She knows all about it. I was set up by the police officers investigating my case.'

'Really?' Adam tried to hide his growing excitement. So that's what she'd meant when she wrote about needing a couple of things from him. A story like this could send newspaper sales through the roof. 'So you want me to print your story?'

'Yes, and I expect payment – the money can go towards my appeal. You can have whatever you want from me as long as you print the truth. Ask my solicitor. They've been forced to reopen the case.'

Adam's thoughts raced. Could he do this to Amy? It wasn't just about revealing her true identity. If she had been involved in some kind of cover-up, it could destroy her career. He would have to complete his checks, speak to his boss and fast-track contracts and payments to obtain an exclusive deal. He had no doubt his paper would go for it, but could he be the one to light the fuse on the bomb? He reluctantly met Lillian's eyes as she proceeded to tear Amy's good name apart.

'She treated me so badly. Despite all the evidence, she was happy to lay the blame at my door. She has a brother and a sister, you know – Mandy and Damien. I begged her to visit them. She thinks she's too good for the likes of us.'

'So Amy knows that you're her mother?'

Lillian's smile broadened as her words hit home. 'She shouldn't be in the police, not with her genes. It's an insult to the victims.' Leaning forward in her chair, she invaded Adam's personal space. 'Do you know she visited the families of Jack's murder victims and said how sorry she was for their loss? What a cheek, knowing her father had killed their kids! And they call me dark.' A gentle chuckle left her lips. 'Believe me, you had a lucky escape.'

Adam fought the urge to recoil as the sickly-sweet scent of deodorant vented from her body. 'I can't imagine news like that would go down easily.'

Lillian snorted in response. 'What they say about me – it's all lies. I was in an abusive marriage. Jack was a monster who forced me to take part. I tried to get out, but back then Amy – or should I say Poppy? – told social services it was all my fault. Nobody would listen to me after that. And then the police set me up.'

Adam's mind reeled. Jack was a monster? A minute ago Lillian had been talking about how her husband would have loved to watch them in bed. Something was very off about this conversation. But Lillian's story was a gift handed to him on a plate. Could he turn down such an opportunity?

'It's all documented,' she said, catching the mistrust in his eyes. 'One of the officers admitted to planting evidence. It's been the basis for my appeal. My solicitor said we have to reverse all the bad publicity in the press. I don't want the public to think I'm some kind of beast. I mean, look at me.' Lillian smiled graciously. 'Do I look like a monster to you?'

Adam decided not to answer. True, in her tracksuit and trainers she did not appear threatening, but there was something chilling about her presence. So far, he was reluctant to believe a word that came out of her mouth. 'So you're after some positive publicity?' he said, edging back in his seat.

'It's only fair you put my spin on things after all the damage you've done. And when it's printed I want you to personally hand it to Amy. Those are my terms. I want you. Nobody else.' She delivered a devilish smile. 'Believe me, it's juicy. You'll be known as the journalist who got the inside story on Lillian Grimes. You could even write a book about it. What do you say?'

'I need to speak to my boss,' Adam said, but his thoughts were with Amy.

'Shame she let you go for such a minor indiscretion,' Lillian said, picking up on his contemplation. 'If I were twenty years younger . . .' Her eyes roamed his body. 'Amy must be mad, fancying that DI Donovan instead of you.'

Adam wanted to ask what she meant about DI Donovan, but he could not get away quickly enough. He checked his watch, feeling his skin crawl. 'I'll run things by my boss and let you know as soon as I can.'

'Don't delay,' Lillian replied. 'I've got stories that will make your hair curl.'

'Right, I'd best be off,' he said, eager to escape.

Adam forced a smile before walking away. He had never been so desperate to be out of anyone's company in his life. He wanted to have a shower. To scrub his face and hands. To get any semblance of that woman out of his thoughts. Yes, he relished the prospect of such a huge story, but it would mean spending more time in Lillian's presence. What a horrible thought.

A pang of regret prickled his conscience as his impulses played tug of war. Only now could he see why Amy had been so upset when he broke that last story on Lillian Grimes a few days after her father's death. How hard it must have been, coming to terms with it all. And then he'd waded in, thinking only of himself.

Still wrestling with his conscience, he left the building. Lillian had presented him with a fantastic opportunity that any other journalist would snap up. It was mind-blowing. But this would affect Amy's career. What if she lost the respect of her colleagues – or, worse still, respect for herself? She wasn't as strong as she led everyone to believe. Beneath that icy exterior lay the heart of a damaged, vulnerable little girl. And now he knew why. If he could not bear to sit in Lillian's company for more than ten minutes, what had it been like being brought up by parents like the Grimeses? In that house, with bodies buried beneath the basement floorboards. Seeing her sister murdered before her own eyes. It did not bear thinking about.

He ran his fingers through his hair, looking both ways before crossing the road. Lillian had said she would give him an exclusive. But why him? And that comment about Amy seeing someone else. It was obvious she wanted to twist the knife. Hadn't Amy been through enough?

Deep in thought, he mulled over his options, oblivious to the drizzle of rain. For once in his life he could be selfless – he owed her that much. 'Easy come, easy go,' he muttered. He would bury the story for Amy's sake. It would never see the light of day.

CHAPTER TWELVE

Amy cast an eye over at the clock on the kitchen wall. As far as she was concerned, 2 a.m. was a perfectly respectable time to sit with a gin and tonic in hand. Outside, the wind howled a wintry chorus, but with the lights off and the radiators still warm, their kitchen was a cosy nook. Cast in the orange glow of the street lamps, Amy watched, entranced, as the rain fell in rivulets against the windowpane. It would have been hypnotic had she not so many thoughts racing around in her head. In times like these, with the world asleep and the dog curled up on her bed, Mr Gordon was the best solution to a long day.

She tipped the bottle of gin towards her glass, topping it up with a measure of tonic until it was full to the brim. 'Whoops.' She chuckled, watching it slosh over the edges. Drawing the glass towards her, she took an unladylike slurp.

'Oh! You frightened the life out of me.' Flora's left hand splayed across her chest as she switched on the kitchen light.

Amy squinted as the flash of the sixty-watt lightbulb temporarily blinded her. Before her, Flora stood in her full-length white nightgown, a smearing of cold cream giving her face a deathly appearance.

'You're pretty bloody frightening yourself.' An impromptu giggle escaped Amy's lips. Her mother was the old-fashioned kind, out of place in the modern world.

'Amy, don't swear,' Flora scolded, approaching her for a closer look. 'Are you drunk?'

'I'm working on it.' Amy took another swig from her glass. She usually tried not to drink on a work night, but she needed a respite from her thoughts. A wisp of a memory bloomed – her adoptive father sitting at this very table with a tipple of brandy, weary after a long day.

'Is that why you're sitting in the dark?' Concern was etched on Flora's face. 'What's happened?' Taking a glass from the cupboard, Flora slid it across the table before pulling up a seat. Amy couldn't help but smile. Her mother was always willing to keep her company, no matter what time it was.

She sat in Flora's presence, her worries tugging at her consciousness once again. 'I've had a pig of a day. It started with the kidnapping of a four-year-old child and ended with her mother being poisoned.' She rubbed the base of her neck, her shoulders stiff from hunching over her computer as she reviewed the investigation. Having exhausted their inquiries, Amy had sent her team home to get some sleep. With the custody clock ticking, Dr Curtis had been bailed pending further reports, and a search of his premises had turned up nothing new. Unfortunately for them, the iPhone seized at the address had been invaded by a virus that had wiped it clean.

At least the phials seized should produce something of value, and they were awaiting lab results. But from whom did they originate? The so-called walking ghost of Luka Volkov, or the equally mysterious Dr Curtis? Some would say the doctor had been through hell, almost losing his wife and his child in one fell swoop. But how much of it was of his own making? Was he trying to silence Nicole before she implicated him in whatever he was trying to cover up? Having located one of Curtis's ex-wives, Amy was pleased to discover she did not live far away. She would call round in the afternoon. And what about Luka Volkov? Would he ring her, as promised? The thought of him made Amy take another sip of gin.

'I saw the appeal on the telly,' Flora said, cautiously eyeing her. 'It was good. You didn't look half as nervous as you used to.'

'I'm getting plenty of practice.' Amy drained her glass. She reached for the bottle of Gordon's, a slight sway in her hand. Good. It meant she would get some sleep. 'You know what really upset me?' She gave her mother a knowing look as she topped her gin up with tonic. 'Work, I can cope with – it's my personal life that drives me to drink. Ever since that woman got in touch, memories of my childhood have come flooding back.' Amy wasn't talking about the comfortable time she had spent with her adoptive parents in their upmarket London home. Nor was she talking about the private education she had been granted or the numerous after-school clubs and trips out with friends. She was referring to a dark and seedy past. Violence that a four-year-old child should never witness, much less be able to comprehend. The scars were embedded deep in her psyche, along with the actions of Jack and Lillian Grimes.

It was when Amy had been scrutinising Dr Curtis that she realised why she was so proficient in recognising the signs of fear. It was not from the hundreds of victims she had dealt with during her time in the police. It was from faces in her past, flashbacks of the victims dragged back to Jack and Lillian's lair.

She looked at Flora, her eyes glistening with emotion. 'I can't keep her out of my head. It's got to the point where I hate going to bed at night.'

'Oh.' Flora's voice was small as she cradled her glass. She didn't need to ask Amy who she was referring to. 'I'm sure things will improve with time.'

An alcohol-induced smile played on Amy's lips. Being both tipsy and annoyed was a novel emotion and she gave it free rein. 'But it won't. The more time passes, the more I remember. It sickens me to think I was there when . . . when . . .' She hung her head as another flashback played on a loop. She was four-year-old Poppy Grimes, the palms of her hands sticky against the black leather seats of her father's car. The radio playing 'Living Doll' on a scratchy frequency. Lillian emitting high-pitched laughter as the lyrics referred to locking someone up in a trunk. Amy could almost taste the boiled sweets her daddy had bought her for being a good girl and keeping quiet. She was their bait. A projection of innocence for lost souls wandering the streets.

She could feel the judder of the car as it came to a halt by the kerb, hear the creak of the rusted car door as an unsuspecting young girl slid inside. A runaway, lured by the promise of a babysitting job and a roof over her head. The girl was hesitant, her hand still on the inside door handle as the car picked up speed. Then came the look Poppy had seen many times before. Eyes that burned with the need for reassurance. *It's going to be OK, isn't it?* But no reassurance was forthcoming. Poppy's lips stayed tightly shut as she rolled her sweet over her tongue.

Reaching across the table, Flora squeezed Amy's hand, making her jerk away in response. 'Maybe you should see a counsellor. You've been through so much. You can't expect to deal with it on your own.'

'And relive it all over again? No thanks.' She gave her mother a watery smile, feeling guilty for snatching back her hand. No one else knew the gory details occupying her mind, and she was going to keep it that way. 'I'm fine, it's just the gin talking. It's been a long day.'

'You could talk to me . . .' Flora looked at her dolefully. They both knew that she would not be able to deal with the horrors of Amy's past. She bit her lip. 'Or Adam. He came for a visit today.'

'Adam? Ugh. And you let him in?'

'What else could I do? I could hardly close the door in his face.'

Flora had received many visitors since her husband's passing, but this was one friendship that did not need cultivating. What was Adam up to now?

'If Charles Manson called, would you let him in for a little chat?' But Amy's joke fell flat as she recalled her heritage. How could Flora bear to have the daughter of serial-killer parents beneath her roof at night?

'He's a sweet boy who made a mistake,' Flora replied. 'He still loves you, you know. He'd do anything to get you back.'

'You call sleeping with someone else the night before our wedding a mistake?' Curled up at her feet, Amy's pug snored, having joined their conversation halfway through. Dotty would have been far more comfortable on her bed, but her beloved pet didn't like to leave her side when she was at home. Amy took comfort in her presence, the warmth of her fur tickling her toes. Who needed a man with devotion like that?

Flora toyed with her glass, having barely touched its contents. 'He misses you. He wanted to check that you were all right.'

'Proper little comrades-in-arms, aren't you?' Amy sighed as the visit played out in her mind: Adam wrapping Flora around his little finger as he tried to worm his way back in.

'I'm sorry, love.' Flora sighed. 'All I want is for someone to look after you.'

'I'm well able to look after myself.' Knocking back the last of her gin and tonic, Amy rose unsteadily to her feet. But her words had been sharp and she caught the hurt expression on her mother's face. 'I'll be fine. I've got you, haven't I?' she said softly.

'And Sally-Ann,' Flora added.

It had not been easy telling Flora about Sally-Ann. Her mother had looked at her with a mixture of surprise and concern at the time. 'But she's dead,' Flora had said.

'That's what everybody thinks,' was Amy's reply. 'But Sally-Ann came to after Jack dumped her body that night. He thought she was dead. So did Lillian. They never spoke about her again.'

Once Flora had got over the initial shock, she had insisted on meeting Amy's biological sister. At first, Sally-Ann was nervous and, suspicious of Sally-Ann's motives, Flora was a little cold. But after a heartfelt chat the two most important women in Amy's life were soon acting like old friends.

After depositing their glasses in the dishwasher, Amy lightly patted Flora on the back. With Amy, hugs were in short supply. With long-buried memories of her childhood working their way to the forefront of her mind, it was easy to see why – but she still loved her mum with all her heart. 'Night night,' was all she could think of to say.

Waggling her rear end, Dotty followed Amy out of the door. Had he been alive, Robert would have been wary of Adam's presence in their home. Right now, Amy missed her adoptive father so much it felt like a physical pain in her chest. Hoisting Dotty on to the bed, she stripped off her clothes and snuggled under the duvet, the faint tap of rain against her window lulling her to sleep. But her slumber provided little respite as her mind processed the day's events in the form of a disjointed nightmare. Nicole Curtis, her blue-painted toenails poking out from behind the sofa. Ellen Curtis being dragged through a derelict house. Moaning in her sleep, Amy could hear the echoes of Ellen's screams. At the end of a long, narrow corridor, her captor's laughter was dark as they forced the child down basement steps. But the face of Ellen's kidnapper was not that of Luka Volkov. It was Lillian Grimes.

CHAPTER THIRTEEN

Since moving in with her mother, Amy had already established her favourite haunts. The Hummingbird Bakery, where she met her sister once a week, as well as the Notting Hill Bookshop and the Ladbroke Arms pub, to name but a few. Then there were her mid-week trips to Portobello Market to stock up on fresh fruit. Her routine and her job underpinned her daily existence and kept her sane.

'Don't say I never give you anything.' She gently laid a tray of freshly baked cupcakes on a table near the office door. The sugary snacks brought a much-needed morale boost; she had picked them up from the bakery on her way to work. Nicole Curtis's poisoning had added an extra layer of intensity to the investigation and everybody was feeling the effects.

'Red velvet, my favourite.' Molly's eyes were lit up as she plucked one from the tray. Her desk was awash with paperwork, as she preferred printing off investigation updates to reading them on-screen.

'You deserve them.' Amy took one for herself. 'If anyone would like to make a round of coffees to go with these, I won't say no.' She handed a cupcake to Paddy, casting an eye over the crossword-puzzle tie hung loosely around his neck. 'How's it going? Have you got five minutes to fill me in?' It was quicker than reading through the vast number of updates uploaded to the system.

'How are you doing? Lillian still hounding you?' Paddy bit into his cupcake as he followed her. He was one of the few people she allowed an insight into her personal life. Given he was living with her sister, it was not something she could avoid.

'Oh, you know, some people are just beautifully wrapped boxes of shit.' Amy's tone suggested that they should leave it there.

Within a couple of minutes they were ensconced in her office, cups of coffee in hand. Her head was still spinning from last night's nightmare. Mentally, she shut the door on her past and homed in on Paddy's words.

His update was as expected. Extra officers were being drafted in to assist with the groundwork, such as viewing CCTV and reviewing automatic number-plate recognition data. As for Luka . . . they may as well have been looking for a ghost. If he was alive, they had no evidence of it. It wasn't as if they could exhume his body. Amy had printed off copies of the paperwork obtained and pinned them to the board in the briefing room. Luka and his mother had died in the fire and then been cremated before officials had the opportunity to examine their remains. And with little family to fight Luka and Sasha's corner, their deaths had been quickly swept aside. The early cremation had been put down to a mix-up in paperwork at the time, but Amy was sceptical. Assuming Luka had escaped the fire, how had a six-year-old boy been able to fend for himself in a strange country after his mother's death?

'Where are we situated with the data on the seized phones?' Amy asked, remembering how shifty Dr Curtis's wife had been when she'd spoken to her at the house.

'The iPhone was wiped clean. Nicole's mobile is still with the tech department. If we're lucky, we'll have it back later today.' He paused to finish his coffee. 'Do you really think Curtis set all this up? Ellen, Nicole – it's got to be connected. But why do it like this? It makes no sense.'

Above them, the wall clock brought with it a sense of impending doom as the minutes since Ellen's kidnapping ticked away. The first twenty-four hours were crucial in any investigation and they were still playing catch-up, thanks to her parents' failure to make the call. In the case of missing children, hope slipped away like sand in an egg timer the longer they were gone.

Amy sighed, feeling a knot form between her shoulder blades. What she needed was a good punchbag session to chase the pain away. 'Maybe Curtis's ex-wife might be able to shed some light on things.' It had been on her agenda to visit the first Mrs Curtis, Shirley, as soon as she could. 'She goes by her maiden name of Shirley Baker now. Lives not far from here, in a flat on St Luke's Road.' Amy rose from her chair. 'Are you all right to hold the fort if I pay her a quick visit?'

'Sure. Hopefully you can find out what makes Dr Curtis tick.'

As she left, Amy was struck with a deep sense of gratitude for the freedom granted in her job. It was good to escape the confines of her office in favour of a change of scene. Hers was not a traditional role. She still had the responsibility of managing the budget and overseeing the investigation but, luckily for her, DCI Pike enjoyed admin, often completing tasks Amy should have dealt with herself.

A quick introduction and a flash of her warrant card were all it took to gain access to Shirley Baker's flat. She was a statuesque woman, her wavy auburn hair tied high on her head with a scarf patterned with cherries. Amy stepped over the toys littering the hall as she followed the first Mrs Curtis through to the kitchen.

'Thanks for seeing me at such short notice,' Amy said, having called ahead and explained the situation. 'I wanted to check if you had any correspondence with your ex-husband with regard to your children.'

Shirley and Dr Curtis had a son and a daughter, and had been married for ten years before they divorced.

'They're all grown up now,' Shirley replied. 'I'm babysitting my grandchildren today. Do you need me to call them down? They're watching television in my bedroom.'

'No need to disturb them. Have you spoken to Dr Curtis recently?'

Shirley nodded. 'Briefly. It's awful, what happened to Nicole.'

Her words may have been sympathetic but Amy caught a hint of insincerity in her voice.

'Have you received any unusual correspondence, noticed anything suspicious?'

'I'd have called the police if I had,' Shirley replied. Amy was satisfied with her answers for now. She glanced at the kettle as it whistled on the gas stove. It was ages since she'd seen an old-fashioned hob kettle, and it suited the quirky kitchen, which was decorated in a seventies style.

'Would you like a cuppa?' Shirley said, following her gaze. 'I was just about to make one.'

'I'd love a coffee. White, one sugar, thanks.' Amy checked her watch, conscious of the time.

She recalled one of the first tasks Paddy had insisted she learn. Back then, her tutor was not quizzing her on police procedures or her knowledge of the law. He was teaching her how to make a decent cuppa. Coffee she could manage, but her tea had tasted like day-old dishwater until Paddy took her to task. 'You'll either be offered or be making plenty of cuppas during your time in uniform,' Paddy told her. 'Take my advice – don't accept a drink in a place where your feet stick to the floor. If you find something scummy floating on your coffee, it's not cappuccino froth.'

Amy gratefully took the coffee and, following Shirley's lead, sat down at the round kitchen table. It seemed barely big enough to squeeze in a family, but property was at a premium in London and Shirley's two-bedroom flat would come with a hefty price tag.

Amy began with an open question in the hope of Shirley filling her in. 'What do you know about what happened to Nicole?'

'Only that she was poisoned. She didn't deserve that.' Shirley relayed what Amy already knew.

'Do you feel your children are in danger?' Amy observed her face for clues. But Shirley wasn't wearing the guarded expression that had been evident on Nicole's face.

'You're the police officer, you tell me.'

'Nicole mentioned a Luka Volkov. Does the name ring any bells?'

Shirley shrugged and played with a coaster. 'My ex-husband worked with many people. I can't remember them all.'

'What makes you think they worked together?'

'It's obvious, isn't it? Unless this Luka is a clothes designer. The only thing Nicole is interested in is fashion, make-up and shoes.'

Shirley was obviously not a fan but, having seen a breakdown of Nicole's shopping habits, Amy could hardly disagree. She sipped her coffee, steam rising from the mug as she gave herself a few seconds to think. 'So you've never received any flowers or gifts that you can't explain?'

'I wish. The nearest I get to presents are the things my grandkids bring home from playschool.'

Amy's grip on the mug tightened. Was Shirley being deliberately obtuse? 'How was your early relationship with Dr Curtis?' she continued. 'Did work ever interfere with your personal lives?'

Shirley snorted. 'Let's put it this way – Hugh has little time for romance. He uses Mensa to find his conquests instead of dating apps.'

'Really?' Amy said. Nicole did not strike her as the academic type.

'The man's a sociopath. His only love is his work.' A tinge of bitterness laced Shirley's words. 'Our children were nothing more than lab rats to him.'

Amy frowned at her sudden change of mood. 'You're not serious.'

Shirley cocked her head as a shriek emanated from a room above. Satisfied it was childish laughter, she sighed. 'I suppose it's why he latched on to Nicole. She was more pliable – I wouldn't go along with his plans.'

'And wife number two? What about her?' Slipping out her pocket notebook, Amy scribbled down a few words as she listened intently to what Shirley had to say.

'Paula was divorced as soon as he found out she was infertile. Watch yourself with him.' Shirley threw her a wry smile. 'If Nicole doesn't recover, he'll be on the hunt for wifey number four.'

'You mentioned his plans,' Amy said, refusing to be drawn into her domestics.

Shirley's smile faded as she relayed the events of the past. 'Hugh's aim was to boost brain power and concentration skills to give children the best start in life. Have you read his work?'

Having no children of her own, Amy had never found the need. 'No.'

'That's the official explanation you'll find in his books.' Shirley's lips parted in a dark chuckle. 'The truth is ugly, not fit for public consumption, and I'm in no position to rock the boat.'

Amy gave her a knowing look. 'Is he helping you out financially?'

Shirley pursed her lips. It was answer enough.

'Please,' Amy said. 'Off the record, if you like.'

Amy's words provided Shirley with enough reassurance to go on. 'Hugh . . . he was blinkered by ambition. He put the kids in the institution through hell to get results.' She paused to sip her coffee, her eyes glazing over as she revisited the past. 'He locked them away for months, put them through a barrage of tests. Those dorms were nothing more than prison cells.'

'But why? I don't understand,' Amy said, struggling to grasp it all.

Shirley's mouth eased into a sardonic smile. 'Why does anyone do anything? For money, of course.'

'Are you talking about the book deals? Television appearances? But those didn't come until later on.'

'You think he funded his lifestyle with a few book deals?' Shirley said, then checked herself. Bit her bottom lip. 'I've said too much. I've got no right to criticise him when he's supported me all these years.'

The melody of a children's TV show carried down from upstairs. Amy imagined Shirley as a young wife, married to Dr Curtis in the early years. Her thoughts held a question. 'You said he treated your children like lab rats?'

Shirley delivered a slight nod of the head, her eyes locked on her mug. 'Sometimes he used a kind of skull cap, with sensors attached. It was going on for ages before I found out. My son came crying to me one day, saying he didn't want to play Daddy's secret game anymore. You can imagine how I felt. At first I thought . . . Well, it's safe to say that all hell broke loose.' She paused as she gathered her thoughts. 'Hugh said it was for measuring brainwave activity. He made them wear it when they were doing their homework. I couldn't believe he used his own children like that.'

But it was all right to test other people's kids? Amy shelved the thought as soon as it appeared. 'Would your son be willing to speak to the police?'

Shirley paused as another giggle erupted upstairs. 'I don't know. He doesn't talk to his father. My daughter's due back tonight, though. She'll be happy to help you, I'm sure.'

Amy nodded as Shirley continued speaking, making mental to-do notes.

'I guess Nicole was prepared to sacrifice her child's freedom in exchange for her lifestyle. But I don't know . . . to deprive your child of a normal life is a terrible crime.' Shirley cradled her coffee mug in her hands with a faraway look. 'She approached me on the street a month ago, said that Hugh had some terrible secret. I told her I didn't want to know.'

'What kind of secret?'

Shirley shrugged. 'She was acting odd. Jittery. It's bad enough she's spending all my children's inheritance . . .' She cleared her throat. Lowering her mug, her eyes went to the clock on the wall. 'I should get back to the kids. Can we continue this another time?'

Amy glanced at a photo frame resting on a dresser in the kitchen. Pasta shells decorated the edges, pressed into putty then painted neon pink. The picture showed two blonde girls wearing wide smiles as they posed. 'Ellen can't be much older than your grandchildren. She must be terrified – if she's still alive.' But Amy's efforts at emotional manipulation fell on deaf ears.

'I've told you everything I know.' Shirley rose from her chair, waiting for Amy to do the same.

Amy sighed. At least she had got a small insight into Shirley's past life. 'Thanks for the coffee. We'll be in touch.'

'He's not a good man,' Shirley continued as she followed her to the front door, 'but he didn't hurt his wife.'

'Why do you say that?' Amy's movements stalled. She had never for a second suggested that he had.

'Oh, come on now, it's the obvious conclusion, isn't it? What if she was gearing up to leave him? By getting rid of Nicole, he had Ellen for life – her kidnapping could have been a ruse to take the attention off him.'

'But you don't think he did it.'

'He hates violence. Mind games are more his forte. According to Hugh, Nicole was poisoned. I can't picture him standing around waiting for her to die.'

But he didn't stand around, Amy thought, recalling how the hood of his car had been warm. And mind games were exactly what the person purporting to be Luka was playing.

CHAPTER FOURTEEN

By the time Amy was summoned to her DCI's office, Pike had obtained and listened to the recording of their suspect's call.

As she took a seat across from Pike, every inch of Amy's body was tense. If it were up to her, she'd be sitting in her department planning their next move, but Pike would kick up a stink if Amy didn't run everything by her first.

'So that's the crux of it. He wants to hit the headlines.' Pike paused the recording as the caller mentioned his demands.

'Seems that way,' Amy replied, putting herself in his shoes. Her gaze fell on a well-thumbed romance novel face down on Pike's desk. She recognised the name of the author, Holly Martin, and knew that Pike inhaled her work. But with everything that was going on, was this the right time to be reading romantic novels? Just what was up with her?

'Whatever his motivation, we only comply with demands when the action is worth the outcome,' Pike said sagely, before sliding the book into her drawer. 'How far will he go to get what he wants?'

Amy paused, giving the question some thought. Her colleagues respected her for her insight. If only they knew what lurked in the recesses of her mind. She imagined her caller's motivations, the driving force behind his words. After a moment, she said, 'People will go to any lengths if they believe in a cause.' She closed her hands on her lap as she explained her reasoning. 'To them, they're justified, the hero in their own story. I could tell that Ellen wasn't welcome in his space but he was compelled to take her just the same.'

'But murder?' Pike replied. 'Nicole could have died.' It was true. Her doctors had cited methanol poisoning, which matched the substance found in the phials at her address. If Amy hadn't performed resuscitation, this would be a murder investigation.

'Did Ellen's kidnapper want to kill Nicole, though? Did murder factor into his games?'

Nicole was obviously frightened. As for Shirley's comments about Nicole spending the children's inheritance . . . Was Luka working alone? It was another angle to investigate. Amy relayed her concerns to Pike, conscious they needed to keep an open mind.

'Hmm . . .' Pike said, unconvinced. 'We'll focus solely on our phone caller for now. We should liaise with the *London Echo*, keep their journalist in the loop.' Her team was already hunting down the letters their caller claimed to have sent to various newspapers each year. Given the *London Echo* had one of the highest readerships, it was bound to be on that list. The stakes were high and it would be worth submitting to Ellen's kidnapper if it meant saving her life.

'Anyone, as long as it's not Adam Rossi.' Amy smiled. But her smile dropped from her face as Pike raised her eyebrows in response.

'It has to be Adam. He's the most likely helpful candidate.'

'Why?' Amy snapped. She would rather walk into quicksand than see him again. If he found out about her connection with Lillian, she would be front-page news.

'Adam is the ideal person to publish this story. Besides, he has more chance of getting approval than the other newspapers – their headlines are all Brexit and terrorist threats.'

'You do know he's my ex-fiancé, don't you?' Amy hated volunteering personal information, but it was worth a shot.

'You'll have to put all pettiness aside for Ellen's sake.' Pike's swivel chair creaked beneath her as she gestured, driving her words home. 'I've made my decision. Give him a call and start greasing those wheels. Now, off you pop.'

Amy strode back to her office, her fists bunched as they swung in time with her strides. Seeing Adam was the last thing she wanted to do.

She walked into the briefing room to see images of the Curtises' living room pinned to the whiteboard. It made sense for them to run Ellen's kidnapping and Nicole's poisoning in tandem. The second day of the investigation and her team's efforts were clear to see. A series of red lines ran like veins across the board, indicating completed tasks to date. Building a picture of the victims' routines was imperative. What they ate, who they spoke to, what they wore. Every facet of Nicole and Ellen's lives was under scrutiny, no matter how trivial. What was the secret that Nicole had approached Shirley about? Was it her husband's ill treatment of his test subjects, or something even worse? Who else had Nicole spoken to? Officers were particularly interested in calls made to a contact saved as 'DM' on her personal mobile phone. The number had come back as unregistered.

Nicole had very few friends of her own. Had she been calling Dr Curtis's old colleague Deborah McCauley? The entry carried a hint of subterfuge. Every other contact was saved by their first name, with their picture, birthday and email addresses, all perfectly detailed.

Amy perused the board, frowning at the comment 'forensically aware' underlined in red. Apart from carrying Nicole's smudged thumbprint, the phials and phone seized at her address were DNA- and fingerprint-free.

◆ ◆ ◆

Amy braved the bitter January winds to make the five-minute bike ride to Arro Coffee on Bishop's Bridge Road. It was Adam's favourite Italian café, and she had arranged to meet him here with the sole intention of buttering him up. They sat at their old spot on the mezzanine, overlooking the main floor. She liked sitting up here, where the scent of good coffee enveloped them like a warm embrace. At the till, two members of staff chatted in Italian. Amy knew the sound of his native tongue put Adam at ease. She was well versed in the tools of manipulation. Perhaps they weren't so different after all.

'*Come va la mia piccola patata?*' Adam asked, tearing a strip of panettone and popping it in his mouth. *How's my little potato* indeed. The term of endearment was a signal to say he wanted to make peace. While dating they'd had the most awful flare-ups, and the next day it was as if they hadn't argued at all. But their truce could be turned on its head just as easily if either of them said the wrong thing.

'I asked you here to talk about the letters.' Her team had already briefed Adam on the kidnapper, although no new correspondence had been received by the newspaper just yet. Amy's spoon clinked against her glass cup as she stirred her flat white. She was pleased to find that her butterflies were dormant and no longer fluttered at the sight of him. Since meeting DI Donovan, she had begun to see Adam in a less favourable light. There was something very artificial about him. Donovan was easy-going and did not strike her as self-obsessed. She preferred his rough charm and steady attitude to life.

Amy forced back a yawn as Adam steered the topic of work back to himself, talking about the accolades he had been awarded for his reporting on the burial sites Amy had helped to find.

She pointedly checked her watch. 'We may need the story printed tomorrow, if you can. To be honest, it was my DCI's idea that we work together. She thinks you'll do a better job because of your readership.'

'Is this connected to Lillian?' Adam asked. 'Because I've been meaning to talk to you about—'

'It's nothing to do with Lillian bloody Grimes,' Amy interrupted, the thought of her biological mother making her gut churn. She checked that nobody was listening before giving him further details of Ellen and Nicole's cases.

'I'll talk to my boss,' he said. 'It depends on the type of story this guy wants to run.' Adam paused to sip his espresso. 'Listen, can we forget about work for a few minutes? I know we parted on bad terms, but you can come to me any time, you know that, don't you?'

Amy's face grew stony. She had Flora to thank for this. No doubt her mother had filled his head with stories of how Amy couldn't cope on her own. It was a small blessing that he didn't know about her relationship to Lillian. 'Weren't you listening?' she said. 'A child's life is at risk. It's the only reason I'm here.'

'And here was I, thinking it would be nice to work together again.' Adam scowled as he swallowed the last of his panettone. 'But you've changed. Become quite a bitch, by all accounts.'

Amy snorted. She was his little potato five minutes ago. Not that it mattered. Right now, all of her emotions were wrapped up in bringing Ellen home.

'Can you help me or not?' Her chair screeched against the floor as she pushed it back with force. 'Because my time is precious right now.'

'I didn't say I wouldn't help you.' Adam reached for her wrist, his anger flaring as she snatched it away. 'Why are you being like this? We have a history together. It means something to me.'

Amy exhaled, willing to stroke his ego if it meant getting back on track. 'I'm sorry,' she said, forcing a smile as she sat back down. 'It's this new team I'm on . . . it's very pressured. I really need your help.' She swallowed her pride, along with the swear word skimming her tongue. She would win Adam around a lot more quickly if she pandered to his ego and acted as the helpless female he wanted her to be. Her thoughts returned to Ellen. She was somewhere in the city. In Amy's experience, it was too risky for a kidnapper to take their charge very far. But was she alive?

'I'll help you,' Adam said, the smile returning to his face, 'although we get lots of correspondence about celebrities. If the allegations aren't backed up, it goes nowhere. If he did send a letter last year, it probably ended up in the bin. The law is strict on what we can publish these days.' His eyes danced over a svelte young barista as she came on duty. The woman turned her gaze towards him, obviously feeling the heat of his stare. Amy gritted her teeth. The old dog. She would never have his full attention now. 'Will you come back to the station?' she said. 'We can go through it together.'

'Or we could go back to your mum's, order pizza, make an evening of it . . . it would be nice to have a proper chat.'

With great effort, Amy quelled the words on her tongue. He had not one iota of concern for Ellen. If Adam had his way, they would be faffing about eating pizza and drinking wine – then they'd fall into her bed. Why else did he want this cosy 'chat'?

'When is your deadline for tomorrow's edition?' she said, grabbing her handbag from the floor.

'Midnight, if we get the letter soon and I shuffle a few things about.' Adam threw a wistful glance at the barista as they prepared to leave. 'But there's no way they'll let me run it on the front page.'

'It's got to be front-page.' Amy tensed, her fingers gripping the lip of her bag. 'I'm serious. A child could die.'

'You're asking me to commit to a story when we don't even know what he's going to say!' Adam pushed his seat back under the table after he had vacated it. He met Amy's eyes, regret crossing his face. 'Fine. I'll run it by my boss.'

'Front-page?'

'I'll do my best. I promise.'

Her ex had let her down so many times. Amy prayed this was one promise he could keep.

CHAPTER FIFTEEN

Amy's head bobbed up as she realised she had begun to doze off at her office desk. Her evening had comprised overseeing the investigation, chasing up leads and liaising with the media department about their latest press release. The caller's letter had been sent to the *Echo* as predicted, and Adam had promised to do his best to print a non-libellous version of his words. Amy stared at the scanned copy. She had read the letter three times but was struggling to absorb it. Surely children weren't tested like laboratory mice here in the UK? She returned her gaze to the printout.

> *I came from Russia, left before the collapse of the Soviet Union. Fear was constantly in the background and you were always being watched. People regularly disappeared with no explanation and any mention of their name was followed by hushed whispers and warning glances through narrowed eyes. I lived in poverty, saw the destitute, but was told we had more than most.*

My mother brought me to England in the hope of a better life. But Dr Curtis showed us little compassion and went back on every promise he made. Our passports were taken. My environment was toxic. My room was windowless and I had little contact with the outside world. Everything I did was monitored, and the tests became increasingly hard to bear. What saved me were the sightseeing trips to London. Without them I would surely have lost my mind . . .

Amy scrolled to the last paragraph on the page.

. . . we were nothing more than prisoners, kept against our will. I was marked, like several others, lab rats for Curtis's use. Just like in my home town, children disappeared and nothing more was said . . .

A shadow at her door made Amy's heart falter. It was their lead CSI. 'Malcolm, what are you doing here?'

'I've come to rescue you, darling. Haven't you noticed everyone else has gone home?' Malcolm's mouth twitched in a smile as he leaned against her office doorway, hands in pockets, ankles crossed. He was the very epitome of suave, and Amy loved being in his company.

'I sent them home an hour ago.' She yawned. 'We're in for an early start.' Stretching her arms, the bones in her shoulders cracked, making Malcolm wince.

'You've finished late every day this week. It's time we got you out of here.'

'But I wanted to talk to you about the case. I got your report and—'

'C'mon now.' Malcolm gently guided her out of her chair. 'I'm up for talking shop, but not here. If we hurry, we can grab a swift one in the Ladbroke Arms before closing time.'

Amy checked her watch: 10.30 p.m. They would have to be quick. 'My bike's out the back and I need to update my planner for tomorrow. I'll meet you there.'

'You're not cycling at this hour, you'll freeze to death. I'll drop you home.' He ushered her towards the door. 'Come along – chop chop. And give your hair a comb, darling, it's a frightful state.'

'Thanks,' Amy said ruefully, reaching for her bag. As she peered into her compact, she had to agree. Quickly running a brush through it, she applied a light coating of lipstick to disguise the paleness of her lips.

Malcolm was right, she was working herself too hard. She needed to ease her foot off the pedal or she would be no use to anyone at all.

As Malcolm stood at the bar, Amy thought of her relationships with her colleagues and how important they had become. In the police, you were part of a much bigger family. While in uniform, you were usually paired up with the same person, who became your 'work husband' or 'work wife'. And conversations weren't just limited to the job. In the wee hours, officers opened up about their personal lives and family problems. But not Amy. It was why she had got on so well with Paddy when he was appointed her tutor after she joined. Talk of home lives was avoided in favour of suspect motivations or the latest crime hotspots. Work was both a passion and a distraction from what was going on at home.

As Malcolm brought their drinks to the table, she knew that he was the same, keeping work and home separate. His wife was a sensitive soul with a love of knitting, and unlikely to want to hear of his latest gruesome research.

'Cheers, darling,' he said, clinking his glass of diet cola against her gin and tonic. Amy gave him a grateful smile before taking a much-needed sip.

'What do you think of this? We found it on the body.' Amy opened the photos app on her phone. She wasn't meant to photograph evidence, but Dr Curtis's reaction to the note had bothered her, and it was something she'd wanted to contemplate at home. She tilted her phone so nobody else could see.

Ladybird, ladybird, fly away home

Your house is on fire

Your child is gone . . .

Luka

'Luka and his mother died in a fire, didn't they?' Malcolm mused. 'Perhaps whoever wrote this set the fire to get revenge on Dr Curtis. Maybe that's why Nicole nearly died too.'

Having committed the image to memory, Amy put her phone away. 'The card doesn't seem recent. It's old and battered, as if Nicole's had it for some time. It seems like a warning, rather than an immediate threat. Why didn't she report it to the police?'

'Perhaps she had something to hide.'

'The letter sent to the paper talks about children going missing from the Curtis Institute, but we've no evidence of that.' Amy sighed, her brows knitted in a frown as she tried to imagine what life had been like in the institute. 'Do you think it's true, what he wrote about Dr Curtis? He's not the nicest of men, but testing children? It all seems so far-fetched.' The possibility of Curtis using children in such a way had plagued Amy's thoughts since her visit to his ex-wife that morning.

'On the contrary . . .' Malcolm paused to sip his drink. 'Have you heard of the Little Albert experiment?'

Amy's puzzled expression relayed that she hadn't.

'You should familiarise yourself with the case.' He crossed his legs, a leather shoe bobbing as he enjoyed his captive audience. 'It involved a chap named John Watson who conditioned a nine-month-old baby to the extent that the child developed irrational fears.'

'Nine months old?'

Malcolm nodded, clearly in his element. 'He started by introducing the baby to a white rat. As expected at that age, little Albert showed no fear. But then Watson made a terrible racket by hammering a steel bar every time the baby touched the rat. He did it again with other animals and objects, until the baby was terrified of them all. The very sight of them made him cry.'

'How was that sanctioned?' Amy asked. It sounded like something out of the pages of a Stephen King novel.

'It was back in 1920, and not the worst experiment by far. It's referred to now by scholars. Some would say we learned a lot from it.'

'Really?' Amy replied, unable to comprehend the justification for such acts.

'It's fascinating,' Malcolm said. 'Mind you, I was shocked at some of the experiments conducted on children when I did my research. It wasn't that long ago that the law changed and such things came to an end.'

'Is that what happened to Luka? He was brought over here on the promise of a scholarship, wasn't he?' Amy's team was still digging, but the details of Luka's past were slowly filtering through.

'So I heard. It reminds me of another case I researched – the Willowbrook Studies.'

Amy smiled. This was why Malcolm had wanted to take her out, and she loved him for it. Like her, he lived and breathed his job and was keen to impart what he had learned.

'It involved some children with learning disabilities who were promised enrolment into Willowbrook State School in Staten Island,

New York. All their parents had to do was to sign a consent form allowing their children to be vaccinated.'

'Something tells me this involved more than vaccinations.' Amy put her glass down on the table after taking another sip.

'Oh, they were vaccinated all right.' Malcolm's face grew serious. 'Fed the faeces of patients with viral hepatitis to track the development of the strain.'

Amy baulked. 'Are you serious?'

'Back in the 1960s this sort of experimentation was rife, and none of it against the law. I researched a whole plethora of cases which were government-approved. One clinic that experimented on children with cerebral palsy had over 1,400 patients die in their care over five years.'

Amy gaped in disbelief. 'That's horrendous. Surely they were arrested when it was brought to light?'

Malcolm shook his head. 'As far as I could see, not a single researcher has been prosecuted for such experimentation. But how could they be, when it was government-approved?'

There was a pause as Amy took it all in. 'Why take a child from Russia? Surely Dr Curtis could have used kids from the UK.'

'There could have been more likelihood of intervention with an English child. Curtis made trips to Russian orphanages before Luka's mother applied for the post.'

'So you think choosing him for his intelligence was a ruse?'

'Let me put it this way. Curtis was a lot more likely to get the family on board if they believed Luka had some special gift. He was clever, yes, and offers of a scholarship made them dream of better days. You have to remember, this was before the collapse of the Soviet Union. Back then, poverty was rife. As for corruption . . . one wrong word could land you in prison. The offer of a scholarship in Britain would have been a dream come true.'

Malcolm's words echoed those of the letter she had read twenty minutes before. 'But that was years ago. Why wait so long for revenge?

Unless seeing Dr Curtis in the media brought it all back.' Amy realised she had answered her own question.

'True, but why did he insist on dealing only with you? He contacted you for a reason. You investigate serious crime. What *really* happened at the Curtis Institute?'

'The building was old, in need of a facelift. It wasn't safe for students to sleep in the dorms, which is why the previous occupants moved out. But Dr Curtis managed to lease it for six months.' Amy reeled off her officers' research to date. 'On the night of the fire, the alarms didn't work and the orderly on duty was on a cigarette break. Luka and his mother were asleep in their rooms. The experiments had wound down by then and the other students had left. According to the paperwork, arrangements were being made for Luka and his mum to travel home.'

'But the fire took care of that,' Malcolm added.

Amy nodded. 'By the time the alarm was raised, it was too late.'

'Or was it?' Malcolm said. 'You've seen the records . . . there's no grave. Perhaps our kidnapper *is* Luka? Maybe he survived the fire after all.'

'Well – that,' Amy said, stifling a yawn, 'is what we have to find out.'

Malcolm did not know it, but he had just read her thoughts.

CHAPTER SIXTEEN

July 1984

From the moment he boarded the plane, Luka felt the walls of the cabin closing in. Even the air seemed thinner as he dragged it into his lungs in short, anxious breaths. In truth, he wanted to be a big boy and make Papa proud. Besides, how could he tell Mama he was scared? She had been brimming over with excitement ever since the date was set, unable to sit still for more than a minute at a time.

His father had remained suspicious, brooding over the doctor's motivations for bringing them halfway across the world. It left Luka in a permanent state of nervousness, and he wasn't sure if it was the good or bad kind. The doctor's visit to his home was brief and did not allay his father's fears. Dr Curtis was an abrupt man, with little time for pleasantries. It was only due to his companion, Deborah McCauley, that Luka was still allowed to go. He could tell by the way her father looked at her that he thought she was pretty. Luka liked her gentle voice, and there was something in her eyes that made him feel a connection, even though they had never met before now. Her long blonde lashes fluttered each time her father turned his attention towards her, and she effortlessly translated his concerns to Dr Curtis. Deborah voiced the doctor's abrupt answers in a way that sounded comforting, softening his explanations to put Ivan's mind at rest.

Luka leaned forward, his world expanding as he stared through the frosted porthole window at the earth rising up from below. 'Look, Mama! I can see England!' he exclaimed – and, smiling, Sasha craned her neck to enjoy the view. Her eyes shone with hope, but the ragged tissue clutched between her fingers told Luka there was fear there too.

After negotiating the airport, they were met by Dr Curtis, who drove them to the institute in his car. Their journey was cloaked in darkness, and by the time they got there, Luka was too tired to take in the sights. 'I'll see you in the morning,' Dr Curtis said, leaving Deborah to bring them in. She was wearing a white lab coat, her blonde hair tied into a ponytail. 'Right.' She clapped her hands together, making Sasha jump. 'You must be exhausted. Let me show you to your rooms.' Luka understood why Mama was jumpy. This creepy old building was not what they had expected at all.

'Rooms?' Sasha tightened her grip on Luka, drawing him near. 'We stay together – yes?'

Deborah smiled. The kind of patient smile you give a toddler when they don't understand. 'We thought it would be best if you had separate rooms. Besides . . . this used to be a university. There are only dorms – no family rooms here.'

'This cannot be right.' Sasha spoke in Russian, pausing for Deborah to absorb her words. 'Luka shares with me.'

Deborah continued walking as if his mama had not spoken at all. She explained that the building had been empty for a year before Dr Curtis leased it for his studies. 'We've had some problems with vandals, so Dr Curtis thought it better to leave the windows boarded up on this floor.'

The absence of windows created an eerie sense of isolation, and Luka was sure he'd just caught sight of a mouse scuttling down the corridor. A flush rising to her face, Deborah led Sasha to her quarters. Despite the damp spores creeping up the walls, the room was dry and warm, with a television in the corner and a thick blue blanket covering a single bed. Deborah showed them to the small communal kitchen across the way.

'I tell you what,' she said conspiratorially, after checking the hall to ensure that Dr Curtis had left. 'We've got a fold-up bed somewhere. Why don't I squeeze it into Luka's room, and you can join him later tonight?'

'I was promised a double room,' Sasha said in her native tongue. 'This is not good enough.'

'It's the best I can do for now,' Deborah replied. 'He won't be far . . . only down the hall.' After giving Luka a kiss and a hug, Sasha reluctantly let him go.

The dimly lit corridor seemed to go on for ever as Luka was shown to his room. Like in his mama's, the windows were boarded and a blue-blanketed single bed was pushed against the wall. As he followed Deborah in, Luka's stomach did cartwheels at the prospect of sleeping in such a strange place. But at least a two-bar heater provided warmth, and he had never heard of an en-suite until Deborah explained what it was. The thought of having a bathroom all to himself seemed beyond luxurious, even a little ludicrous. But one thought hung like a warning in his mind, making his heart beat a little faster than it should.

Was this a bedroom or a prison cell?

CHAPTER SEVENTEEN

'Is it true?' Deborah inhaled a breath and held it in her lungs until she received a response. Most people would dance lightly around the subject of Nicole's poisoning, but she was not most people. Since hearing about it last night, she had not got a wink of sleep.

'Who is this?' Dr Curtis's voice was gruff. Answering the phone was his wife's domain and not many people had his number these days. Deborah knew she was the exception to the rule because they went back such a long way.

'It's me . . . Deborah. Is Nicole really on her deathbed? I rang the hospital, but they won't tell me a bloody thing.' She shot from the hip, did not mess around with sympathetic meanderings. If Nicole died, Hugh would get over her soon enough. Flicking her lighter, Deborah touched the flame to her cigarette, taking a succession of short puffs until it was lit.

'It's serious,' he said, the heat fading from his voice. 'She had a bleed on the brain. The police questioned me for hours.'

Mumbling under her breath, Deborah paced the kitchen floor, menthol cigarette in hand. 'She rang me yesterday. Shit!' she swore again. What if the police were tracing her call?

'They're still looking for Ellen, thanks for asking.'

'I'm sorry . . .' Deborah realised how selfish she sounded. 'But it doesn't end here. You know that, don't you? The police will be knocking on my door . . . and what about Stuart and Christina? It's only a matter of time until they come clean.'

'You think I don't know that?' Hugh said sharply. 'If Nicole dies, I'm looking at a murder charge.'

Deborah's lips puckered around her cigarette as she locked the smoke deep into her lungs. 'You said they questioned you . . .'

'They treated me as if I were a common criminal. Disgusting, it was.' Curtis sniffed. 'Then they grilled me about the experiments and how Luka and his mother died.'

Deborah's frown deepened. 'Why can't they leave the past alone?' She shuddered as a breeze curled around her, as if invoked by the memories of that day. She had first met Curtis through her father, who had been a golfing acquaintance of his at the time. Having decided to study in the field of psychology, she had persuaded Curtis to provide the work experience she needed to progress. How idealistic she had been. How naive.

'The kidnapper's claiming to be Luka.' Dr Curtis's voice brought her back to the present day. 'Taking Ellen and almost killing Nicole . . . I fear for my life. Really, I do.'

Deborah sighed. None of them could have imagined back then just how things would turn out, and now they had the burden of this awful secret to bear. 'What if the police find out? What then?' Taking one last drag of her cigarette, she stubbed it out in the ashtray. She opened the kitchen window, knowing her son Max would complain about the smell of cigarettes later on. It didn't matter that he was thirty-nine, he would always be the beating heart of her fears and concerns. Max loved her. Looked up to her. She could not bear for him to find out what she had done. Things had been different then. She had thought it was for the best. But in the cold light of day, her actions would be viewed as grotesque.

'You'll have to sort out Christina and Stuart,' Curtis said. 'We all need to be singing from the same hymn sheet.' Silence fell between them, and Deborah became aware of her heart as it skipped a beat. She had forgotten to take her medication. She needed to stay on track.

'Aren't you listening to me?' Dr Curtis exhaled sharply in disbelief.

'Can't you do it?' Deborah snapped, riffling through her handbag for her medication. 'Things have changed. I'm not that person anymore.'

'I told you, I'm on police bail. And I've got children's social care crawling all over me, asking about Ellen and the institute.'

Of course, Deborah thought, dry-swallowing a tablet. *It always comes around to his precious experiments in the end.*

'I've kept my silence . . .' His voice grew dark and menacing, his breath heavy on the line. 'If one of them squeals, we all reap the consequences. Remember that. Everything we've built will topple like a house of cards. Do you want to go to prison? Have them discredit our work?'

'Of course not. I'll speak to Stuart and Christina. I'll do it tonight.'

'Make sure you do. You're the ones he'll be targeting next.'

Deborah knew he was talking about Ellen's kidnapper. For years she had told herself that Luka was dead. Closing the door on the past made it easier to bear. It wasn't just the experiments that would cause her life to come crashing down around her. She had a secret. Something else she'd kept hidden over the years. She had spent her whole life atoning for her deeds, but it was never going to be enough.

CHAPTER EIGHTEEN

The mattress springs creaked as Ellen's kidnapper slouched on the edge of the bed. He had come here to get some respite, but there was an invader sleeping beneath his covers, her small form curled up, her thumb firmly jammed in her mouth. *Somebody's sleeping in my bed.* She looked like a modern-day Goldilocks, with her blonde curls forming a halo around her face. Her captor had come here through force of habit, desperate to lock himself away from the suffocating pressures of the outside world.

The never-ending stream of traffic had intruded on his thoughts: cars honking, workmen drilling, the screaming sirens of the emergency services all hours of the day and night. Today he rejected what the world had to offer. But his safe room was named as such for a reason. It was the only place he felt truly at peace. The world was too noisy, too fast, and his senses were overloaded after a busy day. Ellen was in his space, leaving snot stains on his pillowcase and grubby finger marks on the walls. Children should be obedient. Subservient. Unlike Ellen, who had wailed all day to be let out. He'd had to dose her with Night Nurse and Calpol just to get her to calm down.

He watched her, his eyes narrowed, his thoughts dark. Would she survive what lay ahead? Would he? Taking Ellen was meant to change things. She stirred, crying for her mummy in her sleep. Perhaps death would be a blessing and save her from a lifetime of pain.

CHAPTER NINETEEN

Suppressing a yawn, Amy chastised herself for burning the candle at both ends. Sleep had evaded her and the dark rings under her eyes made her look like death warmed up.

'You're in early,' she said, catching sight of Paddy hunched over his desk. 'Did my sister kick you out of bed?' Sally-Ann was a good influence on him. Lately he had not been late for work once.

Opening the office blinds, Amy cleared away some takeaway cartons from the night before. The place stank of curry and the cleaners were late. A stickler for time-keeping, Amy accepted that not everyone shared her enthusiasm for arriving at work when they should.

'Sally-Ann's on a late shift today, sends her regards,' Paddy replied, gathering up empty mugs in preparation for the morning tea round. 'Feck, it's cold out there.' He shuddered in response to the window Amy had flung open.

'Nonsense. You're spoilt, driving to work with heated seats warming your backside. A lungful of fresh air is just what you need to brush the cobwebs away.' Amy had walked to work this morning, as Malcolm had given her a lift home from the pub last night.

Satisfied she had cleared the room of the sour curry smell, she pulled the window in a notch. Bustling through the door, a small grey-haired Italian woman apologised for her tardiness. She was dragging a Henry Hoover, and Paddy helped her find a socket. Given the length of time the detectives spent there, every spare socket was taken up with iPhone and Samsung phone chargers.

By the time the cleaner had finished, the rest of the team had filtered in. They followed Amy into the briefing room. The early start was necessary in order to deal with the day's headlines and the fallout which would ultimately follow. It was D-Day for Ellen, Amy could feel it in her bones.

It all depended on Adam, who had texted in the early hours to say that elements of Luka's letter would appear in this morning's edition. Calling him for confirmation was futile. He had not yet arrived at work and his mobile went straight to voicemail. That was not a good sign.

She checked her watch, her stomach lurching as she realised the time.

'I'll nip to the front counter, see if anything's come in,' Molly said, catching her worried gaze. The sooner Amy saw the headlines, the sooner she could breathe again. But as Molly returned with the *London Echo* in hand, her expression relayed that something was very wrong.

Passing it over, she shook her head. 'It's not on the front page.'

'You're not serious.' Amy laid the newspaper flat on the table as her colleagues crowded around. She found the story printed on page two in a tiny side column. It was a summary of the situation and not Luka's letter at all. Her palms pressed against the desk, she groaned. 'Tell me this isn't happening. Why has Adam gone back on his word?'

A series of collective murmurs filled the room as her colleagues took stock. The caller's cooperation hinged on his letter being on the front page. How would he react to this?

'If we've seen it, then you can bet our suspect has too.' Paddy's face was grim as he scanned the words printed in black and white.

Amy turned back to the front page. 'We need to come up with a valid excuse for Luka as to why Brexit took precedence over this case.' But time was in short supply – and then the desk phone rang. She stiffened, all eyes on her as her hand hovered over the receiver. She pressed the button for the call to go through to speaker and waited until the trace was on.

'You lied.' It was the voice of Ellen's kidnapper. Amy recognised the lilt of his Russian accent immediately.

'You said I'd be front-page news,' he continued. 'You pretty much gave me your word.'

'I'm as much in the dark about this as you are. The reporter guaranteed me front-page placement. We did our best.'

'I should have known I couldn't trust you,' he murmured, his words sharp spikes under his breath.

Amy's grip on the phone tightened. Getting into an argument would do neither of them any good. People like him only listened to what they wanted to hear.

'Tell me where Ellen is and we can run a follow-up tomorrow. The television stations might be interested once they pick it up.'

'Fuck the television stations!' the caller roared. 'Tomorrow is too late. You can go to hell.'

Amy could feel everything slipping away. 'It's never too late, but if you're painted as the villain then nobody will listen. I can give you a voice, but you need to help me in return.' She skim-read the article as she spoke. The piece mentioned Nicole's recent poisoning and the fact that police were looking into a former 'patient' with regard to his daughter's kidnapping. There were a couple of sentences about Dr Curtis being a 'pioneer' in the field of psychology and some 'allegations of mistreatment' being made, but it was unlikely to satisfy Amy's caller. In fact, Dr Curtis was portrayed as the victim, given the poisoning of his wife and the kidnapping of his child.

Amy knew there were constraints. The police media department had advised her against sharing details of the case, while the newspaper's lawyers would have been all over Luka's letter, crossing out anything slanderous. But Adam was a talented journalist. What could have been a vivid and interesting piece appeared dull and washed out. The allegations might be true, but it seemed as if nobody wanted to hear them.

'You're an intelligent man,' Amy continued, listening to his ragged breathing. 'If what you say about Dr Curtis is true, then it needs to be investigated. But you'll lose all sympathy the second they hear you've kidnapped a four-year-old child. We can make a difference. But only if we help each other.'

'I didn't want any of this. But it would have been worth it if the truth about Dr Curtis came out.'

Amy picked up on the strain of resentment running through his words. He sounded serious. Was it really Luka on the line? It occurred to her that, if it wasn't Luka, it was someone who had been through the same thing. Her muscles tensed as she recalled his letter. 'You were kept captive, weren't you? People . . .' She paused, trying to work out where the hell she was going with this. 'People don't get it, do they? They think that, once you're free, everything will be OK. But it's not that easy. Sure, the door may be open now, but in your mind the walls are all around you and sometimes . . .' Amy sighed. 'Sometimes it feels safer that way.' The words flowing from her mouth were the echo of a memory of when she was taken into care. Yes, she had wanted her parents' killing spree to come to an end, but not for social care to tear her home apart. It was fear that had driven her to rebel against her parents. The only way to adjust was to lock away her memories. Memories that were now returning with frightening clarity.

Her caller's silence told her she had hit a nerve.

'It takes time to readjust to the real world,' Amy continued. 'Sights, smells, sounds – they all crowd in on you, and sometimes all you want to do is to go back to where you came from.' Amy kept her gaze on the floor. She could imagine her colleagues' puzzled expressions, their curiosity.

'How . . . how do you know all this?'

'Because I was like you once. Which is why we can't do it to Ellen. None of this is her fault. Please, Luka, let her go.' The use of the name was intentional. Until he told her otherwise, it was how she would address him from now on. She needed to establish a bond.

'It's what Mother wanted,' Luka said faintly, before clearing his throat. 'Be ready. You're about to go on a journey. Wait for my call.'

CHAPTER TWENTY

Amy sat cocooned in her office with the blinds closed as she awaited Luka's call. Her colleagues had questioned her use of his name, asked her if it was wise. But she knew their suspect's actions were coming from a place of deep suffering. By addressing Luka's issues, they might be able to move forward with the case. She drummed her fingers on her desk. It was impossible to concentrate, knowing that at any moment he might give her Ellen's location. She checked the online system, working her way through the completed tasks to date. Safeguarding was imperative, and she set her team to track down Dr Curtis's old colleagues. Had they read Adam's lacklustre newspaper article? This had been Adam's chance to put things right between them. How could he let her down again?

Amy stiffened as her mobile phone rang.

'DI Winter,' she said, holding her breath for a response.

'It's me, Adam. I'm in reception.'

Speak of the devil and he's bound to appear, Amy thought. 'I'm on my way,' she said, before ending the call. Her time was limited, but she could not pass up the chance to tell him how annoyed she was that he had reneged on a promise yet again. As she left her office, she knew she should keep calm, but every time she closed her eyes she saw Ellen's face. Adam's failure to deliver could cost the little girl her life. It did not take Amy long to reach reception.

'About time.' Adam's Italian accent sounded stronger than ever today. 'I'm busy too, you know.'

'In here.' Amy led him into a side room. She had kept him waiting only minutes and sensed an undercurrent of aggression in his tone. The room was stuffy and windowless, the smell of stale sweat lingering in the air. It housed a wonky table with a piece of folded cardboard shoved under one leg, three chairs, and a computer used for taking statements when the need arose. Not that it would come into play now. Her fingers gripped the door handle as she closed it behind them. She was ready to deal with him quickly and get back to work.

A pang of sorrow rose in Amy's chest. In the old days Adam had sometimes called in to see her under the pretence of work. More than once they had exchanged a stolen kiss in this very room before she sent him on his way. But he was the one who had been unfaithful, not her, she reminded herself.

'Why didn't you warn me the story wouldn't make the front page?' she said, the memory of his infidelity seeping bitterness into her words.

'You should be thanking me,' he replied. 'You're lucky it was published at all.'

'It's just a puff piece for Dr Curtis. It's done more harm than good.'

'*Da che pulpito viene la predica!*' Adam waved his arms in the air.

Amy felt a spike of annoyance. 'If we're going to argue, can we at least do it in a language I understand?'

'You don't get it, do you? I can't print slander. There's no evidence for those allegations. I couldn't get it on the front page because the guy who wrote the letter is dead!'

'I'm not sure he is,' Amy retorted. 'And if you'd answered your phone this morning, then at least I could have been prepared.'

'*Me* answer *my* phone? You barely give me the time of day,' Adam fumed. 'Then you click your fingers when it suits you and expect me to dance to your tune.'

'You're a journalist, aren't you? It was to do with work.'

'Then why meet me in Arro and not here? You were leading me on. Now things haven't worked out, you're spitting your dummy out of the pram.'

Adam was right, she had manipulated his emotions purely to help Ellen's case. She drove her hand through her hair. 'I'm sorry if you think I've messed you around, but a little girl is missing. The world doesn't revolve around you.'

'Around me?' Adam's eyebrows shot up in astonishment. 'You've no idea of the sacrifices I've made for you, the opportunities I've turned down.'

'I don't have time for your theatrics.' Amy checked her watch. 'I'm expecting a call from Luka. I need to go.'

'Wait.' Adam's hand hovered over her arm. 'Are you seeing someone named Donovan?'

Amy could not believe her ears. Who had told him that? But a straight answer was not on the cards when she did not know herself. 'What business is it of yours?'

A shadow of regret crossed Adam's face. 'Listen . . . I need to talk to you. I know everything . . .'

But Amy's head was cocked to one side, listening to the intercom in the corridor as it called her name. 'That's me. You need to go.'

Taking a deep breath, Adam blurted out his words as he stood in her way. 'Marry me. Properly, this time. I understand now why your dad didn't want us to be together. But there's no need for secrets anymore.' Reaching out, he took both her hands, but with a look of sheer horror, Amy snatched them away. What planet was he on? She needed to make things clear between them once and for all.

'I'm only going to say this once. We are *never* getting back together. As for getting married . . .' A cold laugh escaped her lips. 'That's the biggest joke I've heard all year.'

'Listen to me,' Adam said, blocking her exit. 'There's no need to be so defensive . . . I know about—'

'No, *you* listen to *me*.' Amy's voice grew louder. 'I was ready to give up my job for you, have kids – the lot. But hey, maybe you did me a favour by sleeping with that stripper. What's the saying again?' She paused as she recalled the phrase. 'A leopard doesn't change its spots.'

'I'm not leaving until you listen.' A thunderous shadow darkened Adam's face. The intercom blared for the second time, demanding Amy's presence. She'd had enough of this.

'You sure about that?' Pulling open the door, Amy grabbed his arm and dragged him into reception. Heads turned in their direction, curious glances from people waiting to be seen.

'You're making a big mistake,' he said in a loud voice, as Amy pulled him through the double doors to the street outside. She didn't care who was watching. This time he had pushed her too far.

'Just remember,' Adam shouted as she turned to go back inside, 'you gave me no choice.'

Cheeks burning, she strode back in. Pushing her tag against the door panel, she allowed herself into the confines of the station, away from prying eyes. But every step she took down the darkened corridor made her regret her show of force. Adam had always been unpredictable, but today she had sensed something darker emanating from his presence. He'd said she was making a big mistake. Something told her this was not the end.

CHAPTER TWENTY-ONE

Adam walked with his hands deep in his jean pockets, his feet dragging against the pavement as he took the route back to work. He was on autopilot, tormented by Amy's behaviour and the way she had treated him. His proposal had been meant to defuse the bomb, not make it explode in his face. He had not expected her to recover so quickly from their parting, much less begin seeing someone else.

He kicked a stone, barely noticing the patter of rain against his leather jacket. If only he'd had such clarity of vision when they were engaged. He had always played the field. He could not recall one girlfriend he had remained faithful to, and there had been quite a few. He blamed his bloodlines, believed the stereotypes about young Italian males. His mother had seemed content to turn a blind eye when his father played around. Yet the thought of Amy seeing someone else evoked an anger he could not control. It had taken all his restraint not to slap her across the face when she dragged him outside and treated him with such disrespect.

It seemed Lillian had been telling the truth about Amy seeing DI Donovan. Who's to say the rest of Lillian's story wasn't true too? He ground his back molars at the thought of Amy and her new squeeze laughing at him behind his back. And to publicly humiliate him like that . . . he didn't owe her anything after the way she had treated him.

Onwards he walked, inhaling the dirty tang of exhaust fumes from the steady stream of passing cars. A bus trundled by as he paused at the traffic lights. He scanned its occupants: shoppers, mums with children too young for school and a pensioner or two. Ordinary people with ordinary lives, so far removed from the likes of Lillian Grimes. His meeting with the psychopathic serial killer played heavily on his mind. He had been shocked to discover Amy's true parentage, but deep inside he had always sensed she was different. If he was honest, it excited him a little bit. He liked pressing her buttons, drawing out the darkest emotions she tried to keep locked within. But he had pushed her too far with his infidelity and thrown it all away.

As for Lillian . . . she was a woman who disgusted and intrigued him in equal measure. He could see how people became entangled in her web. When she demanded your attention it was impossible to say no. It was like driving past a car crash. You knew there was something grisly inside the wreckage, yet morbid curiosity made you feast your eyes on the carnage as you passed. It was why he had become a journalist.

He had expected Amy to crumble, to take him back with open arms. He had underestimated her. Since her father's death she had reverted to who she'd been when they first met. That cold, hard exterior; her unflinching gaze.

His thoughts were interrupted by the light at the crossing as it signalled it was safe to go. *Screw it*, he thought, lowering his head against the rain. Plucking his phone from his jacket, he dialled his boss's number. Tim had been in the industry for over thirty years and had the grey hairs to prove it. With an expanding waistline and a penchant for rich food, he was headed for a heart attack one day. Not that Adam helped ease his stress.

'Where are you?' Tim's deep voice boomed over the line as he picked up the call. 'And why haven't you been answering your phone?'

Adam grimaced. It was Tim who had put the block on Luka's letter, saying the whole thing was a ridiculous hoax. Adam might have agreed with him had he not witnessed Amy's dogged determination. But his boss would not stay angry with him for long.

'I'm on my way back,' Adam said, a smile curling on his lips. 'And have I got a story for you.'

CHAPTER TWENTY-TWO

Amy fixed her expression as Paddy met her halfway down the hall. The hint of cigarette smoke hung on his clothing, even though he was meant to have given up.

'Luka's called,' he said, his steps quickening as he matched her pace.

'What line is he on?' The sound of Amy's heels echoed across the narrow space.

'He wouldn't wait. Said you're to go to Holland Park tube station and he'll call you with Ellen's whereabouts from there.' Concern tightened his features. They were all under pressure to find Ellen safe and well.

'Is there a unit in place?' Amy's thoughts were focused now, her spat with Adam forgotten.

'A covert one. He was very clear – no police involvement. Ma'am Pike wants you to walk there in case a job car scares him off.'

'Suits me.' Amy would use the time to assemble her thoughts. As she reached her office, she tugged on her harness. It evenly distributed her radio, CS canister, handcuffs and extendable baton, all available at the flick of a clip. The old-fashioned term was 'carrying her appointments'. Some officers housed them in their pockets or bags. Some, like Paddy, forgot them entirely. They would rest beneath her coat. Insurance for what lay ahead.

She was informed that arrangements had already been made. A small unit of plainclothes officers would follow her on her journey while Paddy and the team tracked her progress from the office. She prayed the meeting would be productive. The team were chasing every imaginable lead but were yet to come back with a result.

The drizzly weather reflected her mood as she strode to Holland Park, taking short, quick steps. Amy opened her umbrella to protect her hair. Worn loose, it skimmed past her shoulders in brunette waves, giving her less of a regimented look. She had given consideration to her appearance as she dressed this morning. If, by some stretch of the imagination, this was Luka, his problems stemmed from his time in a clinical environment. Her razor-sharp business suit with its white starched shirt was not the best attire to get him on her side. A soft floral blouse combined with a navy coat and matching trousers would do the trick. Her shoes were flat in case she had to give chase. It may have seemed like overkill, given it could be a hoax, but Amy's instincts told her differently. The Curtis family had been singled out, and no demands for money had been made. It seemed obvious that the suspect's actions were born from revenge. Unlike Amy's biological parents, she guessed Luka did not kill for the sake of it, but his acts could clearly be brutal nonetheless.

Despite the puddles and rolling grey clouds, Holland Park Avenue was a pleasant wintry walk. The tree-lined street housed some impressive properties, and celebrities such as David and Victoria Beckham had taken up residence there. With its domed windows and pale brick walls, Holland Park tube station was in keeping with its upmarket surroundings. Retracting her umbrella, Amy focused her thoughts on the job ahead. Standing at the traffic lights, she monitored pedestrians as they passed. Was this a trap? A diversion? Or just a wild goose chase?

But Luka's comments about Ellen had rung true. The colour of her nightdress, the fact that her spectacles had been taken but her slippers left behind. His thoughts on animal fur were another branch of the investigation being pursued. She checked her watch as speckles of drizzle dappled its face. Two minutes past nine. Should she go inside? But her phone signal would inevitably be lost. Relaxing her posture, she reminded herself that she was being watched. Not just by Luka. Her colleagues were relying on her to get this right.

The vibration of her phone was welcome as it alerted her to a call. Lowering her head, she blotted out the world as she accepted the blocked number.

'Where are you?' It was the man claiming to be Luka, his voice tinged with the same faint Russian accent as before.

'Holland Park tube station,' Amy said, not missing a beat. He sounded more assertive this time, focused. It felt as if the dice had been thrown and there was no backing out now.

'Good,' Luka replied. 'I googled you . . . You're quite a celebrity, although you shy away from the media as much as you can. Tell me, Amy . . . I can call you Amy, can't I?'

'I'd prefer it if you did.' Amy was keen to dispense with titles to keep him on side. The fact he was researching online could mean he was bonding with her in some way.

'Why are you drawn to such serious cases when you're uncomfortable with the attention they bring?'

Amy inhaled deeply, the smell of the streets grounding her as she prepared her response. She had been prepped for this phone call. No pressure. Refer to him as Luka if that's what he wants, and allow him to lead the way.

'I don't think of the media when I'm helping victims,' she answered honestly. A lorry rattled past and she strained to listen to the call. 'Where's Ellen? Is she with you? I need proof she's alive.' She wanted to ask if Luka was connected to Nicole's poisoning, but their police negotiator had been firm in his instruction: keep the focus entirely on the child.

'It comes down to justification,' Luka mused, ignoring her question. 'You justify hunting me down because you believe it's the right thing to do. I justify my actions because I have no choice. We are all justified by our wants and needs. Who's to say my reasons aren't just as valid as yours?'

'The law,' Amy replied flatly, her patience running thin.

'And you think your law is always right all of the time? Even if it fails to protect those who need it the most?'

'I presume you brought me here for a reason.' She was taking a risk but was unwilling to waste another minute debating on the street.

'I'm also a victim of crime,' her caller replied. 'The problem is that nobody cares about me. And now the criminal is being rewarded. The accolades, the awards . . . have you seen Dr Curtis's house?' An edge sharpened in his voice. 'He gets all of that, while I live in a box.'

'Did you try to kill his wife?' The words left Amy's lips before she could contain them.

'I gave her a choice: risk her life for the one she loved. Something not afforded to me.'

Amy frowned. What was he talking about? 'If Nicole risked her life to save Ellen, then surely her daughter should be returned?'

'And she will be.' Luka's reply was instant. 'Whether she's found alive . . . that's up to you.'

Found alive? Amy thought. *Does that mean he's already left her somewhere?* 'Then what's the next step?' She eyed a man in a baseball cap reading a newspaper on the corner by the tube station. He'd been staring at that same page since she arrived. Briefly, their eyes met. She exhaled a breath. He was one of theirs. She returned her attention to the call as the kidnapper's voice filtered through.

'I want you to take a walk in my shoes, a trip through my memories, so you fully understand. If I have to kidnap a child to catch your attention, then so be it.' A humourless chuckle ensued. 'It's ironic, given all the children that Dr Curtis used over the years.'

'His wife could have died, and his child is missing. I see nothing to laugh about.' Amy's response was curt. She'd had enough of his teasing. 'What you're doing . . . you might think it will help, but it won't. I know what you're experiencing. Guilt. Depression. Anger. I know because I've been through them myself.' Silence passed as her words sank in. 'I can help you get through this, but only if you let Ellen go.'

A beat passed between them. 'Mother told me you'd do this. Try to make me turn myself in . . . You think it's been easy? Having that kid touch my things . . . in my space.'

But it was his comments about his mother that made Amy's eyebrows shoot up. He was talking about Sasha in the present tense, not the past. 'Mother? You mean Sasha's alive? How—'

'Take the tube to Westminster and go to Big Ben,' Luka interrupted. 'I'll ring you when you arrive.'

Amy noted the word 'arrive'. Did that mean he was already there? 'Why Big Ben?' she said, trying to squeeze out more information.

'It was my first day trip to London. Mama lived for those days when Dr Curtis took us sightseeing. But nobody knew of the darkness behind it all.'

'Sexual abuse?'

'Of course not,' Luka replied, as if the very idea was preposterous. 'Hurry. The tube's coming in, and you haven't got long.'

'Is your mother with you now? Can I talk to her?'

'Don't.' Luka's tone hardened. 'You're not fit to speak her name.'

Amy took a deep breath. For now, the topic of his mother was out of bounds. She remembered the advice she had been given – to keep her focus on the child. 'When I get to Big Ben . . . then you'll tell me where Ellen is?'

'Think of it as a treasure hunt,' Luka replied. 'But this one comes with a timer. So you'd better hurry up if you want to reach Ellen alive.'

CHAPTER TWENTY-THREE

Ellen's kidnapper exhaled the breath he had been holding. The call had gone better than he had thought it would. He had not expected to develop a connection with the detective and it had taken him off guard. Walking the pavement, he turned his face to the sky, feeling better now that Ellen had vacated his room. When he'd first made contact with Dr Curtis and his staff, he had never imagined things would escalate like this. The yearly flowers and messages were meant to be as far as it went. But then, every time he turned on his television he would see Dr Curtis's smarmy face. If he wasn't gloating about his many books, he was talking about his awards. It was obvious the flowers and veiled threats were having no impact at all. Something needed to be done.

His methods were elaborate but, from the confines of his room, it had given him something to focus on. Sourcing the phials, accessing the drugs – it was all in a day's work. Finding the courier had taken longer, but it had been worth the wait. Their conversation had helped dissolve any lingering doubts.

But now the detective was making him unsure of himself all over again. Mama would not want him to back out now. But Mama had not spent her childhood in captivity. By the sounds of it, DI Amy Winter had. He could have ended this quickly, given her Ellen's address without the runaround. Truth was, he enjoyed talking to her. He turned his gaze to the pavement, striding purposefully through the busy London streets. There was no better game than one set against the clock. It added an element of agonising yet delicious suspense. It made him feel alive.

Even while injecting seeds of doubt into his psyche, DI Winter's voice had reeled him in. There was something mysterious about her that made her stand out from the rest – that made her someone like him. He wished she had been there when he needed her, then things would have turned out differently. But, for now, her attention would act as a cooling balm, salving the wounds of his past. Death was too good for the likes of Dr Curtis. Losing everything he owned was justice enough.

His fists clenched in the front pocket of his hoodie as fresh hatred bloomed. Sliding his phone from his pocket, he activated the screen. Soon it would be time to call the detective back. A delicious thrill shot through him. He could be standing right in front of her and she would have no clue about who he really was. It had been worth the risk – taking Ellen – worth every second of listening to her whiny voice. How many people had a cause that they would kill for? Or kill themselves for? Because there was one thing he knew for sure. If the police caught him today, all bets were off.

CHAPTER TWENTY-FOUR

Amy watched as Baseball-Cap Man folded his newspaper and ambled ahead of her into the station. Soon the plainclothes police officer would board the same tube as her. She only hoped he could do so without the suspect recognising who he was.

Within seconds, Amy had relayed the gist of her conversation to DC Molly Baxter, who, in turn, updated Control. Their discussion served to guide her next move and update the officers on the scene.

'OK,' Molly said, sounding focused. 'Take the Central line to Bond Street Underground. That'll take about eight minutes. Then change at Bond Street and take the Jubilee line to Westminster. It's a four-minute journey, and Big Ben is just a couple of minutes' walk away.'

Amy memorised the directions. She knew that, once she entered the Underground, her phone signal could die. Perhaps that was what Luka had wanted all along. Was he watching her? A shudder drove down her spine as her apprehension rose. Brushing past fellow travellers, she entered the gates to reach the platform, her footsteps quickening as the rumble of the tube signalled its arrival. Despite the chill of the morning, she was met with a whoosh of lukewarm air as the train came to a stop.

Her umbrella tucked under her arm, Amy strode through the double doors, gripping the bar above her as she took up space in the central aisle. The compartment was busy but not packed, allowing her enough room to survey her travelling companions. It was the usual mixture of Londoners; at this time of the day, most commuters were already nestled behind their office desks. Briefly, a suited man met her gaze before her eyes flicked to the mothers with small children snuggled in buggies. Next to them were a couple of teenagers running late for school, their headphones blocking out the world as they scrolled through songs on the iPhones glued to their hands.

Amy peered down the length of the carriage, wobbling slightly as the tube train trundled on its tracks. She caught sight of a man in a dark hoodie, his head turned away from her. Could it be Luka? Was he travelling too? But where was the child? Was she walking into a trap?

Her mind examined potential scenarios, none of them good. She checked her watch, the eight-minute journey feeling like eight hours as they passed through the stations. Notting Hill Gate, Queensway, Lancaster Gate, Marble Arch – each one appeared as a flash of white tiles in between tunnels as she sank deeper into her thoughts.

She had to second-guess Ellen's kidnapper. Define his motivations and evoke some empathy. The more she spoke to him, the further she opened herself up to the possibility that Luka was alive. Had the fire been some kind of set-up? A means for him and his mother to escape? He could not have done it alone. She dragged herself back to her childhood, to the painful place that helped her understand the wicked people in the world.

Now that Lillian Grimes had reignited contact, she kept creeping back into Amy's thoughts. But her psychopathic parents had murdered for their own sick satisfaction. Already, Amy sensed that Luka was not like them. His motivation came from a place deep in his heart. His actions were a compulsion, forged by the need to ease his troubled mind. And what about Sasha? Was she in on this too? There was something about the way Luka spoke; it unsettled her to dwell upon it. His comments about Ellen's unwanted invasion were territorial in nature. He was protective of his home. Had he and his mother escaped the fire all those years ago and lived a life underground? His experience in captivity was driving his actions . . . Amy briefly closed her eyes as she put herself in his shoes. What if he had lived his life hidden away from the world? It was bound to damage him psychologically – but enough to commit murder? What would it have been like for her, had she not been adopted? She checked herself. This was no time for sympathy. Sliding her phone from her pocket, she glanced at the screen. No signal. Her thoughts raced. What was Luka planning?

After changing at Bond Street, Amy took the Jubilee line to Westminster. The total journey time of seventeen minutes had never felt so long. Westminster Underground station was a mass of stainless-steel and shiny decor, and as she rushed up the steps to daylight, the juxtaposition of modern and traditional was a sight to behold. Big Ben towered above her, marred only by the scaffolding which masked its beauty against the azure sky. The view was breathtaking, and had she not been so caught up in the moment, she would have taken longer to stop and stare.

Shielding her eyes from the winter sun, she weaved through busy pedestrians. London was not a place you could stand still in for very long. As she scrambled for her phone, she dropped her umbrella, mentally reprimanding herself for bringing it along. Such was the British weather, she was now treated to blue skies and an icy breeze. Finding the nearest bin, she deposited the unwanted item, gripping her phone in her left hand as she waited for it to ring. Was Luka here, timing her movements? Officers were already searching for him on the ground. But without an up-to-date photo, they had very little to go on.

Another question rose in her consciousness. Why her? Had he really chosen her because of an article in a newspaper? But the thought evaporated as her attention was diverted to the ringing of her phone.

CHAPTER TWENTY-FIVE

'Call the bloodhounds off,' Luka said, instantly dispensing with formalities.

'I'm not with you.' Amy took in the scene as she searched for her mystery caller. She was standing near the base of Big Ben, the pavement milling with tourists taking photos and selfies on their phones. The air smelled of icy drizzle and petrol fumes, the day carrying a sense of urgency that made every muscle in her body tense. She peered through the multi-lane traffic at a man across the road holding a video camera. His pot belly stretched the material of his white polo shirt, his baggy jeans were wrinkled and worn. Briefly, he met her gaze, before turning his attention to the structure above. Amy threaded her fingers through her hair. This whole scenario was making her paranoid, but she had a creeping sensation that Luka was not far away.

'Don't play games with me, Detective Inspector,' he replied. 'If you don't call them off, you'll have Ellen's blood on your hands.'

'All right,' Amy replied tersely, scanning the crowds for Baseball-Cap Man. She caught sight of him just as he crossed the road to join her. Fanning her hand, she gestured at him to back off. She returned her attention to her caller. Luka was off on a tangent, musing about old times.

'I studied your face when you saw Big Ben. It's an impressive structure, isn't it? Imagine how I felt when I saw it for the first time.'

Amy's heart skipped a beat. Where was he? More to the point, what would she do if she found him? Take her chances and give chase, or listen to what he had to say? Right now, the choice was not hers to make.

'Dr Curtis brought us here when we first arrived,' he continued. 'I remember, Mama's eyes were like saucers as she took it all in. She did not stop smiling . . . but I did. Because the next day my induction started.'

'Is Ellen with you? Let me speak to her.' Amy tried to steer their conversation back to the child. But Luka seemed determined to have his say.

'One of the first things they did was cut my nails short. Later I realised it was to stop me from making crescent-moon shapes in the palms of my hands. My sightseeing trips came with a very heavy price.'

Avoiding the throng of pedestrians, Amy stood against the black metal railings bordering the landmark as she tried to find some common ground. 'I need to speak to Ellen. You'll have my full attention after that. You can talk for as long as you like.'

Brittle laughter crackled down the phone. 'You know, it's quite a novelty to have you hanging on my every word. You'll find Ellen near the Imperial War Museum. Time is ticking. She doesn't have long.'

'You're kidding me,' Amy said, aghast at the prospect of dragging things out even more.

'She'll be there, I give you my word.'

Turning on her heel, Amy headed back to the tube station from which she had come. Her stomach churned at the thought of Ellen being in danger. 'You'd better not be wasting my time,' she said, searching her pocket for her Oyster card.

'You'll find out soon enough.' Luka ended the call.

Amy called Molly to inform her of her next stop. 'We need a covert unit at the Imperial War Museum, but be quick, time is running out.' She could hear Molly tapping furiously on her computer as she dictated her journey.

'It'll take you ten minutes by tube. We could get a car to you, but there are no guarantees you won't get stuck in heavy traffic.' They both knew a blue-light run was out of the question. It would only scare Luka off. Sighing heavily, Molly's breath ruffled the line. 'Take the Jubilee line eastbound, change at Waterloo and get the Bakerloo line. Then go southbound to Lambeth North tube station. Has he told you anything more?'

'He's twigged the plainclothes officers, but we can't arrest him yet. This could be our only hope of reaching Ellen in time.'

'In time for what?'

Crossing the road at the traffic lights, Amy milled through daytime shoppers as she headed back to the mouth of the tube station. Her blouse was sticking to her, her skin clammy as she gripped the phone. 'Have paramedics on standby, update Control and I'll call as soon as I can.' Shoving her phone in her pocket, she took the escalator down to the inner workings of the station. A pair of headlights beamed from the tunnel as the train rumbled down the tracks.

She jumped on board and was immediately hit by the stench of garlic hanging on someone's breath. At the other end of the carriage, a scruffy man with more hair than he needed was playing an accordion. Not that you could call it music. Amy was tempted to pay him to stop.

She walked the length of the carriage, settling in a section void of noise and questionable odours. Like before, she used the journey time to think, her eyes dancing over her fellow travellers as she studied them.

Exiting Lambeth North station, she followed the signs to the Imperial War Museum. Her throat was dry and she eyed up the coffee stand. What she wouldn't give for a drink. But refreshments would have to wait. Molly's latest update had come in the form of a text. DCI

Pike was unhappy with all the running around. There was a fine line between following a substantial lead and being made a fool out of – if they didn't get anywhere on this leg of the journey, she was to return to the station. As Amy stood on the pavement, the screech of sirens on the busy road made her heart stall. When the police car flashed past, she checked for missed calls to ensure that there wasn't another incident coming in for her team.

In cases such as these, it was easy to become blinkered, but she knew that, back at the station, her colleagues were fighting a rising tide of crime. She noted the presence of uniformed officers across the road. Were they here for her? It warmed her to feel part of such a big family and know they had her back if need be. Crossing at the traffic lights, she broke into a jog, continuing until she reached the tree-lined Lambeth Road. At the entrance to the Imperial War Museum, her phone began to buzz.

'You're running behind,' Luka said.

'You'd better give me something concrete.' Amy's patience was wearing thin. 'If you don't tell me where Ellen is, I'm returning to base.'

'Have you ever been to the museum?' Luka replied, ignoring her request. 'I remember the day Dr Curtis brought me here. I could almost smell the trenches, hear the bombs whistling above my head. I felt this country was powerful. He talked about our studies being immortalised, his findings being used by scholars and students to come.'

Amy ground her teeth. 'Luka, I've done as you asked. Now tell me where she is.'

Luka continued, ignoring her as she spoke over him. 'I remember feeling a little frightened by the enormity of it all. Sometimes when Deborah explained the bigger words, I would catch a glimpse of concern in her eyes. I knew there was more to this study than the doctor was letting on.' Pausing for breath, Luka forced himself to focus. 'I need you to go to one more location.'

'No. No more addresses. It ends here.' Resting her hand on her hip, Amy stood firm. The mention of Deborah's name added an authenticity to proceedings that put her on edge.

'You'll find Ellen near Oxford Street. It will take fifteen minutes on the tube and ten minutes to walk to her location. That's twenty-five minutes – exactly the time she has left.'

'Why should I believe you?' Amy said, yet she found herself heading back to the tube station just the same. Her police radio beeped a point-to-point call from her shoulder harness. It was DCI Pike. She chose to ignore it, unwilling to take the risk of Pike calling the whole thing off. What choice did she have? Luka was their only link to Ellen. She could not walk away now.

'If you don't do as I say, this conversation will haunt you for the rest of your life. Now hurry, there's no time to waste.'

It was true. She could hear the sincerity in his voice. This was a man who knew what it was like to be plagued by regret. As the call ended, Amy phoned Molly and relayed the latest instructions.

'Ma'am Pike has asked you to call her as soon as you can,' Molly replied. 'She's tried reaching you on the radio—'

'I turned down the volume,' Amy interrupted, having enough to focus on with Luka sending her halfway across London. 'Listen, I want you to map the perimeter of Oxford Street. Start at the tube station then work outwards at a nine-minute walk at an average pace. Update Control with all the derelict buildings in the area – houses, empty shops, anywhere he could be hiding her. Tell Paddy we need a search team in but to keep a low profile.' Did Luka want her to experience the bitter disappointment of finding Ellen dead? She couldn't let that happen.

A text beeped through, along with an attachment. Taking a deep breath, Amy prepared herself for what lay ahead. It was Ellen, tears streaking her face as she pleaded with the camera phone. 'Please come and get me,' she cried, her chin wobbling as she spoke. Her childish whimper filtered into a space in Amy's brain where it would play on a loop. Ellen was against a concrete wall from what Amy could make out, poor lighting casting a shadow on her face.

'I want to go home. I want my mummy.' Abruptly, the clip ended. Her adrenaline racing, Amy forwarded it to the team. She noticed the echo as the little girl spoke, the sound of traffic in the distance and the rumbling of heavy engines. Even during that tiny video clip, Amy had gathered a couple of clues. Ellen was in the city. Luka was telling the truth.

The team is on it as we speak, Molly texted. *Take the tube to Oxford Circus. Good luck.*

Amy whispered a silent prayer as she prepared to take the next train.

CHAPTER TWENTY-SIX

Swaying in the Underground train, Amy wondered if stress was intentionally factored into Luka's games. Was Luka Volkov really orchestrating her movements? If so, were his claims about Dr Curtis true? She couldn't help but feel a little sympathy for the boy who had come to England with such high hopes. But it offered no justification for his actions. If Luka had kidnapped Ellen and poisoned Nicole, then he was just as bad as the people at the institution. The latest hospital reports were hopeful – Nicole had fought for her life and was coming through the other side. But the pressure was on for Amy to bring her daughter home.

Her muscles tensed as the doors opened, the tannoy announcing her train's arrival. Bustling past commuters, she offered no apology as her thoughts raced ahead. Surely Luka was not following her now? She would have noticed someone giving chase. But how was he reaching each location before her? With his all-seeing commentary, he was beginning to seem very godlike as he continued to play his game. She only hoped her team was making some inroads. A feeling of foreboding taunted her movements. As she emerged into daylight she welcomed the cold spikes of drizzle on her face. Despite the wintry weather, her armpits were damp with sweat, her clothes itchy against her skin. But the biggest prickle of discomfort came from within. She held her phone aloft, groaning at the lack of reception. Which direction should she go in? Her team would be tracking her radio on GPS. As if in response, her phone buzzed in her hand. She exhaled with relief to see four bars on the screen, a good-enough connection to accept the call.

'I'm here,' she said, panting slightly. She glanced up and down the street, picking out fellow Londoners on their phones. A man with a briefcase, a couple arm in arm. Any one of them could hold the key.

'And here is where we part,' the response came. 'You have five minutes to get to Ellen. Shame, as it's a ten-minute walk. Of course, you could get a cab, but traffic is bad. You'd never reach her in time.'

'Where am I going?' Amy asked, feeling like a runner on the starting blocks.

'Oxford Street, Marylebone Lane.'

There was little time to call Molly, but Amy knew the area well enough to find it on foot. Breaking out into a run, she held the phone to her ear as she raced past bustling Londoners. 'Where is she?'

'You're a resourceful woman,' Luka taunted. 'I'm granting you with enough intelligence to work that out.'

'I can't, not in time. Is she in danger?' Swerving to one side, she dodged a Labrador who shot out in front of her as it escaped its owner's lead. On any other day, she would stop to help, but he would have to fend for himself today.

'Let's just say her whole world is about to come tumbling down.' Luka responded. 'You'll see when you get there.'

'Please!' Amy hated the sound of her voice as he made her beg. 'I don't know where I'm going. Give me something more.' Silence fell between them, and for a moment she thought he had hung up.

'Seeing as it's you, I'll help you out. Head to Welbeck Street. You'll find her there.'

'Luka, wait . . .' But her words were cut short as the line went dead. Her feet pounded the pavement as she ran, her mind focused on the task ahead. Her breath came thick and fast as she relayed the information to Molly, ignoring passers-by as they glanced in her direction. 'What's in Welbeck Street? Any derelict buildings? Maybe leisure centres with swimming pools? What could put her in so much danger that it would risk her life? And on a countdown too?' Amy knew this could be a wind-up and she'd be playing right into Luka's hands. But this had to be the last stop.

Tapping her computer keyboard, Molly brought up the latest information, all the while relaying Amy's instructions to their team. Amy's colleagues were on hand should they find the missing child, and a paramedic was on standby to resuscitate her, if it came to that. 'We've got luxury apartments, a couple of hotels, some private clinics – nothing that stands out. There's an unusual-looking high-rise car park at the end, but that's closed now. Officers are ringing local hotels to make them aware.'

'Get them to check their swimming pools and rooftops,' Amy said, pausing to catch her breath as she reached the long, narrow street. 'It has to be something obvious, otherwise he wouldn't have given me so little time.'

'Unless he set you up to fail.' Molly voiced Amy's concerns. It didn't bear thinking about. An image of Ellen floated into Amy's consciousness. Her gap-toothed smile was enough to melt the hardest of hearts.

Ellen was near, Amy could feel it. But time was slipping away.

She jogged up Welbeck Street, looking left and right. 'Ellen!' she called at the top of her voice. 'Ellen, are you there?' She glared into shop windows and apartment doorways. There were no derelict buildings in this well-to-do location. What could put the girl in immediate danger? Molly informed her that officers were discreetly making house-to-house inquiries. Amy threw a glance behind her, watching the police cars pull up. It was risky, given Luka's instruction, but she was grateful for the backup just the same. Above her, the car park loomed, an ominous grey reflection of her plummeting spirits. She craned her neck, tapping into her intuition.

'That's it,' she whispered, her words barely audible as she voiced her thoughts. 'That's what he meant.' Sliding her radio from her shoulder harness, she brought it to her lips and pressed the button to speak.

CHAPTER TWENTY-SEVEN

The Curtis Institute, August 1984

Luka ran a hand over his freshly cut bristles. His once long and wavy hair was now shaved, and he hated the way the cold air curled around the nape of his neck. He sat on his bed, legs folded, as he checked the label stitched into the collar of his sweatshirt. Subject 5. If he was number five, did that mean there had been four others before him? Was that why they had numbered him? So they could tell them apart? He thought about the children he sometimes saw in the corridor, and of the markings on the inside doors of the cubicle toilets. With some reverence he had traced his fingers over the names 'Martha' and 'Julian' which were scratched into the wood.

He winced at the sight of the red scab crusted over on his wrist. The number was tiny, the size of his fingernail, but it itched like mad just the same. He blew on the inflamed skin to cool the tenderness. Mama would go crazy if she knew. But Deborah said Mama was the 'anxious type', and if Luka had a problem he must go to her instead.

A soft knock on his bedroom door signalled that Deborah was on the other side. 'Are you ready? It's time.'

Sighing, Luka pulled on his grey sweatshirt and shoved his feet into his plimsolls. His head hung low as he followed her down the long, gloomy corridor. A bunch of keys jangled from a chain on Deborah's hip, reinforcing Luka's sense of confinement. Room doors were locked from the outside and people needed special permission to access this floor. Apart from his mama, there were four constants in Luka's life: Dr Curtis and Deborah were there most of the day, while orderlies Stuart and Christina took it in turns to stay overnight. Upstairs, outside workshops ran afternoon classes ranging from music lessons to maths. It was not what Dr Curtis had promised, and Luka spent most of his days completing tests.

His glance flicked to the locked doors. More than once he'd heard crying coming from inside the rooms.

'Today we're going to try something new.' Deborah's voice dragged him from his thoughts. 'Isn't that exciting?' She smiled as they approached the waiting room, but her smile was rigid, the corners of her eyes creasing as she spoke. It provided no comfort in an uncertain life.

Deborah tried to make the tests fun. Just like in the book *Alice's Adventures in Wonderland*, portions of food were placed before him with the words 'Eat me' on a card. They ranged from squares of cake to sweets coloured blue or red, but Luka could pick just one. On other days, four phials were presented with the words 'Drink me' on the side. Luka always picked red, until it gave him a tummy ache. His decision-making was monitored and documented each time. Since taking the tablets the doctor had given him, Luka found it easier to work the patterns out. The drink that made him sick was always top right, unless it was red and then it was bottom left. As the tests became more intricate, Luka was determined to pass each one. But the bitter tablets he swallowed made him see things that weren't there. 'Hallucinations,' Deborah called them, noting them down.

Pausing outside the waiting room, she squeezed his shoulder, catching his worried expression. 'You've got music lessons later. Why don't you focus on that for now?'

Luka's gaze fell to the floor as a sense of trepidation threatened to swallow him whole. 'I want Mama,' he uttered, clasping his hands together until his fingers were tied up in knots.

A soft sigh escaped Deborah's lips as she bent to meet his gaze. 'Sweetheart, your mother's busy in the canteen, feeding the workshop students upstairs. You don't want to worry her now, do you? Think how upset she'd be.'

Luka blinked away the tears beginning to form. The doctor had delivered on his promise of giving her a job, but Mama had dreamed of waitressing in a London café or hotel.

'Now, c'mon . . .' Deborah squeezed his forearm before straightening up. 'Do well today, and you can see her later on.'

The waiting room was a sterile space with paint-blistered white walls and plastic chairs lining each side. In the corner, a mop lay in a bucket of stagnant water, and a selection of well-thumbed comics were splayed on a grubby, glass-topped coffee table in the centre of the floor. But Luka's attention was drawn to the boy hunched in a seat in the corner of the room. Like him, the boy wore a grey tracksuit, but his seemed barely able to stretch over his chubby form. Sniffing loudly, the boy pushed the heels of his palms into his eye sockets to dry his tears.

'Oh.' Deborah frowned as Dr Curtis entered the room. 'Why isn't Sam . . .' She coughed to correct herself. 'Subject Four back in his room?'

But Dr Curtis seemed oblivious to the boy's distress. 'We had a breakthrough.' Clutching a piece of paper, he waved it in the air. 'Come. Let me show you . . .' He gestured Deborah into the adjoining room. Tentatively, Luka stepped forward. Was he meant to go with them?

'Where are you going?' Dr Curtis barked, his bushy brown eyebrows knitting as he scowled.

'I – I . . .' Luka stuttered, looking to Deborah for support.

'Sit down. We won't be long.' She guided him to a seat on the far side of the room. She looked at the other boy, but her gaze did not linger for long. 'Christina will be with you soon.'

Twiddling his fingers, Luka sagged in the chair. He missed his friends. He missed his father too. It had been weeks since his last letter. If Papa were here, he would put Dr Curtis straight. Mama was not good at standing up for herself.

Another sniffle erupted from the corner. Slipping a tissue from his tracksuit-bottoms pocket, Luka rose from his chair and handed it to the boy. Dolefully, he accepted it, his red-rimmed eyes relaying that he had either received bad news or been through something tough. Either way, Luka had to know.

'What's your name?' he asked, claiming the seat beside him. Despite the boy's distress, it felt strangely comforting to be speaking to someone his own age. His time was often spent in isolation. He had a strong urge to befriend the other children he sometimes saw in the corridors, but they weren't usually allowed to mix.

'Sam,' the boy said, making a parping sound as he blew his nose. 'I hate this place.'

'Me too,' Luka said, the words hanging heavy on his breath. None of them was there for fun. 'What's the doc so happy about?'

'I passed some dumb tests,' Sam replied flatly. 'I couldn't do them before. Now they're easy.' He scratched his temple. The faint outline of a sucker was still visible on his skin. The right side of his face jerked upwards in an involuntary twitch.

Luka hated wearing the hat that was the prerequisite for the algebra tests. 'It's for studying your brainwaves,' Deborah had told him last week when she slipped it on. The white cloth cap was covered with circular pads and had a chin strap to keep it in place. Tiny wires connected to a bigger cable which fed into a computer port. But when Deborah started sticking the pads to the side of his face, Luka had baulked. 'It's all right,' she had said, her voice warm. But her words were a betrayal. She would say anything to get him to comply.

'The other kids . . . they've all gone home.' Sam's words cut into his thoughts. 'The workshops are finishing this week too.'

'Really?' Hope lit Luka's face like a beacon. 'Maybe they'll let us go too.'

'I don't have nowhere to go.' Sam lifted his sleeve, displaying his 'Number 4' tattoo. 'You got one of these?'

Tentatively, Luka drew back his sleeve to show that he did.

Sam delivered a narrow smile. 'Then you ain't going nowhere either.'

Luka's mind raced. What did he mean? Didn't the other kids have numbers too? He was about to ask when Sam's face contorted in pain. Rubbing his chest, Sam groaned at the sight of the woman bustling through the door.

Christina's presence put an end to their snatched conversation. A small, stick-thin woman, her eyes were wide as she entered the room. A flash of red drew Luka's attention. Christina painted her nails a different colour each week. So sterile was Luka's environment that he found himself looking forward to the change. But red signalled a warning, and Christina seemed in no mood to talk as she pulled Sam from his chair.

'C'mon, I'm behind schedule,' she said, her face pinched as she pushed him out of the door. Sam tripped over his feet, his hand still planted on his chest. Christina hadn't even noticed he was unwell.

Why had they sent all the other kids home but not them? What did the markings mean? Luka watched him leave, feeling even more nauseous than before.

CHAPTER TWENTY-EIGHT

Tuning into the private police channel, Amy raised a query about the building works taking place. 'What's going on at the car park? There are contractors everywhere.' Welbeck Street car park was a stunning piece of architecture, its facade made up of concrete diamonds which demanded each passer-by's attention. But inside, the building was dark and dingy, a neglected space into which few would venture alone. Amy rarely parked there because of the number of break-ins reported. She had not realised it was closed to the public due to construction.

'I was just about to call you.' Molly's reply was instant. 'It's being demolished today. They're knocking it down to build a hotel. We're trying to call the site manager now.'

'That's it!' Amy said, recalling Luka's words. *Her whole world is about to come tumbling down.* Sprinting towards the building, Amy shouted a warning at the top of her lungs. Reaching into her coat pocket, she pulled out her warrant card, knowing her colleagues were not far behind. 'Stop what you're doing!' she screamed. 'There's a child inside!'

A broad man in a fluorescent sleeveless vest and hard hat ambled towards the plastic fence that had been erected to keep the public at bay.

'Sorry, love, but you're not coming through. We've cleared the building. There's no one inside.'

Amy ground her back teeth in response to his condescension. It was often a by-product of being female and five foot two inches high. Would he have reacted the same way if one of her male colleagues had instructed him to stop? 'It's Detective Inspector, actually,' she said, ignoring his attempt to halt her entry. 'Tell your men to put a stop to this now.' Darting past him, she squeezed through the fence and approached the building where demolition had already begun. Any minute now a wrecking ball could come hurtling towards her, or perhaps an explosion of TNT? But such warnings were whispers in the back of her mind as she searched for the four-year-old child.

'Get back! It's gonna come down! Get the fuck back from there!' The air was peppered with swear words as workmen on the periphery waved in response to her presence. But Amy was too wrapped up in finding the little girl to stop now.

'Ellen!' she shouted, craning her neck left and right. 'Ell—' The force of the blast that followed knocked her off her feet, spewing rubble in the air. Amy coughed to clear her airways as she inhaled a lungful of concrete dust. One of the giant concrete pillars had come down. Radios communicated the news between workers and the on-site machinery fell silent. The dust filtered up Amy's nostrils, tasting chalky on her tongue. Shaking, she rose to her feet. 'Ellen,' she choked, blinking furiously as she tried to clear her vision. In the background, a siren screamed as more of her colleagues reached her location.

Glowering, a heavy-footed man approached. He wore a yellow hard hat and a fluorescent vest, just like the other workers on site. 'You idiot! What the fuck do you think you're doing?' He scowled, his beard white with dust. 'I'm the site manager. You could have been killed.'

Wobbling on her feet, Amy plucked her warrant card from her pocket. Behind her, a spray of water was being directed towards the rubble to keep the dust down. Amy coughed again. Her elbow stung like hell and she realised she'd cut it when she fell. She tucked her warrant card back into her pocket. The building was vast. There was still hope. She refused to believe that Ellen had been caught up in the blast.

'We think there's a child in this building. We're not leaving until it's been searched,' Amy replied. 'How are you doing it? Explosives?'

'In central London?' The man barked a laugh. His face grew serious as he felt Amy's glare. 'Excavators rip through the concrete beams and columns. Then we wet it to keep down the dust. It's done gradually, but with force. Mind you, it's come to a sodding halt now you're here.'

'I see,' Amy said, approaching the remains of what had once been a concrete beam.

'For fuck's sake!' the site manager called after her. 'Come back, it's not stable!'

Amy spun on her heel, her face thunderous as she raised a finger in the air. 'Swear at me one more time and I'll—'

'Boss! I've found something!' A man with a ruddy complexion jumped down from the excavator, pulling the gloves from his hands.

A chill ran down Amy's spine as she caught the expression on his face. 'No,' she whispered. It couldn't be. Ellen couldn't have been there. There was still so much of the building to demolish. But the driver hadn't seen Amy enter the site. Had he missed the little girl inside too?

Amy's legs felt heavy as she approached the rubble. A sense of stillness fell. Swallowing back the dust lodged in her throat, she followed the gaze of the workmen, wishing she could press a pause button on what was to come. Nobody could have survived the weight of a concrete beam bearing down. Her hand rose to her mouth as she drew in a sudden breath. Sticking out of a pile of torn-up concrete was the hem of a child's nightdress, blue with a pink ribbon, exactly as Luka had described. But this one was stained with patches of blood.

The sight of the scrap of material proved to be too much. 'Ellen!' Amy cried, throwing herself on to the rubble and clawing at it.

'Hey!' The site manager lurched forward. 'We've got equipment to clear this lot. You'll never do it like this!' The look on his face relayed that he didn't expect to find Ellen alive.

As Amy tore at the rubble, she paused at the sight of fresh blood. It was only when pain seared in her fingernails that she realised it was coming from her. Grunting, she continued to tear at the rocks, until a gentler voice spoke from behind.

'Ma'am, you're hurting yourself. Let them take care of it. It'll be quicker that way.' The voice was that of a young police officer, and was followed by a firm hand on her arm.

'No! Get off me!' Amy screamed as they tried to lead her away. But her digging was fruitless. She could never move this lot on her own. Her legs shaking and fingernails torn, she glanced up at the gathering crowd and reluctantly stepped aside. She knew what they were thinking. She had failed. She was too late.

CHAPTER TWENTY-NINE

'Don't look so jumpy.' Deborah stared at her guests, mild annoyance sharpening her words. 'Nobody's going to see us here.' It was true. She'd pulled a lot of strings to get a table at Aqua Shard at such short notice. With its breathtaking views of London and its upmarket clientele, they were unlikely to bump into any police here. Like a carrot, she had dangled the invite before them. Fortune had not smiled on Stuart and Christina and she knew they would be unable to resist.

Having finished their appetisers, the wait for their main course seemed like the perfect time to broach the real reason behind the invitation.

'I didn't bring you here for a reunion,' Deborah said, tearing her eyes away from the view.

Christina's face soured as she sipped her sparkling water, her short, cropped hair making her look like an angry pixie.

Across from her, Stuart shifted in his chair, encased in a suit that had seen better days. 'I knew you'd be in touch soon enough,' he said, meeting their gaze. He had changed little over the years. He still sported a buzz cut, was still broad yet lean, despite his advancing years.

Deborah folded her napkin, gracefully straightening her cutlery. 'I'm guessing you've heard about what happened to Dr Curtis? Have the police been in touch yet?' To her, he was Hugh, but only his friends were afforded the honour of using his first name.

'Not yet. I take it you've brought us here so we get our stories straight,' Stuart replied.

'I don't like this,' Christina interjected, her bright pink nails flashing as she toyed with the top button of her blouse. 'I don't like it one bit.'

Deborah looked at her with the interest of a cat observing a mouse. 'We're going to have to deal with it whether we like it or not.'

'Who's behind it all? I mean, it can't be Luka. Not unless he's risen from the dead,' Stuart said.

'I wouldn't be so sure,' Christina replied. 'I've always thought there was something dodgy about that fire.'

Stuart cast her a filthy look. 'Easy for you to say. You weren't there.'

'Hey, I'm just saying,' Christina replied. 'It's been bad enough getting those flowers every year. That card . . . "Ladybird, ladybird . . ." Whoever's behind it wants to hurt our families.'

Deborah's expression darkened. She hated being reminded of the Curtis Institute and all the times she had walked down those creepy corridors at night. Sometimes she could have sworn she heard crying, long after the children had vacated the space. She repressed a shudder as goosebumps broke out on her skin. 'Look. We need to stand together on this, otherwise—'

'Otherwise we're going to jail,' Stuart interrupted, his face tight. 'How we thought we'd get away with it, I don't know.'

'Don't,' Christina squeaked, the colour leaving her face. She reached for Stuart's hand, unspoken words passing between them. His expression melted and he squeezed her fingers.

'The guilt is killing me. I can't bear . . .' The words died in Christina's throat as the waiter arrived with their main course. It was a set meal that Deborah had pre-ordered. Christina was a ditherer and she could not afford to waste time.

Stuart picked at his steak as they fell into silence.

'Eat up, will you?' Deborah grumbled. 'This didn't come cheap, you know.' It had been the same when they worked together. She had to continually keep on top of things and tell them what to do.

Christina delivered a weak half-smile before swallowing a mouthful of steamed fish. The very sight of her made Deborah tense. Here was a woman with the power to tear her world apart. She returned her smile, forced a softer tone of voice. 'There's no need to panic. If they start digging, then tell them the testing was government-approved and you've done nothing wrong.'

'But the government didn't approve what happened.' Stuart gestured with his fork as he directed his concerns towards Deborah. 'Christina's right. It's inhuman, that's what it is. Makes me sick.'

Her nostrils flaring, Deborah inhaled a sharp breath. 'You weren't complaining when you both took the pay-off.' Deborah's finger curled around her steak knife as anger bubbled to the surface.

'This is dreadful. Just dreadful,' Christina said, her words arriving on panicked breaths. 'If my Marcus hears about this . . . He's a vicar, for goodness' sake. He'll fall to pieces.' Christina was on her third husband. She may have come across all sweetness and light, but Deborah knew that past infidelities had split her marriages up.

Slicing off a cube of steak, Deborah popped it in her mouth. It melted on her tongue and brought momentary relief. 'I told you. Stick to the story and we'll be fine.'

'What if he comes after my son?' Stuart said. 'It's all right for you. Your kids are grown up. Toby's only six years old.'

'Is everything to your satisfaction? Can I bring you another drink?' Behind them, the waiter spoke, making Christina jump.

'We're fine. Thank you, Neil,' Deborah replied on behalf of them all. She had flirted with him during previous visits, and they were on first-name terms. But today her smile was tight and he took the hint to leave them alone. *Shame*, Deborah thought, admiring his backside as he walked away. She had been alone for far too long but, for now, dating was not on the cards. She returned her attention to Stuart and Christina, wishing they'd never been involved.

'It's too late to change the past,' she continued. 'But confess now and our families will pay the price.' She glared at Stuart. 'What will become of Toby if you end up in jail?' She turned back to Christina. 'And how would your husband deal with the shame?'

Satisfied she had chastised them both, Deborah returned her attention to her meal. She'd had a long time to contemplate things. It had happened a lifetime ago. Only four people knew the truth and Dr Curtis was paying the price. As long as they kept their silence, it ended there, with him.

CHAPTER THIRTY

'Sure your mum won't mind me coming over so late?' Donovan smiled as Amy greeted him at her front door. He knew all about Flora's adoration of Amy's ex, as she had discussed it with him at length. But Amy valued their late-night phone calls, and after today's events she needed to talk to someone who would understand.

'Of course not, it's my home too.' Amy reached for Donovan's coat, freezing as he took her hand. Closely, he examined the tips of her fingers, which were bandaged after the earlier incident. Heat spread within her, rising as a bloom to her cheeks, but Donovan seemed oblivious to her discomfort as he turned her hand over in his. 'That looks painful. Are you OK?'

'It's fine.' Slowly, Amy freed her hand, making a conscious effort not to snatch it back. Taking his coat, she hung it on the hook in the hall. The injuries to her fingers were superficial and the cut on her elbow had received three Steri-Strips. It could have been a lot worse.

Turning to Donovan, she drank in his form. Adam had always been clean-shaven but Amy liked Donovan's stubble. It suited him. It was nice to see him in jeans and a jumper for a change. Having come straight from work, she'd barely had time to change into an old pair of

Levi's and an oversized sweatshirt before he turned up at her door. The proposed get-together was welcome. The house was warm and welcoming, the sweet aroma of freshly baked cookies hanging in the air. Flora had set the scene before making herself scarce. Fresh flowers in vases, the sideboards polished and a batch of cookies cooling on a wire rack in the kitchen. Adam loved Flora's biscuits, but little did she know it was not Adam who was keeping her daughter company tonight.

'She's gone to see *Mamma Mia!* at the Novello.' Amy knew the theatre trip was an excuse to get out of the house. 'It's been hard for her since Dad died, but she has a good network of friends.'

'And she has you.' Donovan paused at the living-room door.

'Me? Living with me comes with its own set of problems.' Amy paused for breath, realising she had said too much. Being in Donovan's company brought a sense of calm and ease that immediately drew her in. 'I'm sorry.' She flushed. 'You've heard enough about me to last a lifetime.'

Donovan leaned in, his voice deep and warm. 'Yeah, you're a bit of a nightmare all right.'

Seconds passed before Amy realised he was joking, and her face broke out into a smile.

Donovan returned his glance to her bandaged fingers. 'I hear you've had a hell of a day.'

Amy sighed. No doubt word of her meltdown had spread across the force. 'Played. I feel played,' she replied. 'I honestly thought Ellen was under all that rubble. He left her nightdress there just to wind me up.'

'But there was blood on it – wasn't there?'

Amy nodded. Her relief at the absence of a body had been cut short when they saw the blood on the child's nightdress. 'We've had it fast-tracked to the lab. It's Ellen's. It has to be. Which means we could have a murder inquiry on our hands.'

Donovan nodded. 'Sending you halfway across London, then setting you up to fail. He's toying with you.'

Amy had already come to that conclusion and needed answers fast. There was one person who could help her. Someone who was well versed in such games. An involuntary shiver drove its way down her back and she pushed all thoughts of Lillian Grimes away.

'Anyway,' she said, pushing down the door handle, 'there's someone important I want you to meet.'

Donovan gave her a curious look before following her inside. His smile widened as Dotty bounded towards them both.

'Careful,' Amy warned. 'She's funny with strangers. Let her come to you.' But her advice was ignored as he immediately dropped to one knee.

'Hello, lovely,' he said, making a fuss of the dog as she danced around his feet. 'I've got one just like you.'

'You own a pug?' It was Amy's turn to be surprised.

'Yes – Poirot,' Donovan replied, before turning his attention back to Dotty. 'He'd like you very much indeed.'

'You're kidding. You've named your pug Poirot?'

Donovan straightened, brushing off his jeans. 'What's so strange about that? I've got a Staffordshire terrier too. They get on really well.'

'A Staffy and a pug. Sounds like you've got your hands full.' Amy was unable to imagine her beloved Dotty sharing the limelight with another dog.

Donovan was clearly animated by Dotty's presence. 'A couple of years ago we busted a dog-fighting ring and I gave Blackbeard a home. You should have seen him, poor sod. He was a sorry sight.'

'Blackbeard?' Amy warmed to him even more. Their relationship felt like kismet. Here was a man who believed in second chances. Up until now, she had been scared he would judge her for her dark past. Having serial-killer parents was not something you dropped into casual conversation.

But there was a vast difference between being kind enough to adopt an abused dog and understanding the sort of twisted background Amy had emerged from. She shelved her thoughts. Now was not the time.

'He's blind in one eye and has a tuft of black hair under his chin. He was pretty traumatised when I got him, but now he's happy as a pig in . . .' he smiled. 'Mud.'

'That's a myth.' Switching on a lamp, Amy led Donovan through to the kitchen for coffee. 'About the pirates, I mean. They didn't wear eye patches because they were blind. It helped their night vision when they went below deck. They swapped the patch over, you see . . .' She pursed her lips as she caught Donovan's bemused expression. Turning around, she filled the kettle, feeling her cheeks burn. She was a detective inspector, so why did she sound like such a nerd?

'Interesting.' Pushing up his sleeves, Donovan folded his arms. 'We could test the theory, I suppose. Got any dark cupboards?'

Stretching on to her tippy-toes, she plucked two mugs from the top shelf. She poured a little milk into a porcelain jug. It was shaped like a cow, its tail forming the handle. Quirky but functional – just like the rest of her mum's home. 'Now that you mention it, I *had* planned to drag you into a dark space.' She stepped towards him. 'Just you and me . . . somewhere private. Would you like your coffee first or should we get started?' She was teasing him, but she couldn't help herself.

'Get started?' Donovan's eyebrows rose as she offered him a cookie.

'It's why I asked you here. Shall we get stuck in?'

Coughing, Donovan brushed away an errant cookie crumb, almost choking mid-bite. 'Erm . . . whatever you say.'

'You don't know how glad I am to hear that.' Amy took him by the hand. His grip was warm and comforting and, for a second, she regretted her impulsive invitation. But as they reached the door to the wine cellar she knew this would test his character once and for all. The thought gave her pause. Was that what this was about? Testing him to see if he had the staying power to see things through?

Releasing his hand, she opened the door and flicked on the light. She peered down the steps, a cold chill creeping between her shoulder blades. 'Are you coming down? It won't take long.'

'Won't take long?' Donovan said, looking mildly affronted. 'Miss Winter, if I didn't think you were joking, I'd say you're severely under-estimating me.'

'OK, OK.' Amy laughed. 'I just need you to check for spiders, maybe get the Hoover in.'

Donovan followed her gaze into the cellar below. 'Seriously? You want me to hunt for spiders?'

'Yes, well. I need it cleared if I'm going to use it as a gym again. Pike invited me back to her son's place, but we're not on friendly terms anymore.' She registered the disappointment on his face. 'Why? What did you think I'd brought you here for?'

'Where's the Hoover?' Donovan's bemused look suggested he was all too aware of her games.

Within fifteen minutes, every inch of the room had been checked. Amy approached with a mug of fresh coffee and an expression of grati-tude on her face. She had fond memories of her time in this space, which her father had converted to a home gym years ago, but since his death she had been reluctant to come down here on her own.

'Who owns the punchbag?' Donovan said, running his hand down the length of it.

Amy handed him his cup. 'It's mine. Fancy a workout?'

'I might hold you to that. I did a bit of boxing in my youth – some competitions, nothing major.'

Amy could imagine him in the ring. She'd heard rumours that he had run with a troubled crowd in his youth. Joining the police had been his way of going straight. 'It's good for getting rid of pent-up energy,' she replied, inwardly cringing at the double meaning. Stepping forward, she narrowed the gap between them. 'Seriously, thank you. I don't have many friends, and it's been . . . nice.'

Sipping his coffee, Donovan gazed down at her face. 'I'm here any time. You only have to call.'

'You're hardly living around the corner,' she said, referring to his Essex abode.

'What's an hour and a half between friends?' Reaching forward, he tucked an errant strand of hair behind her ear. Amy's heart missed a beat as the warmth of his fingers made contact with her skin.

A sudden gravelly bark was followed by the slam of the front door and she groaned at the intrusion. 'What time is it?' Pushing back the sleeve of her sweatshirt, she checked her watch. 'Don't tell me she's back already?' Flora would be quick to draw inferences.

Amy paused. Would that be so bad? She sighed, knowing she had little choice in the matter. Flora would not have missed Donovan's coat hanging in the hall. 'Would you like to stay for a drink? A proper one?' she said. Her father's spirits cabinet had been left virtually untouched since his demise. She knew he would approve of Donovan being in her life far more than Adam. 'I mean, if you'd rather not, I understand. It's a bit soon to be bringing you back to meet Mum.'

'I'd love to.' Donovan's posture was relaxed as he followed her to the steps.

'Good. Do me a favour, will you? If she jumps to conclusions about us, do you mind not setting her straight? She might give this whole Adam business a break.'

'Yeah, why not?' His smile faded and he gave her a look that was hard to read. Was he hoping for something more between them, or frightened at the prospect? It was impossible to tell. She knew he was recently divorced due to infidelity on his wife's side. They had more in common than just work.

'It's hard getting back into the dating scene, isn't it?' Donovan rested his hand on the stair railing. 'It's changed so much since I was last single. All these dating apps and websites. What's wrong with going out for a drink, meeting in a bar or . . .' He looked at her pointedly. 'Through work?'

'I can't even think about dating yet,' Amy replied, a little more quickly than she meant to.

'But there's nothing wrong with having a bit of fun, is there?' Donovan followed her up the steps. 'Nothing heavy. Just two people enjoying each other's company. Where's the harm in that?'

Amy was about to reply when her mother's voice rose in the hall. 'Amy? Where are you? Are you home?'

Amy smiled at Donovan apologetically. 'Come on,' she said, opening the door. 'I'll get you a drink. You're going to need it.'

CHAPTER THIRTY-ONE

Amy made it to work with only minutes to spare, her legs aching from pedalling her bike against the wind. Last night, the drinks had flowed as she and Donovan curled up on the sofa, chatting about life in the force. She had seen the twitch of Flora's bedroom curtains as she said goodbye to him on their front step. Hopefully, her mother would drop the subject of Adam once and for all.

Standing in her team's office, Amy dragged her thoughts away from Donovan as she watched the officers file in. She curled her fingers around a mug from the tray that Molly had left on the table. A porcelain teapot sat alongside a couple of coffees and a packet of digestive biscuits on the side. Molly had the unenviable task of running the tea club and, come afternoon, there would be nothing left on the saucer but crumbs.

'Can't we afford any choccy biscuits?' DC Gary Wilkes asked, sliding a digestive from the plate. His shirt was cobalt blue, paired with a canary-yellow tie. Pink yesterday, yellow today? Amy made a mental note to find out if he was colour blind.

Molly responded to his quip with a withering look. 'I can only stretch your measly contributions so far. A fiver a week isn't much for biscuits and all the brew-ups you can drink.'

'Yeah, but for the price of a pack of digestives, you could easily get some Jaffa cakes.'

'Jaffas are biscuits, not cakes,' Steve piped up, and a long-running argument about the definition of Jaffa cakes reared its head once again.

Amy's mouth twitched in a smile. They were up to their necks in work but such was the nature of their department. When were they *not* under monumental pressure or dealing with something with the potential to go horribly wrong? These brief moments of office banter helped them stay sane.

Nursing her cup of coffee, Amy thanked them for coming in early. 'I thought we could have a quick round robin pre-briefing,' she said to Paddy. Briefing was not due for another hour, and it was rare for DCI Pike to make an appearance before then. 'Ma'am Pike's been a bit off with me lately. I want the team to present a professional front.'

'Huh,' Paddy snorted, leaning in so only Amy could hear. 'You know what they say . . . you can't make a good impression on wet sand.'

Amy knew there was no love lost between him and Pike, but she was taken aback by the remark. 'I thought it was just me getting it in the ear these days.'

'Far from it.' Paddy checked nobody was listening. 'I mean, she's never been great but, lately, she's lost the plot. We've got the HMIC due in next week. They'll be sniffing around like a dog at a buffet. I hope she gets her act together before then.'

Her Majesty's Inspectorate of Constabulary independently assessed all police forces, and their reports carried a lot of weight.

'Until then, there's always coffee.' Inhaling its aroma, Amy took a sip. Her skin throbbed as the warmth of the mug transferred to the nerve endings in her fingertips. She had taken off the cumbersome dressings, leaving skin-coloured plasters in their place. DCI Pike had torn a strip off her for being so 'wreckless' as to run into the site. But they both knew she would do it all over again if it meant saving Ellen's life.

The case involving the Curtis family had been named Operation Pegasus, taken from a long list of names generated for officers to choose from. Operation Roadrunner would have been more apt, given how their suspect was giving them the runaround this week.

'How are we doing, welfare-wise?' she asked, casting an eye over her officers. They were a small percentage of the number of people working on the case. 'Managing your workloads? Getting enough sleep?'

Heads nodded in unison. 'Good. We've budgeted for overtime for the rest of the week, so fill your boots. Any problems, see me in my office rather than bringing them up during briefing.' Again, knowing murmurs and nods of heads. Amy crossed her legs, happy she had got her point across. 'I've spoken to the hospital. Nicole had an operation for the bleed on her brain and it went better than expected. She was lucky we found her in time. Methanol can be deadly when taken in the wrong way.'

'Methanol . . .' DC Gary Wilkes spoke up. 'Isn't that alcohol?'

'Trust you to know that, Wilkie,' Molly jibed. Her smile faded as she recalled the gravity of the case.

Amy carried on. 'It's the simplest form of alcohol and it looks like Nicole drank it willingly. There was no evidence of a struggle and no bruising on her body. No fingerprints or DNA we can't account for and no forced entry into her home.' She could still see the scene, still hear Dr Curtis's screams, still taste the dried blood crusted on Nicole's mouth. The echo of such horrors would remain in her memory for a while to come. But Nicole was a fighter, pulling through for her child. It was imperative that they found Ellen alive.

'We've had the results back from ANPR,' DC Steve Moss interjected, referring to the automatic number-plate recognition system. 'Dr Curtis's alibi checked out. We clocked him driving to his house minutes before you.'

Amy nodded, recalling that the hood of his car had still been warm. But in some cases, minutes were all it took, and the poison could have been administered earlier that day. Just the same, Nicole had been carrying the weathered card from 'Luka' on her person with the 'Ladybird, Ladybird' rhyme, and Luka's words about Nicole playing her part had rung true. Test results on the other three phials found at the address proved they were nothing more than coloured water. Had she chosen differently, she would have been OK. Had anyone else received such a package? What about flowers? The yearly card? If they had, they weren't admitting to it. The letter sent to the *London Echo* was now police evidence, but one thing bothered Amy as she read the statement covering its seizure. Adam had failed to mention that the same letter had been sent to the newspaper year after year. It seemed Luka had been trying to get their attention for some time.

'Curtis's next-door neighbour, Alison Drew, has come forward,' Steve said, cutting into her thoughts. 'She saw a motorbike pull up to his house on the morning Nicole was poisoned.'

'I didn't see that on the system.' Amy wondered how she had missed it. There were numerous strands of the investigation, and she needed to keep on top of things as they came in.

'The statements are still being uploaded.' Paddy's gaze was apologetic as he stood beside her, mug of coffee in hand. As team sergeant, he should have let her know of any big developments straight away. Amy's idea for an early pow-wow had been justified, not least because Pike was waiting for her to slip up.

Paddy placed his mug on the table. 'Mrs Drew was away during the house-to-house inquiries. She called it in late last night.'

'Do we have a description?'

'Mrs Drew said she was hoovering her car on the drive when a motorbike pulled up next door. The driver was tall, stocky, wearing full leathers and a tinted helmet. He had a package in his hand which he gave to Nicole on the doorstep, but Alison couldn't hear what was being said. Then Alison's phone rang and she went inside. When she went back out a few minutes later the motorbike had gone.'

'That's it, then. The courier delivered the package to Nicole.'

'We checked Nicole's laptop,' Steve said. 'Her history had some shopping sites on it, but no home deliveries due in the last week.'

'Keep working on it,' Amy said, ticking boxes in her mind. 'The motorcyclist might lead us to Ellen. There's still a chance she's alive.'

This nugget of information about the courier could change everything. Luka had said he'd given Nicole a choice, one that had almost killed her. Just who had called at her house that day? Amy flicked through the paperwork, her eyes resting on the photograph of the nightdress they had pulled from the rubble. It was laid flat against brown paper, pictured next to a set of rulers to give it scale. Through his tears, Dr Curtis had identified the clothing as the nightdress Ellen had worn. It was of small comfort that there were no big tears in the fabric, no knife marks or obvious injury sites. Her kidnapper was playing the most twisted of games.

To Amy's frustration, he was still at large, and dangerous. She needed to get inside his mind. Their criminal profiler had drawn up a brief list of things – paranoia, possible former abuse, a socially awkward loner – but she needed more, and there was only one person she knew with that kind of insight.

Amy had received a visiting order to see Lillian in prison. It had been on her mind to bin it. She exhaled a heavy sigh. She sacrificed a little piece of herself every time she was in the same room as her birth mother. But her visits to Lillian helped serve another purpose. They opened her mind to the darkness in others – and, without any viable leads, that was a much-needed attribute.

CHAPTER THIRTY-TWO

A set of sharp knuckles tapped the taxi window, jolting Luka from his daydream. As he lowered the window, the scent of exhaust fumes seeped in. He had been parked with the engine running for five minutes, waiting for the child to come out. It seemed extravagant, a taxi driving him to and from school when the bus could take him straight there.

'Are you here for Toby?' A woman with a beaded necklace bent to speak to him, her considerable cleavage on show. In the distance, the shrill ring of a bell signalled the activation of an alarm within the school.

'Uh-huh,' Luka replied, resting his gloved hands on the steering wheel of the car. His flat cap offered a slight disguise, the wig beneath it itching his scalp.

'We usually have Jeff.' The woman regarded him cautiously, the noise from the alarm dragging her attention away.

'He's in hospital. Fell off a stepladder while changing a light bulb. I'm filling in.'

'Oh, I'm sorry to hear that.' Turning, she beckoned Toby to the car.

Luka's face fell as a boy in an electric wheelchair broke through the group of children on the lawn. *Shit*, he thought. He hadn't known the kid was disabled. When had that happened? His back molars pressed down hard. It was too late to back out now.

'Can you help me with the ramp?' The woman stepped to the side as he opened the car door. 'I need to see to the others. The fire alarm's gone off. It's probably a false alarm, but the fire brigade is on its way.'

Within a few minutes Toby and his wheelchair were secure in the back of the specially adapted car.

'Be careful as you set off, there are lots of children milling about,' she said to Luka, giving them both a brief wave.

'Sure.' Smiling, Luka pictured the semi-conscious Jeff gagged and bound in the boot. Putting the car in gear, he checked his rear-view mirror before pulling away from the kerb. *Wouldn't do to have Jeff call out now, not with so many witnesses around.*

'Who are you?' Toby piped up from the back.

Luka glanced in the rear-view mirror. Toby was a pale little boy, small for his age. A lock of dark curly hair tumbled down over the bluest of eyes. Guilt bloomed from within. Could he really go through with this? The thought was submerged beneath a sudden pulse of pain behind his skull. It was coming. He could feel it in the distance, a dark and treacherous reminder of the torment burrowing in his brain.

'I'm Luka, a friend of your dad's.' His Adam's apple bobbed as he swallowed to clear his throat. 'I'm looking after you until he finishes work.'

Toby chewed on his bottom lip. This was a child who clearly did not like change.

Luka's mouth widened in his most reassuring smile. 'We're going to my place for now. He's coming over in an hour.'

'Daddy said I mustn't talk to strangers,' Toby replied.

But Luka was prepared for such a statement. 'Didn't he mention me keeping you safe? That's why you're in a taxi, right?'

Toby's piercing blue eyes flicked up towards the mirror. 'I . . . I guess so.'

'There you go then. You'll like my house. I've got an Xbox and loads of games.'

'Even zombie games?' Toby's reservations dissipated as his face lit up with glee. 'Daddy doesn't let me play those.'

Given the amount of gore and violence in them, it was hardly surprising, but Toby could play them to his heart's delight as far as Luka was concerned.

'I've got all the games you could want, pizza, chocolate and ice cream too . . .' He paused, manoeuvring a bend in the road. 'Or would you rather that I drop you home and we can wait for your dad there?'

'It's OK.' Dimples pressed into Toby's cheeks as he delivered a toothy smile. 'I want to play zombie games!'

'That's more like it,' Luka replied.

He pressed down the car indicator as he signalled to turn left. A newly purchased tracksuit waited on the bed, just like the one Ellen wore. How would Stuart react when the game began? Would he risk his life to save his son? Another throb of pain pounded on the periphery of his vision. His fingers tightened on the steering wheel. Stuart should think himself lucky he was being given a chance.

Luka rested his forehead against the bathroom mirror. It offered a few seconds of momentary distraction from the pounding in his head. He had felt it this morning and had groaned as he witnessed the flashes of light in his vision. It was a warning of what was to come. He stood back from the mirror, his hand trembling as he searched the cabinet for the slim white box among the shaving cream, shower gel and toothpaste. Each movement, each sound, seemed magnified a hundredfold, and his shoulders inched upwards from the pain. There was a church bell booming in his head, a sledgehammer-fisted monster pounding hard. Slowly, he popped the foil packet from the box, flinching at each sound.

Like two tiny white angels, the Zolmitriptan tablets nestled in the palm of his hand. Ignoring the flash of pain, he threw his head back and swallowed them dry. Chasing them down with a sip of lukewarm tap water, he dragged himself to bed and waited for the pain to ease. In the safe room, Toby was playing 18-rated games and stuffing his face with forbidden food. It was with some relief Luka had discovered that the child was able to take a few steps unaided from his chair. A degenerative condition of some sort had left him recently wheelchair-bound. But there was no room for empathy in his captor's tortured mind. Lying in a foetal position, Luka waited for the pressure behind his skull to ease.

Sounds from outside filtered into his consciousness: the never-ending stream of traffic, a dog barking and . . . he covered his ears as a distant siren pierced his brain. At times like these, with his thoughts circling like predators, he did not have to look far for someone to blame. Minutes passed. His jaw unclenched as he surfaced from the worst of the crippling pain. He no longer trusted his emotions, but he had a job to do.

CHAPTER THIRTY-THREE

Amy's stomach knotted, just as it always did when she visited her biological mother in prison. Each time she strode down the familiar corridors, she vowed it would be her last visit to the woman whose mission it was to make her life hell. Yet Lillian's hold was impossible to escape. As she entered the double doors, a waft of synthetic forest glade rose up to greet her, courtesy of the plug-in air freshener on the wall. It did little to mask the stench of stale breath occupying the room.

Her pulse quickening, Amy glanced around. What was it about Lillian that kept her tightly in her grip? True, during their last few meetings she had been given little choice. Had she refused Lillian, she would have been turning her back on the families whose children were buried in unmarked graves. It was only through emotional blackmail that Lillian had brought her there. Despite the mental cruelty her birth mother relished inflicting, Amy had cooperated with her demands in order to give the families of the victims the peace they deserved.

She had been only four years of age when the police arrested her parents. In recent weeks, Amy's memory of her early years had returned in sounds and smells from which she could not escape. She heard and smelled them in her sleep: the screams of the women in the basement, the sickly air fresheners that masked something horrific in their home. The building had been demolished after Jack and Lillian were sent down, but Amy's repressed childhood memories were not so easily killed. Just a few poisonous words from Lillian could breathe life into them again.

So why had she returned to see the psychopathic woman who delighted in messing with her mind? Amy had learned the hard way that if she did not give Lillian the attention she craved she would seek it by other means. Over the last few weeks, her refusal to let things lie had driven Amy to despair. The phone calls infiltrating her workspace, the constant visiting orders and unwanted letters to her home. They contained instructions to see Damien and Mandy, the biological siblings Amy was accused of having 'turned her back on'. According to Lillian, she wanted the Grimes family to be 'united and supportive' during her appeal.

Amy had tried following the advice she gave to victims of harassment and stalking, telling herself not to respond. The last straw had come when Flora had almost taken one of Lillian's calls. Amy couldn't bear for her old life to merge with her new one. Flora was not as strong as she was. A conversation with Lillian would cause her mother many sleepless nights and Amy could not bear for Flora to be upset. She needed to be protected from the horrors of Amy's past. It was small consolation that spending time in Lillian's world helped Amy better understand perpetrators of similar crimes.

Shuffling behind the other prisoners, Lillian entered the room. Her eyes sought out Amy, narrowing as she found her. Amy knew she would be watching her features, feeding off the slightest sign of distress. When had Lillian grown into such a monster? Many books had been written about her and Jack, but it was all conjecture and no answers were to be found in them. Some experts believed it was Lillian's early abuse that had triggered the need to hurt others in order to gain control. But many victims of abuse lived normal lives, some dedicating their time to help-ing others. What had made the scales tip the other way?

Regardless of her history, Lillian's psychopathic tendencies were wired into her brain. Even if she had been raised in the best of house-holds, she could have turned out the same way. *Could the same be said for me?* The thought hatched in Amy's consciousness. She had read an article about people inheriting psychopathic traits. But surely she would know by now?

Since discovering the truth of her parentage, Amy had spent many evenings dissecting her personality for signs. She was no stranger to manipulating suspects to provide her with answers, but it was always for the greater good. Often blunt, she was not one for physical affection as far as friends and family were concerned. But that did not make her a psychopath and there was no law against enjoying your own company from time to time. She dismissed the thought as Lillian settled into the seat before her.

She looked well, free of the bruises she sometimes sported. Annoyingly, she was growing her hair to the same length as Amy's and even had a little colour in her cheeks.

'Let's get to the point,' Amy said, preferring to bypass Lillian's barbed comments about not taking her calls. 'What do you want from me and how did you get my home number and address?'

'Adam.' Lillian grinned. 'I granted him an audience. He was more than happy to give me your details in exchange for exclusive coverage of my story.' She paused, her eyes roaming Amy's face. When no reaction was forthcoming, she crossed her legs and continued. 'What a cutesy couple you could have made . . . Amy and Adam up a tree, K-I-S-S-I-N-G.' She chuckled. 'It sounds like it was meant to be. Tell me, what's he like in bed? I don't get many male visitors. I thought about him a lot after he left.' Slowly, she licked her lips, delivering a salacious smile.

Amy repressed the urge to shudder. Being in her mother's company made her feel dirty, part of something beyond her control. She knew that Lillian and Jack had used her to lure their victims in. But that was a memory she did not want to recall. Amy took a deep breath as she pushed down the tide of emotions. She didn't want to believe that Lillian had roped Adam in. The woman was a downright liar, winding her up like a clockwork toy. But Amy's last meeting with Adam had not been a happy one. She took a deep breath, vowing to stay strong.

'If you want your exposé, then so be it. My colleagues know all about you. They know I can't help what a vile family I was born into.' Amy's chin tilted upwards in defiance. 'They accept with good grace the decent, loving people who brought me up. They judge me by my actions, not yours.'

But Lillian was not listening; she was looking over Amy's shoulder to the far side of the room. Like many psychopaths, she failed to acknowledge the words she did not want to hear. In Lillian's world, her actions were justified. She had done nothing wrong. 'See her over there?' She pointed to a pale, pock-skinned woman in the corner of the room. Her stringy blonde hair was scraped back off her face, and Amy caught her regarding Lillian with a cautious gaze.

'She's my girlfriend. We call her Mighty Mouse.' Lillian smiled. 'She got banged up for dealing. That's her daughter visiting her. We're proper kindred souls.'

For once, Amy was lost for words. Why the hell would a mother of any kind get together with Lillian Grimes?

'It's amazing what people will do for a little bit of Black Mamba,' Lillian said, as if reading her mind. 'And I've got plenty of connections on the inside.'

Amy was all too aware of Black Mamba. Also known as Spice, the synthetic drug left its users in a zombie-like state. The emergency services were called so often to some prisons they were referred to by inmates as Mambulances. It was not unusual for inmates to deal on the inside in order to make money or garner friends, but Lillian being involved in drugs? This was news to Amy. 'You're dealing? That's risky.'

She was still a police officer, and if intelligence presented itself she would use it to her advantage. Anything to keep Lillian behind bars.

'Me? Deal drugs? Pfft! I don't touch that shit. I just introduced her to people who do.' A smile touched her lips. 'She was ever so grateful . . .' Lillian winked. 'You've got to love the system. Mind you, I won't be seeing her once I get out. Women are fine if there's nothing else on offer, but I do miss a nice rigid—'

'I didn't come here to talk about your sex life,' Amy interrupted, trying but failing to hide her disgust.

The space between them was speared by a titter as Lillian threw back her head and laughed. 'Forgive me. Children don't like hearing about their parents' sex lives, do they? You can blame Adam. He got me all hot under the collar, and I needed some . . . release. As I said to Adam, that DI Donovan must be good in the sack if you dumped the Italian stallion in favour of him.'

Amy's spirits plummeted. How did Lillian know so much about her? But she would not give her the satisfaction by asking. 'I'm warning you. Quit contacting me, or I'll have you done for harassment. If you're arrested, it will go against your appeal – another conviction to add to your long line of offences. You'll never get out of here.' Amy leaned forward, driving her message home. 'I have proof. Plenty of my colleagues have received calls from you in recent weeks.'

'They got a call from someone claiming to be your mother, and I believe the number was blocked. Now, I know that poor delicate Flora won't be up for testifying in court to say it wasn't her. And I also know you won't slap a harassment order on me because you won't want the intrusion into your private life. You can't kid a kidder, Amy.' Lillian's lips parted in a sly smile. 'I'm your mum. I know when you're lying, and it's my guess they don't know about us yet.'

'This is the last time I visit.' Collecting herself, Amy prepared to leave. There was no point in wasting any more time here today.

Another titter in response. 'And how many times have you said that? Yet here you are. Like a boomerang, finding your way back to me.' The air between them cooled as Lillian met her gaze. Her body tense, Amy found herself unable to look away.

'You can blame me all you want, but you can't resist the pull. Poppy Grimes still lives in a little dark place inside you and she's crying out to be free. Can you imagine living life without limits?' She took a slow breath. 'Maybe one day you'll realise that and maybe you won't, but mark my words: I will always be part of your life. It will be *you* making sure of that, not me.' Satisfied, she sat back in her chair. 'So why don't you start by telling me why you're really here?'

Blinking, Amy inhaled a sudden, quick breath. It was as if she had been entranced, and she hated herself for allowing the woman to creep under her skin. She was loath to ask Lillian for help, but they were no further on with finding Ellen and she needed all the assistance she could get. Lillian listened intently as she ran through details of her communications with Luka to date. Spent, she leaned back in her seat, hoping Lillian would provide her with the answers she desperately needed right now. 'Why? Why are they doing this? I don't understand what the kidnapper is getting out of it.'

'You're asking me for help in my capacity as a serial killer?' Lillian regarded Amy with mistrust.

'No,' Amy replied, knowing such accusations would not get her on side. 'But you've lived with one. You know how they work. What's the best way to handle Luka?'

'Just like I handled your father?' The smile returned to Lillian's face.

Amy nodded. She knew Lillian was equally culpable but she would pretend to think otherwise if it meant helping Ellen. Her parents had done untold damage. This was her way of putting things right.

'Then let me tell you. It's the game this Luka is getting off on, not the actual kill.'

It was said with such authority that Amy struggled to maintain eye contact. She clenched her fists beneath the table and the sudden sting of pain from her fingertips brought her firmly back in control. 'Go on.'

'All this drama, pretending to be Luka, setting up the call. He's enjoying the attention. Killing the child will bring it to an end.'

'So you think she's alive?'

'I didn't say that. He wants you to think she is, though. He probably saw where they had marked that concrete pillar and pinned her nightdress to the other side. Not that difficult to do, if you can distract the workers long enough to sneak in.'

'How would he distract them if he was trying to get on site at the same time?'

'Oh, come on, hasn't it occurred to you yet? He's not working alone.'

Amy frowned as she considered the implications of Lillian's words.

'How else has he been able to watch you, stay one step ahead?' Lillian continued. 'And he's had a lot of time to brood on this . . . years, by the sound of it.'

For once in her life Amy was speechless. She had never for a moment considered there was more than one person involved.

Lillian's voice lowered as she leaned forward, speaking so only they could hear. 'Tell me, do you think about the murder victims when you're in bed at night?' Her eyes glittered with dark intent. 'Do you touch their faces, gain a little bit of pleasure from the coldness of their skin? Does your pulse quicken at the prospect of attending a murder scene?'

'Is there anything else?' Amy replied, briefly snapping her eyes shut. She knew she should stay for longer, try to tease out what she could. But the words leaving her mother's lips made her sick to the core.

'Ooh, I'm right, aren't I?' Lillian's eyes grew wide, following her daughter's movements as Amy folded her arms tightly across her chest.

'The only difference between you and me is that you have the law on your side.'

Amy shook her head in amazement. How quickly this woman could change, one moment playing up the fact she was falsely accused and the next trying to reel Amy into her games. Did she have dual personalities? Amy wondered why she was pandering to the type of predator she had spent her career trying to protect people from. Then the alarm activated, telling them visiting time was up. 'Goodbye, Lillian,' she said firmly as she stood to leave. She did not wait for a response before turning and walking away.

CHAPTER THIRTY-FOUR

The Curtis Institute, December 1984

Floating in his chamber, Luka was frozen in fear. Darkness had closed in from every angle. As the water temperature dropped, the cold pricked his skin like a thousand tiny needles. The tests had progressed, and he would have given anything to go back to choosing between coloured sweets and cake. It wasn't the physical discomfort that frightened him, it was the feeling of impending doom. The monsters were coming, and he was too weak to fight them any more. He had promised himself that he would not cry. He would not give the doctor the satisfaction of reading his emotions. Every sob, every wail, had been documented up until now.

It had been weeks since he had been allowed outside. Isolation was part of the experiment – it was as if they *wanted* him to fall apart. The tablets he was forced to swallow were followed by hallucinations which hunted him down mercilessly. Vomiting sessions had carved bony cheekbones into his face and his skin was paper-white from lack of sun. Dr Curtis was pushing him hard and Luka didn't know how much more he could take. His thoughts were stolen by a malevolent presence lurking in his periphery. The monsters were here, dark creatures with bulging eyes and sharpened teeth. He told himself they weren't real. But his pulse pounded as he heard their feet drag, his name on their laboured breaths.

Luka's fists grew rigid as he struggled for air. It was impossible to scream and his heartbeat thundered in his ears. Sucking in a breath, he grasped for purchase in his watery tomb. Eyes open or closed, it made no difference. There was only blackness and the monster looming above him, jaws wide and salivating as it prepared to bite down on his head. Luka pulled at the tube feeding air into his lungs. The thick rubber gloves encasing his hands had reduced his sense of touch. A gargled scream left his lips as water gushed into his mouth. What had he done? Salty water flooded his airways and he gasped for air that would not come.

A sudden slice of light cut through his disorientation as the doors of his chamber were pulled back. Luka chugged for breath, the whites of his eyes rolling in his mask. A set of strong arms rescued him, and he had never been so relieved to see light.

Water gushed from the mask as Deborah lifted it from his head, and Luka coughed and choked, inhaling a desperate breath.

'Slow your breathing,' Deborah said, enveloping him in her arms. 'It's OK. Your pipe became disconnected. You're safe. I have you.'

On shaky legs, he clambered out of the chamber, salt water stinging his eyes and burning his throat.

'Luka. Speak to me. Are you OK?' Deborah swivelled her head towards the doctor, who was standing with a clipboard in his hand.

He frowned at Luka as if he were a lab rat who had failed to find the cheese.

'I hate you!' Luka screamed in his Russian tongue, knowing the doctor would not understand.

Deborah pursed her lips, for once failing to translate.

'I hate you and I wish you were dead!' Luka's words were delivered in an angry stream, cursing the man he hated with all of his might.

'What's he saying?' Dr Curtis snapped. 'He's ruined the experiment, he'll have to go in again.'

Luka dug his fingers into Deborah's forearm at the thought of returning to the tank.

'He's been in there for four hours.' Deborah glared at the doctor. 'He's had enough for one day.'

'I decide when the experiment is complete. I want him back in there now.'

'*Nyet, nyet!*' Luka cried, his body stiff as he tried to clamber away.

'Shhh, it's OK,' Deborah soothed. 'Did you see things? Did they seem real?'

Eyes wide and unblinking, Luka delivered a sharp nod of the head.

A timer beeped to signal the test had come to an end. Deborah turned back to the doctor. 'It's over. You have your results. The hallucinations are hitting him with full force. The fact that he disconnected his air supply can be updated on our records. We've pushed him as far as he can go.'

But the doctor did not seem convinced. 'Such a shame. I was hoping a tweak in medication would keep them at bay.' So that was what the isolation chamber was about. It was the quickest way of finding out if the hallucinations were still there.

'I'll take him back to his room, get him fed. Extract a full update.' Deborah gave Dr Curtis a reassuring smile. 'Besides, Shirley is expecting you home. Aren't you going to the theatre tonight?'

'Very well,' he replied, barely giving Luka a second glance.

'I want Mama!' Luka shivered beneath his towel after Dr Curtis had left.

'Shh, shh, shh, it's OK, you have me,' Deborah responded, her words softly spoken. 'Sweetheart, I'm sorry you were frightened, but I never left your side. We'll change your medication. I won't let anything bad happen to you – ever.'

Luka's chin wobbled, his eyes glistening with tears. 'I want to go home. I don't want to live here anymore.'

'Soon. Just be patient. It'll all be over soon.'

'Why doesn't Papa write? I want my papa.'

Taking a second towel from the radiator, Deborah wrapped it around him, giving his shoulders a squeeze. 'I'll tell you what. You keep going with the last of the tests and I'll speak to your papa. Maybe we could organise a phone call.'

'Really?' Luka said, clinging to the towels and absorbing their warmth. 'I can speak to Papa? And Mama too?'

Deborah nodded, but her features carried concern. 'There's something I need to tell you. Your mama . . . she's not very well. She's been prescribed medication but . . . well, she shouldn't be too stressed. So if you have any worries, come to me. Think of me as your second mother. Yes?'

Luka nodded.

'Now, let's get you into some warm clothes so you can have a bite to eat. We'll skip your medication tonight. Nobody needs to know.'

CHAPTER THIRTY-FIVE

Toby wasn't sure how long the little girl had been there. He had slept facing the wall, feeling her gaze, before he discovered her perched on the end of the bed. Daddy always said he sensed things better than other people, as if he had developed a superhero power to make up for the bodily functions he had lost. This morning he had felt that something wasn't right. Everything seemed off, somehow. School had been fine up until the time the fire alarm was activated. Toby's classmates had bumped into his wheelchair, scrambling out of the classroom for a few extra minutes of fresh air. Then the taxi had turned up, along with the driver with the funny hair and a cap that made him look shifty from the off. I mean, who wears a cap when they're driving? It's not as if it's going to rain inside the car. These were the thoughts that had occupied Toby's mind as he sat in the back of the cab. But Miss Pringle, his teacher, had not seemed worried, and Toby had remembered his father's words.

'Trust me,' he'd said that morning when Toby asked to take the bus to school. 'The taxi is here to keep you safe.' Toby trusted his daddy more than anyone in the world. But today his daddy had been wrong.

Shuffling on his elbows, Toby bore the discomfort as he worked his body into a sitting position. He had not wanted to fall asleep, but a long day at school followed by Xbox games and pizza had made his eyelids feel like two lead shutters he could not keep open. As sleep called, he had clung to the hope that his father would be there when he awoke. But instead, a blonde-haired girl with a piece of tissue paper stuck up her nose sat on the bed.

'Who are you?' Toby said eventually, straightening himself up. He had fallen asleep in his wheelchair but had a vague recollection of someone removing his shoes and lifting him into bed.

'I'm Ellen,' the little girl said, scooting towards him. There was no suspicion in her gaze, only an intense curiosity, which, given the circumstances, seemed odd. She pushed her spectacles up the bridge of her nose, the thick glass making her eyes seem as big as moons. 'What's your name?'

'I'm Toby.' He rubbed his face. How long had he been napping for? He gazed around the room, noting the absence of clocks on the wall. It could not have been any more than an hour or two.

'Have you come to take me home?' Ellen said, her lips parting as she breathed in through her mouth.

Toby stared at her, a flash of incredulity on his face. 'How would I take you home? I'm six! Haven't you seen my wheelchair?' He pointed at the chair next to the bed.

Ellen stared at it, her tongue finding the gap between her teeth as she tilted her head.

'Haven't you seen a wheelchair before?' he asked.

Ellen replied with a shake of the head.

Toby sighed. 'I have it 'cos I can't walk. Not very far, anyway.' He looked her over. Her grey tracksuit was just like his, except hers was stained with chocolate and some kind of purple drink. 'Why have you got toilet paper up your nose?'

'Nosebleeds.' Ellen pulled at the offending plug of tissue, inspected it, then, happy the blood had dried, threw it on the floor. In Toby's house, throwing rubbish on the ground would earn you a telling-off. But was this Ellen's house, or had she been brought here too?

'Where are we?' He lowered his voice, pulling himself to the edge of the bed. 'Where do you live?' He badly needed to pee but wanted to know what was going on. Apart from the guy who'd brought him here, he'd had the room to himself. So why was Ellen here now?

She shrugged in response to both questions, her eyes growing wide. 'The man brought me here. I don't like him. I want my mummy.' She plugged her thumb in her mouth, gave it two sucks and added, 'I want to go home.'

Toby wanted to go home too. Back to his daddy and Jodie. What were they doing now? Had they remembered to feed Thor? His hamster had been a birthday present. They weren't meant to have pets in their block of flats, but Daddy knew the landlord and he said he'd allow it, given it was for Toby. But when Thor had arrived, Toby felt sad because none of the other boys and girls in their block would know how nice it felt to have a pet of their own. Miss Pringle said everybody deserved kindness, not just one or two people. It felt wrong that he was allowed a hamster and they weren't. And now he was the one feeling like a hamster in a cage.

Taking two tentative, wobbly steps, he lowered himself into his wheelchair. The room was big enough to squeeze past the sofa and the single bed. A bunch of games were piled up in the corner and a box of Lego had been upended on the floor. He returned his glance to Ellen. He probably had her to thank for that. After manoeuvring his wheel-chair around the mess, he used the toilet and washed his hands.

There was no way his daddy would leave him somewhere like this. He had tried the door earlier; he knew he was locked in. What would his favourite superheroes do? Should he look for a weapon? Defend himself? Hide? He knew that bad things often happened to kids who were taken by strange men. They'd had talks about stranger danger at school. So why had Miss Pringle allowed him to get in the taxi? He scratched his head, feeling all in a muddle. His stomach was twisted up in knots and his chest hurt from swallowing back his tears. He steered himself back into the room to find Ellen patiently waiting on the sofa. It was up to him to protect them both now.

'See that big piece of green Lego?' he said, nodding to the pile on the floor. 'Can you give it to me?' It was a long, narrow piece of rigid plastic with sharp corners. Lego might not be a weapon, but he knew that it hurt enough for Daddy to swear when he stepped on one in his bare feet. He thought of all the *Home Alone* movies they had watched together. Toby clenched the piece of Lego tightly in his hand. If the man was out to hurt them, then he would fight for all he was worth.

CHAPTER THIRTY-SIX

Head bowed, Stuart scrubbed the inside of the cooking pot until his own warped reflection stared back at him. Dousing it in the water, he set it aside on the draining board. The kitchen was uncomfortably warm, and he dried his hands on his apron before swiping the sweat from his brow.

'The dishwasher's on the blink, so we need this lot done by hand,' his supervisor shouted, stacking food-encrusted pots and pans on the kitchen worktop next to him. Despite the new hearing aids lodged in his ears, George delivered every word at the top of his voice. At the age of fifty-four, his hearing had been restored, but Stuart supposed that old habits were hard to break. Responding with a nod, he got to work. At least he would be left alone, given time to contemplate things. He had seen the way Deborah McCauley had looked at him: as if he was shit on her shoe. She would have had a right laugh if she'd known he worked in the kitchens of the restaurant she'd brought him to. He'd almost cancelled their lunch date, scared his colleagues would show him up. In fact, nobody had recognised him. His charity-shop suit had thrown them off the scent. Back here, in the bowels of the kitchen, nobody was interested in what he looked like, only that he got the job done. It had been the same when he worked for Dr Curtis. The man was so wrapped up in what he was doing to those poor kids that he never gave him or Christina a second thought. Had Deborah kept tabs on them to ensure they kept their silence? He would have spoken up in a heartbeat, had he not been implicated himself.

He watched the dirty water swirl down the plughole as he prepared to fill it with fresh suds and start again. If only it was so easy to make the past evaporate. He thought about Jodie, his girlfriend. She was looking after his son today. As single parents, they stuck together, helping each other out when they could. But now their relationship had progressed to a new level. He had been squirrelling away some savings and had just enough money to buy her a ring. All he wanted for his family was a brighter future. Was it too much to ask?

He squeezed the washing-up liquid bottle, his thoughts on auto-pilot as he worked. It was a catch-22. He wanted to stay at home more to keep Toby safe, but he had to work extended hours to pay for the taxi to take him to and from school. He couldn't win. Toby had been through so much in his short lifetime. His degenerative disease had proved too much for his mother, Kim, to handle and she had given him up. Only recently had he agreed to use his wheelchair. In a way, guilt had crippled Kim too. She hadn't known she was pregnant until long after their one-night stand. By then, the damage was already done. She had tried to get clean too late.

He remembered the day the social came knocking on his door. The day he found out he had a three-year-old son. Discovering that Toby had been dumped by his mother had broken Stuart's heart. He had barely known his own father. He would not have the same thing happen to his son. With the help of social care, they made his high-rise flat into a place fit enough to bring up a kid. Out went the cigarettes and the booze. In came the full-time job. His son had given him a reason to get out of bed. Despite all his problems, Toby had saved him. His son was fuelled with a spirit and determination that put Stuart to shame. Now a monster from the past threatened to blow it all apart.

Methodically, he worked through the pile of pots and pans, raking over his worries until everything was cleared away.

'Oi! Stuart!' George shouted from a couple of feet away. 'You finished yet?'

'Yeah, all done,' he answered, checking his watch. Toby should be home. He'd give it five more minutes and then he'd ring Jodie to check everything was OK.

'Get yourself down to the car park. A courier's asking for you,' George said. 'In future, have your deliveries sent to your home address.' He scratched a pimple breaking out on his chin before turning and walking away.

Stuart scowled. He hadn't ordered anything to be delivered to work . . . Then a wave of fear threatened to engulf him as he undid his apron and hung it on the wall. Had something happened to Toby? The ride down in the lift felt like an eternity and his heart was in his mouth by the time he reached the ground floor.

'What's this?' he said, when the package was thrust into his hands. Wearing a tinted visor, the courier was a leather-clad brick shithouse. Stuart waited for him to produce an electronic device for him to sign. But instead, he retrieved his motorbike keys from his pocket and headed back to his bike. Now Stuart was scared. Tearing open the packaging, he could barely breathe as a ghost of the past raised its ugly head. Encased in black sponge within the cardboard box were four phials. The same as the ones used in Dr Curtis's early tests. 'Who are you?' Stuart asked, advancing on the courier. He didn't care how big he was. 'If you've hurt my son . . .' But his words were drowned out by the roar of the motorbike engine as the courier took off.

Hands shaking, Stuart plucked a black envelope from within the box and scanned the words on the card inside.

There are four phials in this package.

One is poisoned. Three are safe.

Drink one for me to notify police about Toby's location.

Risk your life for the one you love – a choice not afforded to me.

Luka

Stuart's whole world crumbled as he absorbed the words. His boy. Someone had his boy. But Toby needed special care – and without his medication he would fall ill. With a rising sense of dread, Stuart realised that his worst nightmare had come true. A sudden buzzing vibration returned his attention to the package in his hand. Pushing back the sponge, he slid out a mobile phone. The words *Answer me* flashed up on the screen, and Stuart's blood ran cold.

CHAPTER THIRTY-SEVEN

'I needed that,' Amy said as she joined her mother in the kitchen. Despite the pain in her fingers, her early-morning punchbag session had done the trick. Sleep had surprised her after all, granting a full eight hours of rest. The feeling of being refreshed was a novel one, and she felt ready for whatever was thrown in her direction. She did not have long to wait. 'Have you taken Dotty out?' she said, frowning as she noticed the lead missing from the hook in the hall.

'Yes. I . . . I went to get the paper,' Flora replied.

Amy's eyes trailed to the morning edition of the *London Echo* on the kitchen table. It was unusual for her mother to be fully dressed at this early hour, let alone to have taken Dotty for her morning walk.

'What's so interesting that you couldn't wait for the paperboy to deliver it?' Amy asked, switching on the kettle and taking down a cup. 'Would you like a cup of . . .' She stalled, catching the forlorn expression on her mother's face. 'What's wrong?'

The words had barely left her lips before her mobile phone vibrated on the kitchen counter.

'Don't answer it!' Flora's words were brittle as they sliced through the air.

'Of course I'm going to answer it. What if it's work?'

'Don't!' Flora snatched it from the counter, jabbing at the button to reject the call. No sooner had it stopped than the landline rang. Amy swivelled from the phone back to her mother. 'What's going on?'

Pressing her finger to her lips, Flora picked up the home phone. 'Yes? Hello, Patrick.' She paused, pleading with her eyes as Amy advanced to take the call. It was Paddy, but such were her mother's old-fashioned ways that she addressed him by his full name. 'She's out with the dog . . . Yes, she's aware. I'll get her to call you when she comes back . . . No . . . no trouble at all. Thank you. Bye.'

'You're scaring me now.' Amy paled at the prospect of what lay ahead. Her mother was not an assertive woman. There had to be a good reason behind her behaviour today.

'I wanted to be the one to tell you,' she said, sliding the newspaper across the kitchen table. Unfolding it, she exposed the front page for Amy to read.

MET COP DAUGHTER OF BRENTWOOD BEAST, the headlines screamed, stealing Amy's breath. Her gaze fell on the reporter's name. Adam Rossi. He had done it. He had betrayed her in the worst possible way.

'I can't believe he did that,' Flora said, her face soured in disgust.

Amy scanned the page, her heart plummeting as she absorbed the damning words. Here was the passion he was known for, the flair that had been lacking in his piece about Dr Curtis. It spoke of Lillian Grimes as if she were the victim. How the police officer handling the case had adopted her daughter and how details of Lillian's case were later leaked to the press. In another paragraph, it spoke of evidence being planted at the scene, of Lillian's appeal, her claims of innocence and her dreams of being free. It told how her daughter, DI Amy Winter, had turned against her, despite Lillian's recent cooperation in the case of the missing children brutally murdered all those years ago by Lillian's husband, Jack Grimes. 'I was terrified to leave him,' Lillian stated in the interview. 'He raped and abused me, then threatened to kill my children if I went to the police. I never imagined that I would end up in prison for some-thing my husband did.' Amy's stomach churned as the past reared its ugly head all over again.

'Here.' Placing a cup of tea before her, Flora tilted her head. 'Why don't you call in sick? Let things die down a bit before you go back to work.'

Work. The thought hit her like a punch to the stomach. What would her colleagues think of her now? Inhaling a deep breath, Amy pushed the paper away. 'How did you know about this?'

'Winifred rang. Her son runs the newsagent's around the corner. He let me in early so I could have a copy.'

'I'm sorry,' Amy said, painfully aware of the gossip this would gen-erate. 'The tittle-tattle will die down in a few days.'

'It's a bit more than tittle-tattle – what about your job?'

'Don't worry about me. All the important people already know.' Dotty whimpered at her feet, picking up on her unease. Amy bent down, giving her a quick cuddle before casting an eye over the clock on the wall. 'It's time I headed off. What's it like outside? Will I need my hood?' She would cycle to work; the journey would give her time to think.

'It's frosty, no rain forecast for today.' Flora looked at her quizzically. 'Are you sure you're all right?'

'Absolutely. And if anyone rings you up for a quote, tell them to mind their own business. As for Adam . . .'

'Don't you worry, love, he's burned his bridges with me. You stick with that nice Donovan chap.' She paused, as if listening to an incom-ing thought. 'He knows, doesn't he? You've told him?'

Amy forced a smile. 'Of course.' But the words were hollow as they left her lips. How would he react when he found out? Why would anyone want to date the daughter of a serial killer?

'What about Craig?' Flora asked as Amy headed for the door.

Amy sighed. It was a small blessing that her detective inspector brother had taken a week off work. From the day Amy was adopted, he had made her feel like part of the family, even if their competitive natures sometimes got in the way. 'Can you speak to him? I've got to get to work.'

'I'll order a taxi. Tell him in person,' Flora said, with a swift nod of the head. 'I'll bring Dotty too.'

If it weren't for the subject matter, Amy would have been amused to hear of her mother turning up at Craig's door at this early hour. She wondered who Flora would catch him in bed with today. Their mother never refused an opportunity to snoop, and Craig's life was a closed book. 'It's a bit early, isn't it?'

'I'm his mother. It's never too early,' Flora said, riffling in the drawer for the number of a taxi firm.

Amy's legs felt weak as she cycled to work. Forging on, she prepared herself mentally for what lay ahead. The rays of morning sun provided little comfort, and she brushed a strand of hair away from her face, realising her helmet was nestled with her bag in the basket on the front of her bike. Was that what things were going to be like now? Her thoughts unfocused, trailing back to her painful past? Shame encompassed her like a black shroud. She felt dirty, at fault. It was illogical to blame herself for what had happened, but she remained painfully aware that her biological parents had sometimes used her as bait to lure their innocent victims in. If only she could go back to being her four-year-old self and scream at those young girls not to get into the car.

Fear had served to gag her. She had seen far too much at such a young age. Squeezing the brakes on her bicycle, she came to a halt at the traffic lights. What if Lillian was right? Was that why she touched the cheeks of the dead when she attended a murder scene? Why her heart beat a little bit faster at the prospect of dealing with a murder case? *The only difference between you and me is that you have the law on your side.* Lillian's words taunted her as they replayed on a loop.

The toot of a car horn almost made Amy jump out of her skin. The lights had barely turned green, and she gave the driver a dirty look before continuing on her way. The sight of the police station made her stomach lurch. She had known that this day would come, but now, in the middle of a kidnapping case, the timing could not be worse. DCI Pike already knew of her background, which she had since shared with the command team. Would the rest of her colleagues be as understanding? Or would they view her as part of the killer family they despised?

All of this had come at a time when she needed their focus the most. 'C'mon, you can do this,' she mumbled to herself under her breath. But it wasn't her attitude she was worried about. It was that of her team.

CHAPTER THIRTY-EIGHT

The Curtis Institute, December 1984

Slipping out, Luka ran down the hall of the old university, his plimsolls beating against the tiled floor. It was risky, taking off after his music lessons, but Luka could not bear to go through another round of tests. He needed his mama. He needed to go home.

Wincing, he waited for his sight to adjust to the natural light flooding through the expansive windows on either side. A maze of rooms and corridors lay ahead, filled with the chatter of busy students much older than him. He ignored their inquisitive glances, his shoulders hunched, his head hung low. The space was a stark contrast to the fluorescent-lit accommodation in which he spent most of his time. Following the signs to the canteen, his attention was drawn to a large glass counter housing tray upon tray of hot food. The scents of different dishes rose up his nostrils, making him salivate. He thought of the children at home living on the street. Why was it that some people had so much food while others had none?

'Mama!' he called, tears pricking his eyes as his sense of panic grew. Soon they would find him. Clamp a hand on his shoulder and force him back. But he did not recognise any of the faces behind the glass counter where they served food. 'Mama!' The word pierced the air, more insistent this time. A blonde-haired young woman approached him, touching his shoulder. Flinching, he jumped from the contact.

'You OK?' she asked, a gentle curiosity behind her eyes. Her hair peeked out of a white hairnet and she smelled faintly of the spices from the curry listed on the specials board.

'I want Mama,' he cried, feeling like a baby as tears accumulated in his eyes. Pointing towards the kitchens, he gave her an imploring look. He swivelled his head from left to right. Any second now, the orderlies could drag him back to that waiting room in time for the next round of tests.

'You must be Sasha's boy,' the lady replied, leading him through to the canteen staff entrance. 'She told me you were staying in the old dorms.'

Luka caught a faint whiff of crisp, fresh air. Had it not been for Mama, he would have burst through the doors that led into the outside yard. This place had become the worst type of prison, and all he wanted was an escape. But what would happen then? Papa was saving up the money Mama earned and sent home. It would help them through the hard times, for the days Papa was unable to work. Guilt speared Luka's heart like a physical pain. Such thoughts had ensured his silence, but he couldn't take it anymore.

'Luka,' his mama said. 'What are you doing here?' Wiping her hands on her apron, she took him into a side room which was filled with mops and cleaning products of every kind. Upturning two empty buckets, she sat on one and patted the other for him to do the same. 'What's happened?' she asked, her face pale and strained.

His expression screwed up as he tried to find the right words. He remembered Deborah's warning. Mama was ill. He could not upset her by telling her how bad things were. She had lost weight since he last saw her, her thick black hair now streaked with slivers of grey.

'I want to go home,' he finally said. 'I hate this place.'

'You do?' She drew him close, her arm around his shoulders as she met his gaze. 'They told me you liked it here. That you wanted to stay.'

Luka shook his head so fast it felt like a spinning top. Lately, his time with his mama had been rationed to just minutes. Extra hours cleaning the old building as well as serving the workshop students in the kitchen kept her busy during the day. In the evenings, he was so tired from the experiments that he slept. Holding him tightly, Sasha rocked him until his sobs subsided. His tears dampening her apron, he finally drew away.

'Can't we leave this place, Mama? Can't we run away?'

'But where will we go without money?' She asked. 'They send my allowance to Ivan. They've taken our passports too.' She said it with authority. Had she looked for them? Had she thought about leaving too?

'Tell you what,' she said, clasping her palm against his cheek. 'I'll speak to the doctor. The trials will be over soon. If we explain that you're scared . . .'

'But Mama!' Luka blurted. Wasn't she listening to a word he said?

'Shhh, don't fret,' Sasha replied, pausing to kiss his forehead. 'He's a doctor, not a criminal. He can't keep us here against our will.' Just the same, she checked to ensure nobody was listening. Leaning forward, she kept her tone low. 'If that doesn't work, I'll do some snooping. We'll find our own way out.'

Luka slowly nodded. He did not trust the doctor, but what choice did they have?

'I'll speak to Deborah too,' Sasha continued. 'I'll tell her you've had enough.'

But Luka lacked his mama's faith. Deborah was kind and she looked out for him, but she was in no hurry to allow either of them home.

CHAPTER THIRTY-NINE

After securing her bike in the rear car park, Amy accessed the police station through the back. The private entrance was available only to police and today she was grateful for that. Once inside, she made a beeline for the ladies' toilets. Locking herself into a cubicle, she sat on the closed toilet seat. Her legs still felt like jelly and she needed a few seconds to compose herself before facing her colleagues. The muted tones of the tannoy called an officer to the front counter, followed by the urgent footsteps of her police colleagues as they bustled down the corridor. She wasn't the centre of the universe, Amy told herself. Her colleagues were too busy getting on with their work to think about her. So why did her feet feel glued to the floor?

Sliding her mobile from her pocket, she flicked through her texts and missed calls. There were three notifications from Paddy and a voicemail from Sally-Ann, her sister, checking in with her. A text from her brother Craig, asking if she was OK, followed by a smutty one-liner about Flora almost catching him in the act with an ex-lap dancer named Divine. Amy's lips curved into a weak smile, relieved he was playing down the news, which had probably blown his mind. They were all tarred by association – the family who had taken in the daughter of killers Jack and Lillian Grimes. Amy sighed as she scrolled down her phone to find three missed calls from DCI Pike. Rising, she pocketed her mobile, unable to put off the inevitable. She checked her watch. Still on schedule. Despite everything that was happening, she could not bear to be late to work.

'I trust you've seen this.' Pike raised the newspaper in Amy's direction as she entered her office minutes later. Amy stared at the tiny cactus plant gracing Pike's desk. She could not bear to look at the headline again. It stank of betrayal. And this from the man who claimed to still love her. *If that's love, you can keep it*, Amy thought, nodding three times in response to Pike's sharp tones. In the short walk to her DCI's office she had come to a decision. Her father had adopted her because he wanted her to have a better life. She would not betray his memory by throwing everything away now. She was wary but ready to fight. If Pike thought she was kicking her off the team, she had another think coming.

'I owe you an apology,' Pike said. Her response could not have been any more unexpected.

Amy lifted her head, wondering if she had heard right. Was she really saying that she wanted to apologise? She waited before speaking, reluctant to ask Pike to clarify for fear of looking like a fool. Such battles were better fought with carefully chosen words.

'I'm sorry for how I reacted when you came to me about Lillian.' Pike gestured at her to sit down. 'If Robert were here now, he'd give me a serious telling-off.' The mention of his name brought a sad smile to Pike's face. It was true. Robert had treated people as he found them. His beliefs had not been forged from others' opinions or the type of life people were born into. In contrast, Pike had been less than sympathetic when Amy told her about her connection to Lillian Grimes. 'Not that it's an excuse, but I've been struggling to get over Robert's death,' Pike continued, filling the silence between them. 'I should have listened when you said you didn't want to speak to Adam Rossi.' She folded over the newspaper and deposited it in the bin beneath her desk. 'You're a good detective . . . Who am I kidding? You're a brilliant detective, and you've taken everything thrown at you with the integrity I've come to expect. I turned my back on you, and that shows weak leadership on my part.'

Amy opened her mouth to say it was all right, but Pike raised her hand. It was then that Amy realised just how much thought had gone into what she was about to say. 'Poor leadership filters down. This team deserves better than that.'

'Thank you,' Amy replied. 'Hopefully, the rumour mill will die down soon. Today's headlines, tomorrow's chip paper, as Dad used to say.' She should have consoled Pike, told her what a brilliant leader she was, but the words would have felt like a lie. The truth was, her DCI had taken her eye off the ball. Perhaps her admission would signal a new start for them all.

'Have you spoken to the team about it yet?'

Amy shook her head.

'Then do. Get it out in the open. Show them that you've nothing to be ashamed of. Tell them what you're comfortable sharing and leave it at that.'

'I will,' Amy said, even though the thought of talking about her personal life made her inwardly cringe.

'I wish I could turn the clock back,' Pike mused, her eyes falling on a framed photograph on the wall. In the centre of the picture was Amy's father, flanked on either side by new recruits on their passing-out day. At the end of the line-up was Pike. In full uniform, they looked so smart, and Amy felt a pang of shared grief.

'What we had was very short-lived.' Pike cleared her throat. Her eyes watery, she looked as if she were about to cry. Amy had no intention of bringing up their brief affair, but Pike seemed determined to have her say. There was something bizarre about this meeting. They should have been discussing Ellen's case instead of stoking the ashes of the past.

'I hope we can put this unfortunate episode behind us,' Pike said, sniffing back unshed tears.

Amy shifted in her seat. 'Water under the bridge.'

'Good. Because I'm missing our workouts in the gym. Nobody can throw a right hook like you.'

Amy made an effort to smile. She was grateful for Pike's support but a long way off trusting her just yet. 'Have any updates come in?' She steered the conversation back to work.

'The blood on the nightdress has been identified as Ellen's.' Pike sighed, allowing her words to fall like stones. 'The car park where you found it has been released as a crime scene. Apart from some cigarette butts – most likely left by workmen – we've got nothing else of value. Unfortunately, there was no CCTV installed and the security measures put in place by the contractors have not turned up anything so far.'

'This is someone who knows their way around.' Amy felt light-headed, caught in a blood-sugar slump after exercising on an empty stomach that morning. The fact that the blood was Ellen's was something she had prepared herself for. 'I think the kidnapper *is* Luka – that somehow he survived the fire, and maybe Sasha too. How could he get into a building site like that? He can't be working alone.'

'The way this case is going, nothing surprises me anymore.' Pike steepled her fingers as they discussed the possibility of both mother and son still being alive.

Their meeting went far better than Amy could have hoped for. She knew her team would be working hard in her absence, along with dozens of specialist officers assigned to the case. After they had discussed overtime budgets, media liaison and outstanding tasks, the meeting came to an end. Amy rose from her chair. It was time to convince her colleagues to focus their thoughts on the case, rather than today's headlines. People like Luka did not go away quietly and she prayed that he would get back in touch. Every nerve ending prickled as she imagined him on the loose.

CHAPTER FORTY

Amy did not usually concern herself with gossip, yet today she waited outside her team's office just the same. Up until recently, her personal life had been her own business. Now Lillian and Adam had started working together, everything had turned on its head. No amount of list-making or organisational skills could rescue this situation, and she had never felt so exposed. No longer could she contain her history in a black-ribboned box. The past had become a wretched, insistent thing that would not go away.

If her team did not back her one hundred per cent, she might have to consider stepping down. Lillian had enjoyed pushing the notion into her head and, like a hungry worm, it fed on her insecurities. The progeny of Jack and Lillian Grimes had no entitlement to a job such as hers. Who did she think she was, the daughter of murderous parents, dealing with victims' families and relaying sympathy for their pain? Such thoughts made her uneasy as she opened the door an inch and listened for honest responses to her news.

'So, she's known a while?' Molly's youthful voice was plain to hear. 'Fair play to her, she's coping better than I would have. I don't know how she sleeps at night.'

'Don't be fooled by her cool front,' DC Steve Moss replied. 'She's not one to wear her heart on her sleeve.'

Amy inwardly groaned. His observations were correct, but Steve was not a fan and she waited for the slating to come.

'I'd be devastated.' Molly's sentence was punctuated by a couple of chews of her gum. 'Especially in this job. I mean, it's hypocritical, isn't it? Helping the victims her own parents murdered. Ugh. Can you imagine having kids? I'd be worried about passing it on.'

'I'd be more worried about what people were saying about me behind my back.' Steve's words were taut. 'Shouldn't we be focusing on the investigation rather than Winter's personal life?'

'I was only saying.'

'Yeah, I know,' Steve replied. 'Like people were "only saying" about me when I was demoted.' His voice grew louder as he moved around the room, taking the opportunity to make a point for himself. 'You know, if something starts off as a mouse crossing the road around here, it'll be an elephant by the time it gets to the other side.'

'I can't see how we can elaborate any more on Ma'am Winter's story,' Gary Wilkes replied. 'I mean . . . fuck! Having the Beasts of Brentwood as your parents. It doesn't get any worse than that.'

Amy bristled. She thought Gary would have had more empathy. Molly's response didn't surprise her, and she was most likely voicing what many thought. But Steve had shocked her most of all. She had not expected an ally in him, particularly given her frosty reception of him when he joined her team.

'They aren't her parents.' Paddy's voice boomed from the far side of the room. A sudden flurry of movement suggested that they had not seen him enter through the other door. 'Our old superintendent, Robert Winter, was her father. Her mum, Flora, is as lovely as they come. I'm sure Winter would like to know that we all have her back. There are enough people gossiping about this without her own team sticking the boot in.'

'Sorry,' Molly replied quietly. 'I wasn't being mean. I find it interesting, that's all.'

'Yeah, like lots of people found my case interesting,' Steve muttered. 'It doesn't make it any easier on the people involved. We should draw a line underneath it. If you want to gossip, this office isn't the place.'

'Particularly when the person you're talking about can walk in at any minute,' Amy replied, striding in through the door. 'I wouldn't mind you chatting if we could afford the time. I take it we're still no further on with finding Luka.' She looked pointedly at Molly, whose face was puce.

'No, ma'am,' Molly replied.

'Right,' Amy said, inhaling a deep breath as she looked around the room. 'Then I'm going to say this only once. As you're aware, journalist Adam Rossi saw fit to publish a story with details of my biological parents which have recently come to light. I do not consider Lillian Grimes to be my mother, I'm glad Jack Grimes is dead, and I have no ties with Mandy or Damien Grimes.' Amy exchanged glances with Paddy. Coming out in the open about Sally-Ann would leave officers tempted to share the story, and she had taken up enough headlines for now. But Pike was right. She had to face it full on or not at all.

'Can you all do me a favour? Don't speak to the press. They're quick to condemn and will twist your words if it creates headlines trashy enough to sell papers. There are lots of decent reporters out there, but this was written by someone with an axe to grind.'

Amy glanced around the room again, preparing to replace speculation with fact. She was grateful that her team could not hear the pounding of her heart as it reverberated behind her rib cage. 'I was adopted by Robert and Flora Winter at four – almost five – years of age. Robert found me living in appalling conditions when he came to Jack and Lillian's home. He put in a request to foster me with a view to adopt, and he and Flora were approved. I totally understand why they felt it was in my best interests not to focus on it during my youth.

Unfortunately, it has come to light at the worst possible time. I'm still the same person I was before these headlines, and just as determined to make this team the best it can be.' She turned to Molly, whose temperature seemed to be reaching normal levels. 'Has anyone got any questions before we go into briefing?'

'How has DCI Pike taken the news?' Molly asked.

Amy raised an eyebrow. 'Why?'

'Well.' She squirmed in her chair beneath Amy's stern gaze. 'I don't want anyone else managing our team.'

'Why would anyone else manage our team? What have my managerial skills got to do with a newspaper story?' Amy didn't mean to sound so aggressive, but she couldn't help herself. She sensed that those who had wanted to ask questions had now decided against it.

'If DCI Pike has any sense, she'll support Ma'am Winter all the way,' DC Steve Moss replied. 'Best we leave the gossiping to the newspapers and the fishwives that read them.'

Amy watched as Steve rolled up his sleeves, ready to go into the briefing room. 'Any more questions before we close the door on this?' she said, wanting to move forward too.

'What about the appeal? The paper said that Lillian Grimes hopes to be freed.' DC Gary Wilkes's voice rose from the corner of the room.

'That has nothing to do with me.' Amy eyed the clock on the wall. 'The blood on the nightdress has been identified as Ellen's. I want all our focus on the case.'

As the officers filed in before her, Paddy caught her eye. 'Well said. You got through it.'

Amy acknowledged his words with a sharp nod of the head. Ellen's case could soon be progressing to a murder investigation. There was nothing to smile about.

CHAPTER FORTY-ONE

Sighing, Dr Curtis pulled out a plastic bucket chair and took a seat next to Nicole's hospital bed. He was breaking the terms of his bail just by being here and it was only thanks to his supporters in the medical profession that he had been able to sneak in.

He groaned, his joints stiff. His arthritis was playing up for the first time in months. He supposed this was the way it would be from now on. But his discomfort was nothing compared to where he was heading. He approached the prospect of prison with a sense of resignation. He'd always known that one day his past would catch up with him, that not everybody would understand. The modern world wasn't ready to hear of the sacrifices he'd made for advances in medicine. He thought about the tests he had conducted over the years. Some were legitimate, many were not. But they had all provided the basis for the research that had made Zitalin possible. The drug was deemed a lifesaver and, without testing, it would never have got off the ground. But would the police see it that way when the truth was revealed? He had taken drastic measures to protect his methods up until now. Nobody knew of the lethal dosages of Zitalin he had prescribed in the guise of anti-depression medication to Sasha during the last few weeks of her life. She had been an unwitting test subject, and the day he found her snooping in his office was the day he knew she would not come out of it alive. Zitalin worked differently in adults, slowing their movements rather than sharpening their minds. She was a sacrifice, just like the children nobody wanted, whose names he could barely remember anymore. It had come as a shock to discover Luka was alive.

He watched as Nicole's eyelids flickered. The respirator had been removed and she was now breathing on her own. Soon she would surface from her drug-induced coma, but did he want to be there when she did?

Her hand was lukewarm as he clasped it, her skin deathly pale. He had not expected her to survive, yet here she was, battling for her life. Fighting to see Ellen again. But the chances of that happening were low.

'I'm sorry,' he whispered. 'I hope one day you'll forgive me.' Gently, he squeezed her hand, before turning and walking away.

The sideways glances and hushed conversations were driving Amy to distraction. It was why she had insisted on visiting Deborah McCauley herself. *When life gives you lemons*, she thought; if nothing else, she could put her special skills to good use. Given her background, she was particularly deft at detecting signs of fear. A twitch of the eye, flushed skin, the inability to keep still – such emotional leakages were things Amy homed in on.

Deborah McCauley was a woman of means who worked in a private practice part-time. In all likelihood she could afford to retire, but she seemed the type of person who wanted to be kept on her toes. 'Thanks for seeing me at such short notice,' Amy said, admiring the colourful artwork on the walls as she followed her down the hall. Her home had been tastefully decorated by someone with an eye for design.

Deborah walked ahead of her, her sparkly cane tapping against the floor with each step.

'Beautiful house.' Amy cast an eye over a freshly plastered wall in the kitchen. 'You've had some renovation work done.'

'Yes.' Deborah leaned her cane against the glossy breakfast bar before perching on a tall stool. She gestured for Amy to take a seat. 'I expanded the kitchen by knocking down a wall. But you're not here to talk about home decor, are you? What brings a detective inspector to my door?'

Amy glanced at the bar stool and decided to give it a miss. She had yet to perfect the art of getting on them gracefully. High stools did not mix well with legs as short as hers. 'I'm investigating the abduction of Dr Curtis's daughter and the poisoning of his wife Nicole.' She would not waste time in trying to build a rapport. She filled her in on the details already in the press. 'My team's had quite the job, tracking you down.'

'I think Dr Curtis is a fine example of why one should stay private in one's endeavours,' Deborah replied haughtily.

Amy crossed her arms. Now she knew she had not imagined her earlier condescending tone. 'Have you spoken to him lately?'

'Hugh and I parted company years ago. If I kept in touch with every professional I worked with, I'd never get anything done.'

'And you've definitely not spoken to his wife, Nicole?'

Deborah averted her gaze, concentrating intensely on her manicured nails. 'I barely knew the woman. We sometimes bumped into each other at charity functions but that's as far as it went.'

Amy watched her swallow hard before finally meeting her gaze. She was lying and they both knew it. But she would not press her any further just yet. Such questions were better placed in a police interview, if it came to that.

'What about your other colleagues? People you worked with at the Curtis Institute?'

'There were only two, Christina and . . . what was the chap's name?' She tapped her bottom lip. 'Stuart, that's it. Stuart Coughlan. They were orderlies. They helped out during the day and took turns to stay overnight when the dorms were occupied.'

'We need to speak to them urgently. Is there any chance you have their details? And what about the other children involved in the tests? We'll need to see them too.' The words felt sour on Amy's tongue. She made an effort to keep her expression neutral. What sort of person would be involved in testing children? There was a lot more to Deborah McCauley than met the eye.

'The tests were decades ago. What's it got to do with Ellen and Nicole?'

'We're following a strong lead that suggests there's a link. What can you tell me about the orderlies? What do you know about Luka Volkov?'

'He could also go by the name of Lukasha. It means "light", whereas Volkov means "wolf". Quite a combination, wouldn't you say?'

'Do you have children?' Amy asked, feeling it only fair to warn her. 'We can offer safeguarding, just in case Ellen's kidnapper turns his attentions to you.'

'My son graduated with a first-class honours business degree,' Deborah said dryly. 'He's also a black belt in karate – quite capable of keeping himself safe.'

'You must be very proud,' Amy replied. 'But if you see anything suspicious, you should report it to the police.' She cast an eye over the photographs on the kitchen sideboard in an effort to get to know the woman behind the mask.

Her head tilting towards the clock on the wall, Deborah rose to her feet and grasped the handle of her cane. 'I don't mean to be rude, but I've got to get going.'

'Wait,' Amy said, temporarily stalling her movements. 'What can you tell me about the fire that killed Luka and his mother?'

'Really, Officer, I don't like talking about it.' Deborah froze, her expression taut. 'I gave a statement at the time. You must still have a record of it. Now, if you'll excuse me, I've got a manicure booked and I'm going to be late.'

'We have your *original* statement.' Amy dug her heels in. Officers had pored over the old paperwork. 'From what you can remember . . . is there anything about their deaths that doesn't ring true? Ellen's kidnapper . . . he's claiming to be Luka.'

Deborah sighed, leaning on her cane. 'I wish Luka *had* survived. I'd like nothing better than for him to have started again. But they found two bodies in that fire: a woman and a child.'

'Why would someone claim to be him?'

'They could be delusional. Hugh's worked with many patients over the years. Some of them take on the identity of other people to get away from past traumas.'

Amy turned the idea over in her mind. 'No, that can't be it. They know too much.'

'Which means it's someone Luka knew. That, or they're making it up and have convinced themselves it's real. Now, as much as I'd like to do your job for you, I really must insist you leave.'

'Ellen's nightdress was found covered in blood. I'm sure your manicurist can wait.' *Talk about first-world problems*, Amy thought, glancing at Deborah's nails. They looked perfectly fine as they were.

A flush bloomed on Deborah's face. Pulling open a drawer, she reached for a battered blue address book. 'Here,' she said, scribbling on a blank page and ripping it out. 'These are the last addresses I have for Christina and Stuart. Perhaps you can track them down.'

But Amy was not so easily fobbed off. The woman was hiding something; she could not get her out of the house quickly enough. 'Let's play devil's advocate. What if Luka survived? Why would he want revenge?'

'You wouldn't ask me that if you saw where he came from. We saved him from abject poverty. He had his own room, hot meals, private tuition at the institution. He was grateful for everything we did.'

'But what about the testing . . .'

'A bit of aversion therapy and a few minor personality tests. No worse than the ones you did when you joined the police.' But Deborah refused to meet her eye. 'Now, I really must ask you to leave.'

Amy reluctantly followed Deborah as she showed her out. In the hall, the last rays of late-afternoon sun cast a beam through the stained-glass door. Evening would soon be upon them. With Paddy at the helm the office would run smoothly in her absence, but there was so much to oversee. 'We may need a further statement. My officers will be in touch.' Slipping her hand into her suit pocket, Amy pressed a card into Deborah's palm.

'Hugh is the victim here,' Deborah narrowed her eyes. 'So why do I feel like we're all suspects? What happened to Luka and his mother . . . it was a tragic, tragic accident.' She took her jacket from the coat rack in the hall.

'You're not in any trouble,' Amy said, watching her intently. 'We're just trying to put the pieces together.' It was true. She thought of the tangle of red lines across the board in the briefing room. It seemed to double in size as each day passed. It was a giant puzzle of connect-the-dots.

Her mobile phone rang as Deborah opened the front door to allow her outside. She wasted no time in slamming the door behind her, and Amy felt a chill in her wake. She glanced at the screen before answering the call. It was Paddy, and his voice sounded strained. 'Sorry to interrupt, ma'am, but there's been a development. How soon can you get back?'

CHAPTER FORTY-TWO

The Curtis Institute, January 1985

Lying in his dormitory bed, Luka stared at the ceiling, his thoughts swirling in his head. He had not seen Mama in weeks. Silent tears drizzled down the side of his face and dampened his pillow. Christmas had passed with little celebration. Seasons came and went but, in his heart, it was winter, grey and bleak, with storms ahead.

Wiping his tears, he held his breath as a key turned in the lock of his door. Someone was entering his room.

'I heard crying,' Deborah said softly, coming to the side of his bed. 'Are you OK?' Her lab coat was creased, wisps of blonde hair escaping her ponytail and falling into her face.

Sitting up in his bed, Luka blinked away the remnants of his tears. 'I want to go h-home . . .' His words were engulfed by a sob.

'Hey, come here.' Sliding a hand around his shoulders, Deborah pulled him in for a hug. Luka liked this side of her, the kind side, the side that wanted to make everything all right. 'I know you're not happy, but I'm doing everything I can to keep you safe.'

Luka's breath locked in his throat. It was the first time Deborah had admitted he was in danger. The so-called scholarship which had lured his mama in had come to an end. There were no more workshops, no music lessons, just the tests the doctor set and some contact with the orderlies. It was as if everyone was distancing themselves from him, one by one.

'You're such a good boy.' Deborah rocked him gently. 'So sweet and kind.' Pausing, she kissed the top of his head. 'I'll look after you, I promise. I'll take care of everything.'

But the words sounded ghostly on her lips, instilling fear instead of comfort. For a long while, they sat in silence, and he realised that Deborah was crying too.

He had no words to comfort her. It seemed Deborah was as unhappy as him. Was she a prisoner too? Shutting his eyes, he allowed her to hold him close. She smelled of fresh linen, like clothes drying beneath a warm summer sun. Little by little, his world felt brighter. Deborah was on his side.

Wiping her tears, she released him, her face flushed as she kept her voice low. 'It's only natural to feel scared, but I won't let anyone hurt you.' Her eyes searched his face for understanding. 'You trust me, don't you?'

Luka nodded. But there was something he needed to know. He asked her about the number inked on his skin, and why the markings were reserved for the very few. He had not seen Sam since their last meeting. Had he left the institution? Had something bad happened to him?

A shadow passed over Deborah's face at the mention of the name. She exhaled a long, drawn-out breath.

'These tablets you're taking. They make it easier for you to study, yes?'

Sullenly, Luka nodded.

'The more tablets you take, the better your concentration. But then the side effects increase. You understand what I mean by side effects, don't you?'

'The nightmares,' Luka said, referring to the hallucinations that plagued his nights and days.

'Amongst other things,' Deborah said. 'The only way we can find out what dosages are safe is by testing them.'

'Doh-sages?' Luka elongated the word as he memorised it. He'd heard the doctor use it but wasn't entirely sure what it meant.

'How many tablets you take,' Deborah explained. But . . .' She raised a finger. 'There aren't enough children in the study and that's why the doctor pushes you too far.'

'I hate the tablets. They're sucky.' Luka pouted. He hated *everything* these days.

'But they're helping so many children, especially in America. Some kids get distracted, can't focus. Some can barely sit still. The pills help them to learn.' She paused, cocked her head to one side as she waited until footsteps in the corridor had passed. It was Stuart, whistling some obscure tune, as he always did on his night patrols.

Deborah softened her voice, leaned in. 'You, Sam and the other three children, you were earmarked . . .'

Confusion was etched on Luka's face. He had an excellent knowledge of English, but he did not always understand the descriptives people used. Like the other night, when Stuart described the electrics in the institute as 'fried'.

Deborah pursed her lips as she tried to come up with a better choice of word. 'Not earmarked . . . you were *chosen* for these tests because you're the strongest children we have. We're doing so much good here. Think of all the children we've helped.'

But the words seemed like half-truths. The concern in her eyes told Luka she was holding back.

'But Sam . . .'

'Sam's in hospital. He has a heart condition. He won't be coming back.'

Luka remembered the blue tinge to his lips, the way he kept rubbing his chest.

'Don't worry, this will be over soon.' Deborah glanced at him furtively. 'I've got plans.'

'For Mama too?'

Her smile warmed her face as she laid out a bright future for them both. 'One day you'll be living with your mother in a lovely house, and you'll never need to worry about money again.'

Luka followed her gaze as she stared up at the ceiling and described his future life. 'Life is hard in Russia. It's going to be a while before it gets back on its feet. England is the best place for you now.'

'But how?' Luka stared, open-mouthed. His emotions were too big for him to process and he was unable to take it all in.

'I'm working on it. Just give me a little more time. Can you do that?'

Luka nodded, absorbing her words. As she clicked off his lamp, Deborah paused to kiss him on the top of his head. 'Feel better now?' she said when she was standing at the door.

'Yes,' Luka said, giving in to the yawn that rose up in his throat. Tiredness had overcome him, now his fears and worries had been taken away. *Better bread with water than cake with trouble.* The old Russian proverb floated in his mind. It was easier to wait and allow Deborah to take care of things than kick up a stink and cause problems for them both. He thought of the promised phone call from his father, but the door had clicked shut. Tomorrow. He would ask her then. As he nestled under his covers, he thought who was really to blame. The doctor was an evil man. Even Deborah agreed. Perhaps she was scared of him too. Papa had once told him about karma, how people reaped what they sowed.

He thought about what kind of karma the doctor deserved. Papa said such things came when they least expected it, although not always straight away. He remembered more of his father's words: *Your strength is in your silence*. Right now, he needed all the strength he could find.

CHAPTER FORTY-THREE

Amy's footsteps stalled at the traffic lights at the front of the police station. She should have returned through the private car park, away from prying eyes. All too late, she realised the group of people on the footpath outside the station had gathered for her. Peering closer, she recognised a few faces. Her heart faltered. They were relations of the young girls who had fallen victim to her biological parents.

'There she is!' a woman with a high-pitched Essex accent screamed as she approached. 'The Beast of Brentwood's daughter!'

Amy's blood chilled as she became the main attraction. News got around fast. She hurried towards the entrance as the news cameras swivelled in her direction, journalists' questions ringing in her ears.

''Ere, why is she allowed to be a copper?' a thickset man shouted for the camera's attention. 'My taxes pay her wages, that family should be locked away!' By the look of him, it had been a long time since he'd possessed a job, never mind paid taxes, but Amy let it go. She glanced at a uniformed officer who had come outside to tell the crowd to disperse. New in service, he had come to her department for advice more than once. To her horror, he seemed too embarrassed to meet her gaze. 'C'mon, folks,' he said half-heartedly. 'Let her through.'

Amy could have crossed the road, carried on through the back entrance without a word. But skulking away was an admittance of defeat in her eyes. She was not responsible for Lillian and Jack's gruesome misdeeds. She had done nothing wrong. But her gut still churned at the prospect of everyone knowing who she was. Her eyes flicked to the top windows of the building as she pushed her way through the crowd. Several faces peered down at her, but none of her colleagues seemed in a hurry to get involved.

'DI Winter, what have you to say about this morning's news story?' A reedy-looking journalist pushed through the bodies, inserting a microphone under her nose. 'Are you Jack and Lillian Grimes's daughter? How long have you known?'

'No comment,' Amy said, as people and cameras surrounded her. She couldn't turn back now, even if she wanted to.

A woman's voice rose from behind. 'DI Winter, how does the Metropolitan Police feel about having the daughter of Britain's worst serial killers heading up one of their teams?'

'I . . .' Amy said, her words catching in her throat as the enormity of it all hit home. Normally, she would shake off any ugly encounters, but today she felt rooted to the spot. Is that how people saw her? Guilty by association? A sudden jolt made her gasp as something hard hit the back of her jacket. What the hell? She looked over her shoulder to see a man a few feet away holding a tray of eggs. With his ginger beard and steely gaze, he looked familiar. He was the brother of one of Lillian's victims. Amy had visited them when their loved one's body had finally been discovered, decades after her death. The family had every right to be angry. Had they known who she was, they would never have allowed her inside their home. They must see her now as hypocritical, telling them how sorry she was, while at the same time knowing the girl had been raped and murdered under her roof.

Another thought lingered as she answered 'No comment' to the barrage of questions being thrown at her. How had so many people known to gather here at this time? And for the press to be involved too? The whole thing smelled of a set-up.

'Everybody get back!' a strong male voice barked, causing the crowds to part. 'NOW.'

Amy felt a surge of relief as she recognised Donovan's voice. His arm clamped around her shoulders, he whisked her inside the station, her feet barely touching the ground.

Being rescued was a novel experience, and she was glad to get inside in one piece. Pressing her tag against a door sensor, Amy led Donovan into a private office used for printing out reports.

'Are you OK?' he asked, his face creased with concern. The room was empty, apart from a police community support officer who was on her way out.

'I'm fine,' she lied. Shrugging off her jacket, Amy groaned as she caught sight of an egg splattered on the back. 'Ah, no. This is one of my best suits.' She knew she should thank Donovan, but it seemed like an admission of weakness. She prided herself on being self-sufficient – and, given the recent news, she knew she would be going it alone from now on.

'There you are.' His face flushed, Paddy burst through the office door, a wad of paperwork in his hand. 'I heard there was a ruckus. Are you all right?'

'I'm fine,' Amy snapped. 'Honestly, there's no need to fuss.'

'Where was her backup? Anything could have happened.' Donovan shook his head in disgust. 'There were enough of you watching upstairs.'

'Not me, mate,' Paddy replied, his features grim. 'I came as soon as I heard.'

'It all happened so quickly,' Amy said, trying to regain her composure, even though she was shaking inside. She gave Paddy a taut smile. 'I'll be with you in a minute. Best you get back to the team.'

Frowning, Paddy glanced at the paperwork he was holding, as if just realising it was there. 'As long as you're all right.'

'She is now,' Donovan said as Paddy left, his words loud enough for him to hear.

Donovan's protective streak was something Amy had not seen before, and she had mixed feelings about it. 'What are you doing here?' Her voice was cold. She could feel her walls rising. Why *was* he here? Had he come to gape, just like the rest?

'You weren't answering my calls. I was in the area and thought I'd see how you were.'

'Really? In the area? You work in Essex.' Amy's face was set in stone as she uttered the words. None of this was Donovan's fault, yet she was taking her frustration out on him just the same. She folded her jacket, unable to meet his eyes. 'So you've read the headlines then?' she said, filling the uncomfortable silence.

'I had an inkling of your connection to Lillian after our trip to Essex,' Donovan said quietly, referring to Amy's last big case. 'I wondered why she called you Poppy. Then I spoke to one of the drivers, and he mentioned Lillian referred to you as family. But I wasn't going to say anything – at least, not until now.'

A sick feeling grew in the pit of Amy's stomach. So that's why he had befriended her. He'd wanted to know what made her tick.

He reached out to touch her, frowning as she took a step back. 'I wanted to see if you were OK, that's all. I thought you could do with a friend.'

'Well, friends are certainly in short supply right now.' Amy looked into his eyes, surprised to see more than friendship there. She couldn't do it. Could not allow herself to get hurt again. A cold smile graced her face as her internal walls rose another inch. 'Who can blame them? If you've any sense, you'll steer well clear.'

'But what if I don't want to?' Donovan said, taking another step towards her as she turned towards the door. 'I . . .' he faltered. 'I care about you.'

'Care about me? Well, that's pretty stupid of you.' Amy opened the door to leave, barely giving him a second glance. 'I've got work to do. See yourself out.'

CHAPTER FORTY-FOUR

Throwing her car keys into the kitchen dresser drawer, Deborah shouted to her son, Max, that she was home. With one fluid movement, she retrieved a coffee pod and slipped it into the machine. Placing a glass cup beneath the spout, she inhaled the tantalising aroma as it poured. Not that she should be drinking caffeine. The detective's visit had unnerved her, making her as jittery as hell. She had told herself to relax, that nothing could touch her now. So why had a high-ranking officer such as DI Amy Winter come knocking on her door? The attractive young woman had surveyed her with interest, intruding on every facet of her home. Had she sensed her guilt bubbling beneath the surface? Had she suspected her of foul play? But Deborah's worst secrets were buried decades in the past.

'I don't think you should leave the house,' she said, as Max plucked her car keys from the drawer. It was a gently worded command.

'I'm only popping out for groceries. I'll bring you something back.' He turned his brown eyes upon her, pausing as he caught her worried gaze. He might tower above her, but he would always be her little boy.

She reached out and touched his forearm. 'The police were here, it's not safe. Stay home. We'll put a movie on, have a duvet day. I've got some ice cream in the freezer. We can order food from that nice deli you like.' She was grasping at straws, waffling in an attempt to keep him from walking out.

'What am I, twelve?' He chuckled. 'You'll be offering me jelly with my ice cream next.'

She smiled. 'I know you've got things to do, but I've not been feeling very well. I don't want to be on my own.' Using her heart condition was a low blow, but she needed to keep him home. She had always wanted a big family, but the condition that came to light after she gave birth to Max meant having more children had been too much of a risk.

'Fine,' he said, the keys rattling as he dropped them back into the drawer. 'We can put on a box set – but nothing soppy, mind. I get to choose.'

'It's *Game of Thrones* again, isn't it?' She shook her head in mock disgust, pleased she had won him around. The insistent ring of the phone in the hall drew her attention away. 'I'll be right back. There's a leaflet for the deli in the drawer.'

'Yes?' she snapped, picking up the receiver. Her response was sharp, the interruption unwelcome. She rarely received social calls, and she wanted to forget about the past for one day.

'It's me – Stuart,' the voice on the other end responded, making her spirits plummet. Couldn't she have one evening alone with her son?

Lowering her voice, she closed the kitchen door fully before walking to the far end of the hall. She knew from the fear in his words that he was ringing to ask for help.

'He's got Toby. He's got my boy. I don't know what to do.' Stuart quickly relayed the story of the courier visiting his workplace. Just like that, his son had disappeared into the ether, an unwilling pawn in a game he did not understand.

'He sent me phials. Said I had to drink one or my son would die. I was going to call the police but then I saw Toby on FaceTime, crying to come home. What sort of sick fuck is he? Taking my boy like that. Toby needs his medication. He needs his routine—'

'Did you see his face?' Deborah cut through his words. 'The kidnapper . . . did you speak to him?'

'No, he was wearing some kind of mask. I took the drink and he hung up. Should I believe him? He's not given Ellen back.'

'Have you called the police?' Deborah held her breath as she awaited his response.

'He told me not to. Do you think I should?' Stuart's voice broke as he emitted a whimper of despair. 'What should I do? I want my boy back.'

'Just do as he says,' Deborah replied in hushed tones. Feeling like an ant under a microscope, she rubbed the base of her neck. Every inch of her body ached – a side effect of being permanently tense.

'I tried ringing Dr Curtis,' Stuart said. 'Seems like he's washed his hands of us all.'

'Do you blame him?' Deborah struggled to catch her breath. 'His wife almost died.'

'Exactly. We're dealing with a killer. Luka is alive. He's coming for us all.'

'Luka is dead,' Deborah snapped, feeling a build-up of pressure in her chest. Her breath tight, she leaned against the wall, willing her heart rate to slow down.

'Mum?' Max called from the kitchen. He opened the door and poked his head through. 'Oh. Sorry, I thought you were off the phone.'

'It's work,' she mouthed, rolling her eyes in irritation. 'Be with you in a sec.' In his hands was a takeaway leaflet from the deli she had mentioned. She clasped a hand over the mouthpiece of the phone. 'Order my usual. Use my card, it's in my handbag on the side.'

Flashing her a smile, Max withdrew into the kitchen and quietly closed the door. She was so lucky to have him – which is why she had to keep him safe.

Stuart's voice came like an irritant down the phone. 'I'm going out of my mind here. What will I do?'

'Go home. I gave the police your address. They'll be visiting you soon enough.'

'But . . . the kidnapper said not to call them. Why did you do that?'

'Because they wouldn't bloody well leave me alone!' Deborah spat the words. 'Stick to the story and we'll be fine. I've got to go.' A wave of dizziness overcame her as she hung up the phone. She felt queasy, adrift on the deck of a ship with no captain to steer it. Goodness knows how she was going to eat. Her past was clawing for her attention and would not be ignored. She thought of her son, how he would feel if he knew the truth. No matter how much she tried, nothing could make up for her misdemeanours. She had done an unspeakable thing.

CHAPTER FORTY-FIVE

'Sorry, ma'am, have you got a second?' Molly caught Amy on her way to her office.

'Sure,' Amy said, staring at the tropical plant drooping in the corner. It had seen better days. She sniffed, catching sight of a tea bag sticking out of the soil. 'Who's been feeding it tea?'

'Not me.' Molly smiled, looking younger than her twenty-nine years. She wasn't wearing any make-up and her freckles were on show. Amy listened intently as she took a breath to speak.

'It's about Dr Curtis. I didn't want to mention it during briefing as I was waiting to hear back from children's social care.'

'What have you got?' Amy replied.

Much of the briefing had been about Luka, and they had debated whether he was still alive. Her team had mixed reactions and the doctor was not off the hook yet.

'Curtis was a psychologist, but he had a licence to practise as a psychiatrist too. I looked it up, more out of nosiness than anything else, 'cos I didn't know the difference between the two.' Her tongue darted out of her mouth as she licked her lips. The habit came into play when she was excited about something. 'Anyway, it's unusual for someone to practise both. A psychologist can't prescribe medication, but a psychiatrist can. That got me wondering if Dr Curtis had prescribed drugs to the kids in his care.'

Amy's interest was piqued. 'And social care? How could they help?'

'They said that Ellen was on medication – Zitalin. It's big in the US and was hugely popular here in the early nineties. Lots of kids are prescribed it to help with their studies.' Her eyes shone with the discovery. 'I rang Curtis's first wife, Shirley Baker, put the question to her and . . . guess what? Her kids were on Zitalin too – but as soon as she divorced Dr Curtis, they came off the drug.'

Amy smiled at Molly's ability to think outside the box. 'Good job. So that's what she meant about them being lab rats. Curtis is due to answer bail soon, isn't he?' Further interviews were allowed, as long as earlier questions weren't repeated.

Molly nodded, still smiling. The tiniest words of encouragement could make her day.

'Re-interview him when he comes in,' Amy said. 'I don't think we'll have enough to extend his bail but it gives us something new to offer the CPS.' Given Luka was now in the frame, it was unlikely that the Crown Prosecution Service would advise a charge for Dr Curtis, but the theory about children at the institute being drugged would give them food for thought. 'Also,' Amy said, tapping her chin, 'request further intelligence on his finances. His wealth came from somewhere, and it wouldn't surprise me if one of the big pharmaceutical companies wasn't funding his studies back then. You say that Shirley was acting shifty. It makes me wonder if someone is blackmailing them.'

Another thought occurred to Amy. 'But why hasn't Luka specifically mentioned being drugged?' The vagueness of his motives had bothered her all along. She'd toyed with the theory that he was trying to protect the people responsible so he could get to them first. But why involve the police?

Inside her office, the phone began to ring. Amy turned to Molly one last time. 'I've set some new tasks on the system. Let Paddy know if you've any problem keeping up.' The computerised system was used to keep track of the vast number of updates inputted each day. Each entry was time-stamped, and Amy used it to oversee proceedings and set tasks of her own. It was up to her sergeant, Paddy, to chase them up and ensure completion in the timescales she set.

The call was from Amy's brother, Craig. It was only natural for him to be devastated by the news about her biological mother but, after the foray outside the station, she had little energy to deal with it now. She felt horrible for giving Donovan the brush-off earlier on.

'I'm fine,' she lied, after Craig asked her how she was. 'But I haven't got time to talk.' In the privacy of her office, her blinds were half-closed. Her egg-stained jacket hung on the back of her chair, ready for the dry cleaner's.

'Why didn't you tell me?' Craig replied. 'Mum's been so upset.'

'I've only just found out myself.'

'I'm your brother, I should be looking out for you. How were you meant to cope with it on your own?'

'By taking a leaf out of Dad's book and getting on with things.' It was how their father had coped with every situation he encountered. Robert Winter had also been adopted. His mother was only sixteen when she'd had him, and neither had tried to get in touch with the other. Unlike Lillian, who would not give Amy a minute's peace. Ever since Robert died, she'd seemed hell-bent on bringing Amy down – something Adam seemed more than happy to help her with. Amy would not have been surprised if Lillian had somehow organised the scrum of people outside.

'To think you nearly married that chump . . .' Craig said, the sound of his footsteps punctuating his words as he paced the floor. 'I can't believe Adam printed that story. He cheats on you, humiliates you the day before your wedding and now this . . .' His footsteps came to a halt. 'I should give him a piece of my mind.'

Amy smiled. Her brother was a lover, not a fighter. She had stuck up for him throughout their schooling, scaring off any bully who dared approach. But the newspaper headlines were like a punch to the face, connecting Amy to the brutal murders her parents had committed during those dark years. 'Adam's pissed off because he thinks I'm seeing someone else,' Amy said.

'After everything he did? Unbelievable!' Craig exclaimed.

'Looks like I had a narrow escape.'

'You're dealing with this really well.' Craig's voice carried a hint of concern. 'Mum said that's why you went to see Lillian in prison. I remember feeling jealous because she granted you an audience. I'm so sorry. I behaved like an idiot. I should have been there for you.'

'There's nothing anyone can do.' Amy massaged her temples. In truth, she did not want to give it any more of her energy, which was best served focusing on the case. Thanks to the information Deborah had supplied, officers were closing in on Stuart's address. Credit checks had assisted in obtaining the current address of Christina, the other orderly who had worked at the Curtis Institute. Their safety was paramount.

'So who's this new guy on the scene?' Craig said, pulling Amy from her thoughts. 'Mum said he's in the job too.'

'Oh, nobody, we're just friends. I told Mum we were seeing each other so she'd get off my back about Adam.'

'I don't think you need to worry about that now. Listen, I've got to go, but if there's anything you need . . .'

'Don't call you – yeah, I know.' Amy smiled. 'Now, stop being so nice, you're freaking me out.'

'Yeah, that's right.' Craig chuckled. 'But I'm lodging a complaint with the paper. It's about time Adam was taken down a peg or two.'

Thoughts of Adam were quickly discarded as Paddy sharply rapped on Amy's door. 'I'm wanted. Chat to you later,' she said, ending the call. She looked at Paddy. 'What is it?' He swung the door open with an urgency that relayed something was up.

'Two things. We've got an address for Stuart Coughlan. Officers are on their way to Stuart's address.'

Springing from her chair, Amy grabbed a spare blazer from the hook on the wall.

'You can't go, not yet.' Paddy shot out an arm, blocking her departure. 'That's the second thing . . . Luka's on the line, and he'll speak only to you.'

CHAPTER FORTY-SIX

Amy's team gathered around her, the room falling silent as she picked up the phone. Every effort would go into tracing the origin of the call, but their suspect was not stupid. He would not hang around for very long. 'DI Winter,' she said, her tone firm.

But the voice that responded was brittle and pained. 'I'm only going to say this once, so you'd better take note.'

'Is that you, Luka?' Amy was keen to extend every second of their conversation. She was desperate to ask him about Ellen, but the call needed to be handled with care.

'Who else would it be, you stupid cow?' Her caller sucked in a sharp breath between clenched teeth.

Amy could almost feel his pain. 'Are you OK? You don't sound very well.' His health was a big factor. If he fell ill and the children were in captivity, their lives could be at risk.

'Just. Stop. Talking,' he replied. Hesitating, he waited for silence to descend. His mouth sounded close to the receiver, his breath coming in stops and starts. 'I'm not stupid. Nor am I in the mood for games.'

'I know about the drugs,' Amy bluffed. It was a risk, but her sixth sense told her she was on the right track. 'Dr Curtis dosed you with

Zitalin during the trials. Used you as a guinea pig to see how you'd react.'

But the drugs did not appear a subject her caller wanted to tackle, as he failed to respond. Amy tried to second-guess his next move, but all she could hear was his ragged breath. Closing her eyes, she forgot about her colleagues as she put herself in his shoes. 'It wasn't just the drugs, was it? It was the childhood you missed out on . . . normal things that kids take for granted. Birthday parties, mixing with friends.'

'You'd know all about that,' Luka replied. 'I read the newspaper story about you being a Grimes. Is it true?'

'Yes. We're not that different, you and I,' Amy said, the words sticking in her throat. The last thing she wanted was to discuss her past, but she needed to drag out the call and keep him on side. 'I don't have any family photos up to the age of four and I was rarely allowed outside.' A memory bloomed – four-year-old Poppy, her face pressed against the upstairs window, watching children play on the streets below. 'I know how it feels to be an outcast,' she said truthfully. 'The only way you can cope is to become someone else.'

'And did it work?' Luka sucked in a breath as if experiencing a stab of pain.

'For a while. But these things always come back to haunt you in the end.' She paused, reminding herself to put a positive spin on things. They needed to find out Ellen's whereabouts. 'It doesn't have to eat you up. Is Ellen still alive? We're listening. We want to help.'

'It's a shame you weren't around when I needed you,' Luka said. 'On the days I was allowed outside, I used to pray that someone would notice me. I remember being taken to see Number Ten Downing Street. Police were standing before those tall black steel gates. I screamed so loudly in my head for help, willing them to see me. But nobody was looking because they thought I was dead . . .'

'And trying to escape wasn't worth the pain if you were caught,' Amy replied. 'So many times I wanted to ask for help, but I knew they'd kill me if they found out.' A beat passed between them. 'Please. Let me speak to them. Even for a second.' Amy's heart faltered as she realised Luka was handing the phone over.

'Hello?' The voice was that of a boy. In the background, Luka urged him to give his name. 'My . . . my name is Toby,' the child continued. 'We're in a room with no windows—'

'That's enough,' Luka interrupted, but Toby was determined to have his say. 'He took me in the taxi . . .' the little boy shouted. 'I don't know where I am.'

'Shut up!' Luka barked before returning to the phone. A door closed in the background, and Amy's heart was in her mouth as she strained to listen to every sound. Toby's use of the word 'we' had not gone unnoticed. 'Where's Ellen? You promised—'

'Think of it as a relay race,' Luka interrupted. 'Nicole played the game and handed the baton to you. It's not my fault you let the side down. You'll have to be quicker next time.'

Every muscle in Amy's body tensed. Officers were already monitoring incoming calls about missing children. Toby was the name of Stuart's son – why hadn't Stuart called the police? Another thought loomed, darker than the last. Had Luka given him an ultimatum? Just what state was Stuart in?

'If any harm comes to that little boy, you're no better than the monsters who made you this way,' Amy said. But her words were ignored as the kidnapper forged on.

'Stuart earned this call, so I suggest you put it to good use. You'll get Toby back – if you do what I say. Don't worry, it won't involve you speaking to the newspapers – you've had enough exposure for one day.'

Amy glanced at her colleagues, trying to ignore the sting in his words. In the background, her team were working, listening intently to the call. 'What do you want?'

'I want you to shut up. Your voice . . . it's grating on me. No more talking, or I'll finish this, I mean it. I've nothing to lose.'

Keeping her silence, Amy waited for his instructions. This afternoon's events outside the station had distracted her at the worst possible time. She was pleased Luka had volunteered the information – but, for now, it was safer to stay mute.

'Good,' he replied, in response to her silence. He sucked in a tight breath as he seemed to undergo another wave of pain. 'Be at Holland Park tube station. Two o'clock tomorrow.'

Was he on medication? What would affect him so badly that the level of her voice would cause him pain?

'All right,' Amy responded. 'But at least give me Ellen. What have you done with her?' But she was too late. The line was already dead.

Her colleagues collectively exhaled the breaths they had been holding. Amy realised her heart was pounding double time. Adrenaline caused her legs to tremble ever so slightly, a barely discernible movement beneath her trousers. Composing herself, Amy issued instructions to her team. 'Molly, upload the recording of the call and distribute it to all senior officers involved in the case.' She turned to the others, knowing Paddy would follow up with tasks of his own. 'If Luka's taken Toby, then he's not going to stop there. We need to find and safeguard everyone connected with the case, as a matter of priority.' Amy glanced at Molly, who withered beneath her gaze. Her discomfort at hearing about Amy's past was written all over her face. Would things ever be right with her team again? 'I've got a call-on to make. Who's up for a drive?' Amy glanced around the room.

'I am.' The voice belonged to DC Steve Moss. A former inspector himself, he had been demoted following a tribunal with regard to sexual misconduct at work. Regardless of his misdemeanours, he could be relied upon to get the job done.

'In that case, you can come with me.'

'To see Stuart?'

Amy nodded. 'You up for a blue-light run?'

Smiling, Steve grabbed his jacket from his chair.

CHAPTER FORTY-SEVEN

Amy updated Control of her whereabouts as she and Steve jumped into the car. She didn't want to let his loyalty go unnoticed, and their journey across the city would give them time to talk. After fiddling with her car seat, she spoke her mind.

'I'll be honest. Out of all the people to back me up, I didn't expect it to be you.'

She was referring to his reaction in the office when her team had been talking about the news that she was the daughter of Jack and Lillian Grimes.

Craning his neck left and right, Steve exited the car park, cutting through traffic as the blue light cleared his path. He was an expert fast road driver, easily capable of holding a conversation while manoeuvring city traffic at speed. 'I know what it's like to be judged.'

'Which is why I wanted to speak to you in private,' Amy jumped in. 'What really happened to you?'

'You don't want to go digging around in my past,' Steve said, checking the rear-view mirror before pulling back into his lane.

'But I have a feeling you're not content to leave it there. We've got ten minutes before we reach Stuart Coughlan.' She leaned forward, picking up an empty cola can that was rattling around in the footwell. She shoved it into the cup holder, catching Steve's gaze. 'Want to tell me about it?'

Effortlessly, Steve changed gear as he sped through traffic lights. Having cleared the worst of the traffic, he had a relatively straight road ahead. Briefly, his eyes met hers, and he began to relax into his seat. 'I used to train down the gym with Pike, long before you.'

'I didn't know you were friends.' From the way DCI Pike talked about Steve, she thought they were anything but.

'We were more than that, for a little while,' Steve said. 'But she wanted more than I could give her. When I broke things off, it turned ugly.'

'You're talking about your demotion?' This was not Pike's first affair. Amy's father had fallen into the same trap, and Pike had used Amy to get to him.

'At first, I was grateful for her attention,' Steve replied, his eyes fixed on the road. 'I was after a promotion, and Pike promised to put in a good word.' He glanced at Amy. 'I hope you don't mind me saying, ma'am, but you don't seem very surprised.'

'I'm not,' Amy said, unwilling to elaborate. 'I just wish you'd come to me. This sort of thing isn't tolerated anymore.'

'I didn't think anyone would believe me. As she used to say, *I* was the one with the reputation for being a Jack the Lad.'

'So you slept together?' Amy's face soured as she pictured the scene.

'Pike is ambitious,' Steve continued. 'Ruthless, at times. But she didn't set the world on fire as a DC. It makes me wonder how many people she stepped on to get so far.'

Amy was flattered that Steve could be so candid. Then she realised he was thinking like a DI and less likely to be intimidated by her rank. Regardless, it was nice to have the limelight off her personal life. 'She once told me that I was either with her or I was—'

'Standing in her way.' Steve finished her sentence as he negotiated a bend. 'Yeah, she fed me that line too. I'm a dinosaur when it comes to this politically correct stuff, but it pisses me off that because she's a woman she's come out of this squeaky clean.'

'Go on,' Amy said, withholding judgement.

'She pressured me into sleeping with her, using promotion as leverage. We both used each other, but I came off the worst.'

'The probationer,' Amy replied. 'You can hardly blame Ma'am Pike for that.'

'I can when she set me up.' Changing gear, Steve risked a quick glance in her direction. 'And I know you probably won't believe me, but Pike orchestrated the whole thing.'

'How?' Amy shifted in her seat, keeping one ear on the police radio. Updates were flooding in, confirming Stuart Coughlan was alive and well.

'I didn't have sex with that probationer. It was all lies.' Steve's brow creased as he seemed to recall the moment that had sent his career spiralling out of control. 'One late shift she came into my office. She was acting all flirty and plonked herself on my knee. I thought it was a wind-up and was about to tell her to get off when Pike burst in. I'd been set up. Pike doesn't even work late shifts.'

Amy watched Steve's expression as he recounted his story.

'I like a bit of banter as much as the next person, but I never touched that girl.' He slowed the car as he paused at a junction, deactivating the sirens. They were almost at Stuart Coughlan's address and, given he was safe, the justification for the blue-light run had changed. Steve was confident in his decisions, and Amy had come to know him better in the last few weeks. It was unlike him to jeopardise his career for a quick fumble in the office, and he was right, Pike rarely worked late shifts.

'Why didn't you fight it? Tell the truth?'

'My federation rep told me to tread carefully because Pike had some powerful friends at the top. Pike must have got nervous, because she took me aside and said she'd transfer me to our unit if I let the matter drop. I knew I would never get promoted unless I fixed things. I hoped it would be a fresh start.'

'What happened with Molly . . .' Amy began, referring to an incident when he had first joined the team.

'It was banter. For Christ's sake, the girl is gay and dippy as hell. I was joking with her.'

'I'm sorry,' Amy said. 'I didn't give you the warmest of welcomes when you joined.'

'You were only going by what everyone else had told you.'

'I should have checked the facts.' Amy had spoken to a couple of Steve's ex-colleagues who had been keen to repeat the gossip they had heard. She should have gone to the source of all this – the probationer who made the report.

Steve flicked on the indicator as he pulled over at the address. Before them, a high-rise tower loomed. 'I've got a fifteen-year-old daughter, responsibilities of my own. I know it's no excuse, but . . .' They exchanged a glance. 'The culture has changed massively since I joined the police and I'm still getting to grips with it all.'

The big question was: Why? Why was Pike gambling her career and marriage by having mindless affairs?

Steve pulled up the handbrake after parking behind a marked police car.

'I'll make some inquiries,' Amy said, knowing she would have to handle the situation with kid gloves. If Steve was telling the truth, she would get to the bottom of it. For the hundredth time, she wished her father were there to help. He had left very big shoes to fill.

Unbuckling his seat belt, Steve placed a hand on the car door. 'Feel free, but don't make things any worse for me.'

'I'll be discreet,' Amy replied. Stepping outside, she was rewarded with a cool, crisp breeze. She focused her thoughts on the job ahead. Whatever had happened with Steve would have to wait. She had two children to bring home, and Stuart Coughlan was giving her answers – whether he liked it or not.

CHAPTER FORTY-EIGHT

As he paced the confines of his flat, Stuart felt as if his heart was going to explode. It was beating at a rate that seemed impossible to maintain and his guts were all twisted in knots. Dr Curtis didn't want to know. Deborah was only thinking of herself, and Christina . . . she had freaked out when he called her with the news, saying that her family were next. The only person who genuinely cared was his girlfriend, Jodie, who knew little about his past.

'I don't get it,' she said. 'Why did you make those coppers leave?' She put a halt to his pacing as she stood in front of him. He was several inches taller than her, but she glared at him with an insistence that was hard to ignore.

He paused, considering his answer. 'Because they couldn't help. There's a detective on her way over. She knows things about Toby's case. I won't talk to anyone but her.'

'Toby's case? What aren't you telling me?' Jodie looked tired. She had already torn a strip off him for leaving it so long before involving the law. Her hair was unwashed and her eyes red-rimmed, but she held it together for him. She loved Toby with all her heart, but she would leave them both if she knew the ugly truth. A sharp knock at the door made him jolt. Exchanging a glance with Jodie, he turned to answer it.

A determined-looking woman in a business suit raised her warrant card in the air. 'I'm DI Winter. Can we come in?' She was short but authoritative, and Stuart had a feeling he'd seen her somewhere before. Behind her stood a broad-shouldered man who introduced himself as DC Steve Moss. Their combined presence was commanding, and Stuart found himself allowing them into his flat.

'Maybe you lot can explain what's going on.' Jodie looked from Stuart to the police officers, her voice sharp with concern.

'And you are?' DI Winter began.

'Jodie Attreed. She's Toby's childminder.' Stuart sighed. Jodie was not leaving until she knew that Toby was safe. 'She's also my girlfriend. You can say what you like in front of her.'

Stuart led them into his old-fashioned living room, which had been decorated with things from charity shops. Flowery pelmets hung over the windows and the fireplace was cluttered with trinkets and ornaments that Jodie had bought to give the place some warmth. He watched as DI Winter took in the family photos on the wall.

'I need your full cooperation,' the detective said, finally turning her gaze to him. Her eyes were piercing, icy grey, but there was heat behind them. Fire and ice. 'I have an update on Toby,' she continued, and told him about a call from the kidnapper. 'We believe he's safe – for now.'

Stuart swallowed, his throat feeling tight. 'Is it the same person who took Ellen? Is it true? Is Luka really alive?'

'You tell me,' DI Winter replied. 'Apparently, you've spoken to him.'

'What?' Her hip jutting to one side, Jodie leaned against the doorway. 'Who's she talking about, Stuart?'

'Why don't we all sit down?' Steve interjected, leading Stuart to the tired-looking leather sofa. 'Look, mate, I know you're in bits over this, but we can help each other out. There's nothing to say we can't bring

Toby home. But we need to know who we're dealing with. Who have you spoken to? What did they want?'

Home. The thought of seeing his little boy made tears spring to Stuart's eyes. As the officer took notes, Stuart found himself relaying details of the package he had received.

'I don't get it,' Jodie interrupted. 'Why would anyone take Toby? And who's this sodding Lucas you keep talking about?'

'You need to tell us everything,' DC Moss said, ignoring Jodie's outburst. 'Social services will be involved. They'll insist you cooperate.'

Stuart's nostrils flared. 'You're calling the social on me? You think I don't care about my boy?'

'Sit down,' DI Winter commanded as Stuart leapt from the sofa. 'A referral is par for the course. It's no reflection on you. But it's like my colleague said, we can work together to bring your son home.' She hesitated, exchanging a glance with her fellow officer. 'The suspect is due to telephone me tomorrow about Toby's whereabouts.'

'But?' Stuart said. 'There's a but, isn't there? I can tell by the look on your face.'

'We believed Ellen was placed in a dangerous situation and we were working against the clock. I don't want that happening to Toby. The kidnapper's calling himself Luka. I need to know everything about him.'

Stuart wrung his fingers, beads of perspiration breaking out on his hairline. Deborah had warned him to say nothing. But what the police said made sense. Ellen was able-bodied and they still hadn't brought her home. What chance did Toby have from the confines of a wheelchair? A warm hand was placed on his back. It was Jodie.

'Tell them, babe,' she whispered in his ear, her breath smelling of cigarettes and mints. 'Tell them what they need to know.'

Stuart inhaled a deep, strengthening breath. 'Back in the eighties, I was an orderly at the Curtis Institute in West London. There were four of us – Dr Curtis, Deborah McCauley, his assistant, and Christina Watson, who had the same job as me. The pay was good, better than normal, but we signed a confidentiality agreement when we joined.' He looked at Jodie, seeking her approval. She nodded at him to continue. 'It was a trial, government-approved. Psychological testing on children. Different kids came and went, but then Luka arrived with his mother from Russia, and they stayed in the dorms.'

Stuart risked a glance at the police officers, who were taking in every word. 'The dormitories weren't fit for purpose. There were electrical problems, leaky pipes and the fire alarms didn't work. Christina and I were paid to take turns staying overnight.' Closing his eyes, Stuart rubbed his face, dragging his stubbled skin in his wake. The memories he had buried years ago now hit him with full force. 'Near the end of the trial there was a fire. The alarms didn't go off and Luka and his mother died.'

'Oh. Lu-ka, not Lucas . . .' Jodie said. 'For a minute there I thought you meant the bloke from the Hare and Hound. And this is the same Luka that's taken Toby? But how can that be, if he's dead?'

Stuart shrugged. 'Every year I've been getting flowers on the anniversary of their deaths. And I'm not the only one. But nobody wants to talk about what happened back then.' A chill descended as his words hung in the air.

Then he recounted what had happened the day before and watched their faces as he relayed details of the courier who had come to his work address. 'I was too scared to call the police,' he said. 'I didn't know what to do.' But nothing would ease the pain of the guilt he felt. If this was Luka, he understood his anger – the need for revenge. He could still see the faces of the children at the institute, hear their sobs from behind locked doors. His tongue felt glued to the roof of his mouth. He swallowed, giving passage to his words. 'This Luka . . . he started with Dr Curtis a while ago. Took his child. Almost killed his wife.'

'We know a courier turned up at her home. Gave her an ultimatum too,' DI Winter interrupted.

Stuart felt the blood drain from his face. 'And you think that's how she nearly died?'

'She was poisoned, yes,' DI Winter replied.

'Shit,' Jodie blurted, softly punching Stuart in the chest. 'Why did you drink that stuff? You could have been killed. Go to the hospital, get yourself sorted out!'

DI Winter looked from Jodie to Stuart. 'She's right. You should check yourself in, to be on the safe side.'

Stuart cupped his clenched fist. 'I'm not going anywhere until I hear from my boy. He needs his medication. God knows what state he's in.' Stuart had already provided officers with details of Toby's illness. It heightened the urgency and a press appeal was being organised.

Pushing his fingers against his earpiece, DC Moss intently listened to a voice that nobody else could hear. 'They've found the taxi that picked Toby up. The driver was in the boot – alive.'

'Is he in a fit state to give us a description?' DI Winter replied.

'He's on his way to the hospital, but he's conscious, so fingers crossed.'

'Look.' DI Winter pinned Stuart with a gaze. 'It's obvious something happened at the institution. What are you not telling us? What about the drugs?'

'Drugs?' Stuart replied, cursing himself as his voice raised an octave. How did she know about that? 'It was decades ago. I can't remember what medication they were on.'

'It was Zitalin,' DI Winter replied. 'When was the last time you spoke to Deborah, Dr Curtis and Christina?'

'I can't remember.'

'You can't remember?' she repeated. 'Then why do we have CCTV footage of the four of you at the Shard restaurant just days ago?'

'Don't make me talk about it.' Lowering his head, Stuart locked his fingers behind his neck. He could feel Jodie's judgement. He could not bear for her to know.

'I'm sorry, Stuart,' DI Winter said, her expression taut. 'But I'm not leaving here until you do.'

CHAPTER FORTY-NINE

The Curtis Institute, February 1985

Luka darted around a corner as he heard the creak of a side door being pushed open. He recognised the voices of Stuart and Christina, their footsteps urgent as they walked in the other direction. Only a few of the strip lights were on, which meant it was after 8 p.m. It was the only way he could differentiate between night and day.

'We're in way over our heads.' Christina's words were harsh as they echoed along the corridor. 'I didn't sign up for this.'

'Keep your voice down,' Stuart warned. 'What's done is done. Just take the money and go.'

Luka's heart drummed in his chest like a wind-up toy. *Go?* That's why Dr Curtis was pushing him so hard. For the last couple of weeks, things had been building to a climax. The tension was palpable, and everything was spoken in hushed tones. But nobody had mentioned anything to Luka about going home. As for Sam, Deborah must have been telling the truth about his heart condition because Luka had overheard Stuart and Christina whispering that he was gone for good. There were no more sniffles behind closed dormitory doors, no childish voices floating down the hall. All had fallen silent, and the orderlies seemed unable to look Luka in the eye.

He caught a faint whiff of crisp, fresh air as Stuart and Christina slipped through the fire doors. He knew there were steps outside which would lead him into the yard. Had it not been for Mama, he would have run as fast as his legs would take him. Finding Christina's keys had been like a gift placed under his nose. She had been tormented, not thinking straight, and when the telephone rang she had left them on the counter in the waiting room.

Having unlocked his room door, his plan was clear: get Mama and escape. But he stalled as he entered his mama's room. In her place was a thin, emaciated version of the woman he used to know.

'Mama?' Luka's chin wobbled as he approached. Her hair was hacked short, and the pungent smell of body odour hung in the air. Was it really her? Like Luka, the flesh had evaporated from her bones, giving her a pained, gaunt look.

Sitting hunched on the bed, Sasha stared into space. A thin line of drool grew stringy and elongated, falling on to her hands, which were folded on her lap. Luka cast an eye over her grey linen dress, which was baggy, misshapen and stained from morsels of food. A tray of curled-up sandwiches and a small carton of milk lay on her dresser. Deborah was right, Mama wasn't well. But how much of it was of Dr Curtis's making? How could Deborah leave her like this?

'Mama.' He locked his eyes on hers as he sat down on the bed. 'We need to go. It's not safe here.'

Slowly, she took in his expression, her brow knitted in confusion. 'Luka?' she said eventually, raising a bony finger to touch his cheek.

'Yes, it's me. Please, get up. We need to go.' Rising, he slid an arm around her waist, tugging at her gaunt frame. But his mama did not have the energy to leave. Her mind was vacant. She was somewhere else.

Hot tears rose from behind his lids as Luka's frustration grew. Should he run away? Find help? He took a moment to collect himself. He knew what he had to do. 'It's OK,' he said, kissing her on the cheek. Her skin was waxy and deathly cold. 'I'm going to get help. I'll be back soon.' He did not see the figure standing in the doorway until it was too late.

CHAPTER FIFTY

'You know about the Shard?' Stuart said, trying to remember the story he had spun to DI Winter. They were at an advantage. They had been taking notes. They had just recited a police caution, hastening to add he was not under arrest.

'My officers have spoken to your work colleagues.' DI Winter crossed her legs. Stuart's attention was drawn to the cuts on her fingers as she clasped them over one knee. 'One of the waiters was surprised to see you having a meal with Deborah McCauley,' she went on. Apparently, she's a regular. Quite the flirt, by all accounts.'

'When . . . when did you speak to him?' Stuart said, trying to buy himself some time.

'It hardly matters, does it? You're on CCTV. Sounds like you had quite an animated conversation, yet you denied having met recently. I'd like to know why.' DI Winter shifted towards Stuart, narrowing her gaze. In the flat above, the neighbours were having an argument, their words punctuated by the slamming of doors. But the background noise was barely audible to Stuart. All he could hear was the swish of blood in his ears as it pumped through his veins.

'What are you hiding?' DI Winter continued to pile on the pressure. 'Because it could hold the key. Without the full story, we're searching in the dark. Help us turn on the lights. See what we're dealing with.'

Taking a breath, Stuart tried to slow his racing heart.

'Babe, do you need a solicitor?' Jodie said, linking her fingers through his in a show of support. Shaking his head, Stuart softly squeezed in a gesture of thanks.

He mooched forward on the sofa, his elbows clamped to his sides. Time was running out for Toby. The coppers should be out looking for him, instead of sitting here getting nowhere fast. He needed to tell them part of the story at least. He only hoped they would not tie him up in knots.

He took another deep breath. 'I worked at the institute back in the eighties. The money was good but they were strict on confidentiality. They said they could ruin us if we talked about what we saw.' Stuart frowned at the memory. 'By the time it was over, I just wanted to forget. I believed Dr Curtis when he said we were just as much to blame.'

'For what?' DI Winter's voice broke into his thoughts. Jodie was still holding his hand. She gave him another squeeze to signal to go on. He knew she was doing this for Toby. She loved that child like he was her own. He dreaded the moment when she would let go.

'Dr Curtis ran tests on the children, all between six and twelve years old. He gave them doses of Zitalin to check for side effects. The children were treated like prisoners, locked in their rooms at night. I should have said something . . .'

'Why didn't you?' Jodie said, slowly releasing her grip.

Stuart rubbed his sweat-laced palms on his jeans. 'The government had given it the go-ahead. I saw the paperwork. He wasn't breaking any laws.' But Stuart was distorting the truth. The clearance he mentioned was for the psychological trials. It had nothing to do with the drugs.

'What sort of parent would give Dr Freakshow their kid? Tell me that?' Jodie's tone had changed to one of bitter disgust.

'For money,' Stuart replied. 'Sasha and Luka were penniless. They were paid, given food and board. Who was I to judge?'

'Tell me what happened on the night of the fire.' DI Winter steered his focus back. It was just as well. By the look on Jodie's face, she wasn't done with him yet. But he was too worried about Toby to take her judgement on board.

'I was on duty. Every night shift we did a lap of the grounds outside and checked the dorms every hour.' Stuart rubbed his face as the memory of that night closed in.

'Go on.' DI Winter's voice sounded far away as she encouraged him to open up. He was back there, in the depths of the building. He could almost smell the mould spores, hear the rattle of the hot-water piping from behind the crumbling walls. Then there were the other sounds. The echoes of crying children that could not be explained. The memory of that place was branded in his mind.

'The last time I checked Sasha she was sparko, fast asleep. Luka was too. I thought they'd be OK if I left them for a little while.'

'Really?' Jodie interrupted. 'It's bad enough you let them kiddies get hurt. You left them on their own too?'

'If you don't mind?' DI Winter interrupted, her voice stern. Both women stared each other down until Jodie's gaze finally dropped.

'Luka and Sasha were the only ones left in the dorms. I was only gone half an hour . . . an hour, tops.'

He wished he could turn back the clock. How different things would have been if he had done his job properly that night. Sasha and Luka would have been spared, and Ellen and Toby would be safe at home. As for the rest of it . . . His confession to the police was the tip of the iceberg.

He glanced up, realising that all eyes were on him. 'Christina . . . her husband worked shifts. She used to drive over to see me. We'd meet in the car park so we didn't get caught on CCTV.'

'In your original statement you said you were at the far end of the building having a cigarette.'

'I found a way of leaving the institute without being seen on camera. It looked like I was still on duty if anyone checked.' He stared at the thinly carpeted floor, not daring to meet Jodie's eyes. 'We didn't want anyone to know about our affair.' He paused. The police weren't to know that he was leaving the worst of it out. He resented Deborah and Dr Curtis for putting him through this. It was all right for them; their luxurious lifestyles left them little time for remorse. Stuart wished he had never applied for that job, never blighted his life with what followed. Such thoughts haunted his nights and lurked throughout his days. It was why he had been so determined to keep Toby safe. Why had he followed the doctor's instructions and locked Sasha and Luka into their rooms at night?

'When I got back, the whole building was alight. The fire doors were jammed and the corridor was pitch black. The windows were all boarded up, so when the strip lighting blew you couldn't see as far as your hands. I had a torch. I tried to get them out of the building. But I was beaten back by the flames.' His chin wobbled as he spoke, and he brushed back the tears escaping the corners of his eyes. 'I remember feeling like I was coughing my lungs up. The smoke stung my eyes so bad that I could barely see.'

'Sounds like that place was a death trap,' DC Moss said.

'It was.' Stuart took a breath and continued. 'By the time I got to Sasha's room I was too late. She was lying face down on the bed. I turned her over and I . . .' His shoulders shook as a sob escaped his lips. 'I could see that she was dead. By then I could barely breathe. I made it out just in time.' He wiped his nose with the back of his hand. 'Luka didn't stand a chance.'

'And you're sure it was Sasha? One hundred per cent?' Amy asked.

Stuart nodded. 'I remember shining my torch on her face. None of us was trained in fire safety. We didn't have drills and the fire doors shouldn't have been blocked.' He turned to Jodie, genuine remorse in his eyes. 'You're right. I should have said something, but after the fire we were all paid off. Curtis bought our silence. Not a day goes by that I don't feel guilty for my part in it all.'

'So why did you meet in the Shard?' DI Winter's expression relayed that she had not fully bought into his story. A fresh prickle of sweat broke out on Stuart's brow.

'Excuse me.' DC Moss rose, one hand pressed against his radio earpiece as he walked to the door. A final slamming of a door from the couple upstairs put an end to the argument filtering down.

Stuart rubbed his chin, telling himself the interrogation was almost over. 'It was Deborah's idea that we meet up for dinner. She wanted to warn us about Ellen in case the nut that took her came for us.'

'Anything else?' Rising from the sofa, DI Winter exchanged a brief glance with DC Moss as he returned to the room. 'Something's wrong, isn't it?' Panic rose in Stuart's chest as he caught the expression on the detective's face.

'It's not Toby,' DC Moss said, his lips thin. But whatever it was, the news was not good. 'It's Christina Watson.'

'I rang her,' Stuart said reluctantly. 'To tell her about Toby. She has a granddaughter. I wanted to see if she was all right.' He slid his phone from his pocket. 'I can give you her number . . .'

'We won't be needing it.' The room grew dark as DC Moss stood in front of the window and blotted out the fading light.

DI Winter met his gaze with a puzzled frown. 'Why not?'

'The police are already with her. I'm afraid she's dead.'

CHAPTER FIFTY-ONE

Amy sat in her office, quietly fuming. She could not help but lay the blame for Christina's death at the feet of her team. They should have safeguarded her, guessed she would be running scared. Amy was so busy dancing to Luka's tune she did not have time to follow up the taskings she had set. Just minutes after getting off the phone to Stuart, Christina had told her husband she was taking a bath. Had she committed suicide to keep her family safe? Stuart had cried when he recalled Christina saying that her family were next. There was no suicide note, just the word 'sorry' daubed in blood on the tiled bathroom wall.

'She was a self-harmer,' her husband explained when they attended the scene. But he had never expected her to take it so far. Amy knew from experience that a demon manifested from guilt was the most patient of all. Days, months, decades could pass. Guilt did not corrode with time for the tortured soul. For Christina, the burden of her secret had become too heavy to bear.

To top things off, a message on Amy's answer machine left her in no doubt that Lillian had orchestrated the scrum at the entrance to the police station earlier.

'You cow,' Amy grumbled as she listened to her gloating words.

'I hear you had eggs for lunch,' Lillian had quipped. 'Did you enjoy your welcome party when you went back to work?'

Lillian had contacts on the outside, a small band of sick fans happy to do her bidding. Thanks to the power of Facebook, such people were able to form alliances and organise events. Were their own lives so boring they had to worship a serial killer for kicks? How had they manipulated the families of the victims to attend? Could this day get any worse? Slamming down the phone, Amy frowned at the knock on her office door. Her blinds were tightly shut, relaying that she did not want to be disturbed. Couldn't they give her five minutes' peace?

'Come in,' she said flatly, trying to contain the simmering anger bubbling up inside.

It was Paddy, wearing an apologetic grin. 'We're doing a chip-shop run, wondered if you'd like anything?'

Amy's stomach churned at the thought of food. They were no further on with finding Toby, and the CPS had released Dr Curtis without charge.

'No thanks,' she said. 'Is there anything else?' She sighed as Paddy took a seat. The last thing she needed was company. She knew if he stayed that she would only end up taking her anger out on him.

'There is, actually.' He shifted awkwardly in the swivel chair as he unbuttoned the collar of his shirt. It was ten o'clock at night and his tie had been discarded hours ago. 'There's been some mumblings in the camp. I wasn't going to say anything but then I figured you'd want to know.'

Amy's grey eyes alighted on him in disbelief. *Really?* she thought, unable to trust herself to utter the words aloud. *You're going to go there now?*

'The team . . .' Paddy frowned, his discomfort evident. 'Well, ma'am, the team feel you're being too easy on the kidnapper.'

'Do they now?' Amy said. The fact that Paddy had called her 'ma'am' was enough to raise her guard.

'Mmm,' Paddy continued. 'Empathising with him a little too much. I mean, we don't even know if he's Luka. He could be anyone.'

241

'So while Christina Watson was slashing her wrists, the office gossips were busy picking holes in my running of the investigation. Who put you up to this? Was it Molly? Gary? I hope you put them straight.'

'It doesn't matter who it was. The fact is, I agree.' He rose briefly, fully closing the door before settling back down. 'It's bound to affect you . . . all this stuff with Lillian Grimes. It's easy to see how you could empathise with someone like Luka at a time like this. But this guy . . . he's playing on your heart strings. Making a fool of you.'

Amy's jaw clenched as Paddy's words cut to the bone. The dynamics between them weren't always as those between a sergeant and a DI should be. As her ex-tutor, sometimes he slipped back into that role. He should respect her decisions instead of doubting them. She wasn't eighteen anymore. But Paddy continued, oblivious to her darkening mood.

'It's the rubber-band effect.' He checked for understanding, frowning slightly at the scowl on Amy's face. 'You and Lillian Grimes . . . as much as you want to move on from your past, you can't let go. Like a rubber band, you find yourself being dragged back to where you came from. It's why you sympathise with Luka. He spent his childhood in captivity too.'

'I can't believe I'm hearing this.' Amy rose from her chair. 'I thought we'd got over my news. Seems I was wrong.'

'Wait,' Paddy said, as Amy reached the office door. 'I didn't mean to upset you . . .' But his words trailed behind her as she joined her colleagues.

'So,' she said, hands on hips as she stared down her team. 'You think I'm being too soft, do you? Fraternising with the enemy?' Inside, a small voice advised her not to be so silly, to take their comments on the chin. But her anger could not be stemmed, and Paddy's words had made her blood boil. She had not expected to add him to the list of people who had let her down.

A hush descended over the office as keyboards silenced and telephone calls came to an abrupt end.

'You think you can do a better job than me? Then go ahead, be my guest.' Amy paced the length of the room, pausing at Molly's desk, which was littered with glittery pens and coffee-stained paperwork. 'Those tasks I set you. Why hadn't you safeguarded Christina Watson in time?' She turned to Gary. 'Where were you when I asked you to oversee Nicole to make sure she was OK?' She stared at Paddy with unconcealed fury as he approached. 'That's two women we've let down in this investigation. You were meant to oversee the team, make sure everything got done. Christina should have been found in time. Her death is down to us.'

'Boss,' Steve piped up, 'Molly was re-interviewing Dr Curtis and we were focusing on finding the courier. We had no way of knowing the suspect would go after the orderlies too.'

'Why not?' Amy snapped. 'It seems obvious to me. I set those tasks and you all ignored them because you thought you knew best. Now Christina is dead, maybe Ellen too. But that's OK . . .' She threw her hands in the air, her voice taking on a manic edge. 'Because all you're worried about is working with a Grimes! What's the problem?' Amy scanned the room. 'Scared I'll turn into a serial killer overnight? Well, I'll make it real easy for you. Tomorrow morning, I quit. This case and this team. You can speak to Luka. See how far you get.'

Turning on her heel, Amy marched out of the door, but Paddy was close behind.

'Bloody hell, hold up a minute!' he shouted after her, his face flushed. But Amy was in no mood to listen. She stood by every word. Her team no longer had her back.

'Why don't you come back in, we'll—'

'Don't!' Amy's lips formed a thin white line and she raised her palms at him in a gesture to stop. 'I don't trust myself around you right now, so back the fuck off!' It was the first time she had sworn at him. The first time she'd treated him with disrespect. But she had to put some distance between them if there was any coming back from this.

CHAPTER FIFTY-TWO

Amy's footsteps were heavy as she wheeled her bike on the pavement. She would hop on it in a minute, she just needed to catch her breath first. The cool night air played with her hair, and she brushed back the loose strands dancing around her face. Her outburst could cost her dearly. It frightened her how quickly she lost her temper these days. Poppy Grimes, the scared little child she once was, had taken up residence inside her. Now Amy's insecurities had made her lash out for the first time in her career. An undercurrent of anger still lingered. What were her team feeling now she had walked out? Regret? Relief?

She raised her eyes to the sky. The moon was full, occasionally cloaked by some evil-looking clouds. Did that mean it was going to rain tomorrow? Paddy had texted to offer . . . no, *insisted* on giving her a lift home, but her sharply worded response had left him in no doubt that she wanted to be alone. Besides, the cycle home would give her time to think. It would offer her the opportunity to untangle some of the thoughts in her head. She paused to straddle her bike.

'Sleep at night, can ya?'

Venom laced the words, making Amy spin round, ready to assert herself. But her movements stalled as she came face to face with Marian

Price. She was the younger sister of sixteen-year-old Barbara Price, who had been murdered by Jack and Lillian Grimes decades ago. Barbara's brother had thrown the egg outside the station and now Marian had come to say her piece. In seconds, Amy assessed the middle-aged woman's form. Her black puffa jacket could be hiding weapons, up the sleeves, in the lining or inside the hood. Her jeans were tight but the pockets deep enough to conceal a syringe. As for her ankle boots, they were long enough to house a small blade. Her auburn hair was tied up at the back, thick enough to hide a hairpin. Amy did not get her ideas from James Bond movies – this was real life, and these were just a few of the things she encountered during police searches. Just the same, her temper finally dissipated, her stern expression fading to one of sorrow and regret. 'I'm sorry . . .' She hesitated, grasping for the right words. 'But I'm not the one to blame.'

But the annoyance on Marian's face told Amy this would be a one-way conversation. 'You're sorry? Your parents killed my sister. Did God knows what to her first. And then . . .' She stabbed the air with her finger, her words trembling with emotion. '*Then* you had the gall to turn up at Mum's door and act the hero.' Tears shimmered in her eyes. 'What kind of sicko are you?'

'Now hang on a minute,' Amy replied. 'I was just a child back then.'

'So was I,' Marian continued, her features soured with disgust. 'But you weren't a child when you came to update us on the burial sites. It wasn't that long ago. To think I shook your hand. Thanked you for everything you did. That child they used as bait . . . was it you? Did you see my sister? Remember what they did to her?'

Amy danced around the question. 'I have nothing but sympathy for your family. It's why I wanted to help.'

'You shouldn't have come to our house. You weren't welcome there.'

'I had no choice. Lillian Grimes would only help me on the condition that I told the families in person where their loved ones were buried. She's the one who's sick in the head. Surely you remember every-thing my father did to solve the case? Robert Winter – my *real* father. I could have told Lillian no. God knows, I felt like walking away. But I had to let those girls rest in peace.'

'Really? You're telling me the truth?'

'Your mum knew my father. She remembered what he did. Do you think he'd raise me to do anything less?'

'I've been waiting hours to see you. The newspaper headlines . . . they've been going around and around in my head.' Slowly, the heat left her words. 'I shouldn't have come here. But it was such a shock.'

'It was for me too,' Amy replied sadly. 'I'm still coming to terms with it.'

'It was bad enough having to bury my sister, but finding out the killer's daughter had been in our house . . .'

'I don't see myself like that. I'd go mad if I did. I'm Amy Winter. I'll always be a Winter. I hope you can find it in your heart to see things the same way.'

'My brother . . . Some woman messaged him on Facebook, told him where you'd be. I warned him not to bring those eggs.'

'He's upset. We all are. Handling your sister's case is the hardest thing I've ever done. But I had no choice.' They walked side by side, Amy's bike keeping a safe distance between them. They talked about past and present and the pain that would not go away. Her suspicions were confirmed. It was one of Lillian's online groupies who had set up the heckling incident.

Finally, they parted. Shoulders slumped, Marian returned to her car. Another soul tormented at the hands of Lillian Grimes. What would tomorrow's headlines bring? The media were still picking the bones of Lillian's story, and it was a meaty carcass indeed.

Amy was grateful when she got home and discovered her mother had decided on an early night. After quickly checking in on her, she took Dotty for a walk around the block before settling into bed with a cup of Ovaltine. She needed to straighten herself out, and self-medicating with booze was not going to help.

Amy's bedroom had not changed much over the years. Apart from a new double bed, it was still decorated in the Laura Ashley colours her mother had picked. Amy had never been one for pink. Instead, the decor was soft white and dove grey, the one exception the tiny pink cherry blossoms dotted on the cover of her duvet. Snuggling up against plump cushions, Amy opened her laptop and began to research online. There was no way she could sleep, so she decided she may as well put her time to good use. Typing keywords into the search engine, she started looking up the rubber-band theory Paddy had spoken about.

Stockholm syndrome was also referred to as 'trauma bonding' and was defined as the psychological tendency of a captive to bond with their captor. As she read the article she thought of Luka and the things he'd said. The more she spoke to the kidnapper, the more positive she was that Luka Volkov had survived. But what about his possible accomplice? Lillian's theory was not something she had discussed in great detail with her team. After today's incident, it was probably just as well. How would they react if they knew she was going to Lillian for advice? The woman who helped her one minute, then organised a brawl outside the police station the next. Something bothered her about their last conversation but she couldn't put her finger on it.

Describing it as an 'extraordinary phenomenon', the article spoke about the mystery of a 'loving abuser' and the strange and intricate relationships that sometimes formed. Although the victim's behaviour could come as a surprise to even them, it was believed to be a strategy for survival.

Amy had a light-bulb moment as she read the article. Back then, Lillian had always been a strong character, sometimes 'saving' Amy from unbearable situations at home. Putting her to bed when things became ugly, telling her to be quiet for her own good. She had been the head of the household, and when Amy was taken into care the little girl had felt adrift. Then in had stepped Robert Winter, a force for good. He and Flora accepted Amy into their hearts as well as their home. He felt strong, powerful. Which is why Amy took it so badly when he died. Then Lillian wrote from prison and, despite her disgust, Amy had answered the call. Was that why she felt so compelled to visit? Had Lillian become her new bedrock?

She scanned the words, trying to make sense of her life's twists and turns. Stockholm syndrome was defined by several conditions. Usually the victim experienced a situation perceived as life-threatening and, while living in captivity, had to gain permission for every move they made. A small gesture of kindness from their captor would strengthen the bond between them, even make the victim feel that their captor was saving their life. Feeling increasingly uncomfortable, Amy read on.

The syndrome could work both ways, the captor developing powerful feelings for their prisoner. Then there was the victim's inability to escape – the rebound effect. The article spoke of one kidnap victim who had been raped and abused for eight years. Yet when she was told of her captor's death, she broke down and cried. Later, she bought his home, spending time in the rooms she had been forced to clean as a child. Unable to leave the past behind, she was compelled to return.

Sighing, Amy closed the laptop. Was this what life had in store for her? For almost five years of her childhood, she had been brought up by Lillian Grimes. She was not allowed to mix with other children, for fear of what she might say. Her daily life was controlled from hour to hour, and the one time she had slipped away into the basement, she was severely traumatised by what she found. Could she ever hope to recover from such an upbringing? Was she psychologically damaged too? Perhaps that was why people like Luka sought her out. Could she use this childhood trauma to put her skills to good use, or would her experiences serve to replace patience with violence, and empathy with suspicion and regret? She shut down the thought. The internet was vast and filled with theories. She would not self-diagnose just yet.

CHAPTER FIFTY-THREE

Amy drew back her clothes hangers as she decided what to wear. Since when had she become so uptight about work clothes? And who would have thought that blacks and greys could come in so many different shades? Then there were her shirts – rows of stiff white cotton so starched they could stand up on their own. She needed a power suit if she was to face DCI Pike today. No doubt the team had complained about her outburst last night. Where did this leave her now?

She faltered as her phone vibrated on her bedside table. Donovan had tried ringing her last night but she had rejected the call. But as she picked up her phone, it was Paddy's name flashing on the screen. He only rang her mobile when there was something wrong.

'What is it?' she said, cradling her phone between cheek and shoulder as she grabbed a suit from the rack. Her movements were urgent as she threw it on the bed and chose a pair of leather ankle boots.

'Don't cycle to work, I'm coming to pick you up.'

Amy's stomach tightened. 'Why?' Sliding off her dressing gown, she pulled on the black fitted trousers. 'I thought I made myself clear last night. I'm done with you and the team.'

'We messed up. You had a wobble. It's water under the bridge now.'

Secretly, Amy was pleased, but her pride would not allow her to forgive and forget. At least, not until she heard what Paddy had to say. His hesitation filled her with dread. There was more to this than her fallout with the team. 'What is it?' she said, swallowing her pride. 'Have they found Ellen?'

'No, it's not about Ellen,' Paddy said, the tick-tock of his car indicator providing a backdrop to his words. 'Last night Luka spoke to London Talk2Talk radio live on air. He told them all about Toby, spun them a big sob story, and then the subject turned to you.'

Zipping up her trousers, Amy shot her right hand through her shirt. 'You're kidding. What did he say? I thought he was calling me later?'

'Oh, he is. If the eyes of the world weren't upon us before, they've got front-row seats now. I'm surprised you didn't hear about it. It's all over the news and on TV.'

Amy groaned. She had been avoiding the news channels since word broke about her connection to Lillian Grimes.

'I'll pick you up in my car, explain on the way. If you sit in the back, the journos won't see you through the tinted windows.'

Amy cast an eye over the clock on the wall. It was 6.25 a.m. If the journalists were gathering now, what was it going to be like later on? It was fortunate she had recently moved in with her mum and they didn't have her address. 'Where are you?'

'Driving to the nick, but I turned around to get you when I saw the media scrum outside. I can be with you in ten minutes?'

Just enough time to tie up her hair and apply a little make-up to disguise the paleness of her cheeks. Amy ended the call, buttoning up her shirt as her thoughts raced ahead. All she wanted was to do her job unhindered, with her team's full support. Was she asking for too much? Would life ever be the same again?

Sliding into the back of Paddy's Jag, she felt like a reluctant reality-TV star. She could almost hear the narration providing a backdrop to her car-crash life. *Tune in this week to see Amy stumble from one disaster to another. We'll be discussing last night's meltdown, then on to her childhood with Lillian Grimes.* Such thoughts only served to worsen her mood. 'Thanks for the lift,' she said begrudgingly, eyeing Paddy in the mirror as he drove.

He sighed. 'Look. About last night. My timing was off. I didn't mean any offence.'

'As you said, water under the bridge.' She made a silent pact to keep her father's tradition of a stiff upper lip. She could iron out the problems with her colleagues later on. 'What's the story with this radio interview?'

'Another attempt at exposure, given the newspaper story didn't work out. I thought we could log on to the station's website in the briefing room and play it there. I've texted the team and asked them to come in early doors.'

'Right,' Amy said, as Paddy braked at the traffic lights. Regardless of what was said, she should not have stormed out. It was behaviour unfitting for a DI. She tuned into Paddy's narrative as he brought her up to speed.

'The station was running a call-in about missing children, and how white middle-class families get more coverage than ethnic minorities and kids from disadvantaged homes. Luka talked about Toby going missing and how upset he was.'

'So he played the victim?'

'Yup. The presenter presumed he was Toby's father. Can you believe that? But when he started banging on about Dr Curtis they cut him short. We'll know more when we listen for ourselves.'

Their conversation was interrupted by the ringing of Amy's phone. It was DCI Pike, speaking in clipped tones. 'Winter? I need to speak to you urgently. Are you on your way in?'

'Yes, ma'am,' Amy replied, noting her formal tone. 'We're almost at the station.'

'Come straight to my office.' The line went dead as she hung up. This was serious. Was it about last night? Pike never arrived at work before her, much less summoned her before 8 a.m. Surely Ellen and Toby took precedence over all of this. But would Amy be allowed to supervise her team as they investigated the case?

CHAPTER FIFTY-FOUR

'Let me close the window.' Pike rose from her chair as Amy took a seat. 'We don't want the press listening in.' She stretched forward as she pulled it shut, blinking against the early-morning sunshine stream-ing in.

Amy felt a tinge of annoyance at the subtle dig. They would need superhero powers to eavesdrop on this floor from outside. Still, the barbed comment was justified. Since joining the team, she had brought them nothing but grief. Her eyes roved Pike's office. She'd had a visitor, because for once her workspace was clear. No browning apple cores, no books with cracked spines left face down on her desk. As always, the smell of fresh coffee lingered in the air. Amy's mouth watered. She had arrived in such a rush; there had been no time to make a cuppa.

Catching her gaze, Pike poured her a cup. 'I wanted to see you before the briefing,' she said, passing it over.

Amy closed her eyes as she sipped, allowing herself a quick but luxurious inhalation of Colombian fine blend. She had a full day ahead of her, a ton of paperwork to review, her call with Luka and she had no idea what Pike was going to throw up next. Paddy had assured her that last night's incident had gone no further than their four walls but, sitting in her DCI's office, Amy was not so sure.

Pike surveyed her over the rim of her coffee cup. 'I've been thinking about all this press attention. It's not going away anytime soon.'

Amy sighed. They should be discussing Toby's case, not the lime-light being thrust upon her. Why was her senior officer so lacking when it came to serious crime? Yes, admin was necessary, as well as keeping senior officers happy. But behind all of this was a vulnerable little boy and a four-year-old girl who had disappeared into thin air. Amy's frustration grew as the sense of urgency hit home. Thanks to Luka's radio call-in, Amy would be hanged, drawn and quartered if it all went horribly wrong. 'Have you heard the radio show?' she said, in an effort to change the subject. 'Paddy's downloading it now.'

'I'm sure he is, and if there's anything urgent he'll keep us informed.' The smallest of stand-offs passed between them. All that could be heard was the ticking of her wall clock and the dull hum of traffic as commuters battled to get to work. 'I'm talking about damage control,' Pike continued. 'You do realise the command team will be all over this negative publicity like a rash?'

'Of course, but I—'

'Then it's imperative we work out the best way to approach this before they haul me over the coals. Luckily for you, I've got an idea that should help. I'm pitching it to them after the briefing. It's our best shot.'

'I see,' Amy said, her eyes flicking up to the clock on the wall. Each second counted down with damning finality. If Pike wanted to frustrate her, she was doing a good job.

'I know someone with connections in the press. They've suggested we put a positive spin on things.'

'In what way?' Amy kept her emotions in check, hoping it had nothing to do with Adam Rossi. It was his fault they were in this mess.

'We go to a leading newspaper with an exclusive story on you. The Met Police's secret weapon – an officer who has turned her special insight into solving the darkest of crimes.'

A cold smile rose to Amy's face. Her inner child, Poppy Grimes, had awoken from her slumber, igniting a fresh wave of fear that she struggled to control. It was bad enough her story had hit the press, but now Pike wanted to show her off as some kind of Grimes circus freak? *Steady*, she reminded herself as she felt her annoyance rise. *You're skating on thin ice as it is.*

'We could push for a one-off documentary,' Pike continued. 'One of those fly-on-the-wall programmes. They're hugely popular right now. We've had some very positive feedback from previous coverage. I'm sure the command team will be keen to have you on board.'

'And if I choose not to?' Amy kept her response brief. Pike already knew what a private person she was, and she didn't trust herself to say anything more. It was taking all her self-control to stay seated and listen to her babble on.

'I don't see how you have any choice.' Pike paused to sip her coffee. '*You* brought this upon us. The team was set up to generate positive publicity for the force. But there's still time to turn this around.'

'Whose idea was this?' Amy drained her coffee, mirroring Pike's movements. Her supervisor was not the most innovative of leaders. She would not have come up with this on her own.

'A friend of mine gave me the idea. He's a DI on another force.' She delivered a taut smile. 'He's been following your case with interest. You've worked with him in the past.'

Crossing her legs, Amy clasped her fingers together. This couldn't be who she was thinking of. Surely not.

'DI Donovan from Essex Police,' Pike continued. 'We discussed you over dinner last night. You remember him, don't you?'

Amy inwardly cringed at the thought of them together. Was he Pike's latest conquest? And who did he think he was, suggesting more publicity when he knew how protective Amy was of her private life?

What private life? her inner voice piped up.

'Are you all right, Winter?' Pike's question held little sympathy.

Amy would not give her the satisfaction of seeing how upset she was. She had to maintain control. Slowly and deliberately, she checked her watch, her words stone-cold. 'Time for me to go. Paddy should have downloaded the radio call-in by now.' She swallowed back the swell of emotions that threatened to engulf her whole.

'And you're OK with me pitching this to the command team?'

Amy rose from her chair, her eyes not leaving Pike's as she held her gaze. 'As you said, I don't have much choice.' She could still feel her, Poppy Grimes, the ghost of the child she once was. Maintaining a frosty exterior, Amy stood her ground.

Pike's smile quivered. Breaking eye contact, she responded with a nod of the head. Was that fear Amy had caught in her eyes? Now she was equipped with details of her background, Pike seemed a little more hesitant about taking control.

CHAPTER FIFTY-FIVE

A quick pit-stop to the ladies' toilets was needed for Amy to pull herself together. Her behaviour worried her. She was usually the calm one. The one in control. But making contact with Lillian had signalled a change – it had heralded the onset of mood swings which frightened her to the core.

She found Paddy at his desk, staring at a pack of cigarettes he did not have time to smoke.

'I thought you'd given up?'

'They're my emergency pack. Don't tell Sally-Ann. I've not broken into them yet.'

'If my week gets any worse, I may join you.' Amy had never smoked a cigarette in her life. 'Any chance I can listen to that broadcast now?'

'I've already emailed it to you.' Paddy checked his watch. 'We've got time – want me to set it up?'

'You know me too well.' Amy was not technologically minded, and she was keen to get Paddy's input on what he had heard.

'It's not very long,' Paddy said as they both entered her office. Amy paused. On her desk was a box of Milk Tray chocolates.

'They were the best we could get at short notice,' Paddy said, watching as she picked up the card left on top. *To the best DI a team could ask for xx.* It was Molly's handwriting.

Amy felt a pang of regret. 'I don't deserve these.' She had never been so at odds with herself.

'About those taskings – we've updated the system with the previous call-on attempts to Christina Watson's address.'

So they *had* tried to offer Christina safeguarding. It wasn't their fault if she had refused to answer the door. 'I . . . I don't know what to say.' She sat in her chair as the strength left her legs.

'Why don't we leave Luka to do the talking.' Paddy leaned over Amy, clicking the link on her computer. His tie dangled from his neck, sporting a Tetris pattern. She resisted a sudden urge to tug it. Just how many novelty ties did he possess?

Outside her office, her team was working hard in preparation for the kidnapper's next call. She would thank them for the chocolates, and forge ahead. The hunt for the courier was gaining ground. The motorbike plates may have been fake but, thanks to cross-checking the capital's CCTV, they had narrowed his location down to a residential street in Whitechapel. They were closing in, their endless inquiries finally reaping rewards. But would they be quick enough to save Toby and Ellen?

Now out of her coma, Nicole was in intensive care. Soon she would be well enough to see her daughter, and Amy longed for the reunion to take place. Her team were working exhausting hours to make it happen, but Luka kept evading them at every turn.

The radio channel hosted a popular London talk show. They were not short of callers, despite broadcasting in the wee hours before dawn. Amy supposed that if your child went missing, sleep would be the last thing on your mind. As well as fretful parents, there were the insomniacs, night-shift workers and other nocturnal listeners to boost the show's ratings. Which category did Luka fit into?

The female presenter sounded bright for someone working in the middle of the night. Kate Mead was young, cheery and had a velvety-smooth voice that was easy on the ear.

'We have Luka on the line. Welcome, Luka, you're through to London Talk2Talk FM. I believe you have personal experience of a missing child.'

'Hello, Kate, thanks for discussing such an important subject. It's very close to my heart.'

Amy met Paddy's gaze as the conversation flowed. To an outsider listening in, Luka sounded like an average man. His voice was relaxed, free of the mocking tone Amy had come to know. His Russian accent still lingered but his words were easy to distinguish. 'I'm sure our listeners would appreciate hearing about your experiences,' Kate urged. 'You have a missing boy, Toby. Is that right?'

'Yes, I do. He's six years old and in a wheelchair. It's been so upsetting . . .'

'I'm sorry to hear that. What have the police said?'

'Well, that's the problem. They're not doing anything. You hear of these high-profile cases that hit the headlines, but not Toby. They've got no leads, and there's been barely any news coverage of his disappearance.' Luka sighed, his voice forlorn.

'Can I ask where he went missing?'

'From school. He got a taxi but he never made it home.'

'That's shocking. Have the police made inquiries with the taxi firm?'

'Yes. They found the taxi abandoned and the driver tied up in the boot. But it wasn't reported in the news. Is it because I'm Russian? It's so frustrating. I've been driven to such desperate measures. It's why I've come to you.'

'You must insist they organise a re-enactment. I'm . . .' A pause. 'I'm looking at Twitter, and some of our listeners have already started tweeting with the hashtag #TobysArmy. Perhaps you can join in and get a campaign going. See if we can bring some press attention to your son's disappearance.'

A long pause ensued. 'You misunderstand me. Toby's not my son.' His words were delivered in a deadened tone.

'Oh, forgive me, I presumed he was. I take it you're a family member?'

'No. I'm Toby's kidnapper. He's right here with me.'

'I'm sorry . . . what did you say?'

There it is, Amy thought: the realisation she's talking to a dangerous man. *The penny has finally dropped.* Closing her eyes, Amy absorbed the tone and inflection of Luka's words. *Please don't balls this up.* She sent the silent thought to the presenter, even though it was far too late.

'My name is Luka. Luka Ivanovich Volkov. I have Toby Coughlan. I just want my story to be told.'

A pause for breath. 'Can you call the police, let us know where you are?'

'I want to. Toby's frail . . . unwell. But the police will arrest me the minute I try to bring him back.'

'How can we help? How can we get little Toby home?'

'Share my story,' Luka responded. 'It's why I took him in the first place. I want people to know the truth.'

'The truth about what?'

Amy caught a hint of reluctance in Kate Mead's voice. She could imagine a radio producer signalling at her to keep Luka talking, when in reality she was probably desperate to get him off the line.

'The famous Dr Curtis,' Luka said. 'He experimented on children in the eighties and it was all covered up. He should be arrested for what he did.'

'I . . . I'm afraid I can't really discuss Dr Curtis live on air,' Kate stuttered, sounding way out of her depth. 'You need to tell the police where Toby is.'

'I've already called, but they won't listen. The police officer handling my case is Amy Winter – that's right, Lillian Grimes's daughter, the serial killer. Why would someone like that care about one little boy?'

'We care,' Kate replied. 'Please, Luka. Drop Toby off somewhere public. In a safe place where he can be found.'

'The police won't listen. The papers won't listen. And now neither will you. I'll tell them where he is. But I can't guarantee he'll be safe.' A rasping breath crossed the line. 'You . . . all of you are to blame. If he dies . . . it's down to you.'

A loud click filled the air as the line went dead. Silence. A gathering of thoughts. 'Well, listeners, I can see we've had quite an influx of callers. We'll go to them right after this break.'

Leaning forward, Paddy clicked the pause button. 'That's it. Some follow-up calls from members of the public but nothing significant. Toby's father is aware. The family liaison officer is with him now.'

'Right.' Amy nodded, staring into space. Her mind was still on the call.

Paddy straightened, groaning as he rubbed the base of his spine. 'He must have known they wouldn't let him slate Dr Curtis live on air.'

'Definitely. But that's not why he did it. None of what you heard was genuine. By posing as Toby's father, he was playing a game.'

'Why?'

'The same reason he left Ellen's bloodied nightdress at the scene. To get back at Stuart Coughlan. At me. At the system. Who knows? If he gets away with this, we might never hear from him again. He's no serial offender. This is coming to an end, and he's squeezing the last few drops of satisfaction out of it while he can.'

'Then time is running out.'

'Effectively, yes. Whoever the kidnapper is, he's taken on the persona of a dead man who's ready to go back to where he came from. Today's operation may be the only chance we have of bringing him in.'

The words had barely left Amy's lips before Molly threw open the door. 'Have you heard?' Her face was animated, her brows raised. Having gauged their reaction, she reined her excitement in. 'Sorry, ma'am . . . Sarge.'

'Heard what?' Amy relaxed her features. It was nice to see some of Molly's old sparkle back.

'They've arrested the courier. He's on his way in.'

After locking her computer terminal, Amy left her desk. An arrest package had been in place since the early hours. Their next task would be to put together an interview plan that would harvest some results. Solicitors may need to be arranged, disclosure given. But they had only a few hours before Luka was due to call. 'At least this way we'll find out if Luka and the courier are the same person,' Molly said, trotting beside Amy as they hurried to the custody block. 'By the way, have you been in the ladies' toilets?'

'No. Why?' Amy lied.

'There's a big dent on the inside of one of the doors. Looks like someone punched it. Weird, or what?'

'Nothing surprises me in this place.' Amy ignored the sharp sting of her grazed right knuckle as she shoved her hand into her trouser pocket. An image of Poppy Grimes came to her mind's eye. 'Pocket rocket,' Jack had called her, because, even at the tender age of four, she wasn't afraid to use her fists. But it was not aggression that caused little Poppy to lash out – it was pure, unadulterated fear. Amy had spent her whole life trying to overcome her past. Today she'd lost the battle. Poppy Grimes was back. But was Amy strong enough to live with her?

CHAPTER FIFTY-SIX

This time tomorrow it could be all over, Amy thought, her paperwork under her arm as she entered the interview room. Her thoughts went once again to Ellen, and she wondered how Toby was holding up. Were they together somewhere safe? She could not bear to imagine the alternative. Luka seemed to delight in saying how weak and frail the boy was. It was imperative their interview with the courier reaped results.

Pike had advised her to leave the interview to Molly and Steve. 'It's the role of a DC,' she'd said. But Amy had a personal connection with Luka. She could not allow someone else to take control. She had chosen her interview partner wisely. Steve came with a wealth of knowledge but was more likely to take over the interview. Molly was content to be guided by her and follow her lead. Much was said about interview tactics and the 'mind games' police played, but all they wanted was to extract the truth and gather as much evidence as they could.

The courier's name was Jamie Richmond. Background research had revealed a family man who worked in an Argos warehouse and enjoyed riding his motorbike at weekends. His fingerprints were uploaded to the system, confirming he had not been arrested before.

The interview room was in need of a paint job, housing a small table and four chairs. Above the door was a warning light to signal the interview was in progress. Below it, at eye level, was a small peephole. A black strip ran across the wall in a horizontal line. Tapping that would result in an army of police officers racing from their offices to assist. Often, Amy would hear the heavy footfall of boots as yet another false alarm was activated. It didn't matter how many times it went off throughout the station, nearby officers dropped what they were doing every time. Not that Amy thought she needed it today. Beneath Jamie's rough exterior was a man who seemed frightened and insecure. Just seconds in, his presence was enough to tell her that he was not Luka Volkov. He may have intimidated Stuart when he delivered the package, but he withered when confronted by police.

His hair was shaggy but clean, his beard carrying on a couple of inches below his chin. His custody sweatshirt barely stretched over his broad frame. Along with his mobile phone, his clothes had been seized for forensics when he was booked in. Amy was surprised at his decision not to avail himself of the duty solicitor, given the seriousness of the crime. Just three questions into the interview he had progressed from answering 'No comment' to speaking in full flow.

'You're making a big mistake,' he said, releasing his thumbnail from between his teeth. 'It wasn't me who took those kids.'

'There's no mistake,' Amy replied. 'We know exactly who you are.' Normally interviews progressed with open questions, but Jamie seemed unwilling to account for his whereabouts. She changed tactics. Some days you had to work with what you had.

'If you know who I am, then you'll know why he's doing this,' came Jamie's response.

'Doing what? Terrorising children? Killing innocent people? You've got kids of your own. How can you be part of this?' Amy had made it her business to inspect the contents of his wallet and had found the family photo lurking there.

'You'll get Toby back safe. Just do as he says.'

'Like Ellen was safe?' Amy's eyes burned with conviction. 'And Nicole? She nearly died, Jamie. Just tell us what you've done with the children. Toby needs urgent medication. And why was Ellen's nightdress covered in blood?'

'What *I've* done?' Jamie sat bolt upright. 'I haven't touched those kids. I swear.'

But Lillian's words about the kidnapper having an accomplice were strong in the forefront of Amy's mind. Quoting the exhibit number, she slid a photograph across the table. It captured Toby's innocence as he sat in his wheelchair. 'Look at it,' Amy insisted, as Jamie drew away. Sliding the second photo from her folder, she showed him an image of Nicole Curtis, hooked up to a machine in intensive care. 'That's attempted murder right there.'

Jamie's lips thinned as his gaze fell on the picture.

But Amy was saving the most impactful photo for last. Reeling off the exhibit number, she slid the crime-scene photo across the table and pushed it under his nose. It was the image that haunted her nightmares. Ellen Curtis's nightdress, heavily stained with blood. 'You did this. Nobody else – you. And if we don't bring in Luka, you're going to cop the lot.'

Jamie paled. 'No . . . Luka said . . .'

'He said what?' Amy spat, her words filled with contempt.

Jamie rubbed his eyes as if to rid himself of the images forced into his field of vision. 'I don't know who he is. I met him once in a bar. We've been in touch by text ever since.'

'And the phials? Where did you get them?'

'They were sent to my address. I never meant to hurt anyone. I got in way over my head.'

'Tell me everything that happened, starting from the first time you met Toby and Ellen's kidnapper up to the present day.' At last, Amy uttered the open question best suited for the interview.

'I can't,' he said miserably, his head in his hands.

'Then we'll add obstruction to your list of offences.' Amy allowed her words to sink in. 'You can help us or obstruct us. You're going down either way. Which will gain you the most leniency in court?'

'You can still speak to a solicitor,' Molly reminded him. The interruption was fair, but irritated Amy because time was running out. A private solicitor could take hours to arrive. Even the duty solicitor was rushed off his feet. They could not afford the time. His silence spoke volumes as he shook his head. Jamie was going to cooperate.

'I was at a very low point. My wife had just left me, taking the kids with her. Everyone I cared about deserted me in the end.'

Amy focused on his words, a wisp of a thought floating in. 'You were with Luka during the experiments, weren't you?' Next to her, Molly's pen froze on her pad. This was why Luka had chosen him. He was one of the few who understood.

Nodding, Jamie confirmed her suspicions. 'I was known as James back then . . . James Baliss. I changed my name when I got older. I didn't want the doctor finding me again.'

It made sense. Subjects of scientific experiments were often followed up on later in life. But how did Luka catch up with him? And what did Dr Curtis do to make Jamie feel such a way? Had he been drugged too? There were so many things Amy needed to know. But this was meant to be a first-account interview. She'd planned to take what she needed and leave her detective constables to follow up with more.

'You said you met him in a bar?' Amy shifted in her seat. She wanted to get to the meat of the story but needed to obtain some background information first.

'He bought me a drink, said he'd hired a private detective to track me down.' Jamie hunched over in his seat, his gaze on his hands as they rested on the table. 'First I thought he was hitting on me. I was about to tell him to fuck off when he mentioned my tattoo.'

'Your tattoo?' Amy said, trying to move him along.

Pulling up his sweatshirt sleeve, Jamie revealed a tiny tattoo of the number three on his inner right wrist. 'He said he knew where I got it from because he had one too.'

'And did he?' Molly piped up. Amy accepted the interruption. It was important they verified that Luka was who he said.

Jamie nodded. 'Kinda. He had a small ladybird on his inner wrist. It was fresh, still scabbing over. He said it was a cover-up, and his number was beneath. I didn't understand the significance until he explained his plans. It was good to talk to someone who had been through the same thing.'

'Did you remember him from the tests? Do you believe he's Luka? Because our records show that Luka's dead.'

'We were all kept apart. The only kid I knew back then was called Sam, who I saw in passing a couple of times. There was a girl too . . . I can't remember her name. We were numbers as far as Curtis was concerned.' He met Amy's gaze. 'It *was* Luka, though. He knew things that nobody else could.'

'And Deborah McCauley? Stuart Coughlan? Christina Watson? You remember them?'

Jamie's face darkened at the mention of their names. 'Oh yeah, I remember those fuckers. Deborah wasn't too bad, but the others . . . they got everything they deserved.' He blinked, as if remembering his words were being recorded. 'But, eh . . . he told me three of the drinks were harmless. They had pretty decent odds.'

Inside, Amy glowed at the minor victory. The lab had confirmed for the second time that one of the four phials was poisoned, and Jamie had just confessed to delivering them. She was quick to follow up with another question while he was in a talkative mood. 'What about the children? Didn't you think about them?'

'They were well cared for. The calls were all for effect.'

'Where are they? What has he done with them?'

'I don't know. I've not set eyes on them. But Luka swore they wouldn't come to any harm.'

'But you can't say the same for their parents. What happened when you visited Stuart Coughlan?'

'I gave him the package and drove away. I felt like justice was being done.'

'Even though his child is in a wheelchair?'

'That's hardly my fault.' He delivered the words with a shrug.

Amy reassessed Jamie's remorse. The only thing he was sorry about was getting caught. 'You must know something,' Amy replied. 'Toby could die. Is that what you want?'

'Of course not. But the number I texted Luka on isn't working anymore.' He crossed his arms, his chair creaking as he leaned back. 'My job was to deliver the packages. I was a courier, that's all. Hell, I don't even know how Luka's still alive.'

'Can you give us a description of him? It will help your case.'

Rubbing his beard, Jamie seemed to consider it. 'Fortyish, clean-shaven, dark hair, medium build. That's all I remember. We only met once, and I'd had a bit to drink.'

Amy glanced at her watch. She needed to prepare for what lay ahead. She turned to Molly. 'We'll conclude the interview here. Bring him back to his cell and organise a sketch artist. See if he can come up with something better than that.' At least the interview had gleaned something new. If Jamie was telling the truth, Luka had a ladybird tattoo on his right wrist. As Molly gathered up her paperwork, Amy made a mental note to ensure she questioned him thoroughly about the past.

She faced Jamie. 'What's the last thing Luka said to you?' His pause gave her cause for concern. 'We'll be checking your phone, so you may as well cooperate.'

Jamie looked her in the eye, the hint of a smile playing on his lips. 'He texted it in Russian,' he said, remorse fading with each word. 'It's a proverb. I checked it on Google Translate.'

'What does it mean?'

'*Soon it will be our turn to triumph.*'

A shiver crept down the curve of Amy's back. Luka's actions were driven by deep-set convictions. He had no intention of letting the children live.

CHAPTER FIFTY-SEVEN

Amy had not yet forgiven her colleagues for their reaction to her handling of the case, but at least they were getting on with what they had to do. It was not as if they had time to dwell on things. Today their floor was crammed with officers from different departments as they worked together to chase up the latest leads. The more Amy thought about it, the more convinced she was that Luka was not working alone. Had the courier helped him stage Ellen's nightdress in the building site?

On the board in their office was a timeline of the investigation. To the right were images of people of interest. To the left were lists of urgent outstanding tasks. One of them was to contact Luka's father, Ivan Volkov. Intelligence reports had been returned saying he was still alive. Now all they had to do was track him down. Contact with Ivan might provide further leads. In the corner, Steve swore as the printer jammed for the third time.

'Here, let me . . .' Molly said, pulling out the tray and tweaking the paper inside. There was no time for tea rounds today, no banter, no personal phone calls. The air was filled with a sense of urgency as officers chased up every morsel of information that filtered in.

'If I can have your attention,' Amy said, aware that the last time she'd said this, she had stormed out. At times like this she needed to keep up morale.

'I just want to say well done on bringing the courier in so quickly. I know you worked around the clock to make it happen.' It was true. Officers had sat for hours viewing ANPR and CCTV, collating images until they had finally produced a result. 'Jamie Richmond is sitting with the sketch artist as we speak. I'm sure it will help officers on the ground to make a positive identification, which is invaluable at a time like this.' She looked around the room, taking in her colleagues' faces. It was with some relief that she saw they appeared open to her words. 'We're also close to finding Luka's father. If we can establish phone contact, then we can use that as leverage when our kidnapper calls.'

'We've offered Dr Deborah McCauley safeguarding,' Molly piped up. 'She already has CCTV, and we installed a panic alarm this morning.' Amy knew she meant the collective 'we', as she was able to organise such things without leaving her desk.

'What if we're too late for Ellen?' DC Gary Wilkes replied, scratching the back of his head with a pen. 'He didn't mention her in the interview. And then there's the nightdress—'

'We won't be.' Paddy's response was firm as he joined in with the impromptu discussion. 'Failure's not an option as far as the children are concerned.' A hush descended as his words fell like stones.

Amy glanced at her colleagues' tired faces and crumpled shirts, heard their stifled yawns. 'I know you're working long hours, but we can't afford to slow the pace today. Put yourself in Stuart's shoes. He was prepared to drink poison to save his child, knowing there was no guarantee he'd be found alive.' She turned back to the whiteboard, picked up a marker pen and wrote: *Soon it will be our turn to triumph.* 'This is what worries me.' She pointed at the words. 'It's the last thing Luka texted the courier, Jamie Richmond. Luka's got a vendetta against Stuart Coughlan and it's hardly any wonder, given what we know now.'

Amy glanced back at the whiteboard and the long list of outstanding tasks. 'Steve, how are we doing with tracking down staff at the funeral home?' She was talking about Sasha and Luka's cremation after the fire. Someone had to know something, but paperwork was hard to come by, cloaked with an air of secrecy that had plagued them since day one.

Steve gathered his paperwork from the printer and returned to his desk. 'We've managed to track down the funeral director. He's a chap by the name of George Barber. There's only one problem, though . . .'

'What's that?'

'He's got dementia. He's in a care home in Shoreditch. We're visiting him later today.'

Amy felt like swearing, but her bruised knuckles were testament to the fact that some frustrations were better off contained.

She rested her gaze on Gary, seeing a young man who was drunk with fatigue. She took a breath, signalling at Molly to open a window. It was growing increasingly warm, and the air was growing stale.

Her thoughts turned to Luka. He had taken his imprisonment hard, although it had been for just a few months of his life. What had happened to him after that? Had he gone underground? His mention of his excursions seemed odd . . . she imagined him as a child, desperate for the police to rescue him as he mingled with Londoners in broad daylight. She frowned, remembering their last conversation.

'Molly,' she said, knowing she was good with technology. 'Do me a favour, find out when the gates were erected outside Number Ten Downing Street.' Molly gave her a puzzled look but began tapping on her keyboard. 'Got it,' she said as she drew the Wikipedia page up.

'That can't be right . . .' she added, peering at the screen. 'The gates went up in 1989. But the fire . . .'

'Was in 1985.' Amy finished her sentence. 'Which means that either our caller is lying about those trips or Luka survived the fire but remained a captive, somehow. He said he was captive, but who took him there? Did his mother keep him prisoner, allowing him out only on sightseeing trips?' Amy turned to Steve. 'Go back to Stuart. See if you can find any holes in his story about finding Sasha dead. What sort of mental state was she in? If we find her, we'll find Luka. We haven't a second to waste.' Had Sasha been blackmailing Dr Curtis? Pulling Luka's strings all along? But what about the bodies in the fire – who had really died that day?

CHAPTER FIFTY-EIGHT

Luka glanced in his car's rear-view mirror, praying for the pain in his head to ease. The tablets he had taken to combat his migraine had yet to take effect. He shied away from his reflection. These days, he hated what he saw. From what he'd read, Amy Winter had experienced a horrific childhood, yet somehow she found the strength to carry on. Mother had told him not to listen, warned him the detective would get under his skin. If DI Winter had her way, he would be locked up behind bars by now. He could not afford to lose sight of the driving force behind his actions. He had tried to put the past behind him and live a normal life, but Luka was triggered each time he saw Dr Curtis's gloating face in the media. After years of torment, he deserved to have the chance to start again – regardless of the cost. One way or another, this ended today.

Sighing, he answered his mobile phone. The car park was almost empty. Their conversation would be a private one.

'All set?' she said, as if sensing his last-minute doubts. 'Because there's still time to change your mind . . .'

'I've not changed my mind,' he said. She used to hold power over him, but he was not a child anymore. 'We finish what we started and put an end to this for good.'

'But they're only little,' she whispered down the phone. 'They don't deserve to die.'

'Neither did I, but they set up that fire and left me to burn. Whose side are you on?'

'After everything that's happened, you really need to ask?'

'We're so close to ending this.' He winced. His migraine was coming at the worst of times. 'Have you forgotten what they put me through? We finish this and start again.'

'All right, all right,' she replied. 'Whatever you say.'

'So you're ready?'

'I'm ready.'

'Good. You know what to do.'

Luka had wanted Stuart to suffer, but Stuart hadn't chosen the poison – fate had given him a helping hand. If he was fair, then Toby would be returned to him. But Luka was teaching him a lesson: that promises were often broken and life could be cruel. Unless DI Winter had superhuman powers, she would not be winning today. Like Ellen, Toby was as good as dead.

CHAPTER FIFTY-NINE

As she walked the route to Holland Park tube station, Amy used the time to reflect. She had declined the offer of a lift. The journey was short and she could not afford to be seen arriving with backup in tow. Safety evaluations had taken place and deemed her to be at low risk. Luka fed off her empathy. He would not cause her harm.

Above her, the sky was slate grey, the pavement edged with frost. She walked head first into the icy breeze, her heart burning with the need to bring Toby and Ellen home. Luka could prove to be slippery, disappearing into the ether from which he had come. She had made her wishes clear. No arrests until they had extracted Toby's location.

Approaching the station, she stood at the traffic lights and surveyed the crowd. The sketch artist's composite had been released just in time. Amy glanced at the beggar sitting on the pavement, his back against the tube station wall. He looked a little too clean for someone who lived outside. Was he undercover? What about the man tying his shoelaces at the entrance? She drew her gaze away. Luka could be watching too, and she didn't want to bring attention to either of them.

Crossing the road, she stood on the pavement as a stream of pedestrians flowed around her. She checked her watch, tapping her right foot. The phone in her hand felt like a bomb about to detonate and she gripped it tightly as it rang. 'DI Winter.' Her words were sharp and to the point. 'Where is Toby? I need to speak to him.'

'What's the rush?' Luka replied. 'Ellen is such an annoying, whiny child. I much prefer Toby. He's quiet and insightful.' He chuckled, but the laugh sounded bitter and forced. 'At least I don't have to worry about him running away.'

'Ellen *is*?' Amy picked up on his use of the present tense. 'Is she with you? Can I speak to her?'

'Careful,' Luka replied, an edge to his voice. 'If I hang up, then you'll never find out. You don't want that on your conscience, not with everything else you've done.'

'We're not here to talk about me.' Amy lowered her head, imagining the look on her colleagues' faces. Today, Pike had insisted she wear a recording device. They could hear every word.

'We are if I say we are,' Luka replied. 'Because the way I see it, I'm the one in the driver's seat.' Another forced laugh. 'There's a clue there. Can you figure it out?'

Amy frowned. A clue? Is this how they were playing today's game? At least she wasn't alone. Right now, her colleagues would be unpicking everything he said.

'We're very alike, you and I,' Luka continued. 'Both of us have come back from the dead. How does it feel to resurrect Poppy Grimes?'

Amy stilled. Another clue. She had been right about Luka. Like her, he had shed his skin and become someone else. But when? How much of his life had been spent in captivity with someone else at the helm? They may have something in common, but she was dedicating her life to helping others. She was not like him at all.

'What a contrast, your parents being serial killers and you a detective inspector in the police. The psychologists must be having a field day with it all.'

Each word dug like sharpened nails into her skin. She knew her colleagues would have thought the same thing. But this case had taught her that being different was not so bad. From now on, she would hone her skills, put them to good use by helping those unable to help themselves. It would not be easy taming Poppy Grimes, but she was no longer going to spend the rest of her life hiding her away.

'Go to St Paul's Cathedral,' Luka said, issuing his next demand.

Amy stood firm. Two children were in danger. She would not be Luka's puppet anymore. 'No,' she said. 'Not until I know Ellen and Toby are safe.'

'Take the Central line eastbound . . .' Luka continued, ignoring her outburst.

'I said no!' Amy shouted, attracting the glance of a passer-by as she raised her voice. But the shopper did not register on Amy's radar. 'I saw the blood on Ellen's nightdress. Is she dead? What have you done with her?'

'Ellen's with Toby. But if you don't believe me, then to hell with you.' His words were followed by silence as he ended the call.

Immediately, Amy's police radio beeped as she was alerted to another call. It was Pike, her tone shrill as she voiced her disapproval. 'Why didn't you stick to protocol? What have you done?'

'He'll call back. I'm sure of it,' Amy said. 'He's planned for this. He won't hurt those kids until he's had his fun.' She'd thought long and hard about what she was going to say. No longer would she take his demands lying down. The beep of her mobile phone signalled a picture message from an unknown number. Her hand fell to her chest as she exhaled in relief. It was Toby and Ellen, playing Lego together. There was no way of knowing when the picture had been taken, but at least it was proof that Ellen had still been alive after her nightdress was found. 'Go,' Pike said, as Amy described the photo. 'Don't wait another second. Go and bring those kids home.'

◆ ◆ ◆

Amy glanced around the tube carriage and took a vacant seat. Next to her, a silver-haired woman murmured under her breath about her daughter, fretting over her choice of men. But she was easily in her sixties. Was that what it was like when you had kids? How was Stuart coping, knowing his child's life was in someone else's hands? It was a terrifying prospect that such a helpless child was so heavily reliant on Amy and her team. Her thoughts raked over the embers of Luka's call. What did he mean about being in the driver's seat? Was he talking about Toby? Perhaps he was in a car, or on a fairground ride? What sort of situation involved a race against time?

She reached St Paul's Cathedral, the January winds chilling her face as she scanned the street for signs. Fifteen minutes had passed. How much time did she have left? In a way, this was easier than before, as she didn't have to continually update base. This operation had trebled in size since it began, and there were a lot more officers on the ground.

Her phone rang. It was Luka. 'I see you made it. Nice suit, by the way. Very sharp. I prefer it to that flowery blouse you had on the other day.'

Amy's eyes narrowed. Luka was here, in the crowd. But where were the children?

'St Paul's Cathedral is the last place I visited as Luka. Everything changed after that.'

'Why are you telling me this?' Amy said, changing tack. 'Throwing another pity party for one?'

'Who are you to judge me, with your past?' Luka snapped. 'We're all entitled to start again. You joined the police to run away from what your parents did.'

But this time Luka's words were failing to hit their mark. 'There's a paperwork trail of my reinvention,' Amy said. 'My time in social care. Adoption records. What happened to you? Where have you been hiding all these years?' Amy danced around the subject of his mother, hoping he would let something slip.

Luka exhaled an exasperated sigh. 'It's too late to explain now. Putting things right is the only way to leave Luka behind.'

'Kidnapping vulnerable children is hardly putting things right.'

'I'm giving them up – it's down to you to get there on time.'

'How am I meant to do that? I need an address.' She held her breath as he considered her words.

'OK, I'll tell you where they are. One last journey. Who knows, if you find them, maybe it will undo some of the harm printed about you in the papers.'

Amy's pulse quickened. Had she made a breakthrough? Dare she hope he was going to help her find the children in time?

CHAPTER SIXTY

The Curtis Institute, February 1985

Standing in Sasha's doorway, Deborah watched the scene unfold. It was bad enough that Luka had escaped from his room. The last thing she had wanted was for him to find his mother in such a state. The woman was suffering a mental breakdown. It happened sometimes with people when they were left too long with their thoughts. Deborah had not told Luka that his mother had sneaked a pair of scissors into her room and had used them to hack off her hair. And now he was here, as white as chalk as he took the scene in. No wonder he thought Sasha was being mistreated – but, in truth, she had done it to herself. They'd had no choice but to sedate her as they worked out their next steps. Besides, as Dr Curtis had said, Sasha knew far too much for her own good.

'Let me go!' Luka squealed, trying to dodge Deborah in the doorway. But Deborah had not come this far for things to end like this.

'Hey, what are you doing?' she said, wrestling him into her arms. 'Luka, wait. I'm not the enemy here.'

'Let me go!' Luka cried for a second time, squirming in her grasp.

Sasha craned her head in their direction and Deborah caught the spark of defiance still lurking behind her eyes. Somewhere within her drug-induced state, Sasha was screaming to get out.

'Luka, calm down,' Deborah said firmly. 'You're upsetting your mother. You know she's not well.'

'That's your fault,' Luka huffed, breaking free of Deborah's grip. 'You did this to her!' From the corridor, Stuart and Christina approached.

'I take it these are yours?' Deborah said, extracting the bunch of keys from the door and waving them under Christina's nose.

Extending her palm, Christina took them into her possession. 'Sorry,' she mumbled. 'I only put them down for a minute.' She glared at Luka with ill-concealed contempt. 'Do you want me to take him back to his room?'

'I'll take care of it,' Deborah said, rubbing the little boy's back as he calmed down. 'You should have finished your shift hours ago.'

Christina flushed, exchanging a glance with Stuart. 'I . . . I stayed on to look for my keys.'

'C'mon,' Deborah said to Luka. He gave his mama one last wistful glance before being led away.

'Where are you taking him?' Christina said, as Deborah led him towards the fire doors.

'Outside, to my car. Don't worry, we won't be long.'

'But you can't . . . he's my responsibility.'

'Like your keys were your responsibility?' Deborah placed one hand on her hip. 'Would you like me to call Dr Curtis? See what he thinks of all this?' She was met with silence. 'I didn't think so.'

◆　◆　◆

Luka inhaled a lungful of cool night air as they walked across the car park. Turning his face to the sky, he sought out the moon, sighing as it came into view.

Deborah wondered if he was thinking about his father; he had not heard from him in so long. It was cruel to keep them apart, but she was trying to do the right thing. Sitting in the safety of her car, she did her best to reassure him. Time outside was what Luka needed, a brief change of scene. She had to show willing if he was to trust her again. She allowed him his outpouring, listened as he relayed his concerns.

'It ends tomorrow night,' she said calmly. 'That's when you'll leave this place for good.'

Luka's eyes narrowed with mistrust. 'You promise? And Mama too?'

'I won't just promise.' She looked at him solemnly. 'I swear on my life. This ends tomorrow – for your mother too.'

◆　◆　◆

Dr Curtis's voice was thick with sleep as he answered the phone. 'Hello? What's wrong?'

'It's Luka.' Deborah's tone was flat, her emotion spent after getting the boy back to bed and staying until he fell asleep.

'And it can't wait until the morning? What time is it?' His voice drew away as he murmured to his wife, 'Go back to sleep. I'll take this in the study.'

Deborah gathered the courage needed to deal with what lay ahead. 'He stole a set of keys and made it as far as Sasha's room. It's only down to me that they didn't escape.' A wave of sadness fell as she thought about Luka, asleep in bed. He trusted her. Could she betray him like this?

On the other end of the line she heard the creak of a door closing. Of the phone being cupped close to Curtis's mouth. 'We'll have to bring forward the fire,' he said, his words level and low. He had discussed it twice with her this week, how he had planned to erase his past mistakes. Sasha had discovered their secret; and, with the drugs infiltrating his system, it was a miracle Luka had survived this long.

'Leave it to me. You can't risk getting involved,' Deborah replied. 'You have copies of everything, don't you?' She was talking about his studies and the reports that were fit to be made public.

'Of course. Are you sure you're up to it?'

'Tomorrow night. No survivors. Make sure you have an alibi.' There was an audible click as Deborah swallowed, easing the tightness in her throat.

'Very well.' The doctor spoke on the exhale, uttering the two words that would bind them together for decades to come. 'We'll speak in the morning, go over the fine details one more time.'

Leaning back in her seat, Deborah felt her muscles relax. She was in control. Everything was going to be OK. She had told Luka he and his mother would be leaving the institute. She hadn't promised they would be alive.

CHAPTER SIXTY-ONE

One last journey, he'd told her. Amy contemplated Luka's words during her tube ride to Tower Hill. A quick liaison with her colleagues had informed her that they were working hard behind the scenes. An undercover crew was already awaiting her arrival but Amy's thoughts were laced with dread. Her stomach growled, reminding her it had not yet been fed. She reached into her pocket, plucking out the protein bar she had fished from her office drawer before she left. She barely noticed the taste, chewing automatically as she mentally ticked through their actions to date.

DC Gary Wilkes was at the care home, talking to the funeral director responsible for cremating Sasha and her son. Molly had been tasked with speaking to Luka's father using an interpreter via LanguageLine, now they had got him to a phone. Her updates to Amy had come as text messages as she relayed snippets of their conversation. But what had he been told about Luka's death? Had he travelled here all those years ago? Grieved for his wife and son? Scrunching up the wrapper, she shoved it deep into her pocket, ready to depart at the next stop. The carriages were getting busy, with people escaping the city streets. If she never took another tube, it would be too soon.

As she came up the escalators, Amy's phone informed her of a voicemail. It must have been urgent for Molly to call. She listened to her update. Her words were used sparingly, conscious that she must not tie up the line for very long. As she drew the phone away from her face, Amy closed her eyes briefly and willed some positive vibes to come her way. *Please God*, she thought, praying to anyone that would listen. *I'll go to church, donate to charity, but please make this come good.*

As her phone rang, she directed all of her focus to the call.

'So, you're here, but I'm sorry. You're probably too late.' It was Luka, sounding pained.

Amy's pulse picked up speed as she surveyed the crowd. She could hear traffic in the background. A car beeped across from her, and through the receiver of her phone. Goosebumps prickled on her skin as she realised he was near.

'I've done everything you asked,' she said, feeling breathless with emotion. 'Where are the children?'

An edge of misery mounted in Luka's voice. 'I'm sorry. I can't help you. I've got to go.'

'Got to go? What the hell?' Amy screamed down the phone.

'It's over. I can't deal with this anymore. The pain. It's coming back. I need to lie down somewhere dark. I'm not strong enough to see this through.'

'What would your father think?' Amy said, watching a man across the road. There was something about the way he was slightly crouched, holding his hand to his forehead. His peaked hat only partially disguised his face. As he turned to face Amy, she caught sight of his features before averting her eyes. It was the man in the artist's sketch. And she was not the only person who had noticed him. Two men in bomber jackets were drawing near. Tall and muscular, one of them put a hand to his ear. They were listening to instructions. But who was issuing them? *Not yet*, Amy thought. *Wait. Hold back.* Her eyes flicked to a woman in

Lycra jogging on the spot. Her head was bowed. Was she undercover too? Her footsteps stalled as she approached him.

'My father's dead,' Luka replied, after a long pause.

'Then how has my colleague spoken to him today? Ivan's alive, Luka, and he wants to talk to you.'

'No . . . he can't be. I . . .' A sharp intake of breath. Standing across the road, Luka returned his hand to his head.

'He knows about Ellen and Toby. He wants you to let them go. He spoke in Russian. He said the real Luka would never harm a living soul.' Silence. Amy had one last shot at making this work. 'I'm telling you the truth. There was something he said. Something that only you would understand.' Amy watched as Luka leaned into his phone. Watched as the police gained ground. *Not yet. It's too soon.* 'He said this was *not* the time to make your silence a source of strength.'

'Yes,' Luka sniffled. 'It was something he said to Mama before she left. And he's alive? He's really alive?'

'Yes. He wants to see you. He doesn't care about what you've done, as long as you let the children go.' The last sentence came from her, but time was running out. She needed answers fast.

'I'm sorry. But I set you up to fail. They're in a breaker's yard miles away from here.' Luka checked his watch. 'You'll never reach them in time.'

'Where?' Amy stiffened as she watched the men surround him. They nodded to the woman closing in. A few feet away, a homeless man was getting to his feet. Amy tried to catch their attention but their focus was all on Luka, who appeared to be in crippling pain.

'They're sedated, in the boot of a car about to be crushed.' He paced the footpath, oblivious to the movement around him. 'I'm sorry . . . I wanted Dr Curtis and Stuart to suffer – to pay for what they did.'

'Where? Please, Luka. For me,' Amy said, still trying to catch the officers' eyes. She might not be able to reach the children, but they had units on standby. Her heart hammered as she imagined Toby and Ellen, their helpless bodies curled up in an abandoned car. In her mind's eye she could see the crusher, hear the sound of metal splintering bone. Her muscles tensed as she watched the officers through the passing traffic obstructing her view.

'All right,' Luka replied. 'I'll tell you. But you'll never reach them in time . . .'

Amy watched in horror as the undercover officers closed in. Couldn't they hear? He was about to give her the location. She wanted to scream at them to back off. Briefly, she caught the female undercover officer's eye and gave a violent shake of the head. But Luka was watching her and followed her gaze.

'Where? Tell me!' Amy repeated, their eyes locking. It was too late for him to hide.

'I told you no police!' he shouted, his voice panicked as officers closed in. From all around him, they crept from their vantage points. He was surrounded at every turn. Throwing his phone on the ground, he sprinted, stopping dead as a car drew to a halt and more officers flooded out. He had nowhere left to go. Nowhere except across the road towards her. But the traffic was not letting up. It was too big a risk. Looking around him one last time, he gritted his teeth and ran.

'No!' Amy shouted. Time seemed to move in slow motion as he spotted a gap in the traffic and sprinted across. But his decision had been ill-timed, the pain creasing his face and stalling his movements. The screech of brakes was deafening, and Amy watched, horror-struck, as Luka was thrown into the air.

CHAPTER SIXTY-TWO

With a sickening crunch, Luka's body hit the windscreen of the car. The treble tragedy made Amy's stomach lurch as she clasped her hand over her mouth. Luka's life could be snuffed out in a matter of seconds. He was the only hope they had. Panicked voices ensued as she radioed for an ambulance, updating Control about the scene. Running towards the site of impact, she was forced to listen to one sickening crunch after another as a domino effect took hold and cars piled up behind. The sound of screeching metal felt like nails against chalkboard as Luka's body flopped forward on to the road. Traffic ground to a halt, plain-clothes officers rushing out to stop oncoming cars. Rage flooded Amy's system as she knelt down to check for signs of life. She had been on the cusp of finding Toby and Ellen, on the brink of Luka giving himself up. She recognised the weariness of being caught up in something so dire, knew how he felt being part of a situation he'd hated for so long. Blood streaked down his temple, his right leg at an angle that suggested broken bones.

'Luka, can you hear me?' She cupped his face with her hands. His eyes fluttered open, a moan passing his lips. Already she could hear the wail of sirens as the ambulance came to assist.

'Is he alive?' A male officer spoke from above her, while others checked on drivers caught up in the scene.

'No thanks to you!' Amy spat, briefly assessing the rest of his body for injuries. 'You were meant to hang back.'

After mumbling something about following orders, he crouched down to help. Slowly and gently, she rolled Luka into the recovery position, assisted by the officer, who had nothing more to say. They had moved in without her authority and gone above her head. There was only one person who would have panicked enough to issue the order to arrest. Someone who had no clue of how people like Luka felt. DCI Pike. The betrayal bit deeply.

'Luka,' she said, squeezing his forearm. 'Where are they? Please tell me.' She prayed this would not be a dying declaration. Why should his father have to lose him a second time? Luka's eyelids fluttered, but his eyes were unfocused, and there were no words on his lips.

'Back off!' she screamed at the people crowding around him. 'Give him some air.' Hot anger drove tears behind her lids, and she swallowed them back. She could almost hear Ellen and Toby crying out in fear. The sound would haunt her nightmares if she could not get to them in time. Hands trembling, she touched Luka's cheek, praying for warmth. 'Luka,' she whispered, bending over until her lips brushed his ear. 'Please, tell me where the children are.'

The tiniest of groans escaped from between his lips. 'Mother knows,' he said, before passing out.

Heavy footsteps broke the stillness as paramedics gathered around her in a flash of green uniforms and equipment bags. A warm sticky substance laced Amy's fingers as she raised them from the ground. Blood was oozing from the back of Luka's head at a frightening rate. Making room for them to work, she gave the paramedics a quick rundown of events. 'If he says anything – utters a syllable – please tell us. There are children's lives at risk.'

He was still breathing, but only just. Working quickly and diligently, officers took control while Luka was treated at the scene.

◆ ◆ ◆

With some trepidation, Amy climbed into the back of the ambulance, squeezing herself into a corner seat. Having updated base, she left uniformed officers to take control. Officers were being drafted in to search all breaker's yards and an appeal was soon to go live. But even if they put a stop to all the cars in England being crushed, Toby still needed medication and specialised care. He was a long way from being out of the woods. They needed to pin down his location, and it had to be soon.

As the paramedics hoisted Luka on board, she wanted to ask them how things looked. But she knew from experience how much she hated being asked for updates early on in an investigation. Was this the same? She could see by their grim faces and the haste of their actions that Luka's life was hanging by a thread. As the ambulance weaved in and out of traffic at speed, Amy felt her stomach churn. She had never been the best of travellers and hated being in the back seat. Medical supplies rattled in compartments as she gripped the sides. One of the paramedics turned and gave her a sympathetic smile.

'We'll be there soon.' The ponytailed girl seemed too young to hold such a responsible role, but her movements carried a confidence beyond her years.

'How's it looking?' Amy said, no longer able to hold back the question on her tongue. 'Can he speak? He's the only one who can help me.'

'At the moment we're looking at broken bones and a serious head injury. It could be some time before he's able to talk, if at all. Sorry.'

Amy gave a tight nod. She had always felt a sense of camaraderie with members of the emergency services, and they worked well with the police, helping each other along. But today, no comfort was being offered. All she could do was go to the hospital with the slim hope he could utter a couple of words. But with each minute that passed, that hope faded, along with the chances of finding the children in time. Amy took a deep breath to settle her stomach as another wave of nausea rose. Her colleagues' voices buzzed on the radio and she pushed her earpiece, which had become dislodged, back into her ear. She knew she should speak to DCI Pike, but it sounded like everything was in hand. She had learned to be wise with her words when updating Control. All updates made over airwaves were recorded and transcribed into a report. That was something the Independent Police Complaints Commission could be trawling through later on. DCI Pike's voice sounded worried. She should never have intervened.

A blast of cold air kissed Amy's skin as the back doors opened, seconds after the ambulance came to a juddering halt. Her muscles stiff, she climbed out, watching as paramedics lowered Luka from the ambulance, his head and neck in a brace. The trolley rattling against the pavement, they wheeled him into the hospital with Amy following close behind. Luka himself was a crime scene. His clothes would be seized, a blood sample and forensics taken as soon as police were allowed.

'I'll have to ask you to wait here,' the paramedic said as they came to a set of double doors. Amy watched, helpless, as their best chance of finding Toby and Ellen was wheeled away.

CHAPTER SIXTY-THREE

'Here. Get this down you.' The smell of salt and vinegar filled Amy's senses as Paddy shoved a bag of chips under her nose.

'I don't have time.' Amy was too busy sorting through the paperwork she had just printed off.

'Eat,' Paddy said. He was not taking no for an answer. Minutes later, he followed up with a mug of tea. It was ten o'clock at night. Since returning from the hospital, Amy had been caught up in a whirlwind of investigative tasks. Overseeing briefings, liaising with crime-scene operatives and media support, and updating her supervisors. Today had taken its toll. She wolfed down the chips, realising that all she had eaten up to now was a protein bar. She had come back to the station, guns blazing, but DCI Pike had been nowhere to be seen. 'I can't believe she's not here.' Amy spoke her thoughts aloud. 'And I'm not buying that rubbish about her being sick.'

'She was pretty green around the gills when she heard Luka was mown down.' Just as Amy had feared, Pike had panicked during the operation, instructing officers to move in.

'If only she'd waited a few more seconds.' Amy paused to swig her tea. It was missing sugar but it didn't matter, it tasted like nectar right now.

'I don't suppose you've had any updates on Luka?'

'He's the same – serious but stable. They think he'll pull through but it's too early to tell if he has brain damage.' Amy turned her chair to face her old friend. 'What am I doing here? I should be on the ground, visiting scrapyards, looking for the missing kids like everyone else.' Luka's clothes had been searched. There was no identification on his person, nothing except a set of keys, which were seized by police.

'We've got plenty of boots on the ground. Your time is best spent here.'

Frustrated tears built up behind Amy's eyes and she swallowed them down. 'For all the good I'm doing.'

'Boss, give yourself a break. You haven't stopped all day.'

Amy sucked the salt stinging her fingers before turning back to her desk. 'There are answers here somewhere . . . I can feel it. His mother is at the heart of this. And the way he was clutching his forehead. He suffers from migraines, I can tell. Do you think Zitalin caused them, from when he was drugged as a child?'

'It's a bit extreme, isn't it? Almost committing murder to get rid of a headache?'

'Migraines are nothing like headaches. If you'd had one, you'd know.' Casting the chip wrapper aside, Amy looked through the paperwork on her desk. 'They are a painful reminder of Luka's past. A constant drumming beat that won't let him move on. Besides, there was someone else in the background. He wasn't working alone.' Her eyes fell on an update that had come in earlier that evening. 'Ahh . . . bingo!'

'What is it?' Paddy said, craning his neck to look.

'Every time Luka spoke about Sasha, he referred to her as Mama. But when he talked about present day, he used the term "Mother". Don't you see?'

Paddy frowned. 'I'm not with you.'

'Remember the ultimatum Stuart was given? To risk his life for the one he loved. Luka wanted them to know how it felt.'

'Riiiight . . .' Paddy said, which basically meant he was in the dark.

'Luka was saved from the fire but his mother was left to burn.' She pointed at the copy of the police statement taken earlier that day. 'It's written here in black and white. Stuart said he found Sasha dead in her room – but not Luka. That's when he was beaten back by the flames.'

'And you believe him? What's that got to do with Luka's ultimatum?'

'Stuart and Nicole were given the chance to risk their lives for the one they loved – something not afforded to Luka. Luka was deprived of the chance to save Sasha from the fire.'

Amy tapped her chin, feeling answers drawing near. 'Someone's been helping him. Someone who knows who he is.'

Paddy pointed at the custody photo sitting among the paperwork. 'The courier. Jamie Richmond.'

'Yes, but there's someone else, right under our noses.' Shifting the papers on her table, she fanned them out like a deck of cards. She had printed off everything she could about the people involved in the case – their financial information, plans of their houses, details about their family, friends, closest relatives – as well as witness reports, a list of police who had investigated the fire at the institute and newspaper reports. 'Dr Curtis was so proud of his achievements.' She pointed at a newspaper piece about his latest accolade.

'Proud enough to commit murder?'

'Pride can be a terrible thing.' Amy's eyes narrowed as a memory surfaced. Dr Curtis's home and all the framed plaques and photos on the wall. Then Stuart Coughlan's humble accommodation, family photos littered across the mantelpiece along with some tatty ornaments. Inhaling sharply, Amy drew her hand to her mouth.

'What is it?' Paddy said.

'It might be nothing.' But Amy's pulse had picked up speed. 'Let me see . . .' She searched through the paperwork and found Gary's report. George Barber, the funeral director, had dementia, and his words were disjointed and made little sense. But Amy had insisted that Gary made a note of every single one. 'Who is he?' she said, tapping her finger against the paperwork.

'The funeral director,' Paddy replied.

'No. Who *is* he? And who is he talking about here?' Colour rose to her cheeks as she reread the report. She picked up the phone.

'Who are you ringing?'

'Intelligence. I need something more in-depth.' She turned to Paddy. 'Do me a favour, will you? Those keys we seized from Luka. Book them out and bring them to me.'

'For what?'

'We're going on a trip. If I'm right, we may be able to save Toby and Ellen after all.'

CHAPTER SIXTY-FOUR

'Are you sure about this?' Paddy said, exiting the car as they parked outside the address.

'No. Which is why I haven't called it in.' Amy shook the bunch of keys loose from her jacket pocket, her shoulders hunched against the speckle of hailstones falling from the sky. They were the keys that had been taken from Luka, booked out of the system for her use.

Amy's hand rose to the Yale lock and the first silver key slotted in with ease.

'Shitting hell,' Paddy whispered as he met Amy's triumphant gaze. 'So Luka's been living here all along?' He touched her arm as she pressed forward. 'We should wait, call it in. This needs to be handled properly.'

'Like they handled Luka properly?' Amy shook her head. 'We're doing this my way.' Time was running out for Toby and Ellen, and they had every right to enter the property to save the children if their suspicion was strong enough.

A sharp nod of the head relayed that Paddy had her covered.

'We don't have long until she gets back,' Amy whispered as they entered the hall. She had already rung the homeowner and asked to meet her at the station, but she was sure to return home when she discovered Amy was not there.

But footsteps on the upstairs landing told them she was still home. Raising her finger to her lips, Amy instructed Paddy to step to one side as the woman descended the stairs.

'Going somewhere?' Amy said, nodding towards the suitcase in Deborah's hand.

Open-mouthed, Deborah looked from Paddy to Amy, the colour draining from her face. 'I thought you were at the station. What are you doing in my house?'

Opening her palm, Amy showed her the set of keys. 'Courtesy of Luka. Or should I say Max?' Amy rattled off a police caution, informing her she was under arrest before signalling to Paddy to search the house. Amy's gaze was on Deborah's left hand, which was hidden behind her back. As she took another step forward, she could see why. Deborah was holding a knife.

'Get back from the door,' said Deborah, dropping her suitcase on the steps and raising the knife to chest height.

'You don't think we're going to let you leave, do you?' Amy replied. 'We've spoken to your dad in the care home. We know about Luka – his key fits your door.' Amy's call to the intelligence team had borne fruit, confirming Deborah's family connection with the undertaker.

Deborah's features twisted as she realised she was cornered. 'I should have known my father couldn't let things go.' Their family spat was most likely why Deborah had taken her mother's maiden name. True, the funeral director's words were rambling but, as quite often with dementia, memories of the past were sharper than the present day. It was when he had mentioned the name Max that everything fell into place.

'She was only fourteen . . .' he'd said. 'We didn't even know . . . When the baby was born it was too late. There was only one thing to do . . .' That was when Amy had pieced it together. A secret child.

Deborah had given birth at the age of fourteen and the little boy was stillborn. Using his undertaking business, Deborah's father had disposed of the body to spare the family shame. But the deed had come back to haunt him. Had Deborah used their guilty secret to claim another favour? There was so much yet to uncover. What about the other children in Curtis's care? Deborah had been young when she began working for the doctor. How had she coped with what she found there?

Luka had fulfilled a long-buried need that had been eating away inside Deborah since the age of fourteen. He was also the same age as her child, Max, would have been, had he lived.

'You took him,' Amy said. 'You saved Luka from the fire and raised him as your own.'

Mother. The word had played on Luka's lips. Yet he always called Sasha 'Mama'.

He had been referring to Deborah. She was his mother now. Had she forged a birth certificate? Given him the name Max, the little boy that never was?

'Why all this?' Amy said, watching Deborah intently for any sudden moves. 'You could have stayed as you were. Nobody would have known.' Deborah had lied about her son having a university degree and a black belt in karate. For someone so proud of her child, there was not one photo of him to be seen. No graduation pictures, no martial-arts trophies – no evidence he had ever existed. She had home-schooled her son, kept him prisoner all these years. He was a living ghost. By the time he was given his freedom, he was no longer able to cope.

'You think I don't know that?' Deborah gesticulated with the knife. 'Max . . . Luka needed closure. He bought the flowers online and sent them every year. Even now, Luka is a part of him, right down to the marrow of his bones.'

Amy understood. Poppy Grimes would never leave her. The best she could do was live with the shadows of her past. Some were fleeting, some were dark, but they could not hurt her anymore.

'Where's Toby and Ellen? Luka said they were at a scrapyard.' Paddy loomed over Deborah, his voice firm.

Amy's eyes stayed trained on Deborah's knife. 'They're not in any scrapyard, are they? You couldn't kill those kids, any more than you could kill Luka all those years ago.' The pieces were finally slotting into place. Luka had started by threatening Dr Curtis and the others, while Deborah tried to protect him from the police. But living in isolation had left Luka severely disturbed and she had been unable to keep a lid on it all.

'I thought if I helped him I could make him see sense, but his migraines have affected his thinking. He's not well.'

Amy took a cautious step forward, her hand extended, palm up. 'And you probably counselled him yourself, because you couldn't risk anyone finding out that he was Luka, not Max. It's time to finish this, Deborah. Give me the knife.'

Lashing out with the blade, Deborah forced the officers back. 'He's Max. As far as I'm concerned, Luka died in that fire.'

Amy did not have time to argue. The children were her priority and she had an idea where they were. 'Toby's in the panic room, isn't he, along with Ellen?' The plans of Deborah's house had made for interesting viewing; Amy had checked out a recent planning permission she had applied for. Not once had Deborah mentioned a panic room when she was safeguarded by police. Her CCTV cameras weren't there to catch intruders – they were there to watch Luka's every move.

'I want to see my son.' Sidestepping them both, Deborah edged down the hall. She was going to him, just as she had done all those years ago, finding comfort in the depths of despair. The wild look flashing in her eyes told Amy that Deborah had been affected by events of the past too. She wobbled on her feet, walking without the benefit of her cane, which was propped against the wall.

'Put down the knife.' Amy advanced, her eyes flicking to Paddy, who was to her right. She watched as he slowly reached beneath his jacket for his baton on the clip of his harness. For once, he was wearing his full set of appointments, and now he had a choice: use CS gas or his baton to subdue the suspect and protect them both. Unlike Amy, he reacted badly to gas, and spraying it at such close contact would temporarily blind them both. Amy's police radio was nestled beneath her jacket. If she could get to the emergency button, she would be placed on an open mic. GPS would bring backup to her location and Deborah need not know she had called for it.

Her eyes darting from Amy to Paddy, Deborah reached the kitchen door. 'You were wrong about the children. They're not in the panic room. They're at a breaker's yard in Peckham. I drove the car there myself . . .'

'No,' Amy said, dread filling her core. Reaching beneath her blazer, she pressed the emergency button on her airwaves. She had nothing to lose now. But Deborah caught sight of the movement. Still holding the knife, she seized her opportunity and pulled open the door.

'No you don't!' Amy and Paddy bundled forward. Knife or not, they were not about to let her go. With a flick of his wrist, Paddy extended his baton, bringing it down on Deborah's arm.

'Ah! My arm!' Her words were punctuated by the clang of the kitchen knife as it dropped to the tiled floor. 'You've broken it!' Bending over, Deborah gripped her forearm, her face screwed up in pain.

But their safety came first, and Paddy dragged Deborah's hands behind her back and snapped cuffs on her wrists. 'Are you all right?' Amy asked, as Paddy recited the caution.

'Go!' he said, no further explanation needed. She was already halfway out of the room.

'The suspect states that the children are in a breaker's yard in Peckham,' Amy said, updating Control. Left and right she darted through Deborah's home, until she found the living room. She had memorised the house plans, but now, standing in the room filled with books of every kind, she struggled to find a way in. Where was the door?

She thought of Toby, in desperate need of medication, and wondered what state they would find Ellen in. 'Toby! Ellen!' she called. 'It's the police! Can you hear me?' Amy said a silent prayer. *Please let them be here and not in the breaker's yard.* Her eyes lit on a bookcase filled with medical journals of every kind against the far wall. Grunting, Amy pushed it, exhaling with relief to discover a small white door disguised as a panel in the wall. It opened with a click as she pressed against it, and Amy slid through.

'Ellen? Toby?' She scanned every inch of the room. In the corner a wheelchair sat empty. 'No,' she said as she cast her eyes over an unmade bed. Three specks of blood dappled the pillowcase. What had Luka done? And then she heard it, the smallest of whimpers, followed by a sob. Dropping to her knees, Amy's heart did a somersault as she peered under the bed. 'They're here,' she informed Control. 'They're safe.'

'It's OK,' she said softly, coaxing the children out. In his hand, Toby clutched a piece of Lego to his chest. He shielded Ellen, who peeped out from over his shoulder like a frightened rabbit in the undergrowth. A lump rose in Amy's throat as she took in the scene, gesturing for them to come out. 'It's all right, I'm a police officer. You're safe now.'

Ellen's eyes were wet with tears as she clambered out from under the bed. Dragging himself from beneath it, Toby's features crumpled too. 'I want my daddy,' he sniffed, his chin wobbling as he spoke.

Amy's heart melted and she opened her arms wide. 'It's OK,' she said, encompassing them in a hug. 'You're safe now.'

CHAPTER SIXTY-FIVE

The Curtis Institute, February 1985

'Wake up! There's a fire, we have to go!' Deborah's voice grew insistent as she shook Luka's shoulder hard.

His eyes snapping open, Luka's heart missed a beat. He had been dreaming of Papa . . . of home. But as he took in his surroundings, he realised he had awoken to a living hell. In the distance, he could hear crackling, feel the stench of burning plastic rising in his nostrils as he rose from his bed. Beneath his door, a thin film of acrid smoke drifted through. 'Fire? Mama . . . where is Mama?' He choked on his words.

'Stuart's gone to get her. Come now, there's no time to waste!' Throwing a blanket around him, Deborah scooped Luka up in her arms. He gazed up at the sprinklers as they negotiated the corridor. Why wasn't the fire alarm ringing? His eyes streaming, fear gripped his being as the ceiling tiles began to melt. Strip lighting popped and fizzed overhead, plunging them into darkness and sprinkling them with glass.

'Keep your head down!' Deborah shouted, crouching over him as the flames licked her heels. He bounced in her strong arms, wondering if they would make it out. Was Mama safe? Was she waiting for him? The plan was that Deborah would sneak them both out when Stuart was on his break. There had been no mention of a fire when she had explained earlier in the day. A rush of fresh air hit his face as they reached the sanctuary of outside. But they were at a part of the building he did not recognise. Peeping from beneath the blanket, he was jolted from Deborah's arms, and he realised he was being deposited in the back of a car. 'Cover yourself up.' Deborah's words were breathless, her face holding a determination he had not seen before. 'You need to keep your head down.'

Luka frowned. He did not understand. Shaking Deborah's hands from his shoulders, he wanted to run back the way he had come. 'Mama!' he cried, rasping for breath, his words punctuated by a series of coughs. 'We need to go back! Mama!' All he could hear was the roar of flames and distant sirens growing closer. Luka trembled, the feeling of dread coming in waves until he could hardly breathe.

As he tried to escape the confines of the car, Deborah tightened her grip. Her face was red and blotchy, her eyes bulging as she spoke. 'Lie down. I'll come back to find your mama as soon as I've taken you somewhere safe.' She brought her hand to her mouth as her breath erupted in a cough.

'No,' Luka cried, his throat scratchy and dry. 'We need to go back now!'

'Listen to me!' Deborah clutched his shoulders and delivered a gentle shake. 'The sooner I get you somewhere safe, the sooner I can find out where Stuart has taken Sasha. But we need to get to her before the doctor does. We can't afford to wait.'

The journey to the house took minutes and, under cover of darkness, Deborah sneaked him in. There was a bed, a television, even toys. This was a little boy's room. Luka's face wrinkled in confusion. As she laid him on the duvet, Deborah stroked his hair. Why wasn't she rushing back, like she had promised? The ring of her phone in the hall made them both jump. Her words were short as she took the call, simply saying she was on her way. Briefly, she returned to Luka. 'I need you to be a brave boy. Can you do that for me?'

Luka nodded, but inside his belly it felt like there was a host of rats clawing to escape. Minutes later she returned, wearing a change of clothes, her face clean, her hair brushed. 'I'll find your mother and bring her here. Can you stay until I get back? There's a fridge . . . food and drinks. A television you can watch.'

Luka's eyes danced around the room. As if reading his thoughts, Deborah spoke. 'It's a safe house. I did this for you both.'

'What about Mama?' Luka said. 'I want her here with us.'

'I know.' Deborah stroked his hair. 'You can both hide here until we get you home. I'll be back soon. Can you hang on until then?'

Luka nodded.

'That's my boy.' Deborah smiled, concern evaporating from her face. She pointed to a door in the corner of the room. 'There's the bathroom. You can clean yourself up. There's pyjamas and clean clothes in the wardrobe too. Make yourself comfortable. I'll be back soon. This is your home now.'

It felt like a lifetime before she returned. The room was windowless, just like the place he had come from, but for the first time in months Luka felt safe. At least now there was hope. Deborah cared about them both and would help them start again.

As the door slowly opened and Deborah walked in, Luka's heart fell like a stone.

'I'm so sorry,' she wept. 'Sasha . . . she didn't make it. I'm sorry, sweetheart.'

Luka's screams eventually gave way to giant, shuddering sobs. Taking him in her arms, Deborah did her best to console him. The fire was a tragic accident. It seemed a two-bar heater Sasha had been using set light to her bedclothes. She was asleep when it happened and the faulty electrics deactivated the alarms. Stuart had not been at his post.

By the time he discovered the fire, he was beaten back by the flames. If it hadn't been for Deborah, Luka would be dead too.

For a while, he blamed her for Mama's death. She should have let him back inside. But it was not Deborah who insisted on locking the doors at night. Not Deborah who made his mother take those drugs. It was not Deborah who had neglected her duty, leaving the institution when she should have been doing her rounds.

But Luka wished he could have gone back inside – even if it had meant risking his life. Later, when he was older, Deborah told him about the darker side of the experiments and how Dr Curtis had black-mailed her into keeping quiet about their use of drugs. If the truth came out about the pharmaceutical company, then Deborah would go to prison too.

As for Sam? The truth was, he had died in his room. The fire chiefs mistook his body for Luka's because nobody was looking for Sam. When Luka asked about his father, Deborah had more bad news to share. 'I should have told you sooner,' she said, imparting the news that Ivan had been killed when the mine he was working in collapsed. Almost overnight, Luka was orphaned. It was too much to bear. Through the weeks and months of his grief, Deborah remained steadfast. He would live the life she had promised him. She would help him begin again. That was when Luka Volkov died and Maximus McCauley was born.

CHAPTER SIXTY-SIX

'Please. Don't charge my son. He's been through enough.' Deborah's face crumpled as she negotiated her way through the police interview the next day. Across from her sat a male and a female detective. The man was called DC Moss; the woman's name she had already forgotten. She looked like she was in her twenties but seemed quite capable of holding such a responsible role.

'It's our job to gather evidence. The Crown Prosecution Service makes the decision to charge,' DC Moss said, looking at her arm as she nursed it. 'How are you doing with that?'

'It's fine,' she replied. It was badly bruised but not broken, and right now she was only interested in protecting her son. 'Hugh . . .' She paused, rethinking the use of his first name. 'Dr Curtis is behind everything. He's the one who imprisoned those children at the institute. The rest of us were bystanders. He pushed them to their limits in the name of drug research.'

'We're looking into it,' the young officer piped up, just as Deborah caught sight of the name DC Molly Baxter on her folder.

'I've got paperwork, copies of all his test results. It's in a safety-deposit box.' Deborah watched as the officers exchanged a glance. She wasn't stupid. She had kept the evidence as leverage in case she got caught. 'It was all his idea to light the fire at the institute,' she continued. 'I pretended to go along with it so I could save Luka. Dr Curtis . . . he never had any intention of letting him go home.'

'Yet you never saw fit to report him to the police,' DC Moss interjected.

'I couldn't. My father would have gone to jail. Back then, he was my mother's carer. She wouldn't have been able to cope without him.' Memories of her mother filled her with a sense of sadness. How disappointed she would be in her now, if she were still alive. Not to mention how Luka would feel when he discovered she had left Sasha to die.

'There were five children in the Zitalin study.' Deborah's words were heavy with regret. 'I didn't know about Julian and Martha until the fire, when I read some of the paperwork Dr Curtis had told me to burn.' She glanced at the officers across from her, then to the camera recording her every move. 'It said that Julian had died of convulsions a month into the study and Martha . . . she died in her sleep.' Deborah knew her father had taken pay-offs for cremating their bodies on the quiet. But where were their parents? Were they runaways? Or had they come from the children's home Sam originated from?

Deborah thought about the orderlies. Would Christina have ended her own life if she hadn't been pressured into keeping quiet? A pang of guilt hit her. 'I was taken on at the same time as Stuart and Christina, just after Jamie, child number three, ran away.' She knew Luka had found him again, and together they had conspired for revenge.

'Dr Curtis desperately needed another child to finish the Zitalin trials. That's where Luka came in.'

'And child number four?' DC Baxter piped up. 'You mentioned there were five children.'

Deborah frowned as she recounted her words. 'Oh, yes, number four was Sam. He died of heart failure after Luka joined us.' That was the day they had all been bound into a secret which would span over decades. 'Dr Curtis is a monster,' Deborah said, her thoughts floating back to the orderlies. 'He got Christina and Stuart to give Sam his medication so they would be implicated if anything went wrong. As for me . . . by the time I found out what he was really like, it was too late.'

'So you felt justified in helping Luka kidnap Ellen and Toby?' DC Baxter's voice brought her into the present day.

Deborah picked at a thread on the cuff of her blouse. 'I tried to help Luka live a normal life as Max. Yes, he had episodes, but I thought it was under control. That was, until Dr Curtis started popping up on television. That's when the migraines began.'

'Let me get this straight.' DC Moss scratched his cheek. 'You're saying that Luka was driven to commit a crime because he saw Dr Curtis on TV?'

Deborah sighed. 'It was like he was two different people. My kind and loving son Max, who supported animal-rights charities, and Luka, the little Russian boy who wanted revenge.' She looked from one officer to the other. 'It started with the flowers, but then he tracked down Jamie. When I found out about the kidnapping I pretended to go along with it. What choice did I have? Luka had already spent years hidden away. I couldn't bear for him to go to jail.' Deborah shook her head. 'There was no stopping him once the idea took hold. I looked after Ellen when he took Toby. She suffered from nosebleeds – poor mite. I bought them toys . . . tried to make them as comfortable as I could.'

'And the plan was for you to dump them at a breaker's yard in Peckham?'

'He would never have gone through with it. He knew I would never have hurt those kids.' Deborah tried to sound convincing but, deep down, she wasn't sure. It had taken her some time to persuade him to use Ellen's nightdress at the building site as a substitute for the little girl herself. 'And where were you when he needed you?' She glared at the officers, trying to allocate blame. 'Everybody let him down. That's why he made that police officer jump through hoops. He liked being the one in control.' Her gaze fell to her clasped hands resting on the table. She knew who was really to blame in all of this. Her actions had been for her own selfish gain. From the moment she had first met Luka, all she could see was her little boy, Max. Selfishly, she had taken him, moulding him into the son she had lost. But their relationship was tainted by the past, and nobody in the world could replace her secret child.

CHAPTER SIXTY-SEVEN

'I thought it only fair that you hear the news from me.' DCI Pike looked different today. Her face carried a sense of peace Amy had not seen in a long time. A sad smile crossed Pike's lips. 'It's been a tough year, but I hope we can put it behind us and be friends.'

Friends? Amy swallowed the acidic response on her tongue. Pike knew how let down Amy had felt when she issued the order that caused Luka to bolt. With the limelight solely on her, Amy had taken the flak. Her actions could have been career-breaking and her job was the one thing that kept her sane. Finding Toby and Ellen in the panic room had been one of the highlights of her time on the force. These were the moments she lived for. But there was more digging to do. Details of the children in the doctor's care were slowly filtering through. Julian, Martha, Sam, Jamie and Luka would finally have a voice. Amy would not rest until they followed up every lead. Her hunch about the pharmaceutical company had been justified. Dr Curtis had two sets of tests: the legitimate results concerning his usual subjects, and another, secret set for the tattooed children. These results had been sent to pharmaceutical company Novo-Hynes, which had funded Curtis's studies for years. Stuart was offering his full cooperation, which would hopefully gain him leniency in court. While not directly involved in the children's deaths, he and Christina had turned a blind eye.

Luka was conscious, fortunate to have survived his ordeal. Seeing his father again would be a groundbreaking moment, and Amy hoped it would go some way towards putting things right. Not that she would convey any of this to DCI Pike. Amy's disappointment in her senior officer was expressed without words. She would not share her private thoughts with a person she no longer trusted or even liked.

'I hear you've been talking to Steve.' Pike was referring to DC Moss and the part she had played in getting him demoted. 'It's regrettable how things turned out between us, but it's never too late to put things right.' She turned her gaze towards the window. Amy shifted in her seat as she took in her expression. Were there tears gathering in her eyes? 'I've taken early retirement,' Pike continued. 'Let's say I was encouraged to do so.'

As her words sank in, Amy wondered if she had heard right. 'You've quit the police?'

'Yes, and I've a good idea who my replacement is. The role needed some fresh blood from an outside force.'

'Oh . . . I see. I'm sorry to hear that.' But was she? She was glad Pike was facing up to things, including her sexual harassment of Steve Moss. But losing her job . . . the woman lived and breathed the police. It was bound to hit her hard. 'What are you going to do now?'

'Between us, I'm going to concentrate on my marriage. We're relocating to Devon, hoping for a fresh start.'

Amy imparted a hesitant smile. How her husband had put up with her infidelities this long, she did not know. But there were two sides to every story, and she would not be quick to judge.

'This job's changed me, and I don't like who I've become.' Plucking a tissue from a box on her desk, Pike dabbed the tears forming in the corners of her eyes. 'The official line is I'm retiring because my role as a DCI has been made obsolete. I thought I owed you an explanation.'

'I'm shocked,' Amy replied. 'I hope the decision to go wasn't down to anything I said.'

Pike sniffled before blurting a humourless laugh. 'No offence, but you're not that influential. On a brighter note, the command team are very pleased with you. They want to capitalise on what you bring to your role. Just imagine when the story comes out. Teamed with a new DI, you'll reach stratospheric levels of success.'

Thoughts of further publicity made Amy bristle, but she was glad the command team were behind her. Pike was right, a good leader could take them even higher. Be an example to other forces implementing similar teams. 'So there's a DI taking over your position? How is that going to work?'

'You'll share the same rank but he'll be responsible for overseeing the team. I'm sure you'll work well together.'

'So it's a he?' Amy held her breath. As much as she mistrusted Pike, sometimes it was better the devil you know.

The clock on the wall ticked a few more seconds before Pike passed on the news. 'DI Donovan is going to make an excellent addition to the team.'

'Donovan?' Amy's mouth fell open as she lost all composure. 'Not DI Donovan from Essex Police?'

'Yes, he's been primed for the role. 'Nice chap, very personable, and he's got a lot of time for you. He has a daughter living in London and wants to relocate to the Met.' She rose from her chair and turned to the coffee pot. 'Would you like some?' she said, filling a cup.

'No,' Amy said on autopilot, her head spinning with the news. Donovan was moving to London? Leading her team? This was a joke. It had to be. But then she thought about his visits to the area, how he had happened to be around when she got pelted with eggs. His dinner with Pike. Had he been using Amy to get inside information on the role? No. She was a decent judge of character, and he was too genuine for that. But still . . . How was she meant to work with him every day?

Pike was too busy singing his praises to notice Amy's rising panic. 'He's got some amazing commendations and is just what this team needs. I'm sure you'll get on famously.'

'I don't know what to say.' The words tumbled from Amy's mouth as she acclimatised herself to the news. Donovan must have known he was joining the team, yet he hadn't breathed a word. But Pike was right. Things were going to change.

CHAPTER SIXTY-EIGHT

'May I say how honoured I am to spend a rare day off with you. How long has it been since you've taken one? Ten days? Two weeks?' The comment came from Sally-Ann, who had guilt-tripped Amy into spending some 'sisterly time' together. But the words were delivered with a smile. Sally-Ann was well aware of the challenges that working in the police brought, particularly given she was living with Paddy, Amy's right-hand man.

Amy returned her smile. 'I can think of worse ways to spend my day. Being surrounded by cats and kittens is just the therapy I need.' As far as Amy was concerned, it had been an excellent idea to visit their local cat shelter. Not that Dotty would have approved, but this visit was to complete Sally-Ann's family, not hers. As they ambled past the outdoor enclosures with the sun on her face, everything felt well in Amy's world. But peace was there to be shattered, and as her mobile phone rang, Amy was tempted to ignore the call. 'It's Adam,' she said, plucking the phone from her jeans pocket and eyeing the display.

'Go on, answer it,' Sally-Ann said. 'I want to hear what the scumbag has to say for himself.'

There was a time when Amy could not have shared her personal life even with her sister. But what she had with Adam was over, and she was finally in a place where she could move on. Snatching up the phone, she accepted the call before she could change her mind. 'Hello, who's this?' she said, giving her sister a wink. She would not give Adam the satisfaction of knowing she still had his contact details saved on her phone.

'It's me, Adam.' He sounded deflated, dissolving the smile from Amy's face.

'Have you got a minute?' he said. 'Can we talk?'

'I think the time for talking is over . . .' Amy began to say.

'Please. It's important.'

'What's wrong?' Amy frowned. She may have washed her hands of him, but she no longer wished him ill. She watched as Sally-Ann bent down at an enclosure and stroked a tabby cat through the wire mesh.

'Look, I won't keep you. I just wanted to say I'm sorry. I took our break-up badly. I let Lillian get under my skin. I should never have printed that story. That woman . . . she has a way of making you do things . . . she egged me on.'

Amy's sympathy began to fade. Even now, Adam could not take responsibility for his deeds.

'The damage is done. It's too late for apologies.' She frowned. What did he want her to say? Surely she had made her feelings clear?

'Anyway . . . I was thinking we could balance it out if you gave your side of the story too.'

'You're kidding,' Amy blurted out with a laugh.

'Think about it. Lillian's had her say, now you can respond. Or we could interview you both together . . . pit her argument against yours.'

'Adam, I need you to warm up your few remaining brain cells and work with me.' Amy's voice dripped with sarcasm. She was enjoying having her say. 'From now on, all I want from you is the silent treatment. I don't want to hear your bullshit. I don't want to see your face and I certainly don't want to receive your calls. You get me?'

'If you'll just let me explain,' Adam replied. 'We could meet up over coffee, discuss it properly.'

Amy marvelled at his cheek. 'I'd rather stick my head in the oven than spend another minute with you. Enjoy your playtime with Lillian. I'm never letting you close enough to hurt me again.' Pressing the power button, she switched off her phone. She glanced at Sally-Ann and saw admiration on her face. 'I try to be nice,' Amy said. 'But my mouth doesn't always cooperate.'

'Good for you,' Sally-Ann replied, chuckling under her breath. 'Look at this little girl.' She pointed to a skinny grey cat housed in its own enclosure. A handwritten sign tied to the mesh gave her the name of Taz. 'She's had a lifetime of cruelty, and she's only three years old.'

All thoughts of Adam dissipated as Amy read the sign. The cat was not the prettiest of creatures. A line of shaved fur revealed a shock of stitches running across her back.

'I'm having her.' Sally-Ann smiled, not in the least put off as the cat shied away from her touch. 'I'll win her round.' A cold breeze enveloped them as a cloud passed over the sun.

'There's something I wanted to ask you,' Sally-Ann said, eyeing up a family who were cooing over the kittens. 'I wasn't going to bring it up, but seeing as Adam's killed the mood . . .'

'Is it about Lillian?' Amy sensed her sister's concern. Together, they walked away from the enclosure.

'Yeah. Is it true? Is the appeal really going ahead?'

Amy nodded. 'It's gaining momentum. You know what that means, don't you?'

Her head bowed, Sally-Ann seemed burdened with the weight of her plight. 'I'm going to have to give a statement, aren't I? God, the thought of her knowing I survived makes me sick.'

As an older sibling, Sally-Ann had suffered at the hands of her cruel parents a lot more than Amy had. Yet she had found the strength to revert to her old name. Amy could never imagine calling herself Poppy again.

Sally-Ann stared at the gravel drive as they headed back towards reception. 'How much do you remember about our childhood?'

'Enough. Too much. Although I'm not sure how reliable my memory is. The more I see Lillian, the more I remember, which is why I throw myself into work.'

'It's just that I . . .' Sally-Ann took a breath, her palm flat on her chest. Inhaling slowly, she tried to assemble her words. 'It's just that I may need your help . . .' Another deep breath. Her hand circled her chest. It was the beginnings of a panic attack. Amy recognised it instantly. Flora had suffered from them for years.

Amy touched her arm. 'It's OK. Take a deep breath. Focus on my words. In and out . . . nice and steady. You're safe here. We don't need to talk about it right now.'

Breathing through her panic attack, Sally-Ann stood beneath one of the trees bordering the driveway. Gradually, her breath returned to normal. She gave Amy a grateful smile. 'I'm OK now, thanks.'

'Do you want to talk about it? You said you needed my help.' Amy knew she was going back on her earlier reassurance, but she needed to know what was wrong.

'It's just stuff from the past. I can't bear the thought of it all coming out.'

'I'm here for you,' Amy replied. 'Whatever it is, I've got your back.' She would never forget how Sally-Ann had hidden her from their drunken father in the basement of the Grimes family home. Had she not acted so selflessly, Amy could have taken the full force of an anger dark enough to kill.

Sally-Ann stood rooted to the spot beneath the tree.

Amy recognised her expression. Her gaze was far away, in an unspeakable place.

Sally-Ann reached out to the bark of the leafless tree, her fingers tracing its grooves as she tried to ground herself. 'I stood by and allowed my parents to be sent down for my murder. Yes, there were others, but the fact they killed their own daughter made a big impact on their case. Now I'm worried what will happen when I come forward. There's a very real chance Mum will be freed.'

Amy was also dreading the excavation of their past. There were secrets buried in her psyche and things that Sally-Ann was still struggling to get to grips with. But Lillian was an abomination. She must never be set free. Sally-Ann's use of the word 'Mum' sickened Amy. Why couldn't she call them Lillian and Jack? It was a stark reminder that, in some ways, they were worlds apart. She looked away from her sister as she tried to conceal her emotions. 'We can testify, tell the jury what we've seen.'

Sally-Ann shook her head, her face haunted by shadows of the past. 'Mum was promiscuous. She slept with lots of people and had a filthy tongue. But I never saw her murder anyone. Dad, yes, but not Mum. She was too clever for that.'

'But I saw her,' Amy replied. 'She killed one of the women who got a little too close to Jack.'

'You were so young. Do you think the court will give any credence to your testimony?' Sally-Ann stepped away from the tree, dry-washing her hands. 'Thanks to Adam's story, a lot of people have changed their minds about Mum. She's being backed by No Choice. They're helping to fund her appeal.'

Amy knew about No Choice, an anti-police movement set up to assist victims coerced into crime because they feared for their lives.

'Up until now, the major stumbling block was that Mum allowed her daughter to be killed to save her own neck. When it comes out I'm alive . . .' Sally-Ann stared glumly into the distance. 'She's an evil woman but I can't lie in court.'

'Then why call her Mum?' Amy said, unable to contain the question a second longer. 'You said it yourself: she's evil. Why don't you call her Lillian, like me?'

Sally-Ann sighed, her face grim. 'Because I'm sick of fighting it. She's my mum, always will be.' She turned to face Amy. 'I'm not as strong as you. I tried pretending I was someone else, but the stress of it was making me ill.'

'Then you must do the right thing.' Amy followed Sally-Ann's lead as they took the path. Lillian's appeal was a blight on the horizon, but there was more to her sister's behaviour than that. She was hiding something, and the prospect of Lillian being freed was a reality neither of them was ready to face.

ACKNOWLEDGMENTS

Coming to the end of a book always feels like a huge accomplishment, but I haven't done it alone. I'd like to thank my editors, Jane Snelgrove and Ian Pindar, for their valued insights. It has been a pleasure working with you on this book. Thanks also to Eoin, Laura, Jack, Hatty, Nicole, Shona and the team at Thomas & Mercer. I feel very privileged to work with people who are as passionate about my writing as I am. I'd like to give thanks to Tom Sanderson, whose cover designs leave me in awe.

I want to thank Madeleine Milburn, Hayley Steed and the wonderful team at the Madeleine Milburn literary agency – a more dedicated bunch of professionals you could not meet.

A special mention of gratitude to my supportive fellow authors, in particular to Angie Marsons and Mel Sherratt, two truly inspirational (and hilarious) people I feel proud to call my pals. Also, to my ex-colleagues in the police who are still up against it, you are never far from my thoughts. To the organisers of such events as Theakston's Crime Writing Festival, Bloody Scotland and Killer Women – thanks so much for having me at your events.

To the wonderful bloggers and book clubs on Facebook who read and promote books: THE Book Club, the Crime Book Club, Book

Connectors, Crime Fiction Addict and The Book Trail to name a few. To my all-important readers, words are not enough to express my gratitude for your support. I hope you continue to enjoy my offerings. Thanks also to Amy Jane Hinton for assisting with my research into all things Russian.

Last, but certainly not least, to my family, both in Ireland and the UK, especially my husband, Neil, who encouraged me to take the leap of faith and leave my job to write full-time. Thank you for believing in me. To my children: near or far, you inspire me every day.

ABOUT THE AUTHOR

 A former police detective, Caroline Mitchell now writes full-time.

She has worked in CID and specialised in roles dealing with vulnerable victims – high-risk victims of domestic abuse and serious sexual offences. The mental strength shown by the victims of these crimes is a constant source of inspiration to her, and Mitchell combines their tenacity with her knowledge of police procedure to create tense psychological thrillers.

Originally from Ireland, she now lives in a pretty village on the coast of Essex with her husband and three children.

You can find out more about her at www.caroline-writes.com, or follow her on Twitter (@caroline_writes) or Facebook (www.facebook.com/CMitchellAuthor).